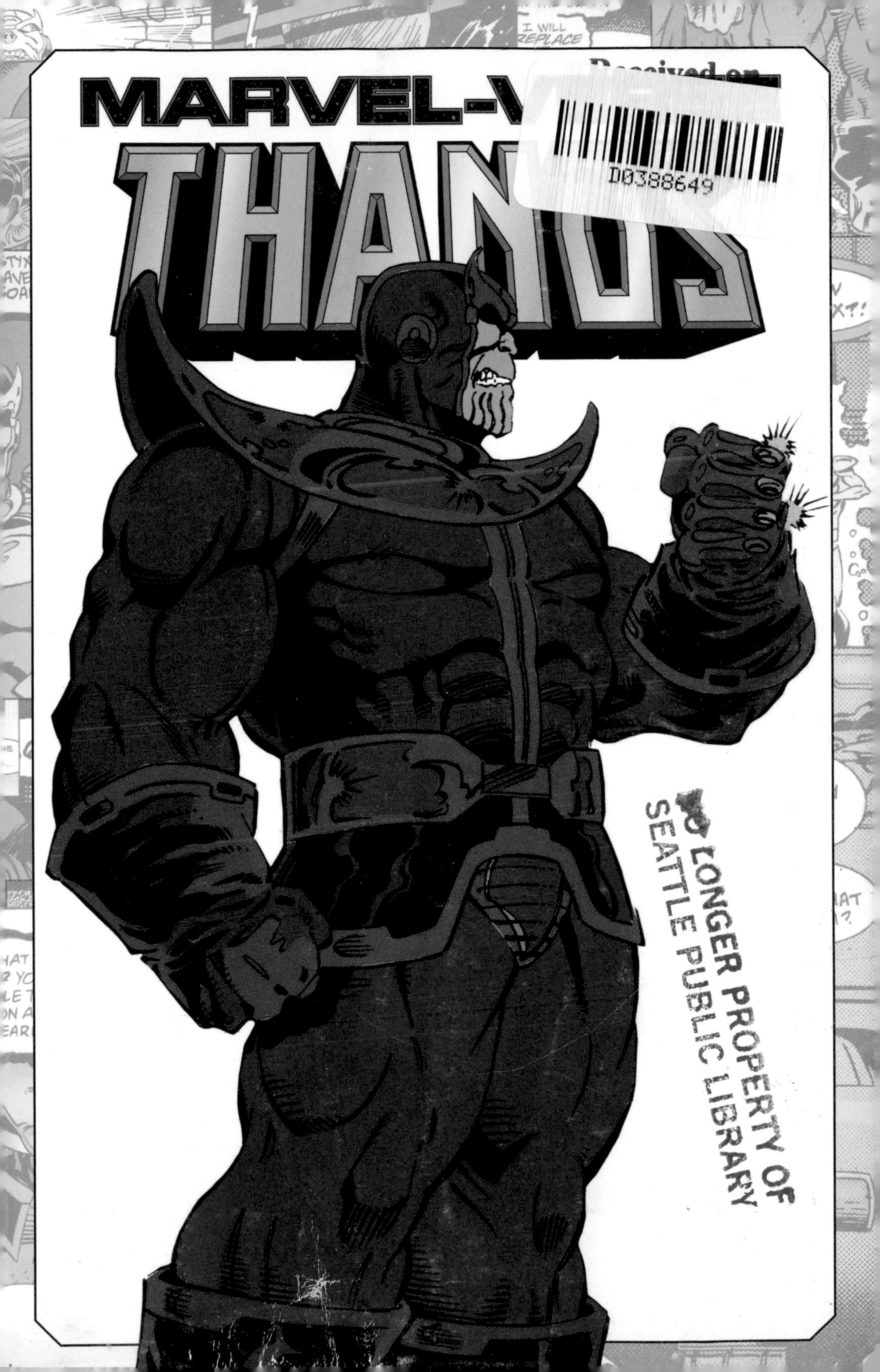
I WILL REPLACE
MARVEL-V
THANOS

MARVEL-VERSE THANOS

IRON MAN #55

PLOTTER/PENCILER: **JIM STARLIN**
SCRIPTER: **MIKE FRIEDRICH**
INKER: **MIKE ESPOSITO**
LETTERER: **JOHN COSTANZA**
EDITOR: **ROY THOMAS**

SILVER SURFER #45

WRITER: **JIM STARLIN**
PENCILER: **RON LIM**
INKER: **TOM CHRISTOPHER**
COLORIST: **TOM VINCENT**
LETTERER: **KEN BRUZENAK**
EDITOR: **CRAIG ANDERSON**

MARVEL HOLIDAY SPECIAL 1993 "YULE MEMORY"

WRITER: **JIM STARLIN**
PENCILER: **RON LIM**
INKER: **TERRY AUSTIN**
COLORIST: **TOM VINCENT**
LETTERER: **BRAD K. JOYCE**
EDITOR: **RENEE WITTERSTAETTER**

CAPTAIN MARVEL #33

PLOTTER/PENCILER: **JIM STARLIN**
SCRIPTER: **STEVE ENGLEHART**
INKER: **KLAUS JANSON**
LETTERER: **TOM ORZECHOWSKI**
EDITOR: **ROY THOMAS**

SPIDER-MAN #17

WRITER: **ANN NOCENTI**
PENCILER: **RICK LEONARDI**
INKER: **AL WILLIAMSON**
COLORIST: **GREGORY WRIGHT**
LETTERER: **CHRIS ELIOPOULOS**
EDITOR: **DANNY FINGEROTH**

KA-ZAR #11

WRITER: **MARK WAID**
PENCILER: **ANDY KUBERT**
INKER: **JESSE DELPERDANG**
COLORIST: **JOE ROSAS**
SEPARATIONS: **DIGITAL CHAMELEON**
LETTERER: **TODD KLEIN**
EDITOR: **MATT IDELSON**

COLLECTION EDITOR: **JENNIFER GRÜNWALD**
ASSISTANT EDITOR: **CAITLIN O'CONNELL** ASSOCIATE MANAGING EDITOR: **KATERI WOODY**
EDITOR, SPECIAL PROJECTS: **MARK D. BEAZLEY** VP PRODUCTION & SPECIAL PROJECTS: **JEFF YOUNGQUIST**
RESEARCH: **JESS HAROLD** & **JEPH YORK** BOOK DESIGNERS: **STACIE ZUCKER** WITH **JAY BOWEN**

SVP PRINT, SALES & MARKETING: **DAVID GABRIEL** DIRECTOR, LICENSED PUBLISHING: **SVEN LARSEN**
EDITOR IN CHIEF: **C.B. CEBULSKI** CHIEF CREATIVE OFFICER: **JOE QUESADA**
PRESIDENT: **DAN BUCKLEY** EXECUTIVE PRODUCER: **ALAN FINE**

MARVEL-VERSE: THANOS. Contains material originally published in magazine form as IRON MAN #55, CAPTAIN MARVEL #33, SILVER SURFER #45, SPIDER-MAN #17, KA-ZAR #11 and MARVEL HOLIDAY SPECIAL #2. First printing 2019. ISBN 978-1-302-92118-7. Published by MARVEL WORLDWIDE, INC., a subsidiary of MARVEL ENTERTAINMENT, LLC. OFFICE OF PUBLICATION: 135 West 50th Street, New York, NY 10020. © 2019 MARVEL No similarity between any of the names, characters, persons, and/or institutions in this magazine with those of any living or dead person or institution is intended, and any such similarity which may exist is purely coincidental. **Printed in Canada.** DAN BUCKLEY, President, Marvel Entertainment; JOHN NEE, Publisher; JOE QUESADA, Chief Creative Officer; TOM BREVOORT, SVP of Publishing; DAVID BOGART, Associate Publisher & SVP of Talent Affairs; DAVID GABRIEL, SVP of Sales & Marketing, Publishing; JEFF YOUNGQUIST, VP of Production & Special Projects; DAN CARR, Executive Director of Publishing Technology; ALEX MORALES, Director of Publishing Operations; DAN EDINGTON, Managing Editor; SUSAN CRESPI, Production Manager; STAN LEE, Chairman Emeritus. For information regarding advertising in Marvel Comics or on Marvel.com, please contact Vit DeBellis, Custom Solutions & Integrated Advertising Manager, at vdebellis@marvel.com. For Marvel subscription inquiries, please call 888-511-5480. **Manufactured between 8/23/2019 and 9/24/2019 by SOLISCO PRINTERS, SCOTT, QC, CANADA.**

10 9 8 7 6 5 4 3 2 1

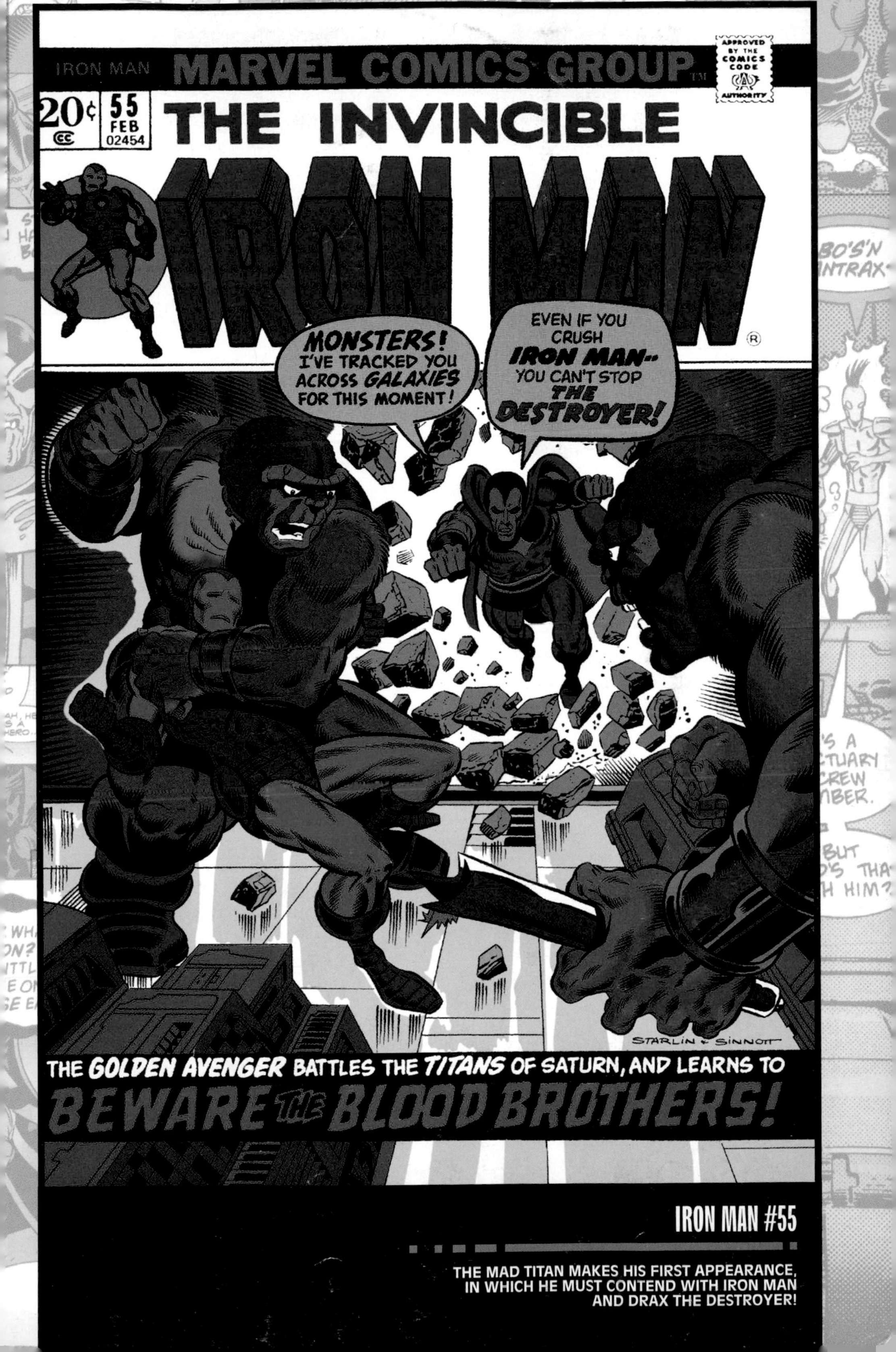
IRON MAN
MARVEL COMICS GROUP
APPROVED BY THE COMICS CODE AUTHORITY
20¢ 55 FEB 02454
THE INVINCIBLE
IRON MAN
MONSTERS! I'VE TRACKED YOU ACROSS GALAXIES FOR THIS MOMENT!
EVEN IF YOU CRUSH IRON MAN-- YOU CAN'T STOP THE DESTROYER!
STARLIN & SINNOTT
THE GOLDEN AVENGER BATTLES THE TITANS OF SATURN, AND LEARNS TO
BEWARE THE BLOOD BROTHERS!

IRON MAN #55

THE MAD TITAN MAKES HIS FIRST APPEARANCE, IN WHICH HE MUST CONTEND WITH IRON MAN AND DRAX THE DESTROYER!

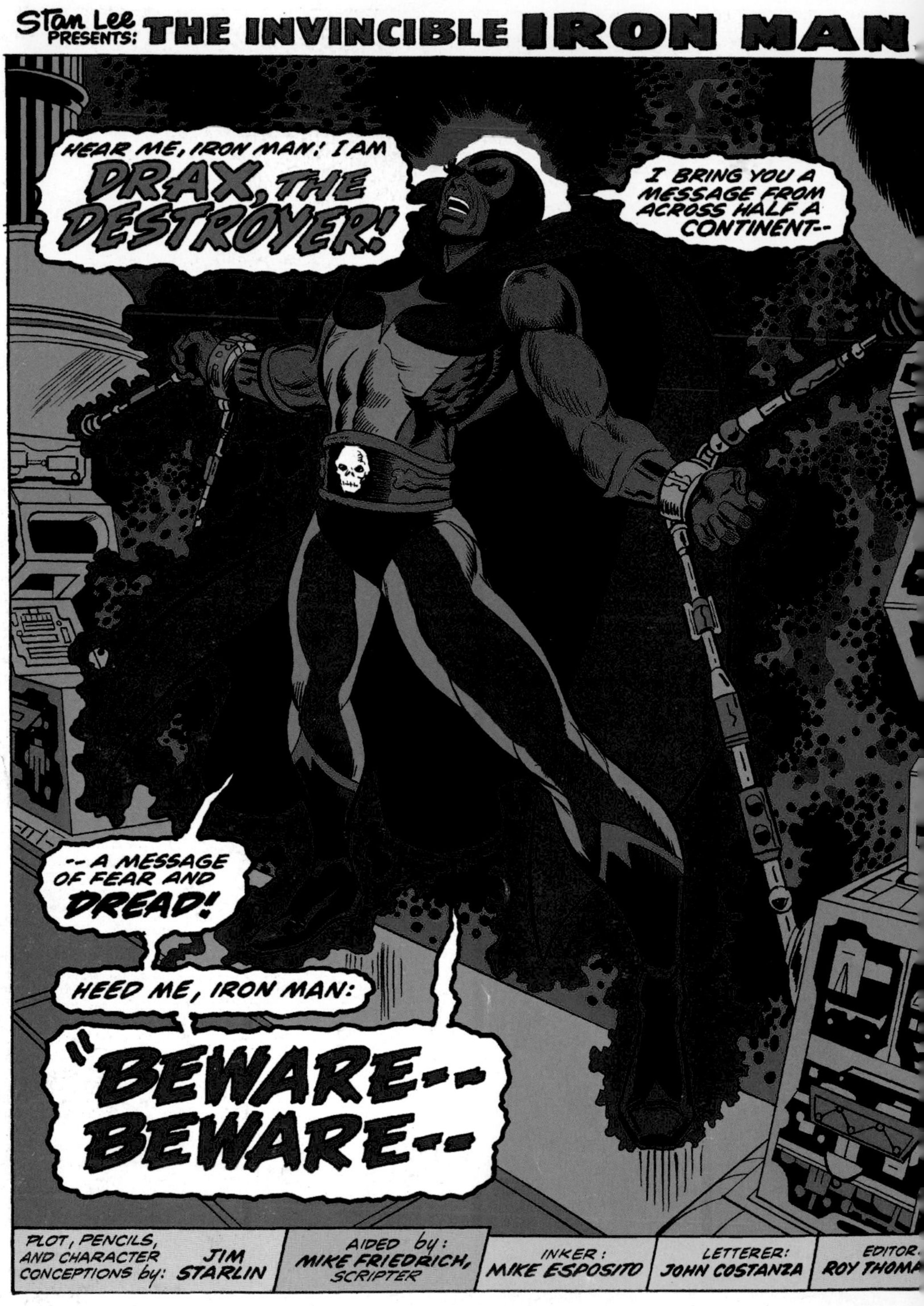
STAN LEE PRESENTS: THE INVINCIBLE IRON MAN
HEAR ME, IRON MAN! I AM DRAX, THE DESTROYER!
I BRING YOU A MESSAGE FROM ACROSS HALF A CONTINENT--
-- A MESSAGE OF FEAR AND DREAD!
HEED ME, IRON MAN:
"BEWARE-- BEWARE--
PLOT, PENCILS, AND CHARACTER CONCEPTIONS by: JIM STARLIN
AIDED by: MIKE FRIEDRICH, SCRIPTER
INKER: MIKE ESPOSITO
LETTERER: JOHN COSTANZA
EDITOR: ROY THOMA

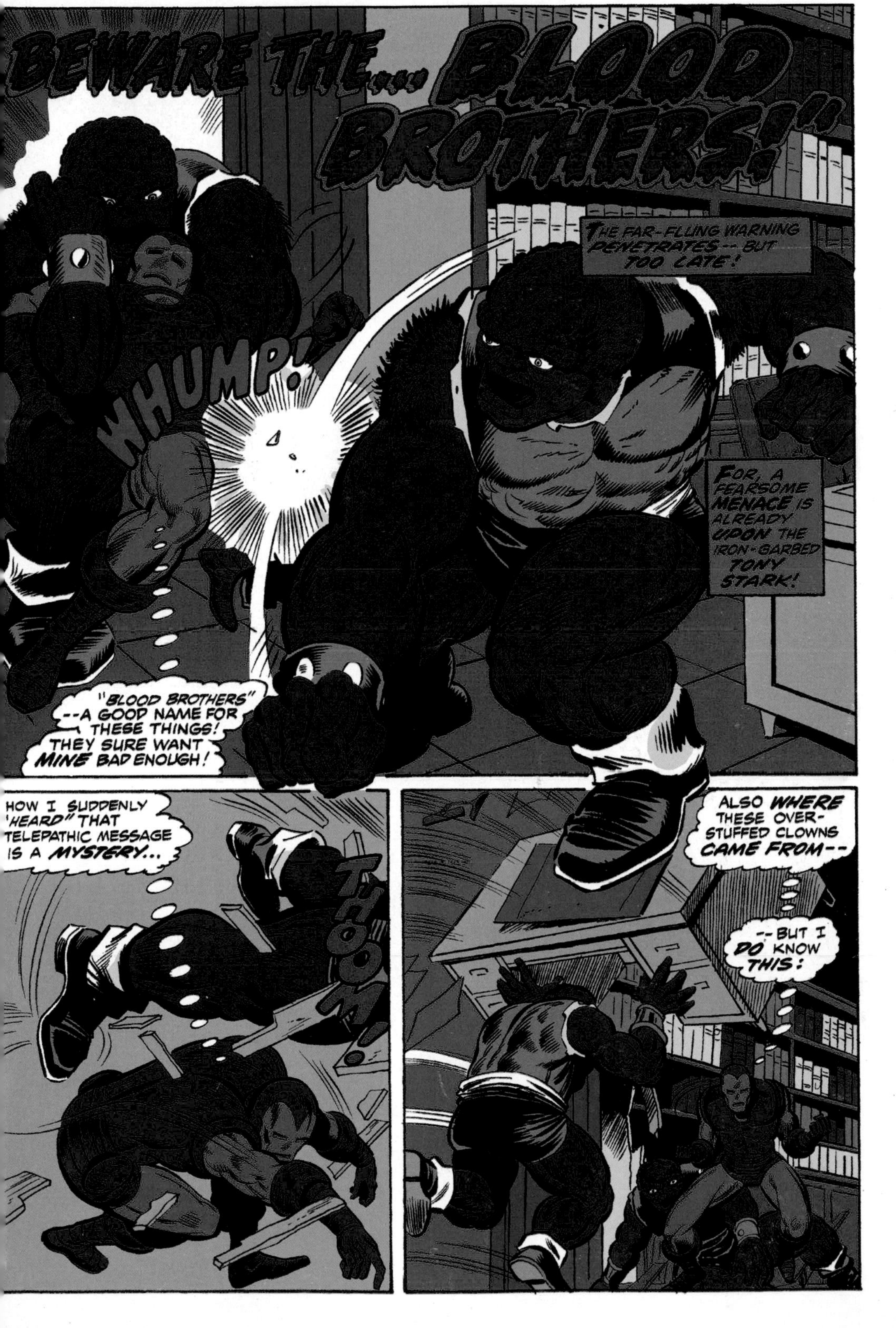
"BEWARE THE... BLOOD BROTHERS!"
THE FAR-FLUNG WARNING PENETRATES -- BUT TOO LATE!
FOR, A FEARSOME MENACE IS ALREADY UPON THE IRON-GARBED TONY STARK!
WHUMP!
"BLOOD BROTHERS" --A GOOD NAME FOR THESE THINGS! THEY SURE WANT MINE BAD ENOUGH!
HOW I SUDDENLY 'HEARD" THAT TELEPATHIC MESSAGE IS A MYSTERY...
THOOM!
ALSO WHERE THESE OVER-STUFFED CLOWNS CAME FROM--
--BUT I DO KNOW THIS:

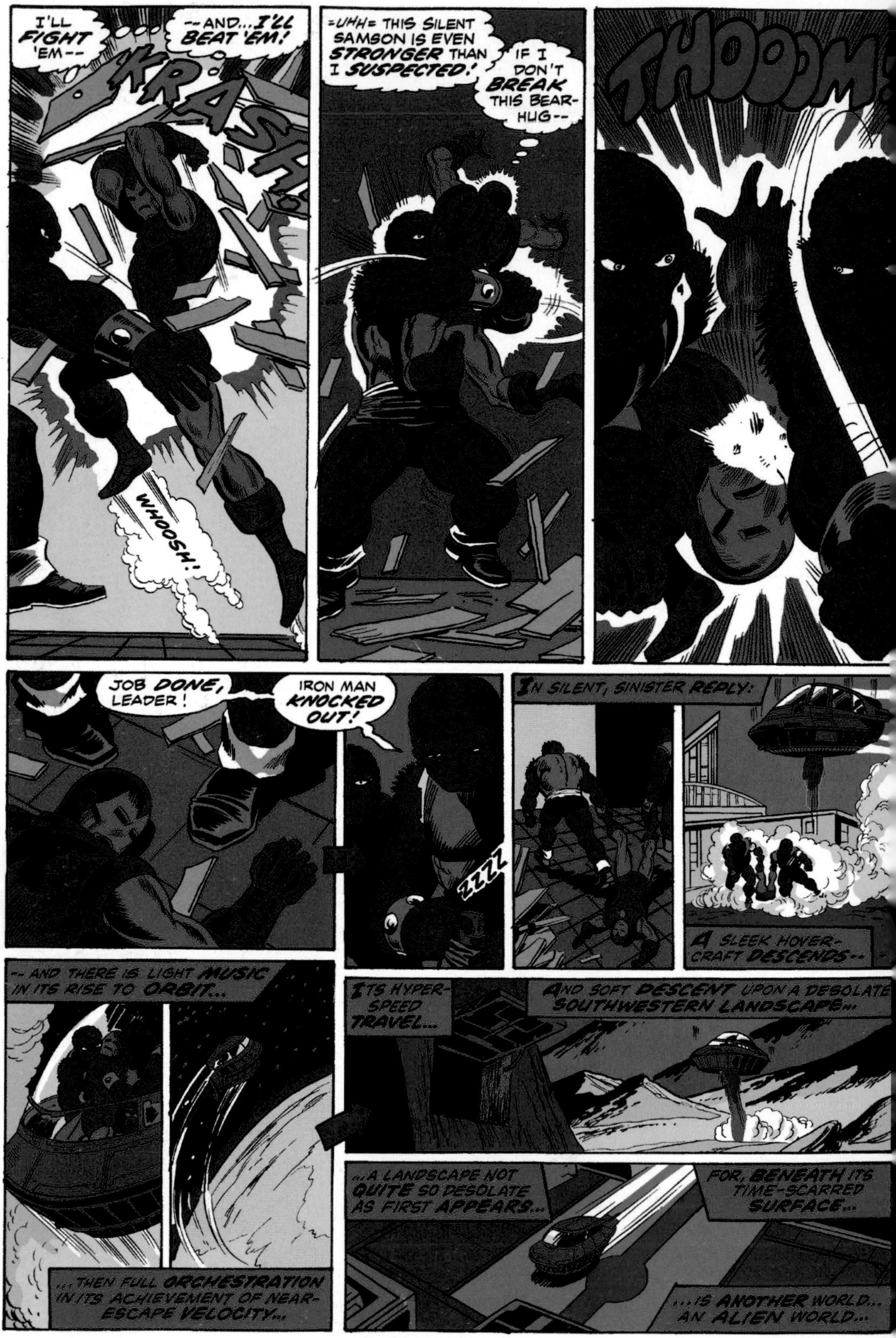
I'LL FIGHT 'EM--
--AND... I'LL BEAT 'EM!
KRASH
WHOOSH!
=UHH= THIS SILENT SAMSON IS EVEN STRONGER THAN I SUSPECTED!
IF I DON'T BREAK THIS BEAR-HUG--
THOOOM!
JOB DONE, LEADER!
IRON MAN KNOCKED OUT!
ZZZZ
IN SILENT, SINISTER REPLY:
A SLEEK HOVER-CRAFT DESCENDS--
-- AND THERE IS LIGHT MUSIC IN ITS RISE TO ORBIT...
...THEN FULL ORCHESTRATION IN ITS ACHIEVEMENT OF NEAR-ESCAPE VELOCITY...
ITS HYPER-SPEED TRAVEL...
AND SOFT DESCENT UPON A DESOLATE SOUTHWESTERN LANDSCAPE...
...A LANDSCAPE NOT QUITE SO DESOLATE AS FIRST APPEARS...
FOR, BENEATH ITS TIME-SCARRED SURFACE...
...IS ANOTHER WORLD... AN ALIEN WORLD...

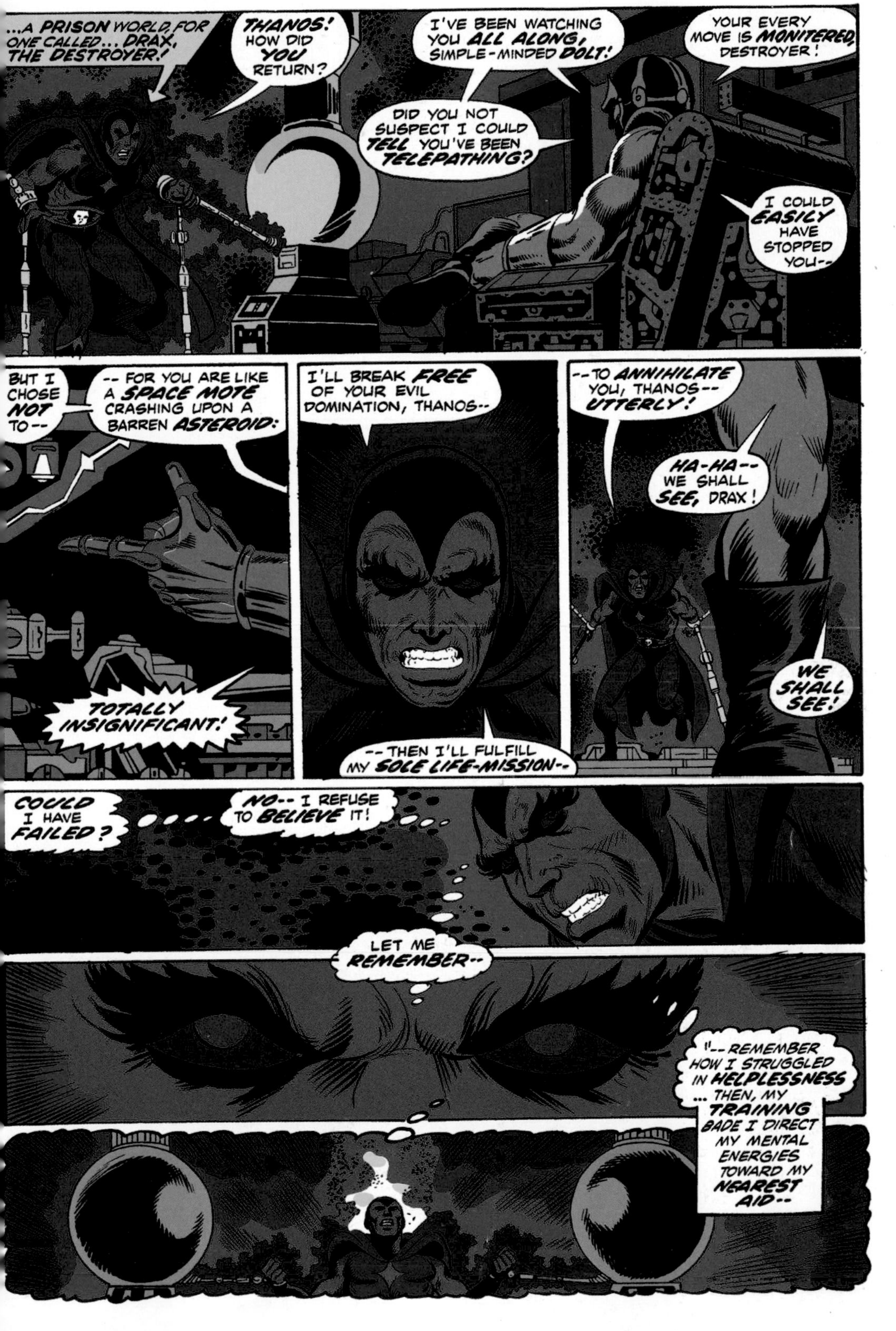
...A PRISON WORLD FOR ONE CALLED... DRAX, THE DESTROYER!
THANOS! HOW DID YOU RETURN?
I'VE BEEN WATCHING YOU ALL ALONG, SIMPLE-MINDED DOLT!
DID YOU NOT SUSPECT I COULD TELL YOU'VE BEEN TELEPATHING?
YOUR EVERY MOVE IS MONITERED, DESTROYER!
I COULD EASILY HAVE STOPPED YOU--
BUT I CHOSE NOT TO--
-- FOR YOU ARE LIKE A SPACE MOTE CRASHING UPON A BARREN ASTEROID:
TOTALLY INSIGNIFICANT!
I'LL BREAK FREE OF YOUR EVIL DOMINATION, THANOS--
-- THEN I'LL FULFILL MY SOLE LIFE-MISSION--
--TO ANNIHILATE YOU, THANOS-- UTTERLY!
HA-HA-- WE SHALL SEE, DRAX!
WE SHALL SEE!
COULD I HAVE FAILED?
NO-- I REFUSE TO BELIEVE IT!
LET ME REMEMBER--
"-- REMEMBER HOW I STRUGGLED IN HELPLESSNESS ... THEN, MY TRAINING BADE I DIRECT MY MENTAL ENERGIES TOWARD MY NEAREST AID--

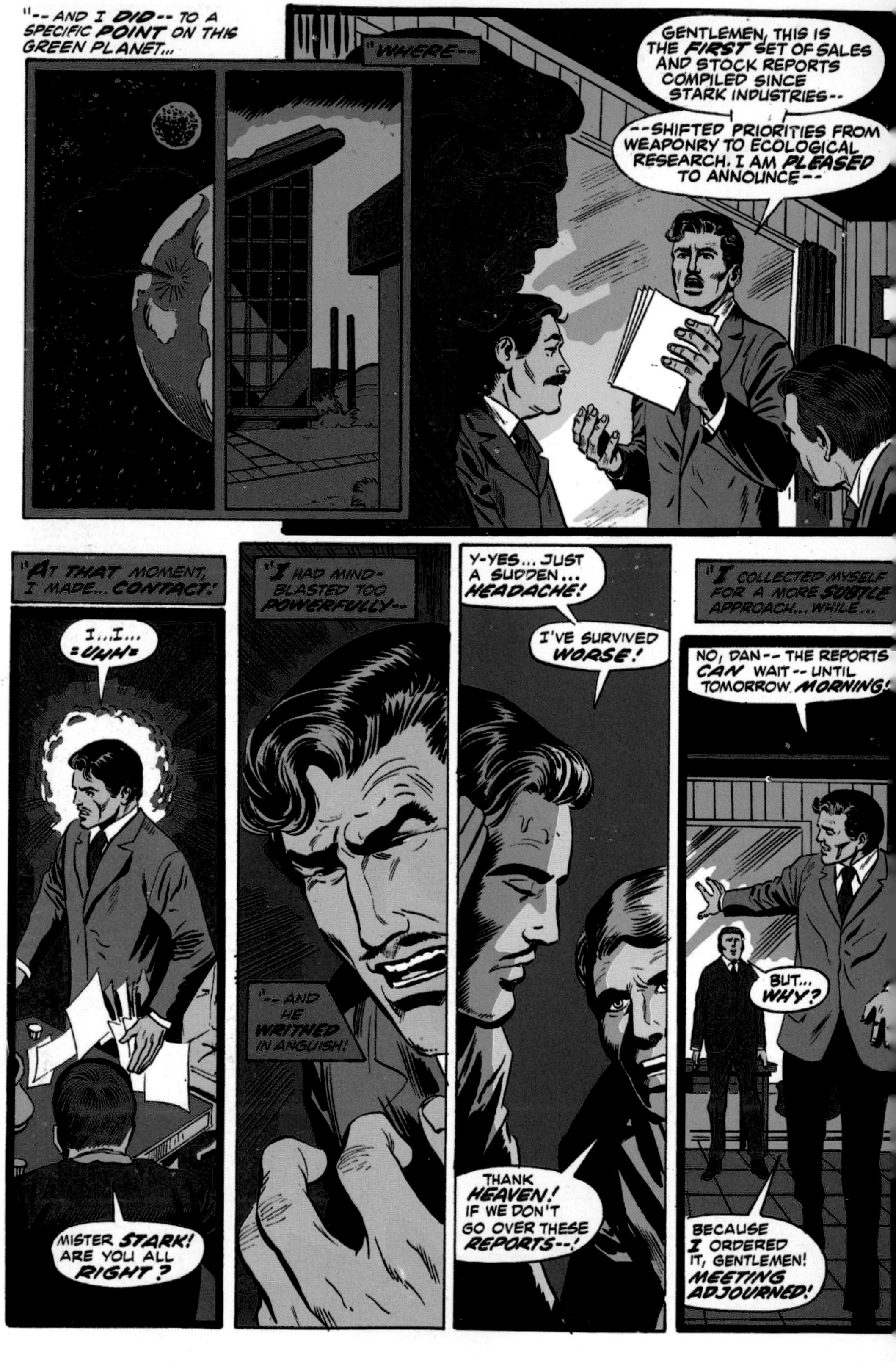
"-- AND I DID -- TO A SPECIFIC POINT ON THIS GREEN PLANET...
"WHERE--
GENTLEMEN, THIS IS THE FIRST SET OF SALES AND STOCK REPORTS COMPILED SINCE STARK INDUSTRIES--
--SHIFTED PRIORITIES FROM WEAPONRY TO ECOLOGICAL RESEARCH. I AM PLEASED TO ANNOUNCE--
"AT THAT MOMENT, I MADE... CONTACT!
I...I... =UHH=
MISTER STARK! ARE YOU ALL RIGHT?
"I HAD MIND-BLASTED TOO POWERFULLY--
"-- AND HE WRITHED IN ANGUISH!
Y-YES... JUST A SUDDEN... HEADACHE!
I'VE SURVIVED WORSE!
THANK HEAVEN! IF WE DON'T GO OVER THESE REPORTS--!
"I COLLECTED MYSELF FOR A MORE SUBTLE APPROACH... WHILE...
NO, DAN -- THE REPORTS CAN WAIT -- UNTIL TOMORROW MORNING!
BUT... WHY?
BECAUSE I ORDERED IT, GENTLEMEN! MEETING ADJOURNED!

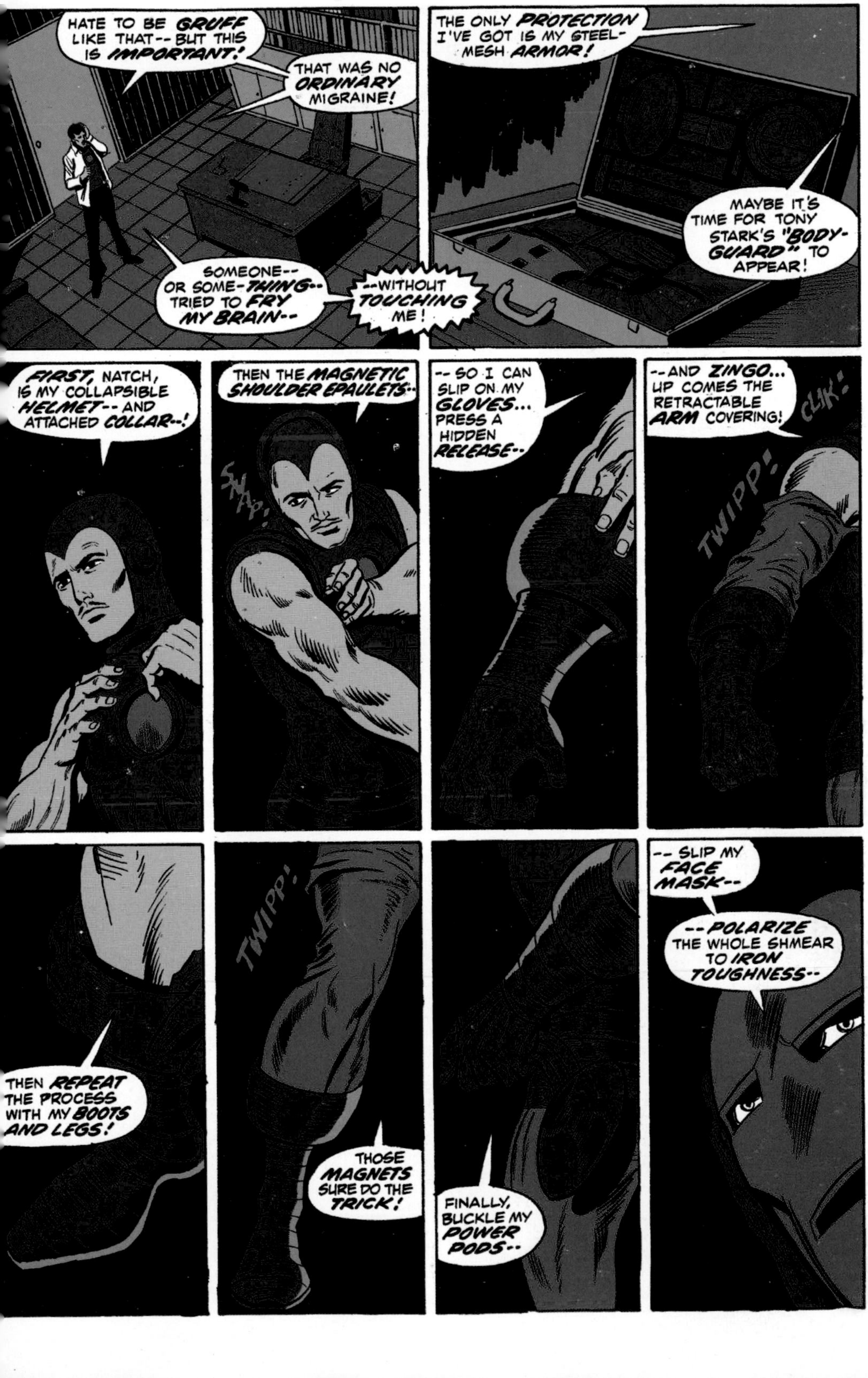
HATE TO BE GRUFF LIKE THAT-- BUT THIS IS IMPORTANT!
THAT WAS NO ORDINARY MIGRAINE!
SOMEONE-- OR SOME-THING-- TRIED TO FRY MY BRAIN--
--WITHOUT TOUCHING ME!
THE ONLY PROTECTION I'VE GOT IS MY STEEL-MESH ARMOR!
MAYBE IT'S TIME FOR TONY STARK'S "BODY-GUARD" TO APPEAR!
FIRST, NATCH, IS MY COLLAPSIBLE HELMET-- AND ATTACHED COLLAR--!
THEN THE MAGNETIC SHOULDER EPAULETS--
SNAP!
-- SO I CAN SLIP ON MY GLOVES... PRESS A HIDDEN RELEASE--
--AND ZINGO... UP COMES THE RETRACTABLE ARM COVERING!
CLIK!
TWIPP!
THEN REPEAT THE PROCESS WITH MY BOOTS AND LEGS!
TWIPP!
THOSE MAGNETS SURE DO THE TRICK!
FINALLY, BUCKLE MY POWER PODS--
-- SLIP MY FACE MASK--
--POLARIZE THE WHOLE SHMEAR TO IRON TOUGHNESS--

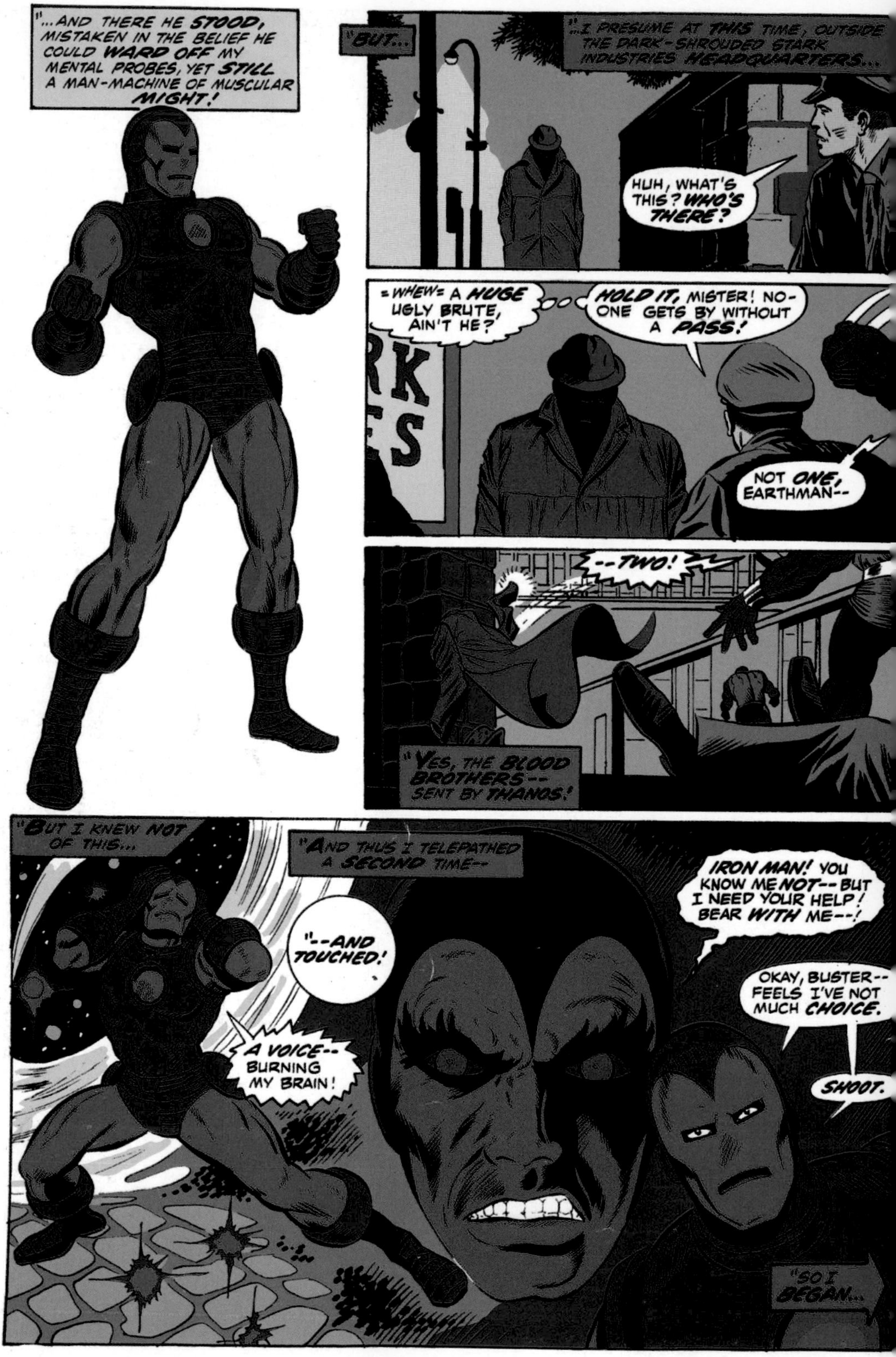
"...AND THERE HE STOOD, MISTAKEN IN THE BELIEF HE COULD WARD OFF MY MENTAL PROBES, YET STILL A MAN-MACHINE OF MUSCULAR MIGHT!
"BUT...
"...I PRESUME AT THIS TIME, OUTSIDE THE DARK-SHROUDED STARK INDUSTRIES HEADQUARTERS...
HUH, WHAT'S THIS? WHO'S THERE?
=WHEW= A HUGE UGLY BRUTE, AIN'T HE?
HOLD IT, MISTER! NO-ONE GETS BY WITHOUT A PASS!
NOT ONE, EARTHMAN--
--TWO!
"YES, THE BLOOD BROTHERS--SENT BY THANOS!
"BUT I KNEW NOT OF THIS...
"AND THUS I TELEPATHED A SECOND TIME--
"--AND TOUCHED!
A VOICE--BURNING MY BRAIN!
IRON MAN! YOU KNOW ME NOT--BUT I NEED YOUR HELP! BEAR WITH ME--!
OKAY, BUSTER--FEELS I'VE NOT MUCH CHOICE.
SHOOT.
"SO I BEGAN...

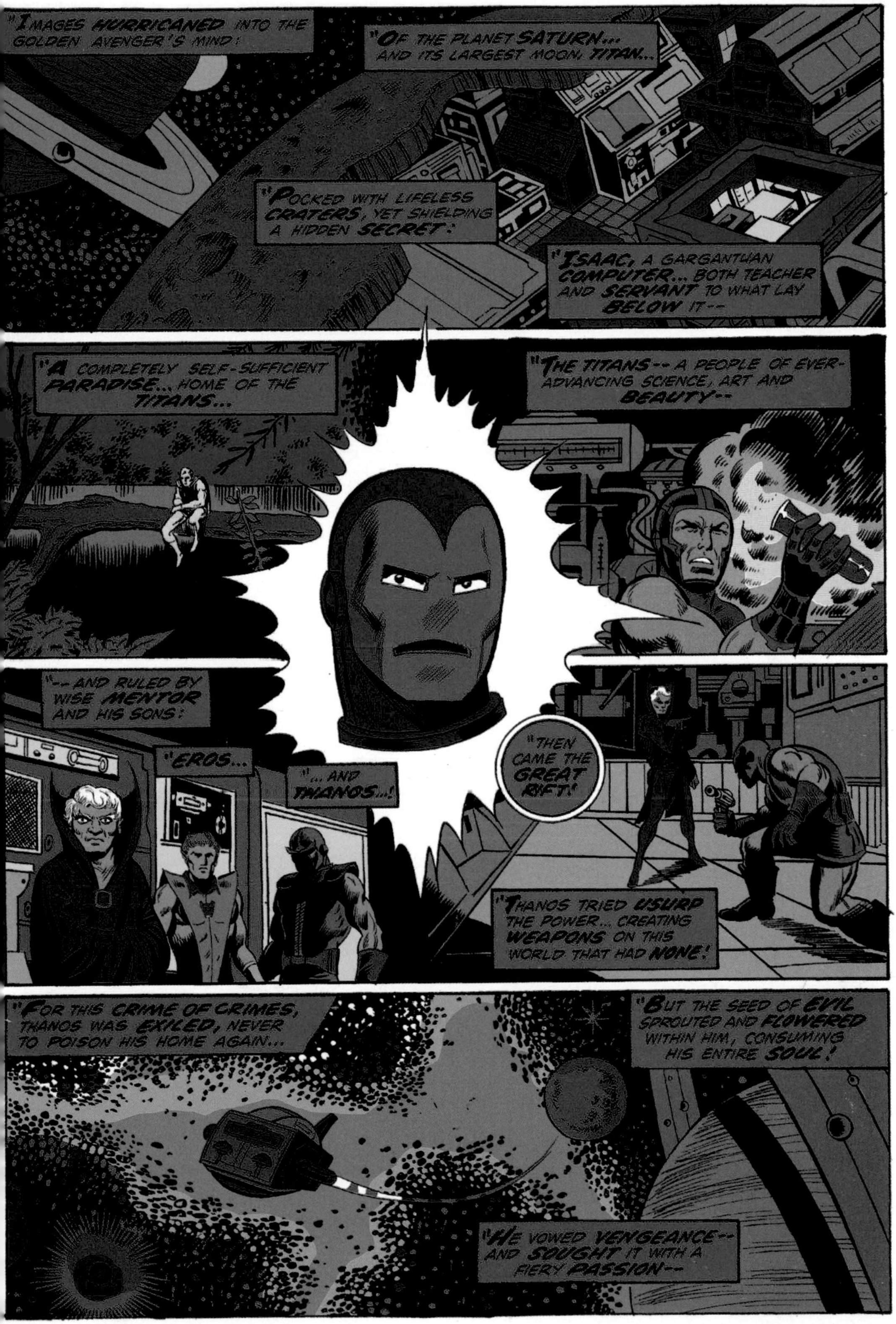
"IMAGES HURRICANED INTO THE GOLDEN AVENGER'S MIND:
"OF THE PLANET SATURN... AND ITS LARGEST MOON, TITAN...
"POCKED WITH LIFELESS CRATERS, YET SHIELDING A HIDDEN SECRET:
"ISAAC, A GARGANTUAN COMPUTER... BOTH TEACHER AND SERVANT TO WHAT LAY BELOW IT--
"A COMPLETELY SELF-SUFFICIENT PARADISE... HOME OF THE TITANS...
"THE TITANS-- A PEOPLE OF EVER-ADVANCING SCIENCE, ART AND BEAUTY--
"--AND RULED BY WISE MENTOR AND HIS SONS:
"EROS...
"...AND THANOS...!
"THEN CAME THE GREAT RIFT!
"THANOS TRIED USURP THE POWER... CREATING WEAPONS ON THIS WORLD THAT HAD NONE!
"FOR THIS CRIME OF CRIMES, THANOS WAS EXILED, NEVER TO POISON HIS HOME AGAIN...
"BUT THE SEED OF EVIL SPROUTED AND FLOWERED WITHIN HIM, CONSUMING HIS ENTIRE SOUL!
"HE VOWED VENGEANCE-- AND SOUGHT IT WITH A FIERY PASSION--

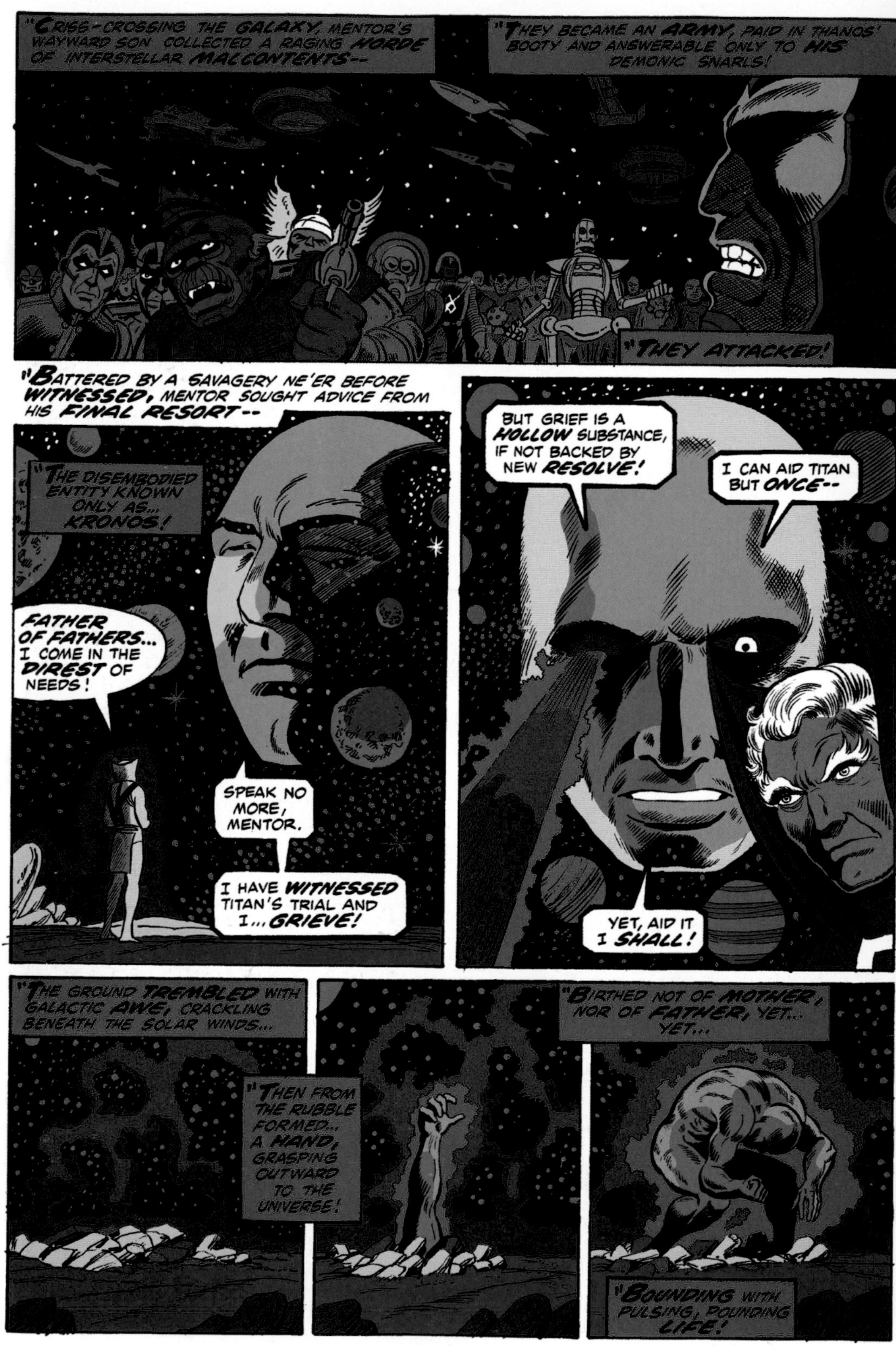
"CRISS-CROSSING THE GALAXY, MENTOR'S WAYWARD SON COLLECTED A RAGING HORDE OF INTERSTELLAR MALCONTENTS--
"THEY BECAME AN ARMY, PAID IN THANOS' BOOTY AND ANSWERABLE ONLY TO HIS DEMONIC SNARLS!
"THEY ATTACKED!
"BATTERED BY A SAVAGERY NE'ER BEFORE WITNESSED, MENTOR SOUGHT ADVICE FROM HIS FINAL RESORT--
"THE DISEMBODIED ENTITY KNOWN ONLY AS... KRONOS!
FATHER OF FATHERS... I COME IN THE DIREST OF NEEDS!
SPEAK NO MORE, MENTOR.
I HAVE WITNESSED TITAN'S TRIAL AND I... GRIEVE!
BUT GRIEF IS A HOLLOW SUBSTANCE, IF NOT BACKED BY NEW RESOLVE!
I CAN AID TITAN BUT ONCE--
YET, AID IT I SHALL!
"THE GROUND TREMBLED WITH GALACTIC AWE, CRACKLING BENEATH THE SOLAR WINDS...
"THEN FROM THE RUBBLE FORMED... A HAND, GRASPING OUTWARD TO THE UNIVERSE!
"BIRTHED NOT OF MOTHER, NOR OF FATHER, YET... YET...
"BOUNDING WITH PULSING, POUNDING LIFE!

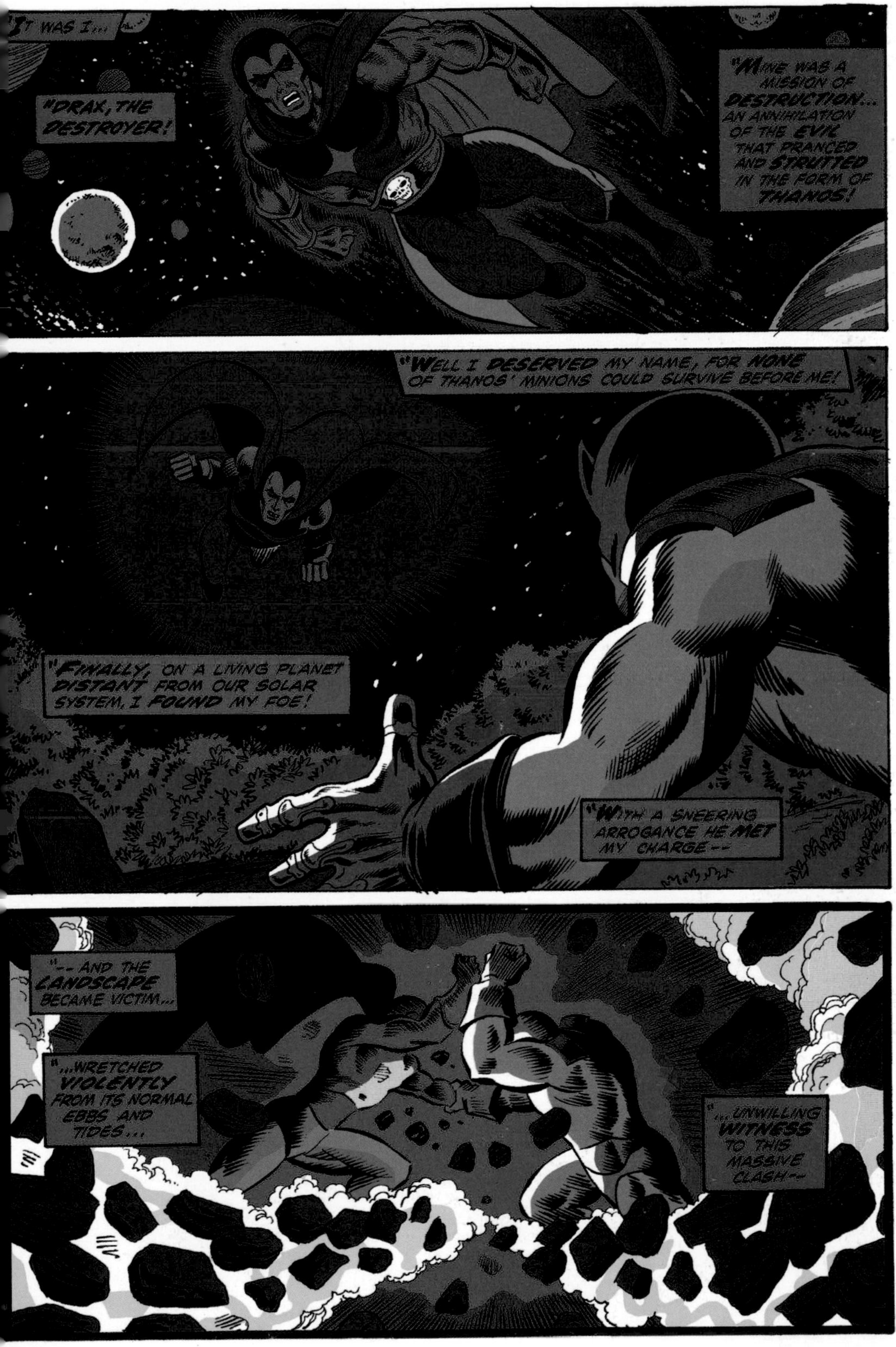
"IT WAS I...
"DRAX, THE DESTROYER!
"MINE WAS A MISSION OF DESTRUCTION... AN ANNIHILATION OF THE EVIL THAT PRANCED AND STRUTTED IN THE FORM OF THANOS!
"WELL I DESERVED MY NAME, FOR NONE OF THANOS' MINIONS COULD SURVIVE BEFORE ME!
"FINALLY, ON A LIVING PLANET DISTANT FROM OUR SOLAR SYSTEM, I FOUND MY FOE!
"WITH A SNEERING ARROGANCE HE MET MY CHARGE--
"--AND THE LANDSCAPE BECAME VICTIM...
"...WRETCHED VIOLENTLY FROM ITS NORMAL EBBS AND TIDES...
"...UNWILLING WITNESS TO THIS MASSIVE CLASH--

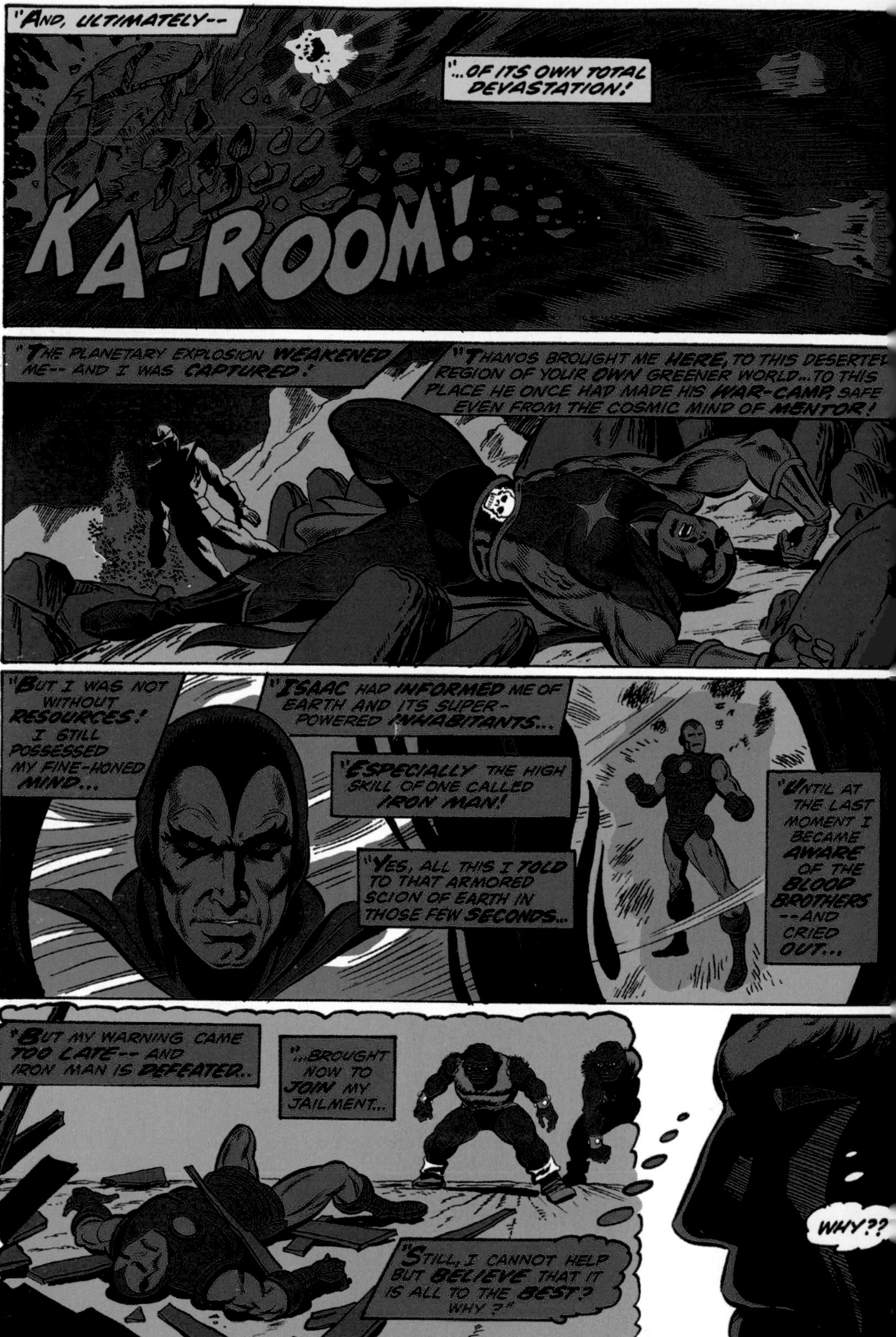
"AND, ULTIMATELY--
"...OF ITS OWN TOTAL DEVASTATION!
KA-ROOM!
"THE PLANETARY EXPLOSION WEAKENED ME-- AND I WAS CAPTURED!
"THANOS BROUGHT ME HERE, TO THIS DESERTED REGION OF YOUR OWN GREENER WORLD...TO THIS PLACE HE ONCE HAD MADE HIS WAR-CAMP, SAFE EVEN FROM THE COSMIC MIND OF MENTOR!
"BUT I WAS NOT WITHOUT RESOURCES! I STILL POSSESSED MY FINE-HONED MIND...
"ISAAC HAD INFORMED ME OF EARTH AND ITS SUPER-POWERED INHABITANTS...
"ESPECIALLY THE HIGH SKILL OF ONE CALLED IRON MAN!
"YES, ALL THIS I TOLD TO THAT ARMORED SCION OF EARTH IN THOSE FEW SECONDS...
"UNTIL AT THE LAST MOMENT I BECAME AWARE OF THE BLOOD BROTHERS --AND CRIED OUT...
"BUT MY WARNING CAME TOO LATE-- AND IRON MAN IS DEFEATED...
"...BROUGHT NOW TO JOIN MY JAILMENT...
"STILL, I CANNOT HELP BUT BELIEVE THAT IT IS ALL TO THE BEST? WHY?"
WHY??

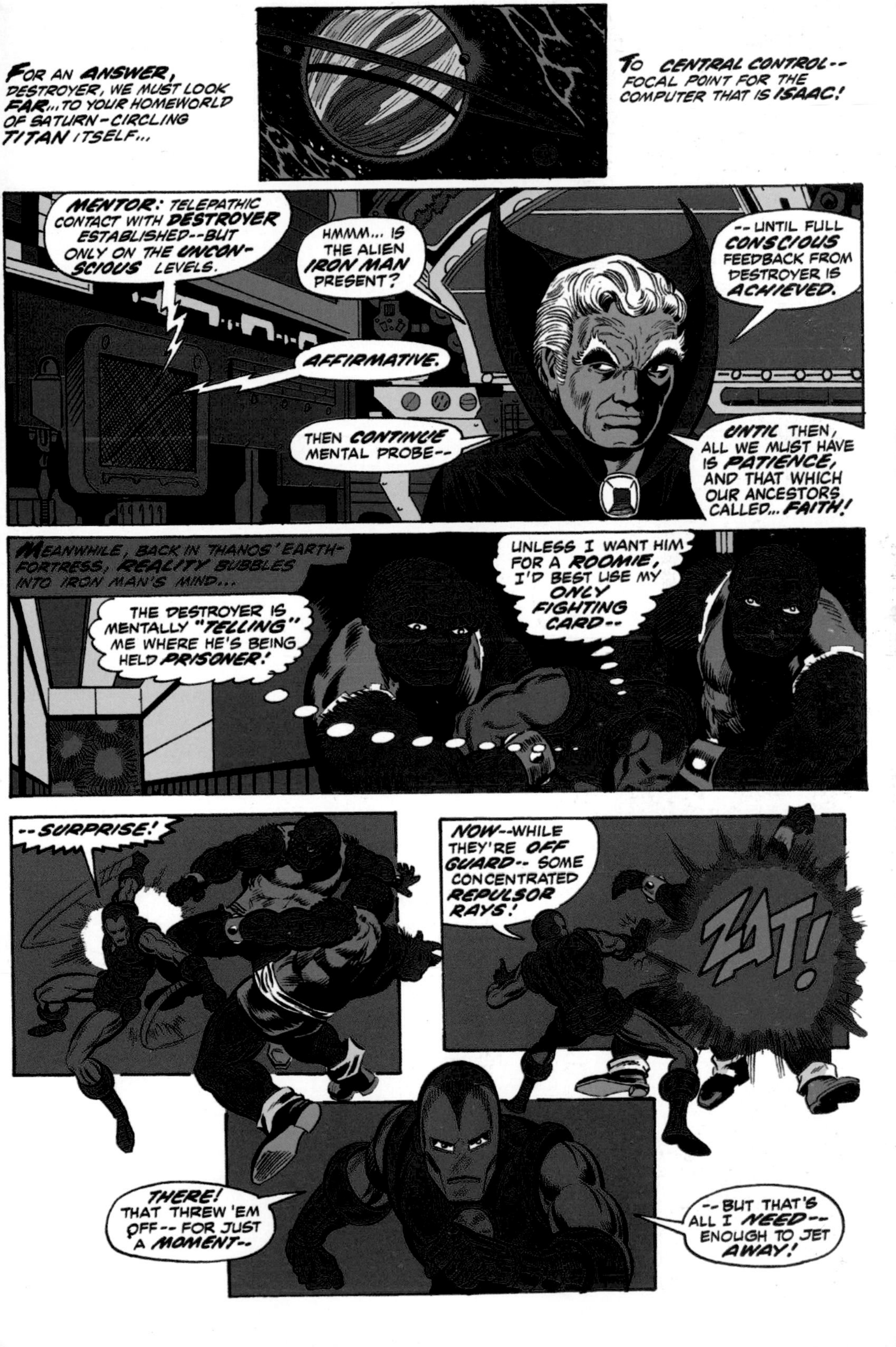
FOR AN ANSWER, DESTROYER, WE MUST LOOK FAR... TO YOUR HOMEWORLD OF SATURN-CIRCLING TITAN ITSELF...
TO CENTRAL CONTROL-- FOCAL POINT FOR THE COMPUTER THAT IS ISAAC!
MENTOR: TELEPATHIC CONTACT WITH DESTROYER ESTABLISHED--BUT ONLY ON THE UNCONSCIOUS LEVELS.
HMMM... IS THE ALIEN IRON MAN PRESENT?
AFFIRMATIVE.
THEN CONTINUE MENTAL PROBE--
--UNTIL FULL CONSCIOUS FEEDBACK FROM DESTROYER IS ACHIEVED.
UNTIL THEN, ALL WE MUST HAVE IS PATIENCE, AND THAT WHICH OUR ANCESTORS CALLED... FAITH!
MEANWHILE, BACK IN THANOS' EARTH-FORTRESS, REALITY BUBBLES INTO IRON MAN'S MIND...
THE DESTROYER IS MENTALLY "TELLING" ME WHERE HE'S BEING HELD PRISONER!
UNLESS I WANT HIM FOR A ROOMIE, I'D BEST USE MY ONLY FIGHTING CARD--
--SURPRISE!
NOW--WHILE THEY'RE OFF GUARD-- SOME CONCENTRATED REPULSOR RAYS!
ZAT!
THERE! THAT THREW 'EM OFF-- FOR JUST A MOMENT--
--BUT THAT'S ALL I NEED-- ENOUGH TO JET AWAY!

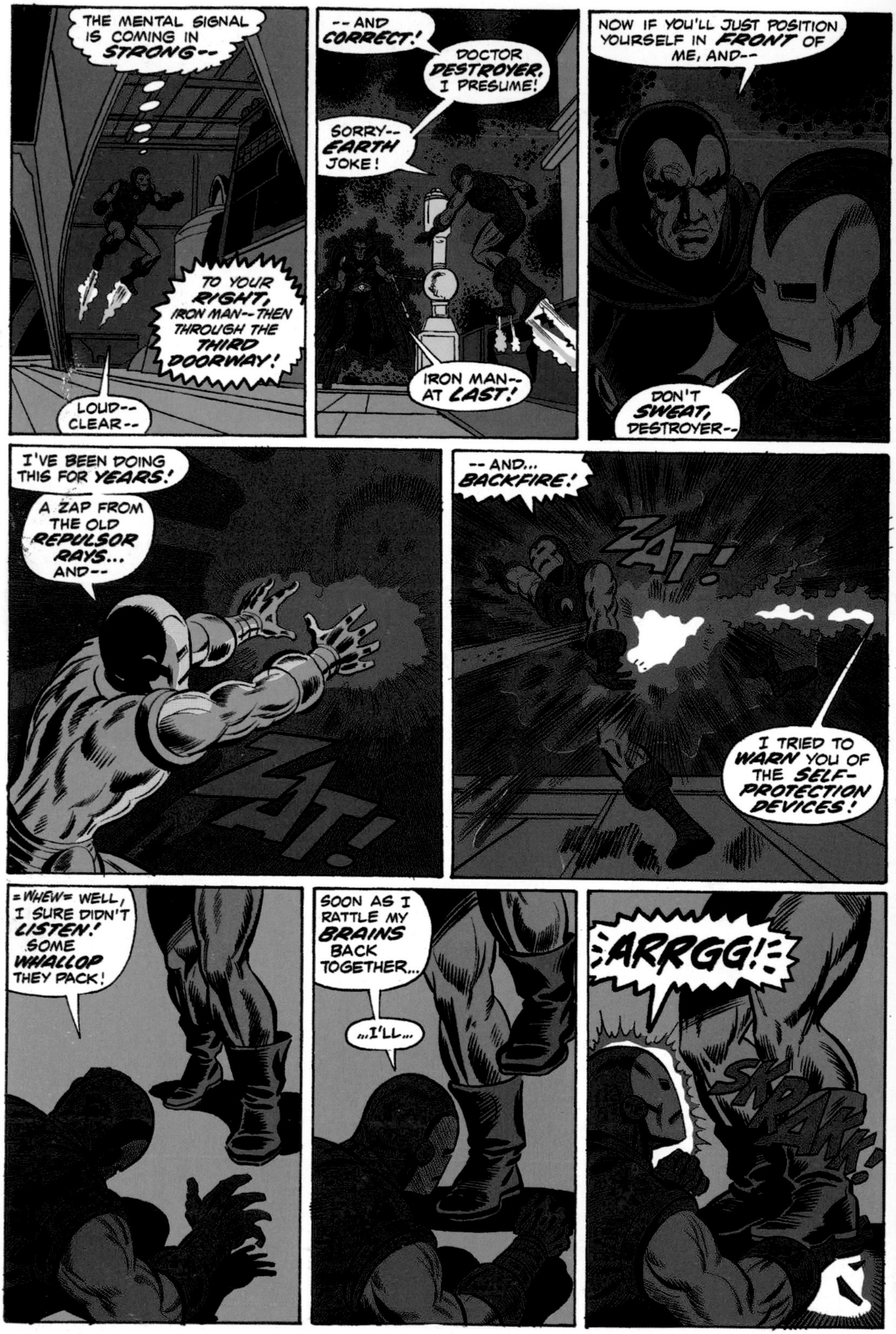
THE MENTAL SIGNAL IS COMING IN STRONG--
TO YOUR RIGHT, IRON MAN--THEN THROUGH THE THIRD DOORWAY!
LOUD-- CLEAR--
--AND CORRECT!
DOCTOR DESTROYER, I PRESUME!
SORRY-- EARTH JOKE!
IRON MAN-- AT LAST!
NOW IF YOU'LL JUST POSITION YOURSELF IN FRONT OF ME, AND--
DON'T SWEAT, DESTROYER--
I'VE BEEN DOING THIS FOR YEARS!
A ZAP FROM THE OLD REPULSOR RAYS... AND--
ZAT!
--AND... BACKFIRE!
ZAT!
I TRIED TO WARN YOU OF THE SELF-PROTECTION DEVICES!
=WHEW= WELL, I SURE DIDN'T LISTEN! SOME WHALLOP THEY PACK!
SOON AS I RATTLE MY BRAINS BACK TOGETHER...
...I'LL...
ARRGG!
SKRAK!

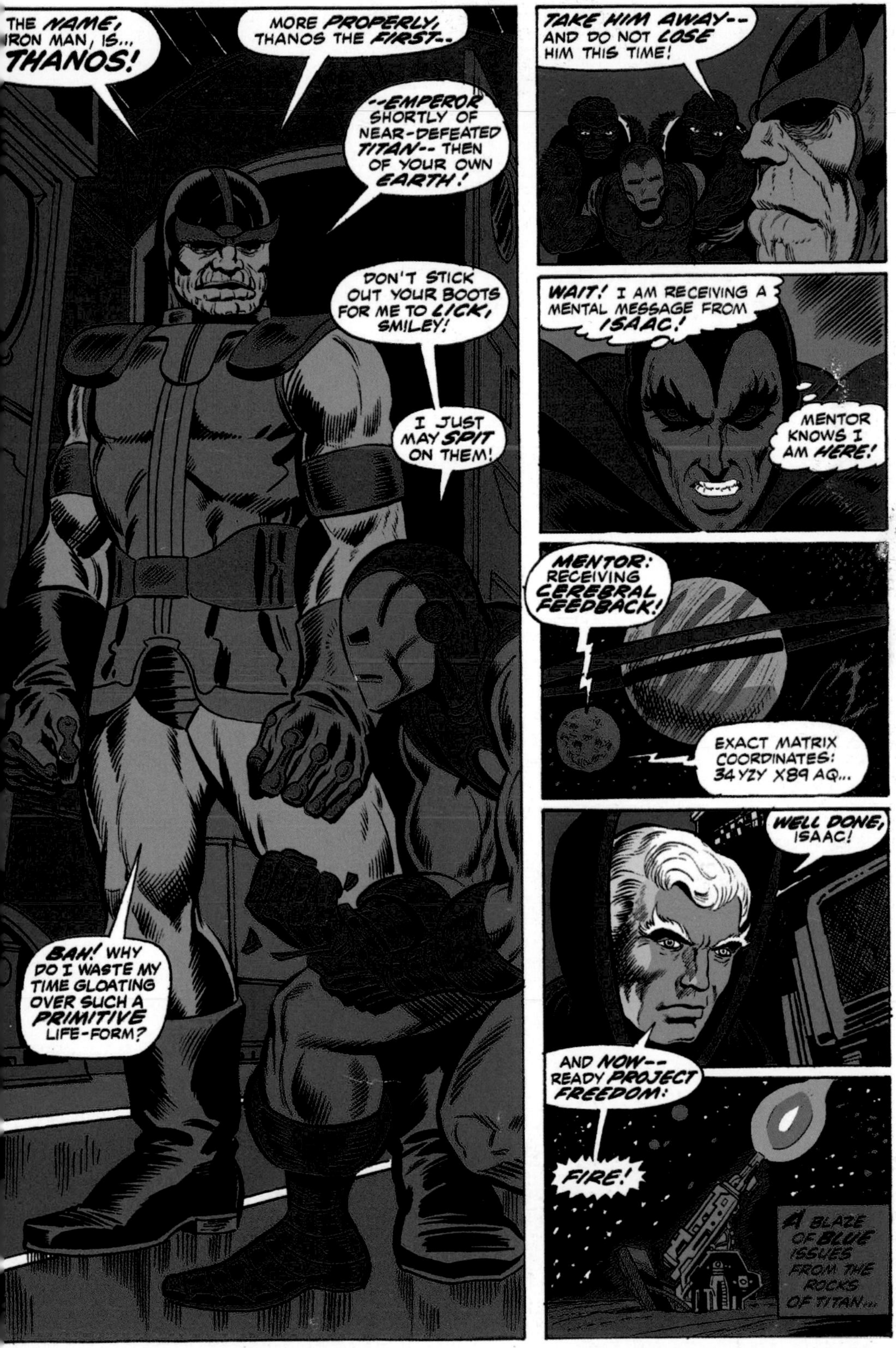
THE NAME, IRON MAN, IS... THANOS!
MORE PROPERLY, THANOS THE FIRST--
--EMPEROR SHORTLY OF NEAR-DEFEATED TITAN-- THEN OF YOUR OWN EARTH!
DON'T STICK OUT YOUR BOOTS FOR ME TO LICK, SMILEY!
I JUST MAY SPIT ON THEM!
BAH! WHY DO I WASTE MY TIME GLOATING OVER SUCH A PRIMITIVE LIFE-FORM?
TAKE HIM AWAY-- AND DO NOT LOSE HIM THIS TIME!
WAIT! I AM RECEIVING A MENTAL MESSAGE FROM ISAAC!
MENTOR KNOWS I AM HERE!
MENTOR: RECEIVING CEREBRAL FEEDBACK!
EXACT MATRIX COORDINATES: 34YZY X89 AQ...
WELL DONE, ISAAC!
AND NOW-- READY PROJECT FREEDOM:
FIRE!
A BLAZE OF BLUE ISSUES FROM THE ROCKS OF TITAN...

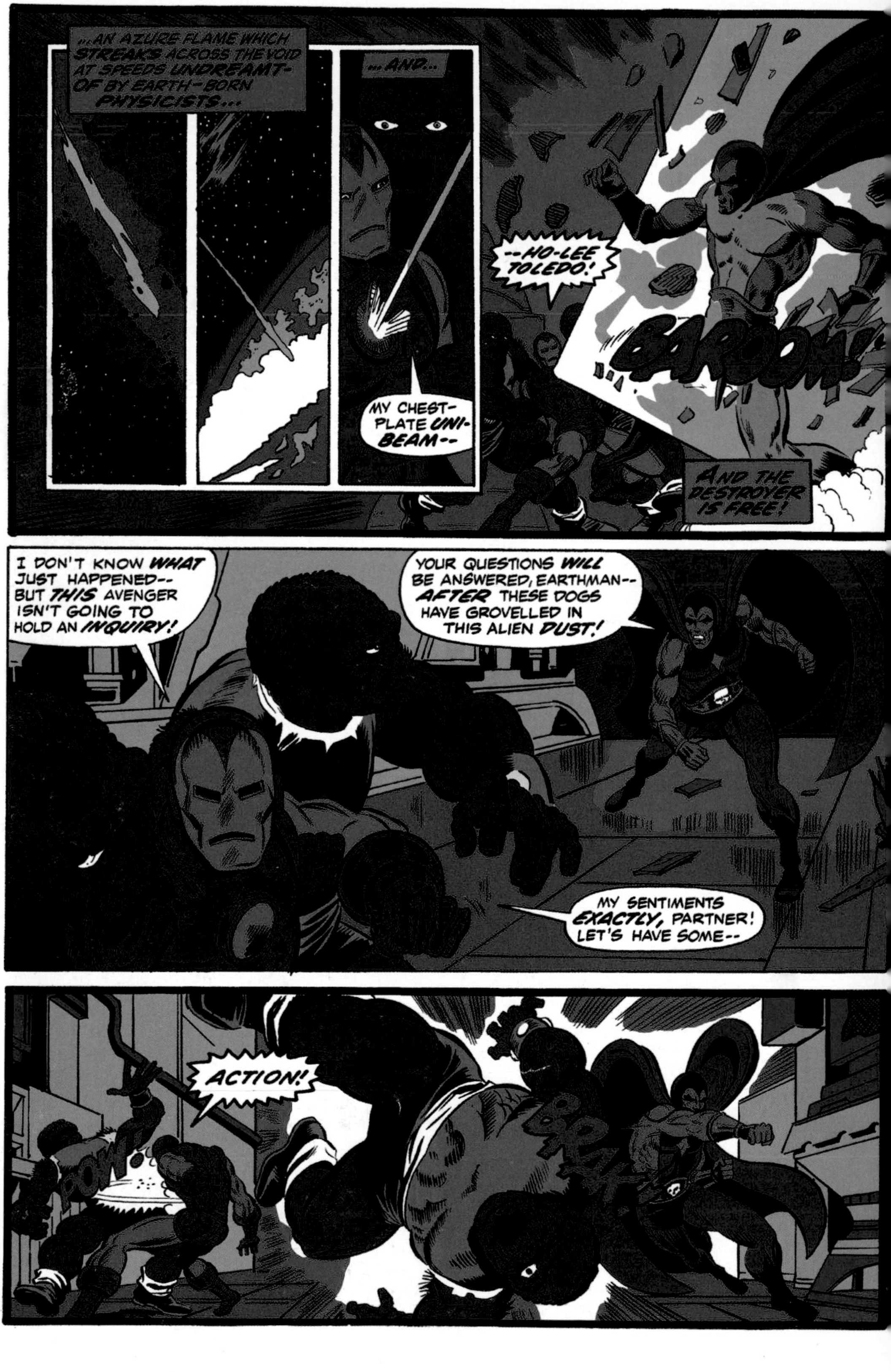
...AN AZURE FLAME WHICH STREAKS ACROSS THE VOID AT SPEEDS UNDREAMT-OF BY EARTH-BORN PHYSICISTS...
...AND...
MY CHEST-PLATE UNI-BEAM--
--HO-LEE TOLEDO!
BAROOM!
AND THE DESTROYER IS FREE!
I DON'T KNOW WHAT JUST HAPPENED-- BUT THIS AVENGER ISN'T GOING TO HOLD AN INQUIRY!
YOUR QUESTIONS WILL BE ANSWERED, EARTHMAN-- AFTER THESE DOGS HAVE GROVELLED IN THIS ALIEN DUST!
MY SENTIMENTS EXACTLY, PARTNER! LET'S HAVE SOME--
ACTION!

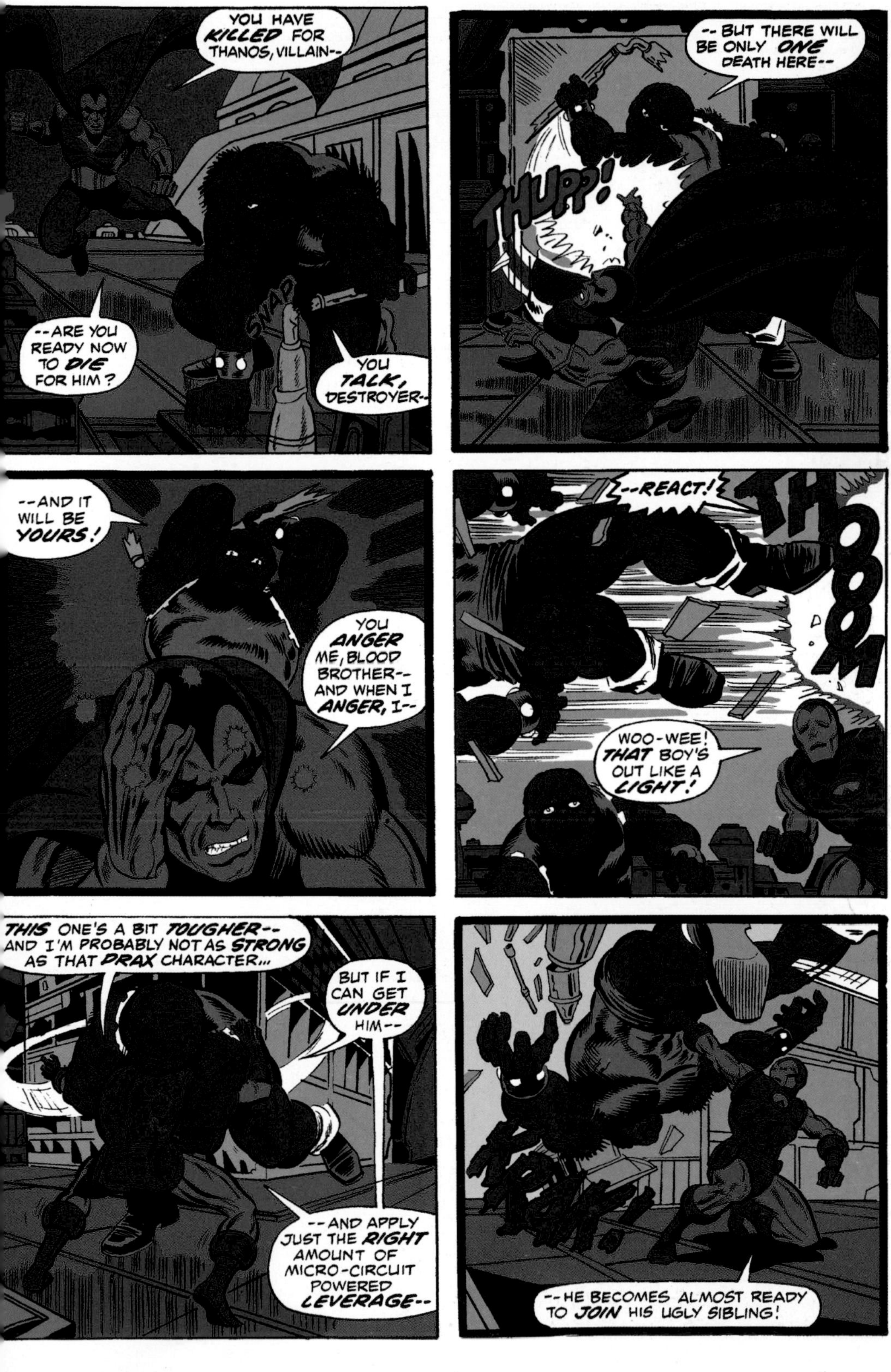

YOU HAVE KILLED FOR THANOS, VILLAIN--
--ARE YOU READY NOW TO DIE FOR HIM?
SNAP
YOU TALK, DESTROYER--
--BUT THERE WILL BE ONLY ONE DEATH HERE--
THUPP!
--AND IT WILL BE YOURS!
YOU ANGER ME, BLOOD BROTHER--AND WHEN I ANGER, I--
--REACT!
THOOOM
WOO-WEE! THAT BOY'S OUT LIKE A LIGHT!
THIS ONE'S A BIT TOUGHER--AND I'M PROBABLY NOT AS STRONG AS THAT DRAX CHARACTER...
BUT IF I CAN GET UNDER HIM--
--AND APPLY JUST THE RIGHT AMOUNT OF MICRO-CIRCUIT POWERED LEVERAGE--
--HE BECOMES ALMOST READY TO JOIN HIS UGLY SIBLING!

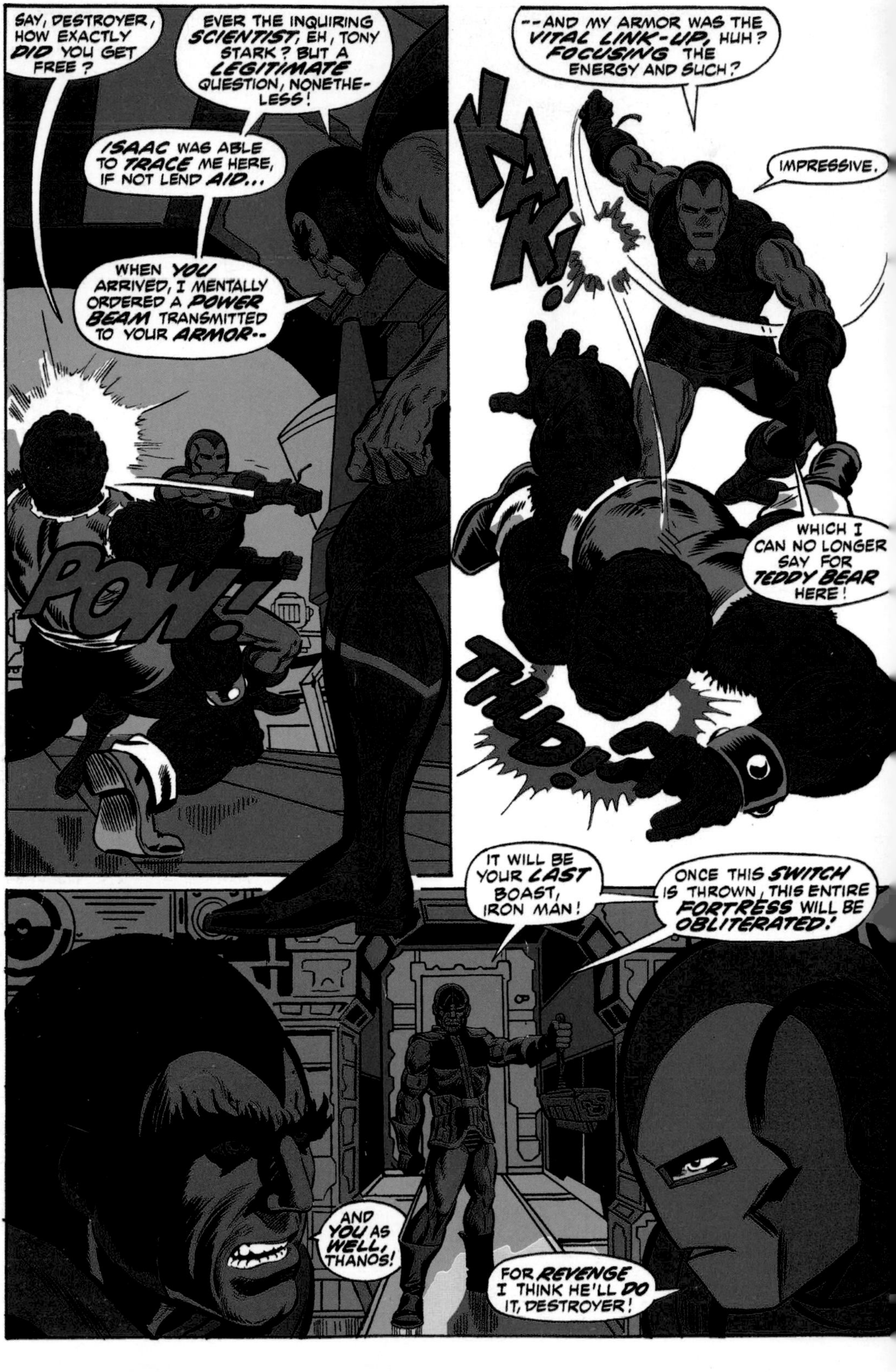
SAY, DESTROYER, HOW EXACTLY DID YOU GET FREE?
EVER THE INQUIRING SCIENTIST, EH, TONY STARK? BUT A LEGITIMATE QUESTION, NONETHELESS!
ISAAC WAS ABLE TO TRACE ME HERE, IF NOT LEND AID...
WHEN YOU ARRIVED, I MENTALLY ORDERED A POWER BEAM TRANSMITTED TO YOUR ARMOR--
POW!
--AND MY ARMOR WAS THE VITAL LINK-UP, HUH? FOCUSING THE ENERGY AND SUCH?
KAK!
IMPRESSIVE.
WHICH I CAN NO LONGER SAY FOR TEDDY BEAR HERE!
THUD!
IT WILL BE YOUR LAST BOAST, IRON MAN!
ONCE THIS SWITCH IS THROWN, THIS ENTIRE FORTRESS WILL BE OBLITERATED!
AND YOU AS WELL, THANOS!
FOR REVENGE I THINK HE'LL DO IT, DESTROYER!

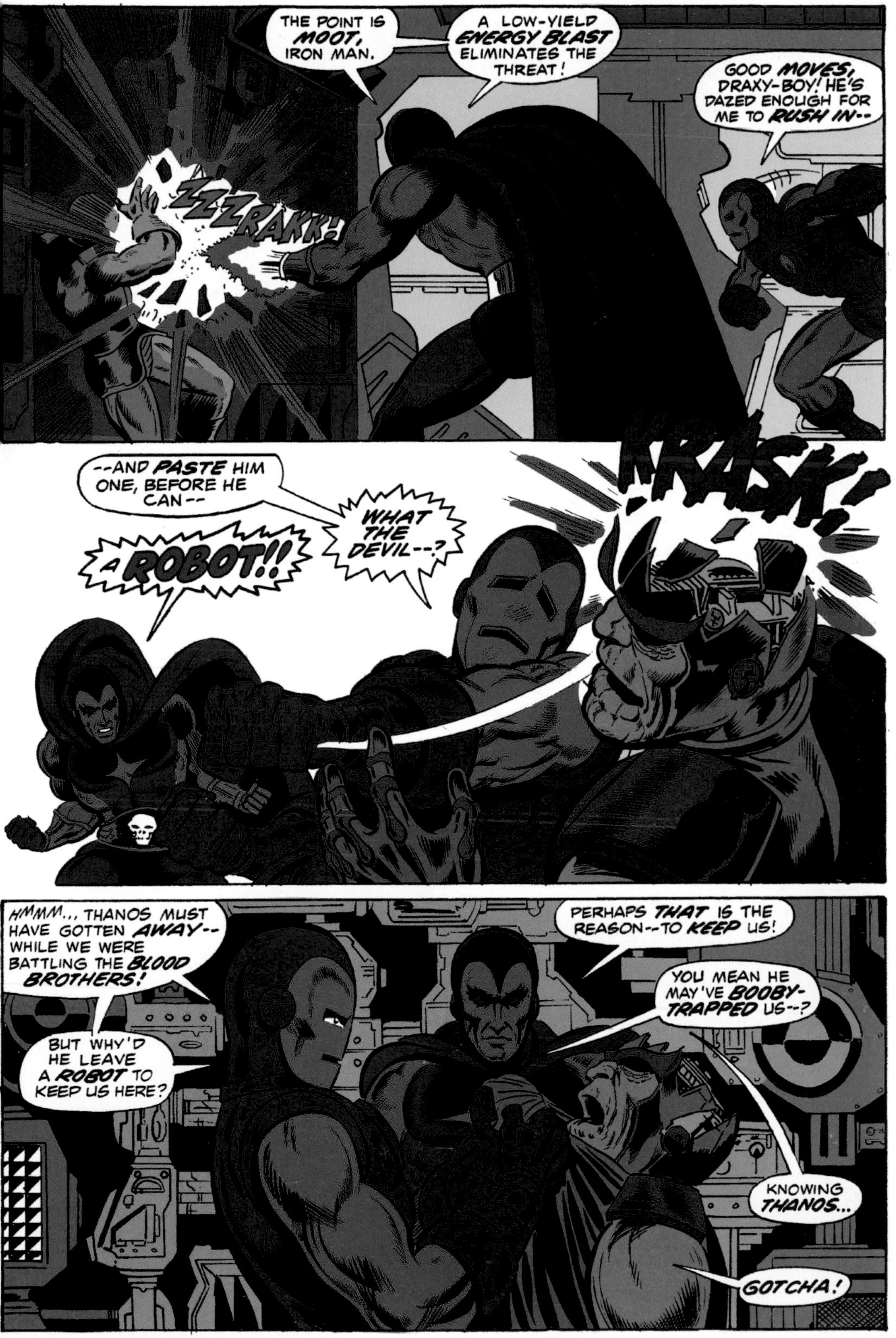
THE POINT IS MOOT, IRON MAN.
A LOW-YIELD ENERGY BLAST ELIMINATES THE THREAT!
ZZZRAKK!
GOOD MOVES, DRAXY-BOY! HE'S DAZED ENOUGH FOR ME TO RUSH IN--
--AND PASTE HIM ONE, BEFORE HE CAN--
KRASK!
WHAT THE DEVIL--?
A ROBOT!!
HMMM... THANOS MUST HAVE GOTTEN AWAY-- WHILE WE WERE BATTLING THE BLOOD BROTHERS!
BUT WHY'D HE LEAVE A ROBOT TO KEEP US HERE?
PERHAPS THAT IS THE REASON--TO KEEP US!
YOU MEAN HE MAY'VE BOOBY-TRAPPED US--?
KNOWING THANOS...
GOTCHA!

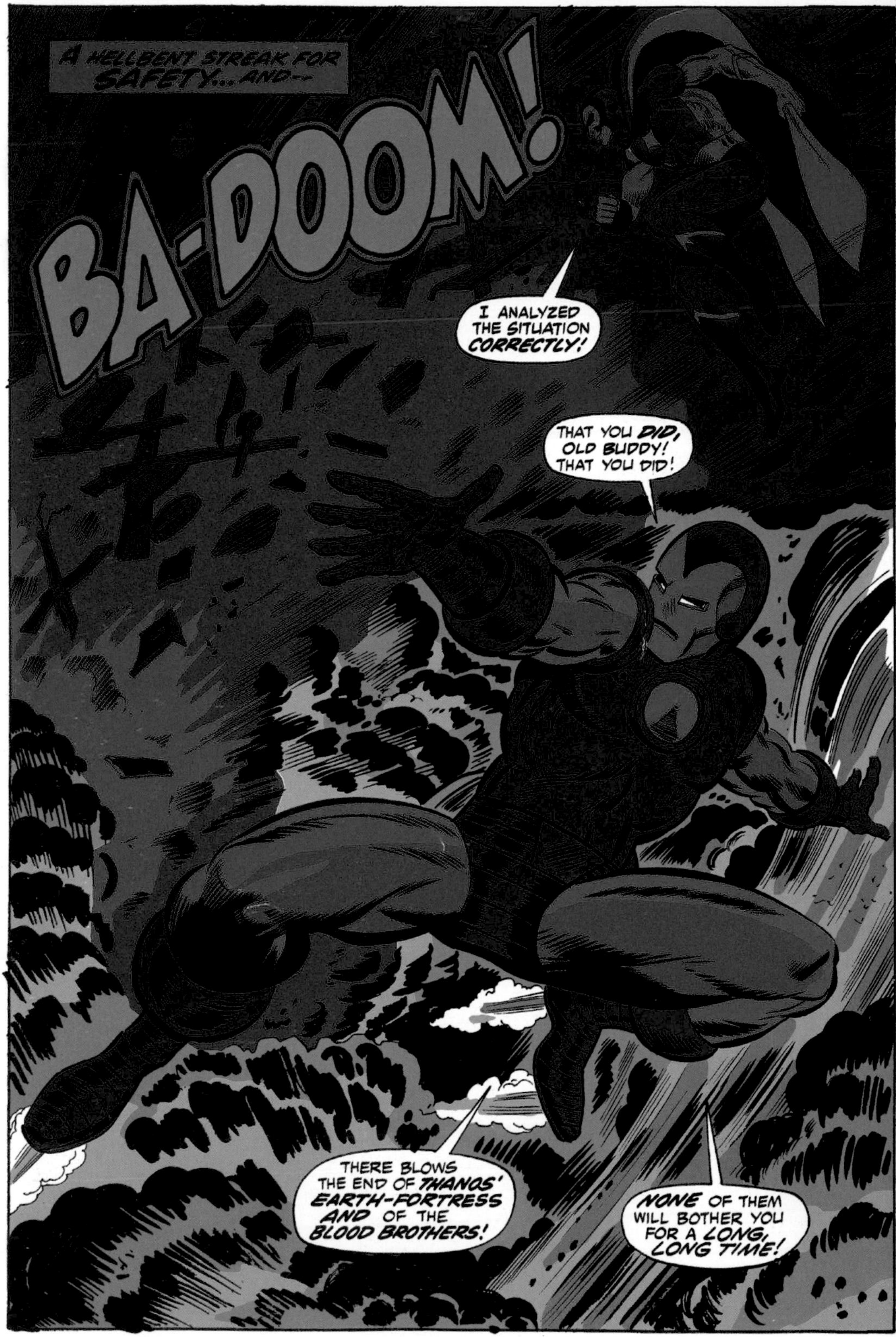

A HELLBENT STREAK FOR SAFETY... AND--
BA-DOOM!
I ANALYZED THE SITUATION CORRECTLY!
THAT YOU DID, OLD BUDDY! THAT YOU DID!
THERE BLOWS THE END OF THANOS' EARTH-FORTRESS AND OF THE BLOOD BROTHERS!
NONE OF THEM WILL BOTHER YOU FOR A LONG, LONG TIME!

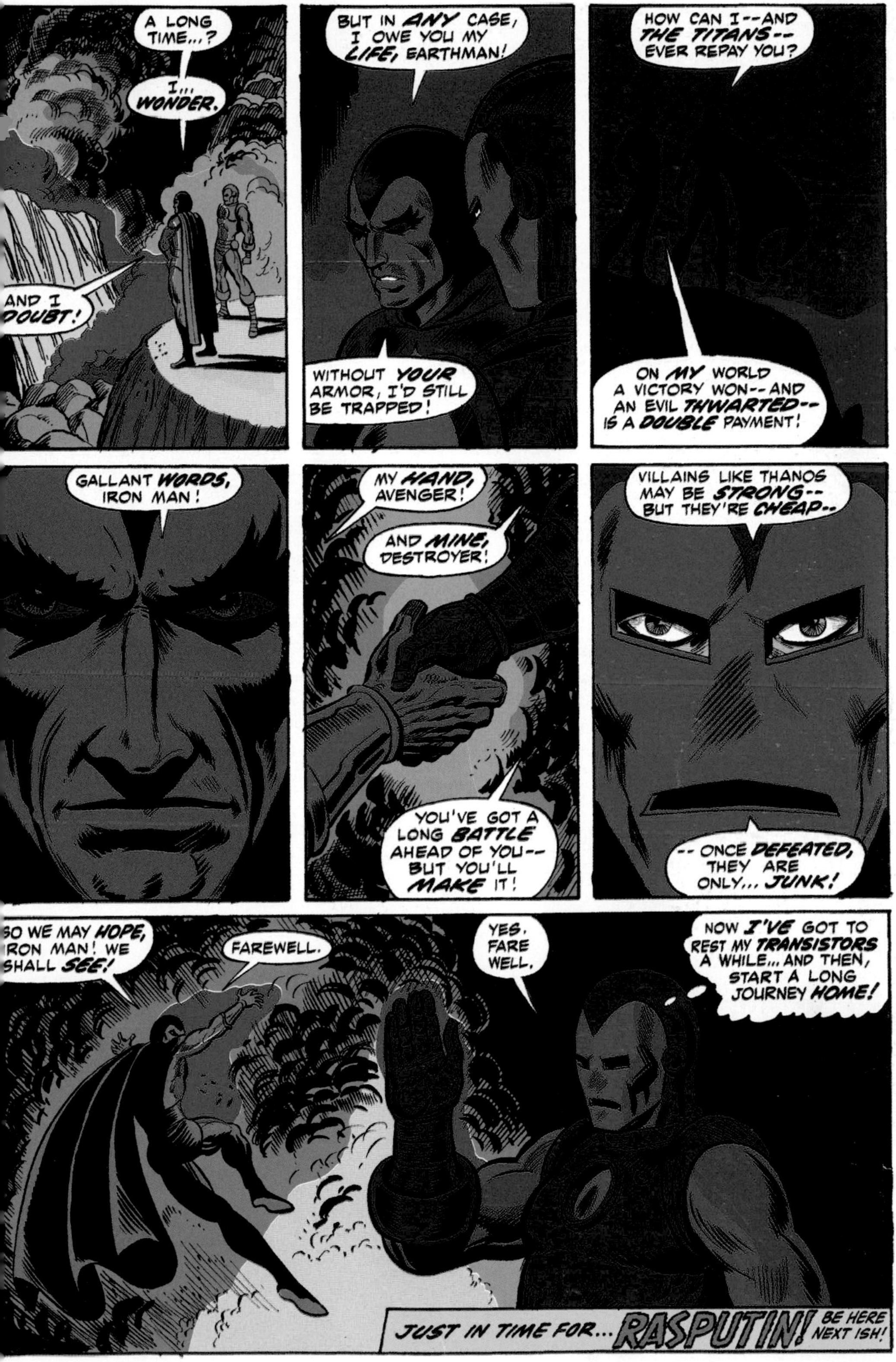
A LONG TIME...?
I... WONDER.
AND I DOUBT!
BUT IN ANY CASE, I OWE YOU MY LIFE, EARTHMAN!
WITHOUT YOUR ARMOR, I'D STILL BE TRAPPED!
HOW CAN I--AND THE TITANS--EVER REPAY YOU?
ON MY WORLD A VICTORY WON--AND AN EVIL THWARTED--IS A DOUBLE PAYMENT!
GALLANT WORDS, IRON MAN!
MY HAND, AVENGER!
AND MINE, DESTROYER!
YOU'VE GOT A LONG BATTLE AHEAD OF YOU--BUT YOU'LL MAKE IT!
VILLAINS LIKE THANOS MAY BE STRONG--BUT THEY'RE CHEAP--
--ONCE DEFEATED, THEY ARE ONLY... JUNK!
SO WE MAY HOPE, IRON MAN! WE SHALL SEE!
FAREWELL.
YES. FARE WELL.
NOW I'VE GOT TO REST MY TRANSISTORS A WHILE... AND THEN, START A LONG JOURNEY HOME!
JUST IN TIME FOR... RASPUTIN! BE HERE NEXT ISH!

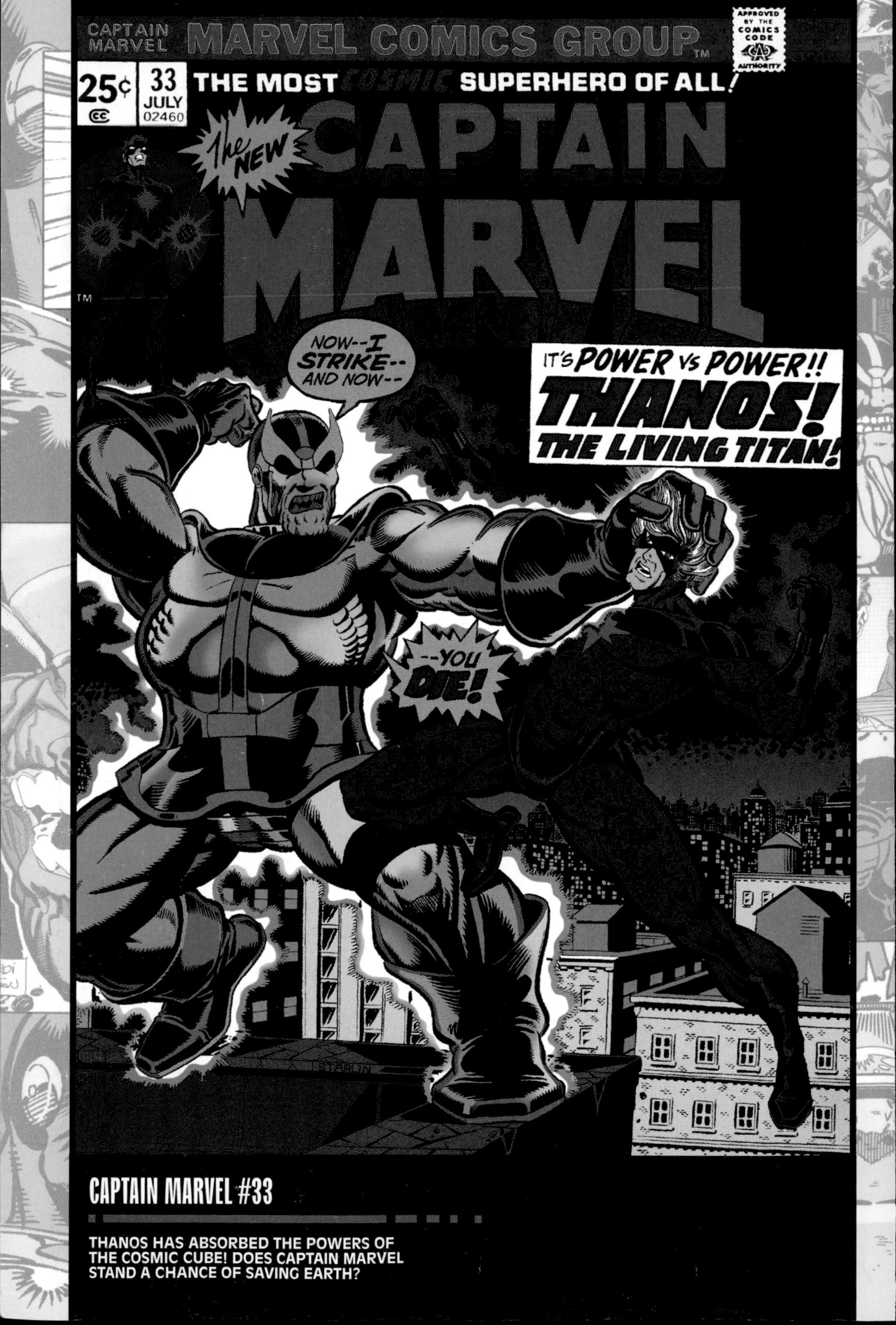
CAPTAIN MARVEL
MARVEL COMICS GROUP
APPROVED BY THE COMICS CODE AUTHORITY
25¢
33 JULY 02460
THE MOST COSMIC SUPERHERO OF ALL!
The NEW
CAPTAIN MARVEL
NOW--I STRIKE-- AND NOW--
IT'S POWER VS POWER!! THANOS! THE LIVING TITAN!
--YOU DIE!

CAPTAIN MARVEL #33

THANOS HAS ABSORBED THE POWERS OF THE COSMIC CUBE! DOES CAPTAIN MARVEL STAND A CHANCE OF SAVING EARTH?

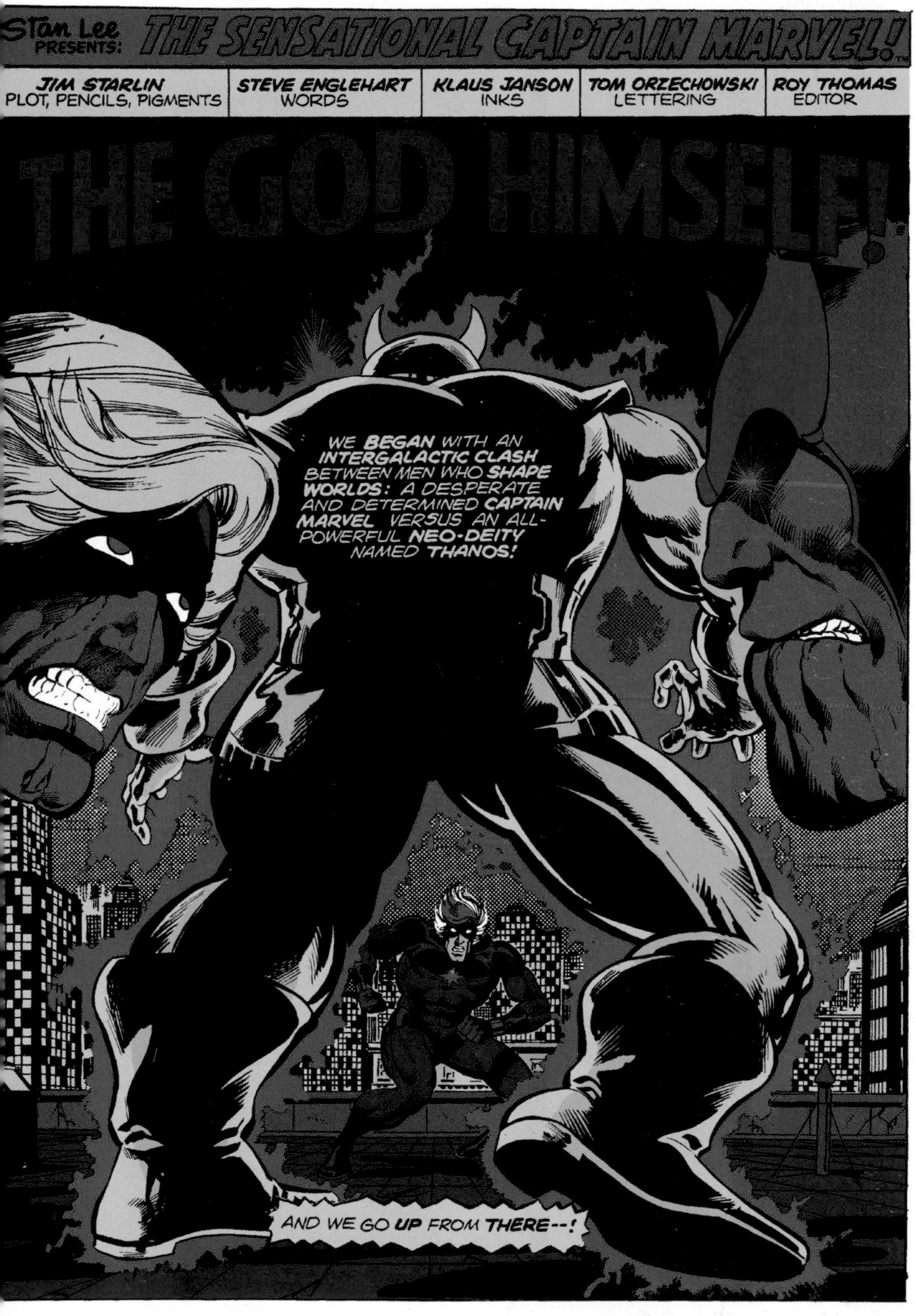
Stan Lee PRESENTS: THE SENSATIONAL CAPTAIN MARVEL!
JIM STARLIN PLOT, PENCILS, PIGMENTS
STEVE ENGLEHART WORDS
KLAUS JANSON INKS
TOM ORZECHOWSKI LETTERING
ROY THOMAS EDITOR
THE GOD HIMSELF!
WE BEGAN WITH AN INTERGALACTIC CLASH BETWEEN MEN WHO SHAPE WORLDS: A DESPERATE AND DETERMINED CAPTAIN MARVEL VERSUS AN ALL-POWERFUL NEO-DEITY NAMED THANOS!
AND WE GO UP FROM THERE--!

WHAT, YOU MAY WELL ASK...

? ...IS GOING ON HERE?

WELL...

BEFORE THERE WAS **CAPTAIN MARVEL**, BEFORE THERE WAS **THANOS**, THERE WAS **SATURN**, THE SIXTH PLANET FROM THE SUN... AND ITS **SATELLITE TITAN**.

TITAN WAS A **DREAM WORLD**--A LAND OF **LIGHT** AND **PEACE** AND **WONDROUS JOY!** TITAN WAS A **GARDEN OF EDEN** WITHOUT A LURKING **SERPENT!**

BUT IN THE END, THE SERPENT **CAME**, IN THE FORM OF THE DARKLING **SON** OF TITAN'S **CREATOR**... AND THE SERPENT'S NAME WAS **THANOS!** AS **PRINCE**, HE TASTED **POWER**...

...AND IT WAS A DELICACY HE FOUND HE **CRAVED!** WHEN HE DARED, HE BUILT A **WEAPON** -- THE **ULTIMATE CRIME!** HIS **FATHER, MENTOR,** ORDERED **EXILE!**

THUS, **DEPART** THE DREAM WORLD THANOS DID, TAKING **NONE** OF THE **PEACE** AND **JOY** WITH HIM. HIS HEART WAS FILLED WITH THUNDEROUS **HATRED**--

--AND HIS **EYE** WAS FIXED ON HIS **FATHER'S POWER!** AS HE CLEARED THE DREAM WORLD'S **ATMOSPHERE**, HE LAUNCHED TWO STREAKING **MISSILES**...

...WHOSE PRE-PROGRAMMED **DEATH-WISH** HURLED THEM INTO THE TWIN **POPULATION** CENTERS OF TITAN, **INFLICTING** THEIR WISH WITH SCREAMING **FINALITY!**

MOST OF TITAN, THE **PEOPLE** AND THE **DREAMS, DIED** IN THAT TERRIBLE ATTACK. AMONG THEM WAS ONE CALLED **SUI-SAN,** SHE WHO WAS **MOTHER** TO THANOS.

BUT THAT SLAUGHTER DID NOT STOP THE WARLORD, THANOS. HE **RETURNED** TO TITAN, AND **REPOPULATED** IT WITH AN ARMY OF ALIEN **OUTCASTS** --

--AS THE **FIRST STEP** IN HIS PROJECTED **CONQUEST OF THE UNIVERSE!** HIS **SECOND** STEP WAS TO CAPTURE THE **COSMIC CUBE** FROM **EARTH!**

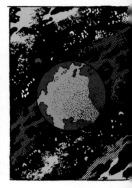

HOWEVER, MIGHTY **KRONOS**--A GOD, PERHAPS, OR SOMETHING NEAR--CREATED **DRAX THE DESTROYER** TO COUNTER THANOS!

THE DESTROYER CAME TO EARTH TO DO **BATTLE** WITH THE WARLORD, AND HERE MET **IRON MAN.** THEIR **UNITED COMBAT** AGAINST THANOS SIGNALED THE **OPENING ROUND** IN HIS **CAMPAIGN** AGAINST EARTH!

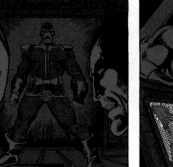

THANOS **WITHDREW,** AFTER THAT, TO SECRETLY PLOT THE TAKING OF **RICK JONES.** RICK UNKNOWINGLY POSSESSED INFORMATION CONCERNING THE **LOCATION** OF THE COSMIC CUBE. THUS, WITH TWO **SKRULLS** AT HIS SIDE--

--HE ENGINEERED A **CLASH** BETWEEN RICK'S ALTER EGO, **CAPTAIN MARVEL,** AND THE ORANGE-SKINNED BEHEMOTH CALLED THE **THING.'** THIS LED TO MARVEL/RICK'S **CAPTURE**--

--AND THE SUBSEQUENT **THEFT** OF RICK'S KNOWLEDGE! LATER, THE CAPTAIN EXECUTED THE FIRST OF **SEVERAL** ESCAPES--

--ONLY TO FIND HIS RETURN TO EARTH MARKED BY BATTLE WITH A TERRAN SUPERVILLAIN WHO HAD **ALLIED** WITH THANOS, AND THE **DISMAL DEFEAT AT THE CONTROLLER'S** HANDS!

AT THE **CLIMACTIC** MOMENT, HOWEVER, CAPTAIN MARVEL **VANISHED** FROM THE EARTH, AND APPEARED BEFORE **EON,** ANOTHER CREATION OF KRONOS'. EON GRANTED MARVEL THE GIFT OF **COSMIC AWARENESS.**

KRONOS HAD **FORSEEN** THAT ONLY **THIS SKILL** COULD HOPE TO VANQUISH A POWER-CRAZED TITAN THAT HELD THE **COSMIC CUBE!**

YET, KRONOS HAD BEEN **UNABLE** TO PREDICT THAT THE CUBE WOULD GIVE THANOS THE **INFINITE** POWER NEEDED TO IMPRISON EVEN **HIM**-- THE POWER TO IMPRISON **ALL** HIS FOES WITH THE SLIGHTEST **THOUGHT**--

--YES, **EVEN** THE POWER TO BRING ABOUT THE **GRAND TRANSFORMATION,** TO CHANGE HIS VERY **SOUL** INTO THE STUFF OF THE **UNIVERSE**... IN OTHER WORDS...

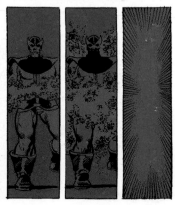

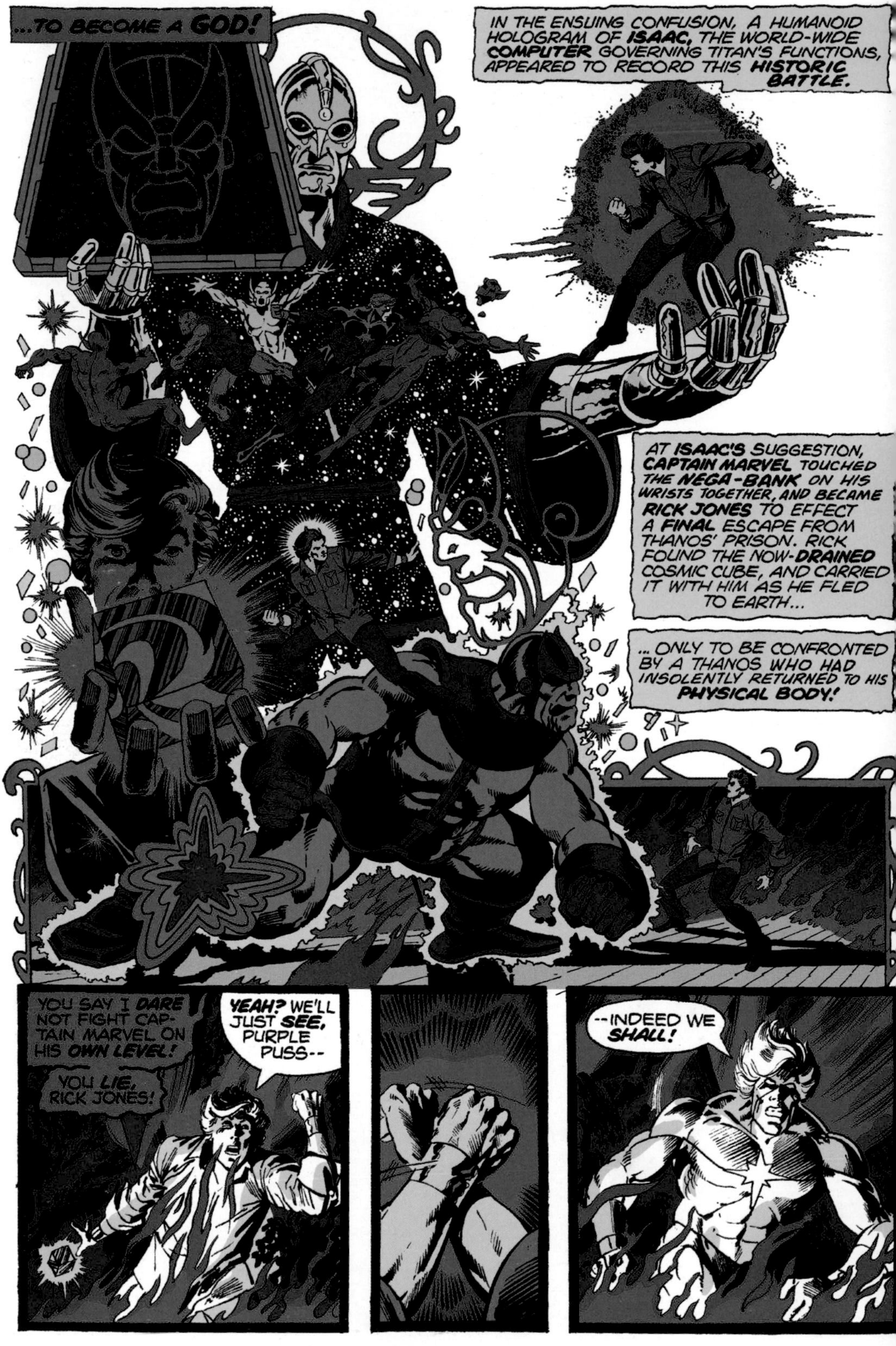

...TO BECOME A GOD!
IN THE ENSUING CONFUSION, A HUMANOID HOLOGRAM OF ISAAC, THE WORLD-WIDE COMPUTER GOVERNING TITAN'S FUNCTIONS, APPEARED TO RECORD THIS HISTORIC BATTLE.
AT ISAAC'S SUGGESTION, CAPTAIN MARVEL TOUCHED THE NEGA-BANK ON HIS WRISTS TOGETHER, AND BECAME RICK JONES TO EFFECT A FINAL ESCAPE FROM THANOS' PRISON. RICK FOUND THE NOW-DRAINED COSMIC CUBE, AND CARRIED IT WITH HIM AS HE FLED TO EARTH...
...ONLY TO BE CONFRONTED BY A THANOS WHO HAD INSOLENTLY RETURNED TO HIS PHYSICAL BODY!
YOU SAY I DARE NOT FIGHT CAPTAIN MARVEL ON HIS OWN LEVEL!
YOU LIE, RICK JONES!
YEAH? WE'LL JUST SEE, PURPLE PUSS--
--INDEED WE SHALL!

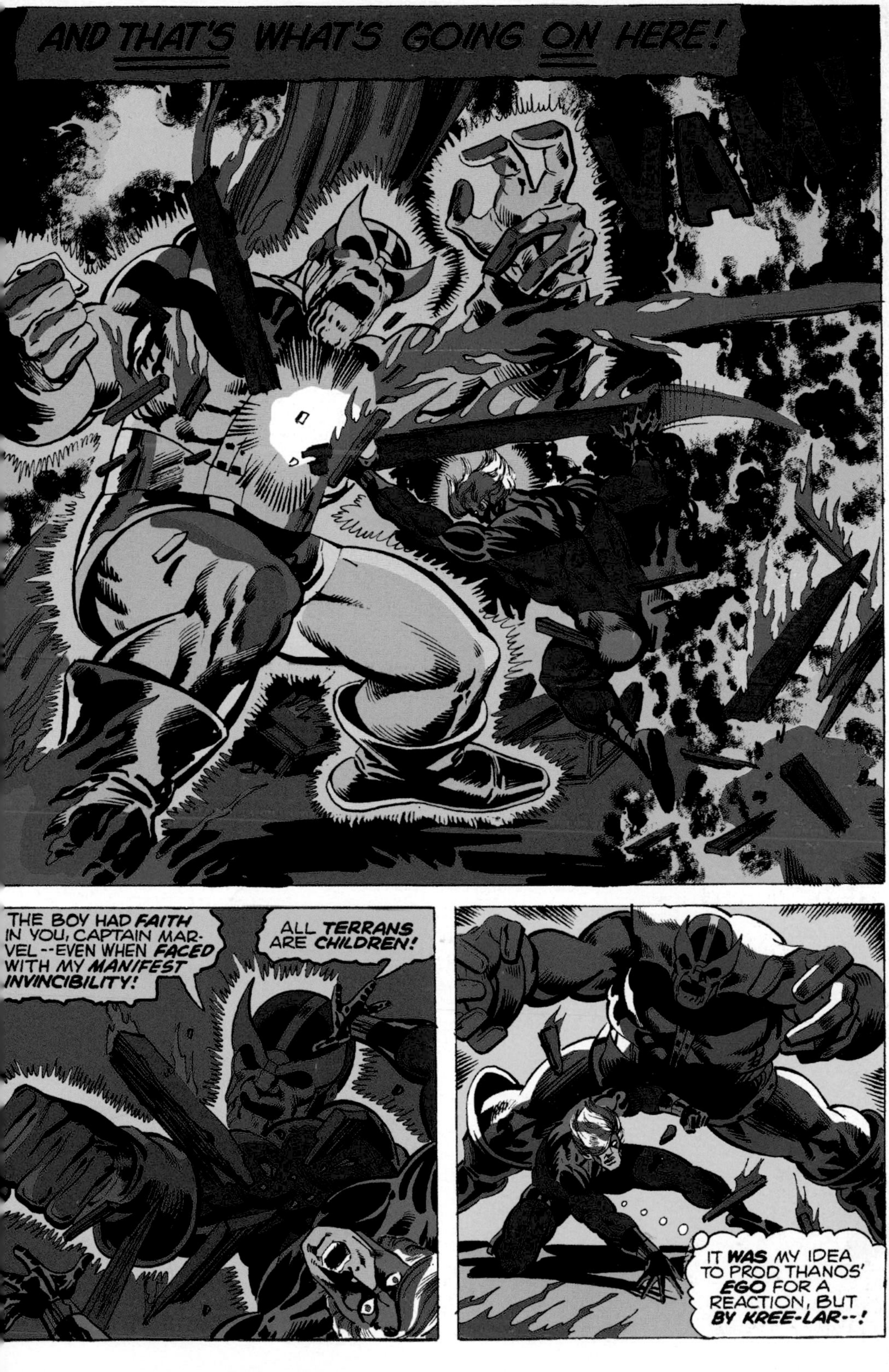
AND THAT'S WHAT'S GOING ON HERE!
VAM!
THE BOY HAD FAITH IN YOU, CAPTAIN MAR-VEL--EVEN WHEN FACED WITH MY MANIFEST INVINCIBILITY!
ALL TERRANS ARE CHILDREN!
IT WAS MY IDEA TO PROD THANOS' EGO FOR A REACTION, BUT BY KREE-LAR--!

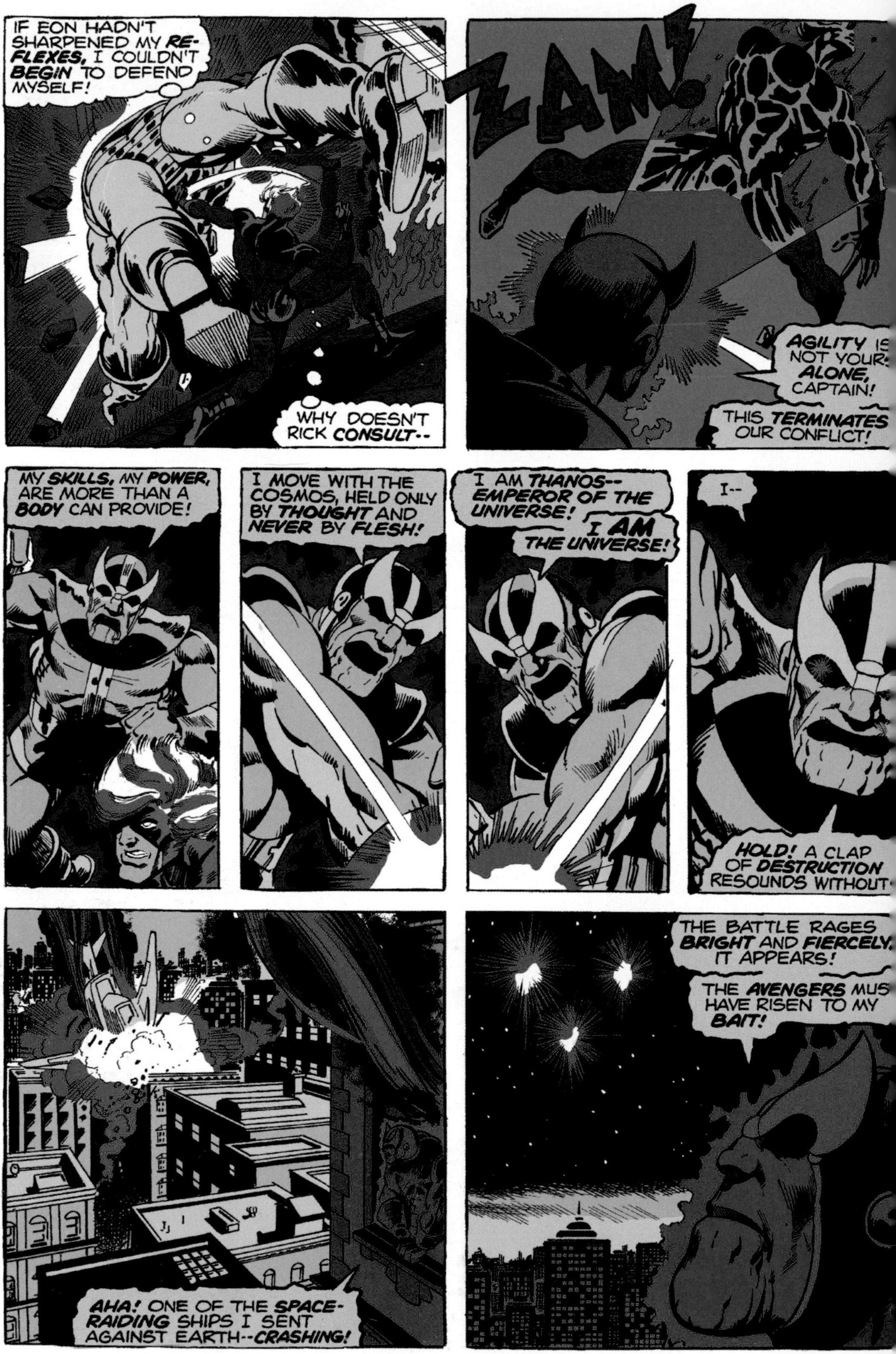
IF EON HADN'T SHARPENED MY REFLEXES, I COULDN'T BEGIN TO DEFEND MYSELF!
WHY DOESN'T RICK CONSULT--
ZAM!
AGILITY IS NOT YOURS ALONE, CAPTAIN!
THIS TERMINATES OUR CONFLICT!
MY SKILLS, MY POWER, ARE MORE THAN A BODY CAN PROVIDE!
I MOVE WITH THE COSMOS, HELD ONLY BY THOUGHT AND NEVER BY FLESH!
I AM THANOS-- EMPEROR OF THE UNIVERSE!
I AM THE UNIVERSE!
I--
HOLD! A CLAP OF DESTRUCTION RESOUNDS WITHOUT!
AHA! ONE OF THE SPACE-RAIDING SHIPS I SENT AGAINST EARTH--CRASHING!
THE BATTLE RAGES BRIGHT AND FIERCELY, IT APPEARS!
THE AVENGERS MUST HAVE RISEN TO MY BAIT!

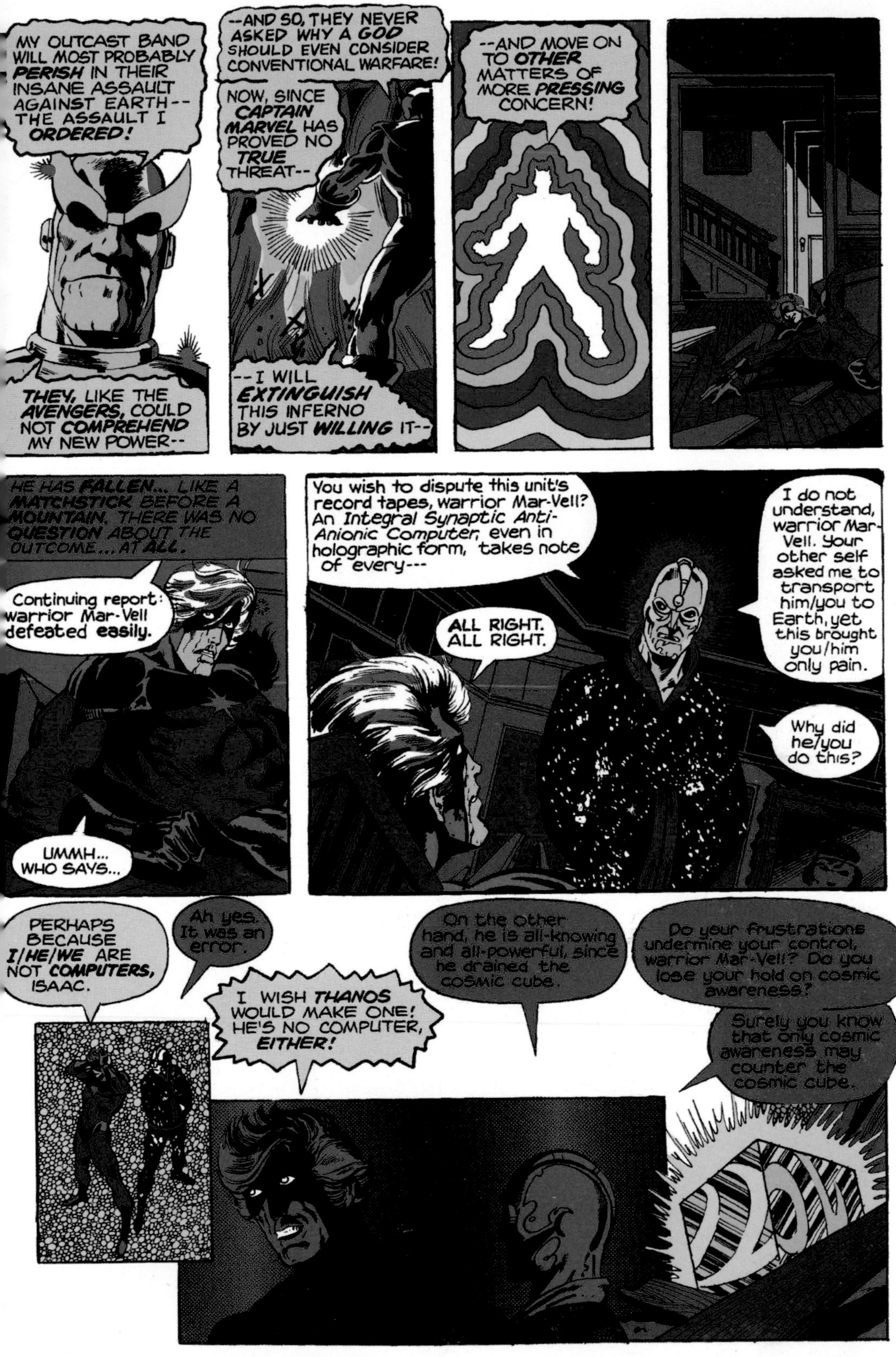
MY OUTCAST BAND WILL MOST PROBABLY PERISH IN THEIR INSANE ASSAULT AGAINST EARTH-- THE ASSAULT I ORDERED!
THEY, LIKE THE AVENGERS, COULD NOT COMPREHEND MY NEW POWER--
--AND SO, THEY NEVER ASKED WHY A GOD SHOULD EVEN CONSIDER CONVENTIONAL WARFARE!
NOW, SINCE CAPTAIN MARVEL HAS PROVED NO TRUE THREAT--
--I WILL EXTINGUISH THIS INFERNO BY JUST WILLING IT--
--AND MOVE ON TO OTHER MATTERS OF MORE PRESSING CONCERN!
HE HAS FALLEN... LIKE A MATCHSTICK BEFORE A MOUNTAIN. THERE WAS NO QUESTION ABOUT THE OUTCOME... AT ALL.
Continuing report: warrior Mar-Vell defeated easily.
UMMH... WHO SAYS...
You wish to dispute this unit's record tapes, warrior Mar-Vell? An Integral Synaptic Anti-Anionic Computer, even in holographic form, takes note of every---
ALL RIGHT. ALL RIGHT.
I do not understand, warrior Mar-Vell. Your other self asked me to transport him/you to Earth, yet this brought you/him only pain.
Why did he/you do this?
PERHAPS BECAUSE I/HE/WE ARE NOT COMPUTERS, ISAAC.
Ah yes. It was an error.
I WISH THANOS WOULD MAKE ONE! HE'S NO COMPUTER, EITHER!
On the other hand, he is all-knowing and all-powerful, since he drained the cosmic cube.
Do your frustrations undermine your control, warrior Mar-Vell? Do you lose your hold on cosmic awareness?
Surely you know that only cosmic awareness may counter the cosmic cube.

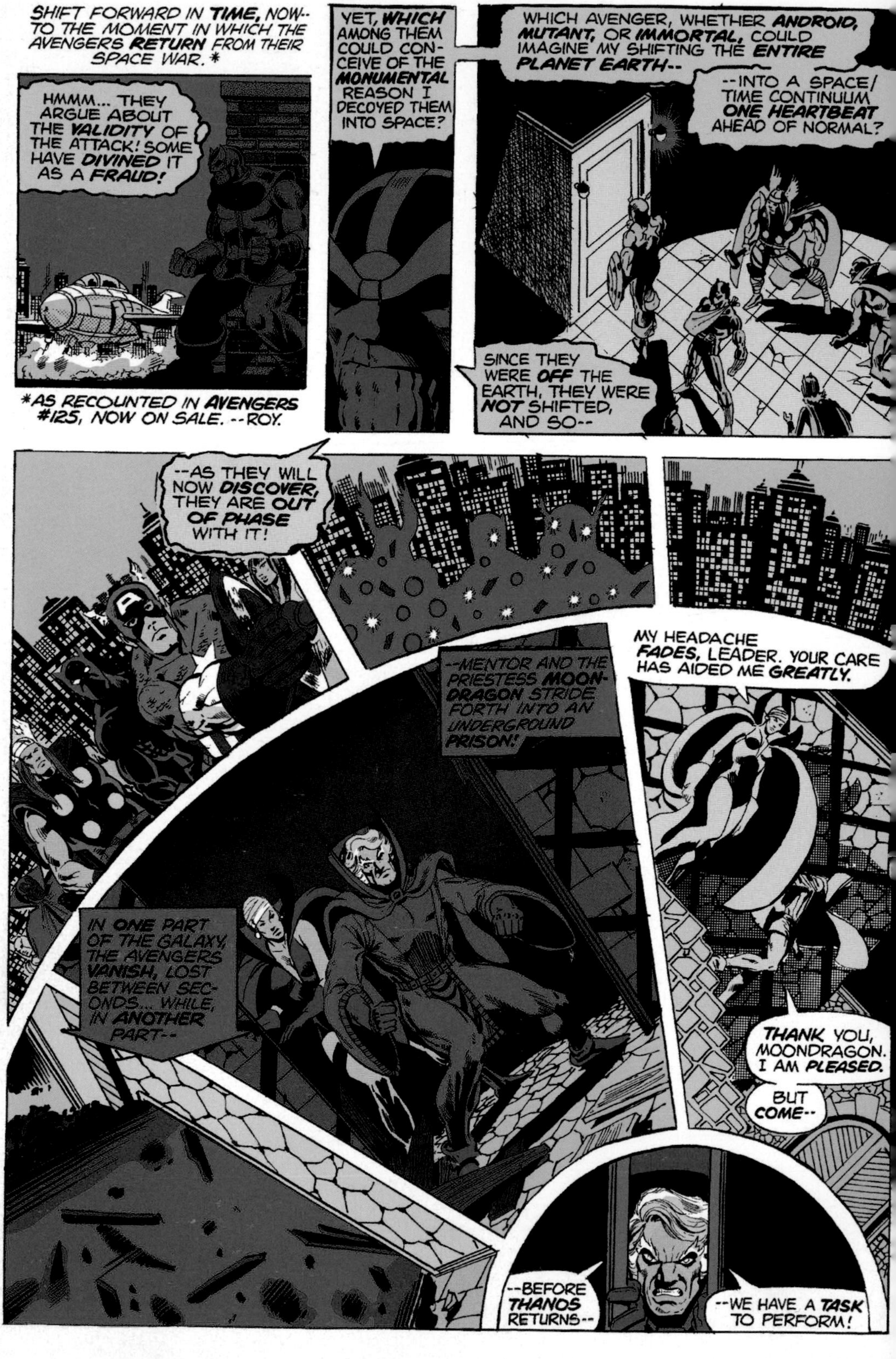
SHIFT FORWARD IN TIME, NOW-- TO THE MOMENT IN WHICH THE AVENGERS RETURN FROM THEIR SPACE WAR.*
HMMM... THEY ARGUE ABOUT THE VALIDITY OF THE ATTACK! SOME HAVE DIVINED IT AS A FRAUD!
*AS RECOUNTED IN AVENGERS #125, NOW ON SALE. --ROY.
YET, WHICH AMONG THEM COULD CONCEIVE OF THE MONUMENTAL REASON I DECOYED THEM INTO SPACE?
WHICH AVENGER, WHETHER ANDROID, MUTANT, OR IMMORTAL, COULD IMAGINE MY SHIFTING THE ENTIRE PLANET EARTH--
--INTO A SPACE/TIME CONTINUUM ONE HEARTBEAT AHEAD OF NORMAL?
SINCE THEY WERE OFF THE EARTH, THEY WERE NOT SHIFTED, AND SO--
--AS THEY WILL NOW DISCOVER, THEY ARE OUT OF PHASE WITH IT!
IN ONE PART OF THE GALAXY, THE AVENGERS VANISH, LOST BETWEEN SECONDS... WHILE, IN ANOTHER PART--
--MENTOR AND THE PRIESTESS MOONDRAGON STRIDE FORTH INTO AN UNDERGROUND PRISON!
MY HEADACHE FADES, LEADER. YOUR CARE HAS AIDED ME GREATLY.
THANK YOU, MOONDRAGON. I AM PLEASED.
BUT COME--
--BEFORE THANOS RETURNS--
--WE HAVE A TASK TO PERFORM!

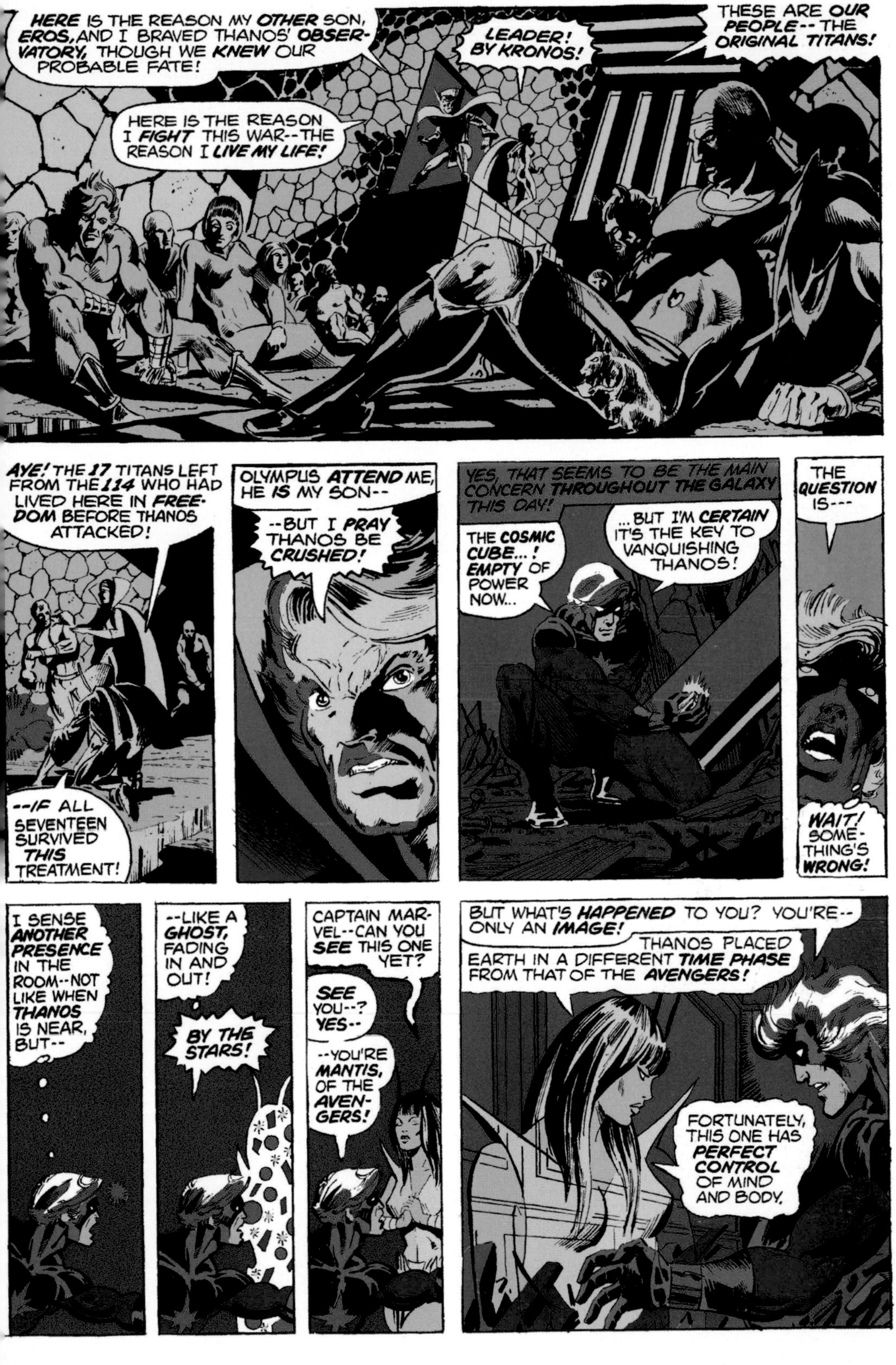

HERE IS THE REASON MY OTHER SON, EROS, AND I BRAVED THANOS' OBSERVATORY, THOUGH WE KNEW OUR PROBABLE FATE!
LEADER! BY KRONOS!
THESE ARE OUR PEOPLE-- THE ORIGINAL TITANS!
HERE IS THE REASON I FIGHT THIS WAR--THE REASON I LIVE MY LIFE!
AYE! THE 17 TITANS LEFT FROM THE 114 WHO HAD LIVED HERE IN FREEDOM BEFORE THANOS ATTACKED!
--IF ALL SEVENTEEN SURVIVED THIS TREATMENT!
OLYMPUS ATTEND ME, HE IS MY SON--
--BUT I PRAY THANOS BE CRUSHED!
YES, THAT SEEMS TO BE THE MAIN CONCERN THROUGHOUT THE GALAXY THIS DAY!
THE COSMIC CUBE...! EMPTY OF POWER NOW...
...BUT I'M CERTAIN IT'S THE KEY TO VANQUISHING THANOS!
THE QUESTION IS---
WAIT! SOMETHING'S WRONG!
I SENSE ANOTHER PRESENCE IN THE ROOM--NOT LIKE WHEN THANOS IS NEAR, BUT--
--LIKE A GHOST, FADING IN AND OUT!
BY THE STARS!
CAPTAIN MARVEL--CAN YOU SEE THIS ONE YET?
SEE YOU--? YES--
--YOU'RE MANTIS, OF THE AVENGERS!
BUT WHAT'S HAPPENED TO YOU? YOU'RE--ONLY AN IMAGE!
THANOS PLACED EARTH IN A DIFFERENT TIME PHASE FROM THAT OF THE AVENGERS!
FORTUNATELY, THIS ONE HAS PERFECT CONTROL OF MIND AND BODY.

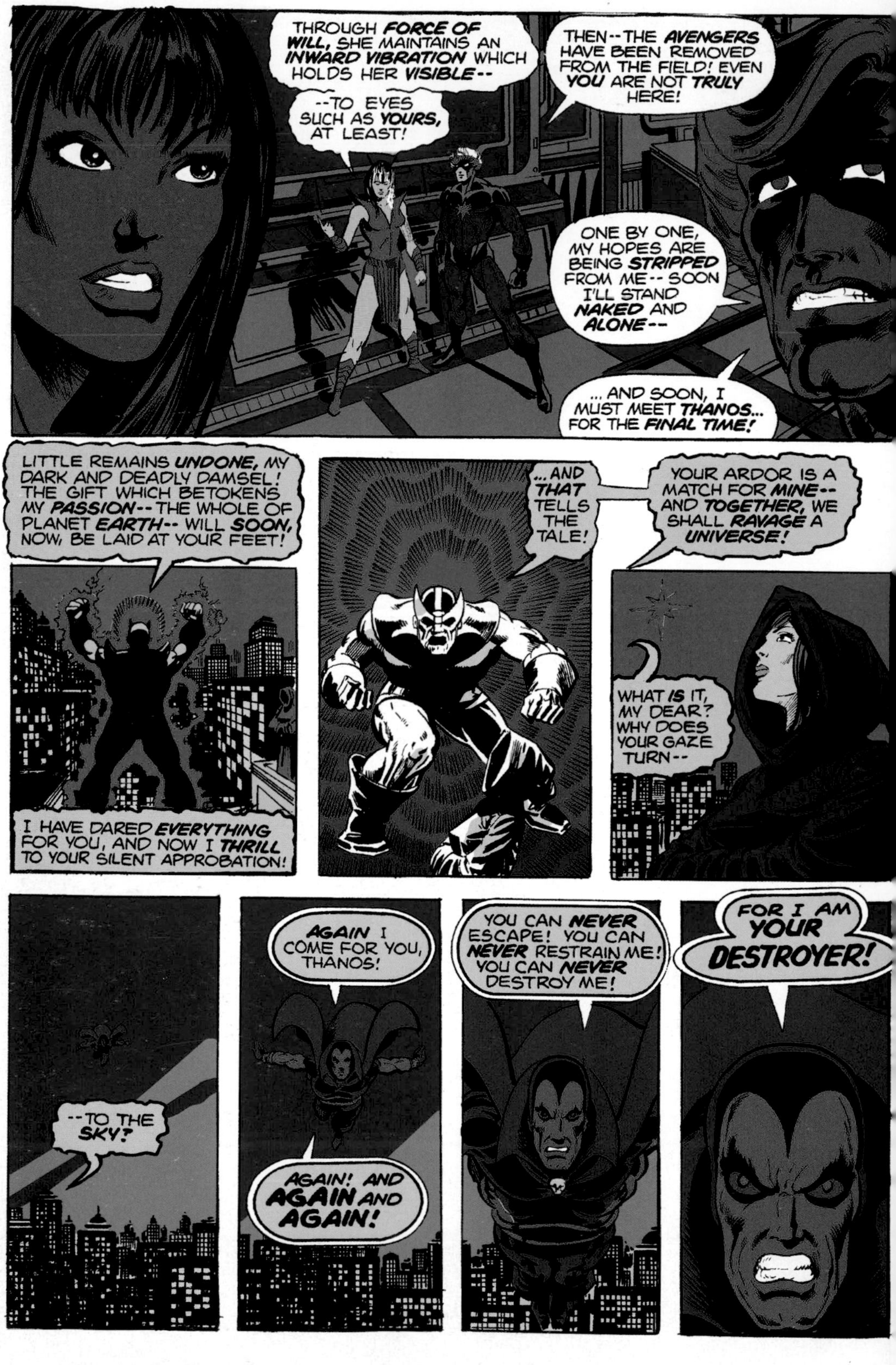
THROUGH FORCE OF WILL, SHE MAINTAINS AN INWARD VIBRATION WHICH HOLDS HER VISIBLE--
--TO EYES SUCH AS YOURS, AT LEAST!
THEN--THE AVENGERS HAVE BEEN REMOVED FROM THE FIELD! EVEN YOU ARE NOT TRULY HERE!
ONE BY ONE, MY HOPES ARE BEING STRIPPED FROM ME-- SOON I'LL STAND NAKED AND ALONE--
... AND SOON, I MUST MEET THANOS... FOR THE FINAL TIME!
LITTLE REMAINS UNDONE, MY DARK AND DEADLY DAMSEL! THE GIFT WHICH BETOKENS MY PASSION-- THE WHOLE OF PLANET EARTH-- WILL SOON, NOW, BE LAID AT YOUR FEET!
I HAVE DARED EVERYTHING FOR YOU, AND NOW I THRILL TO YOUR SILENT APPROBATION!
...AND THAT TELLS THE TALE!
YOUR ARDOR IS A MATCH FOR MINE-- AND TOGETHER, WE SHALL RAVAGE A UNIVERSE!
WHAT IS IT, MY DEAR? WHY DOES YOUR GAZE TURN--
--TO THE SKY?
AGAIN I COME FOR YOU, THANOS!
AGAIN! AND AGAIN AND AGAIN!
YOU CAN NEVER ESCAPE! YOU CAN NEVER RESTRAIN ME! YOU CAN NEVER DESTROY ME!
FOR I AM YOUR DESTROYER!

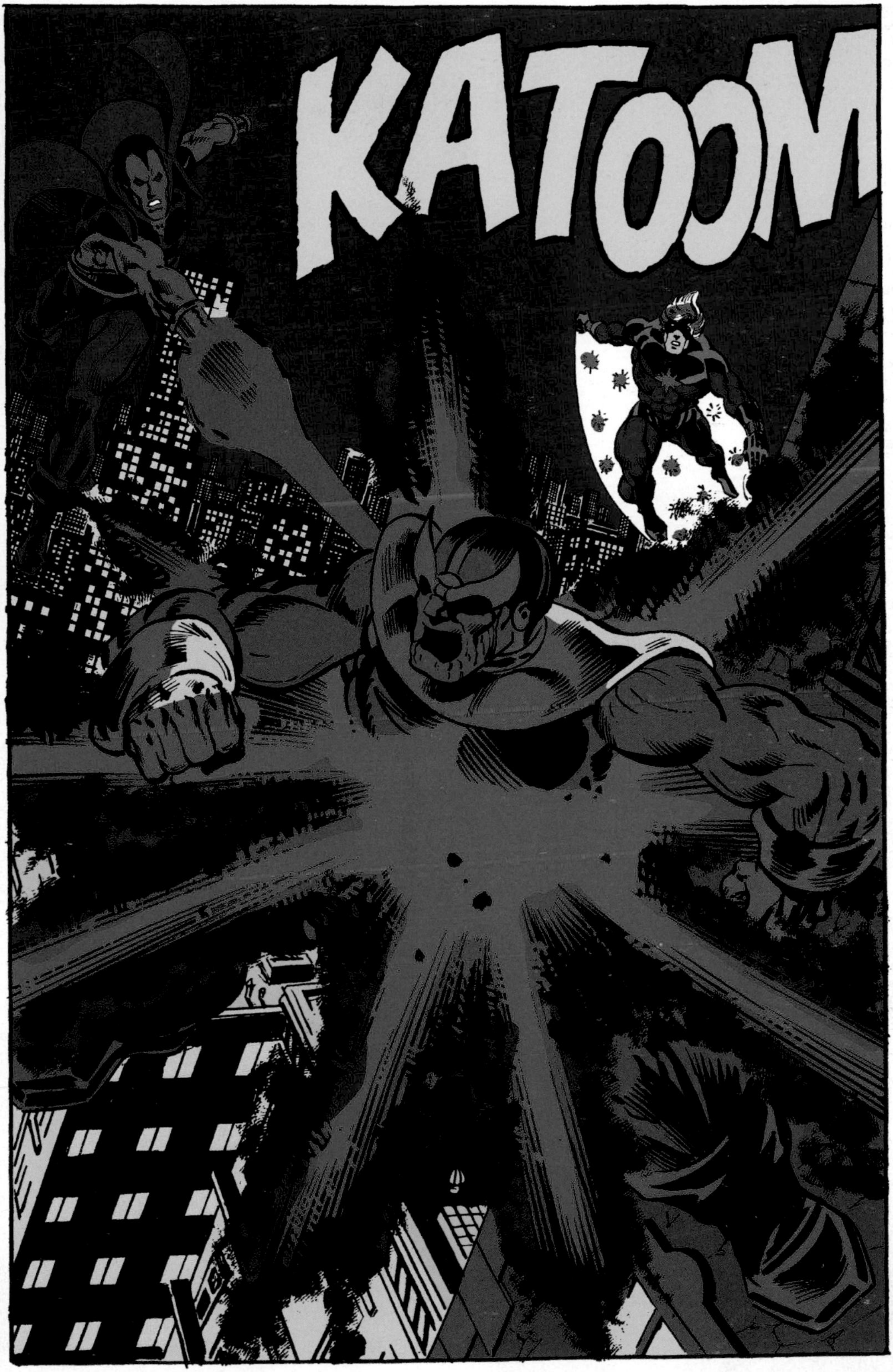
KATOOM

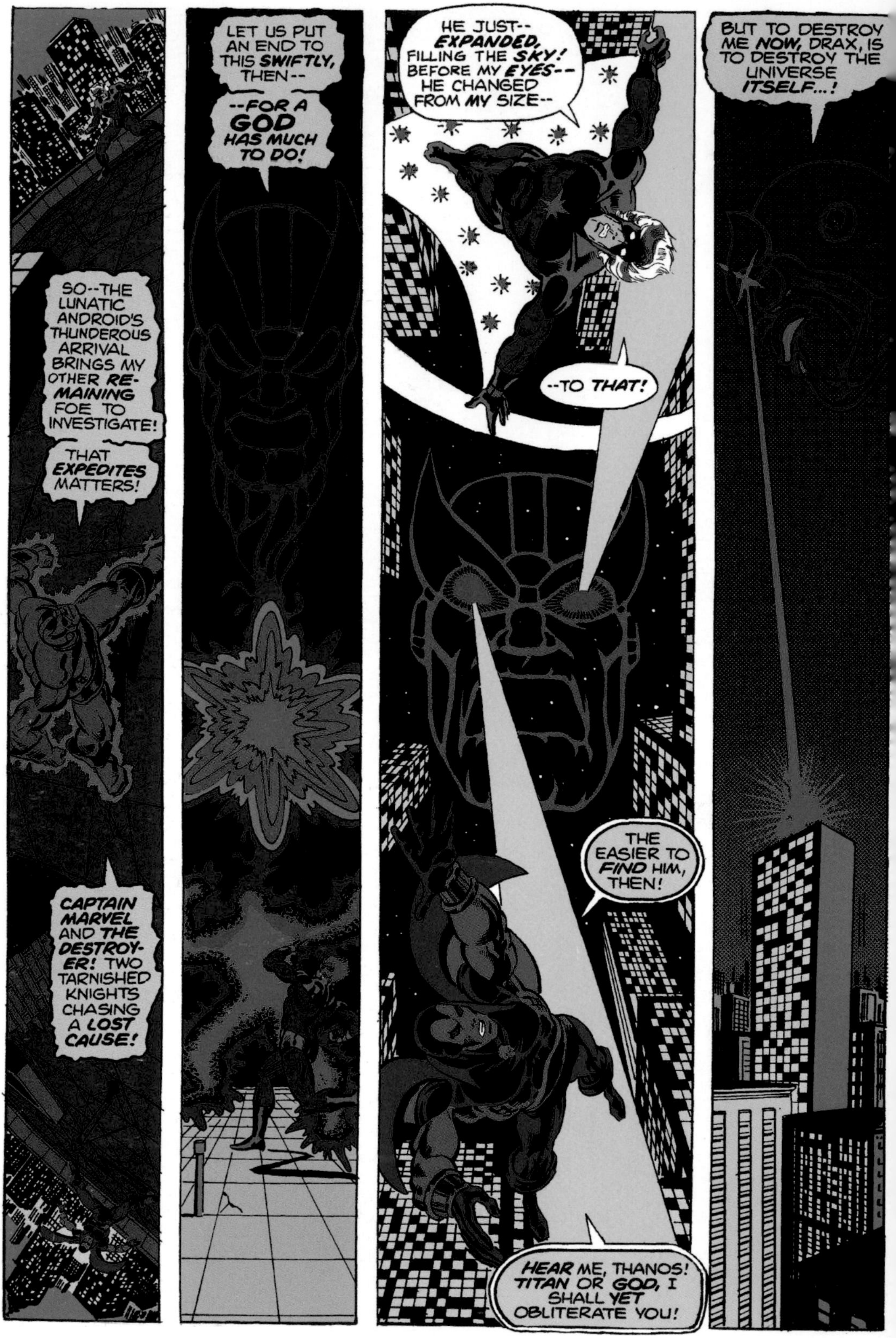
SO--THE LUNATIC ANDROID'S THUNDEROUS ARRIVAL BRINGS MY OTHER RE-MAINING FOE TO INVESTIGATE!
THAT EXPEDITES MATTERS!
CAPTAIN MARVEL AND THE DESTROY-ER! TWO TARNISHED KNIGHTS CHASING A LOST CAUSE!
LET US PUT AN END TO THIS SWIFTLY, THEN--
--FOR A GOD HAS MUCH TO DO!
HE JUST-- EXPANDED, FILLING THE SKY! BEFORE MY EYES-- HE CHANGED FROM MY SIZE--
--TO THAT!
THE EASIER TO FIND HIM, THEN!
HEAR ME, THANOS! TITAN OR GOD, I SHALL YET OBLITERATE YOU!
BUT TO DESTROY ME NOW, DRAX, IS TO DESTROY THE UNIVERSE ITSELF...!

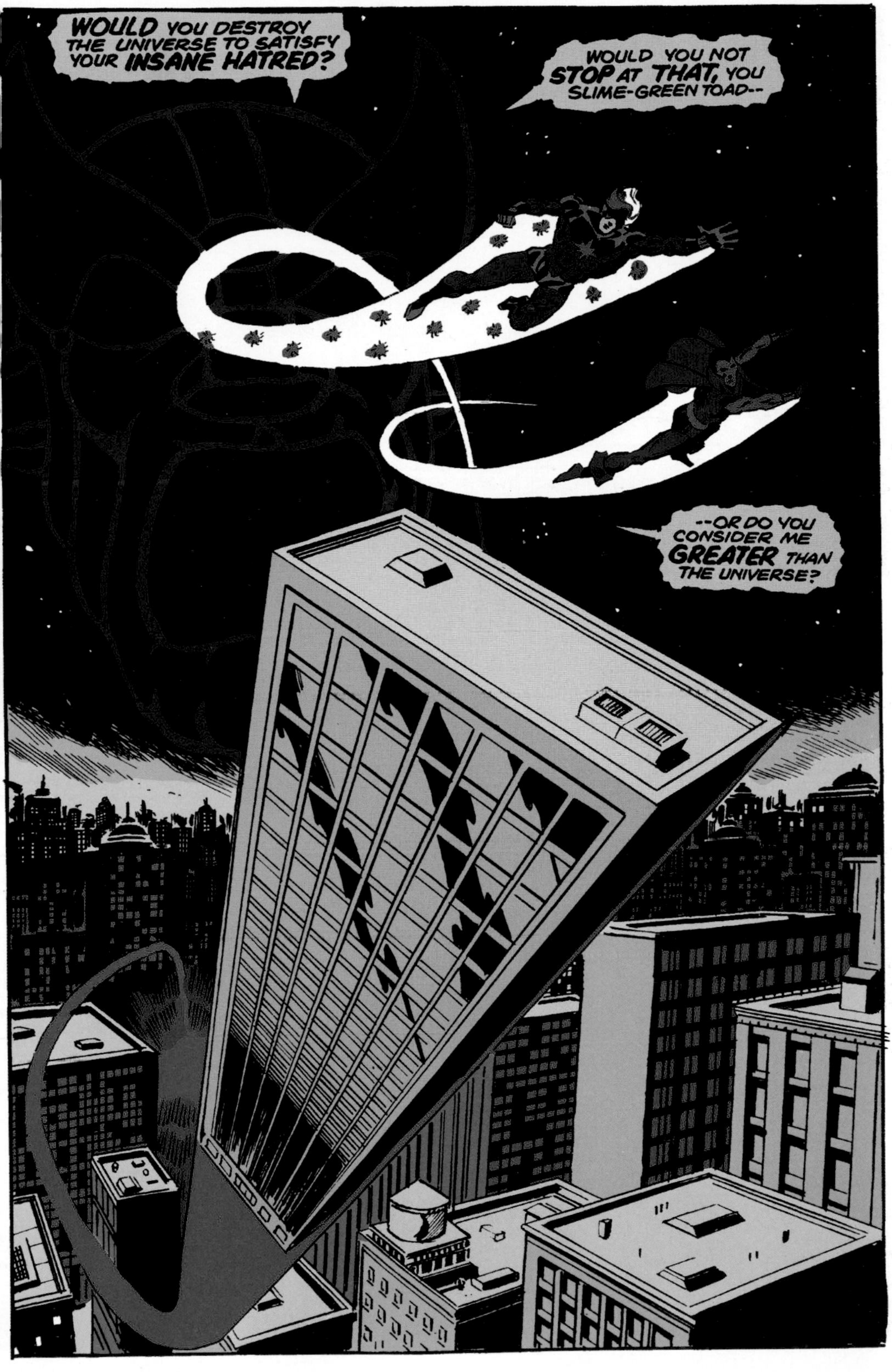
WOULD YOU DESTROY THE UNIVERSE TO SATISFY YOUR INSANE HATRED?
WOULD YOU NOT STOP AT THAT, YOU SLIME-GREEN TOAD--
--OR DO YOU CONSIDER ME GREATER THAN THE UNIVERSE?

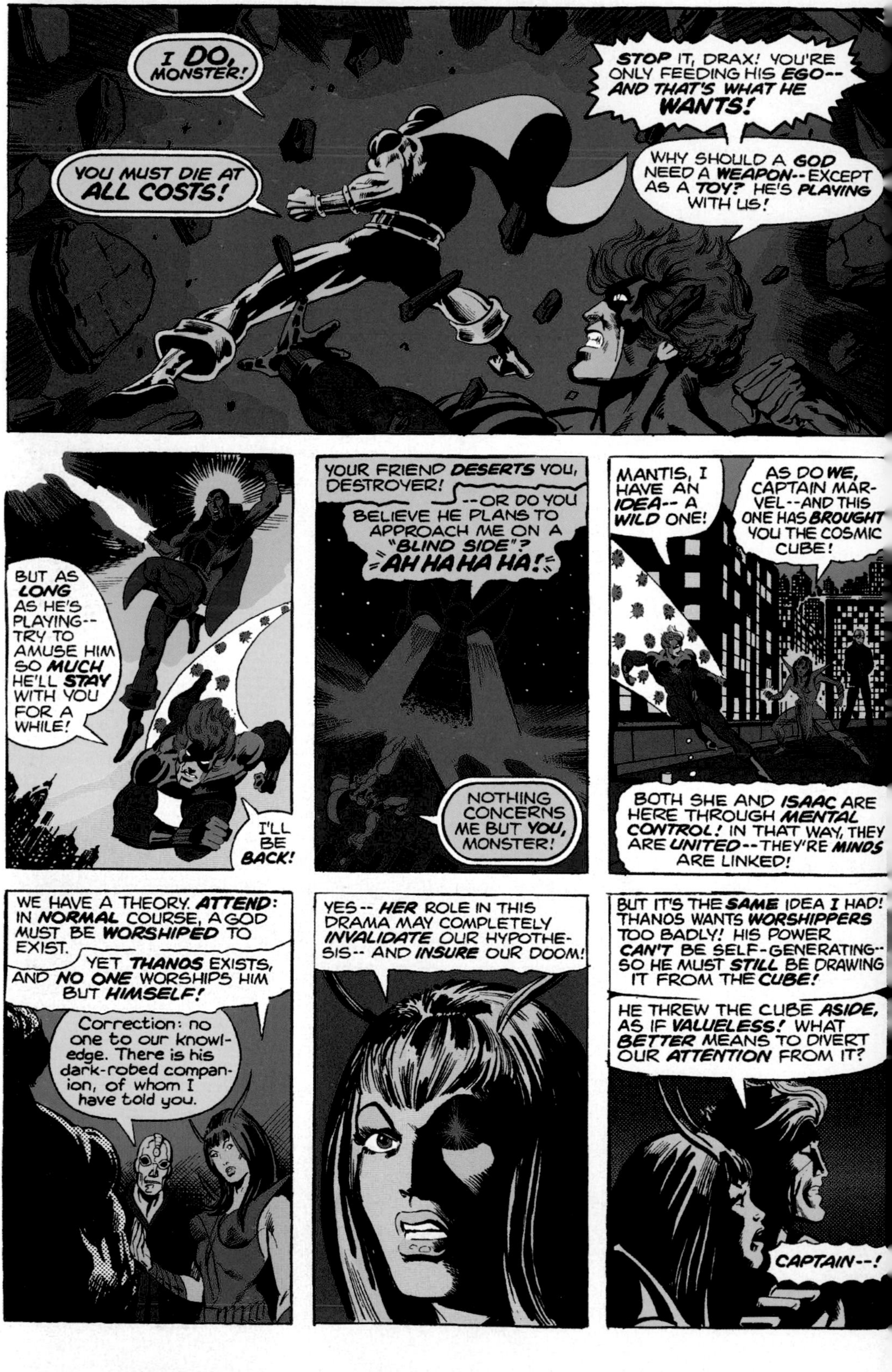
I DO, MONSTER!
YOU MUST DIE AT ALL COSTS!
STOP IT, DRAX! YOU'RE ONLY FEEDING HIS EGO-- AND THAT'S WHAT HE WANTS!
WHY SHOULD A GOD NEED A WEAPON--EXCEPT AS A TOY? HE'S PLAYING WITH US!
BUT AS LONG AS HE'S PLAYING-- TRY TO AMUSE HIM SO MUCH HE'LL STAY WITH YOU FOR A WHILE!
I'LL BE BACK!
YOUR FRIEND DESERTS YOU, DESTROYER!
--OR DO YOU BELIEVE HE PLANS TO APPROACH ME ON A "BLIND SIDE"? AH HA HA HA!
NOTHING CONCERNS ME BUT YOU, MONSTER!
MANTIS, I HAVE AN IDEA-- A WILD ONE!
AS DO WE, CAPTAIN MAR-VEL--AND THIS ONE HAS BROUGHT YOU THE COSMIC CUBE!
BOTH SHE AND ISAAC ARE HERE THROUGH MENTAL CONTROL! IN THAT WAY, THEY ARE UNITED--THEY'RE MINDS ARE LINKED!
WE HAVE A THEORY. ATTEND: IN NORMAL COURSE, A GOD MUST BE WORSHIPED TO EXIST.
YET THANOS EXISTS, AND NO ONE WORSHIPS HIM BUT HIMSELF!
Correction: no one to our knowl-edge. There is his dark-robed compan-ion, of whom I have told you.
YES-- HER ROLE IN THIS DRAMA MAY COMPLETELY INVALIDATE OUR HYPOTHE-SIS-- AND INSURE OUR DOOM!
BUT IT'S THE SAME IDEA I HAD! THANOS WANTS WORSHIPPERS TOO BADLY! HIS POWER CAN'T BE SELF-GENERATING-- SO HE MUST STILL BE DRAWING IT FROM THE CUBE!
HE THREW THE CUBE ASIDE, AS IF VALUELESS! WHAT BETTER MEANS TO DIVERT OUR ATTENTION FROM IT?
CAPTAIN--!

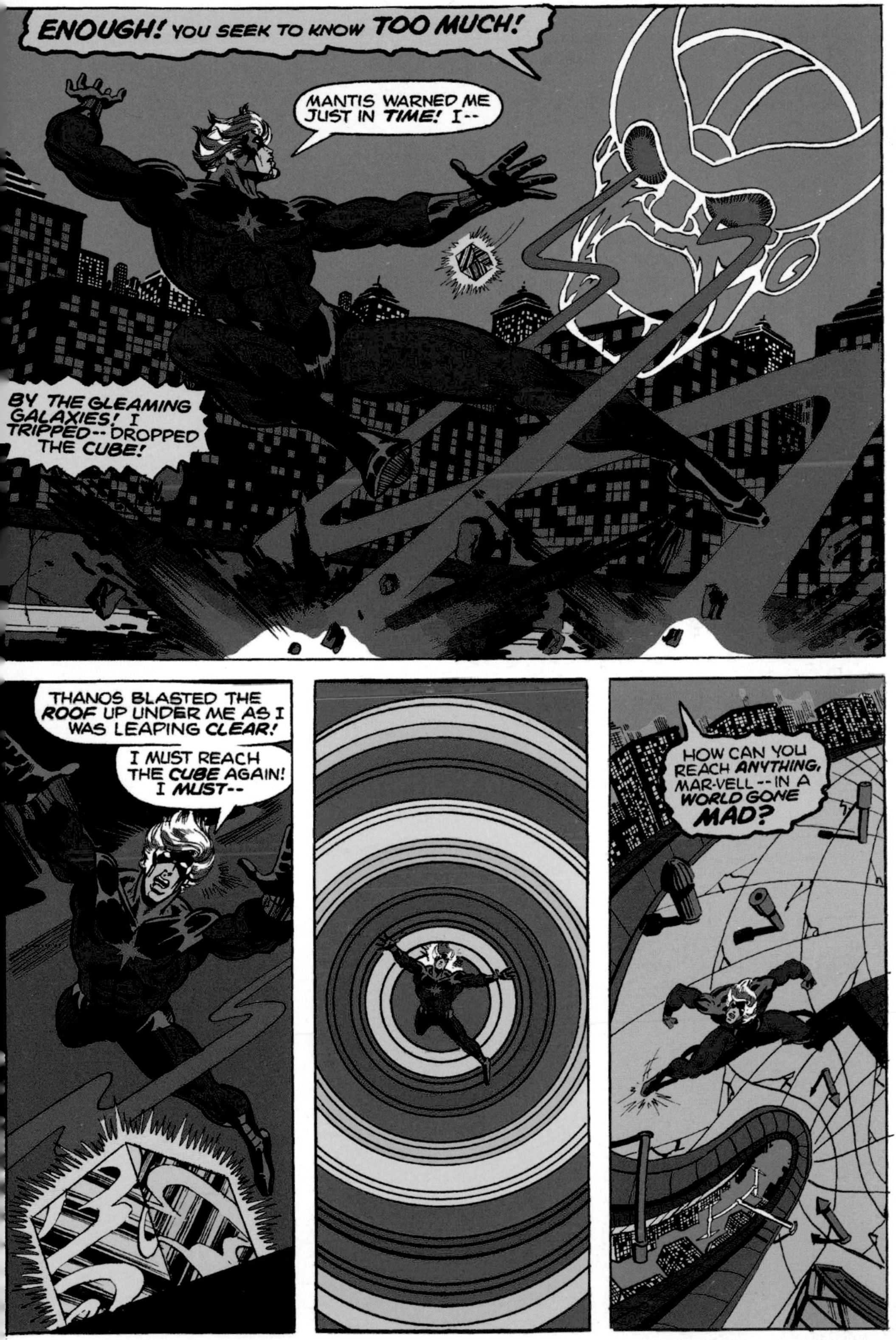
ENOUGH! YOU SEEK TO KNOW TOO MUCH!
MANTIS WARNED ME JUST IN TIME! I--
BY THE GLEAMING GALAXIES! I TRIPPED--DROPPED THE CUBE!
THANOS BLASTED THE ROOF UP UNDER ME AS I WAS LEAPING CLEAR!
I MUST REACH THE CUBE AGAIN! I MUST--
HOW CAN YOU REACH ANYTHING, MAR-VELL--IN A WORLD GONE MAD?

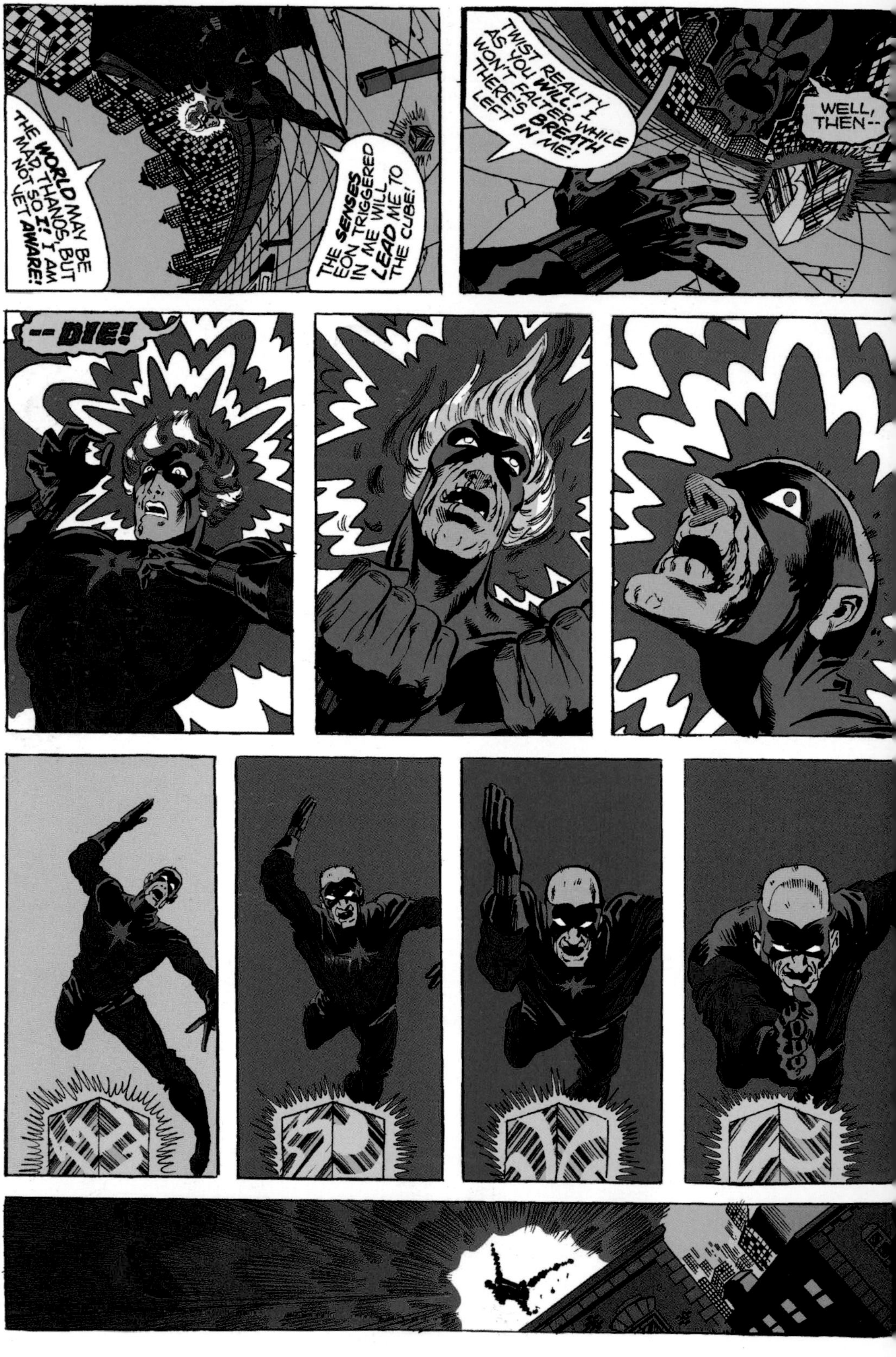
THE WORLD MAY BE THE MAP, THANOS, BUT NOT SO I! I AM YET AWARE!
THE SENSES EON TRIGGERED IN ME WILL LEAD ME TO THE CUBE!
TWIST REALITY AS YOU WILL, I WON'T FALTER WHILE THERE'S BREATH LEFT IN ME!
WELL, THEN--
--DIE!

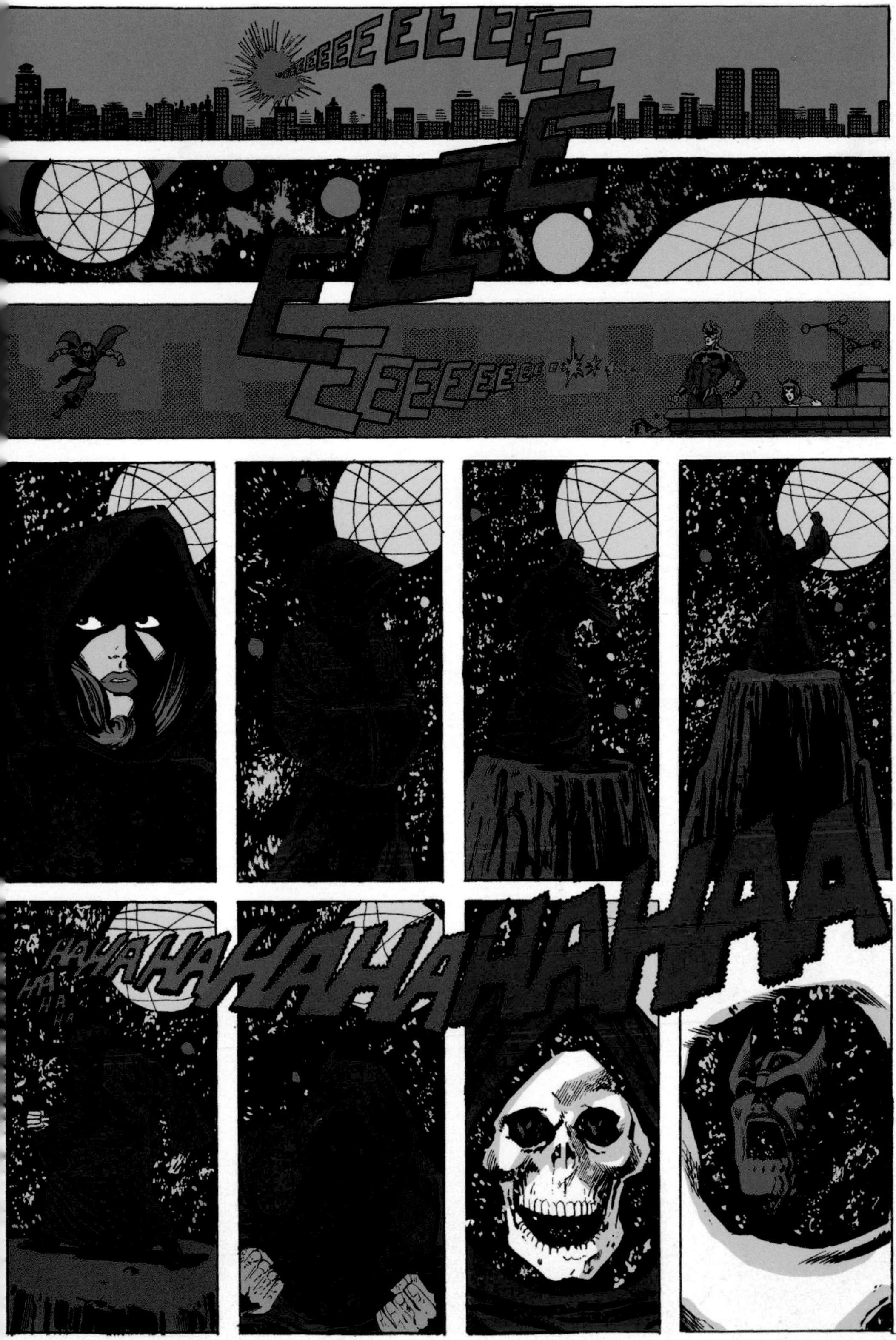
HAHAHAHAHAHAHAHAA
HA HA HA HA

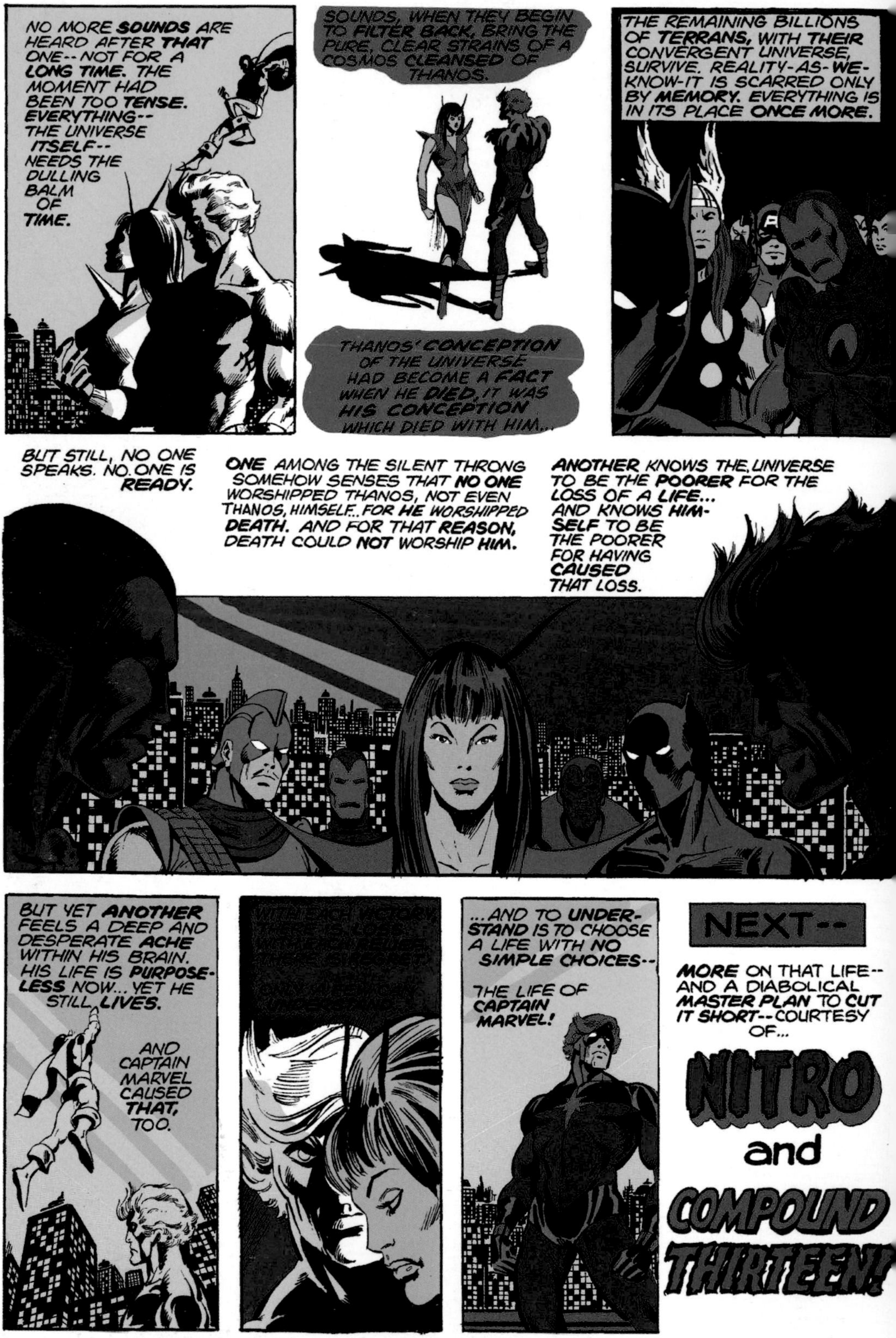
NO MORE SOUNDS ARE HEARD AFTER THAT ONE--NOT FOR A LONG TIME. THE MOMENT HAD BEEN TOO TENSE. EVERYTHING--THE UNIVERSE ITSELF--NEEDS THE DULLING BALM OF TIME.
SOUNDS, WHEN THEY BEGIN TO FILTER BACK, BRING THE PURE, CLEAR STRAINS OF A COSMOS CLEANSED OF THANOS.
THANOS' CONCEPTION OF THE UNIVERSE HAD BECOME A FACT WHEN HE DIED, IT WAS HIS CONCEPTION WHICH DIED WITH HIM...
THE REMAINING BILLIONS OF TERRANS, WITH THEIR CONVERGENT UNIVERSE, SURVIVE. REALITY-AS-WE-KNOW-IT IS SCARRED ONLY BY MEMORY. EVERYTHING IS IN ITS PLACE ONCE MORE.
BUT STILL, NO ONE SPEAKS. NO ONE IS READY.
ONE AMONG THE SILENT THRONG SOMEHOW SENSES THAT NO ONE WORSHIPPED THANOS, NOT EVEN THANOS, HIMSELF.. FOR HE WORSHIPPED DEATH. AND FOR THAT REASON, DEATH COULD NOT WORSHIP HIM.
ANOTHER KNOWS THE UNIVERSE TO BE THE POORER FOR THE LOSS OF A LIFE... AND KNOWS HIMSELF TO BE THE POORER FOR HAVING CAUSED THAT LOSS.
BUT YET ANOTHER FEELS A DEEP AND DESPERATE ACHE WITHIN HIS BRAIN. HIS LIFE IS PURPOSELESS NOW... YET HE STILL LIVES.
AND CAPTAIN MARVEL CAUSED THAT, TOO.
...AND TO UNDERSTAND IS TO CHOOSE A LIFE WITH NO SIMPLE CHOICES--
THE LIFE OF CAPTAIN MARVEL!
NEXT--
MORE ON THAT LIFE--AND A DIABOLICAL MASTER PLAN TO CUT IT SHORT--COURTESY OF...
NITRO and COMPOUND THIRTEEN!

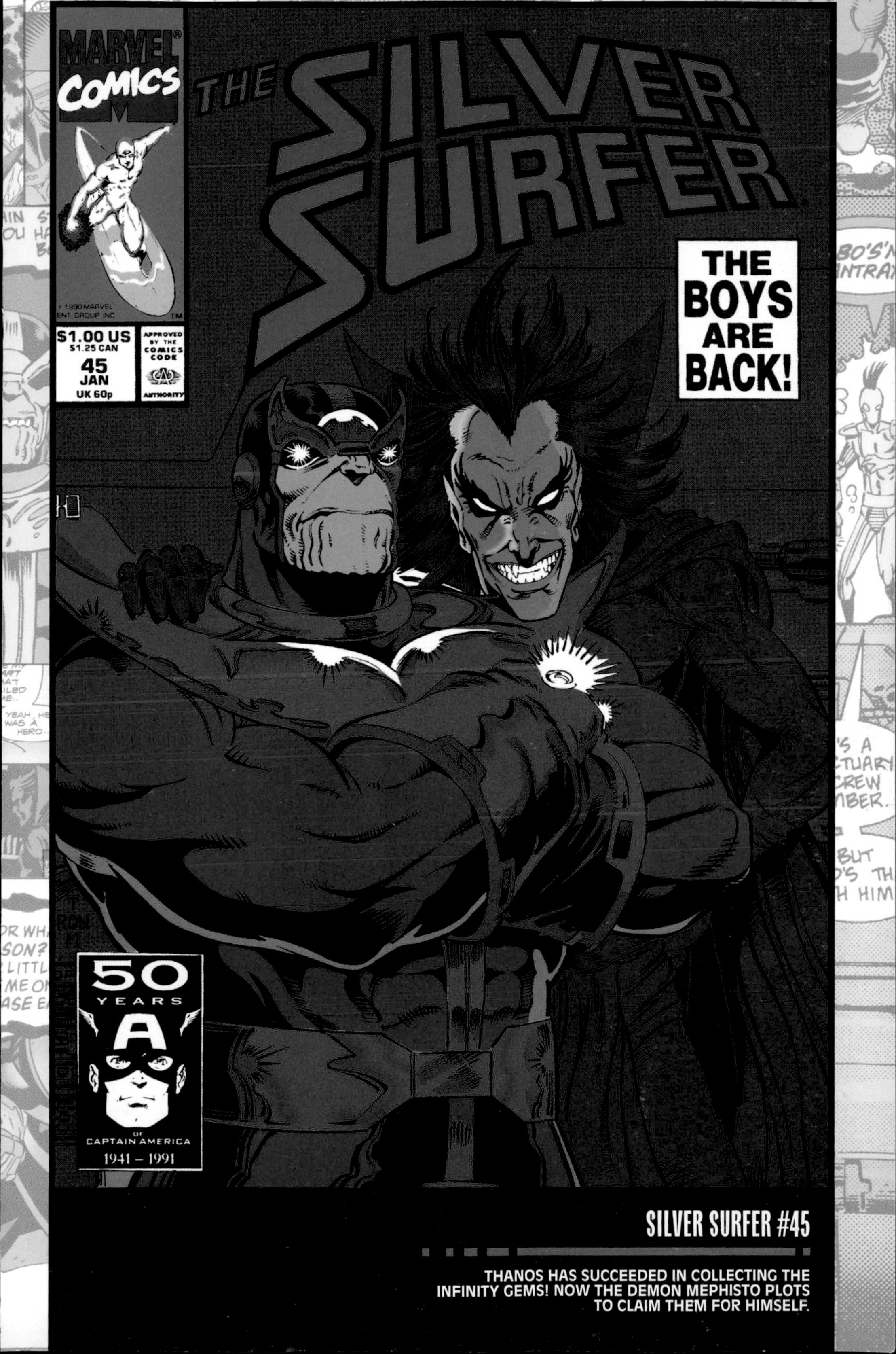
MARVEL COMICS
THE SILVER SURFER
© 1990 MARVEL ENT. GROUP INC.
$1.00 US
$1.25 CAN
45
JAN
UK 60p
APPROVED BY THE COMICS CODE AUTHORITY
THE BOYS ARE BACK!
50 YEARS OF CAPTAIN AMERICA
1941 – 1991

SILVER SURFER #45

THANOS HAS SUCCEEDED IN COLLECTING THE INFINITY GEMS! NOW THE DEMON MEPHISTO PLOTS TO CLAIM THEM FOR HIMSELF.

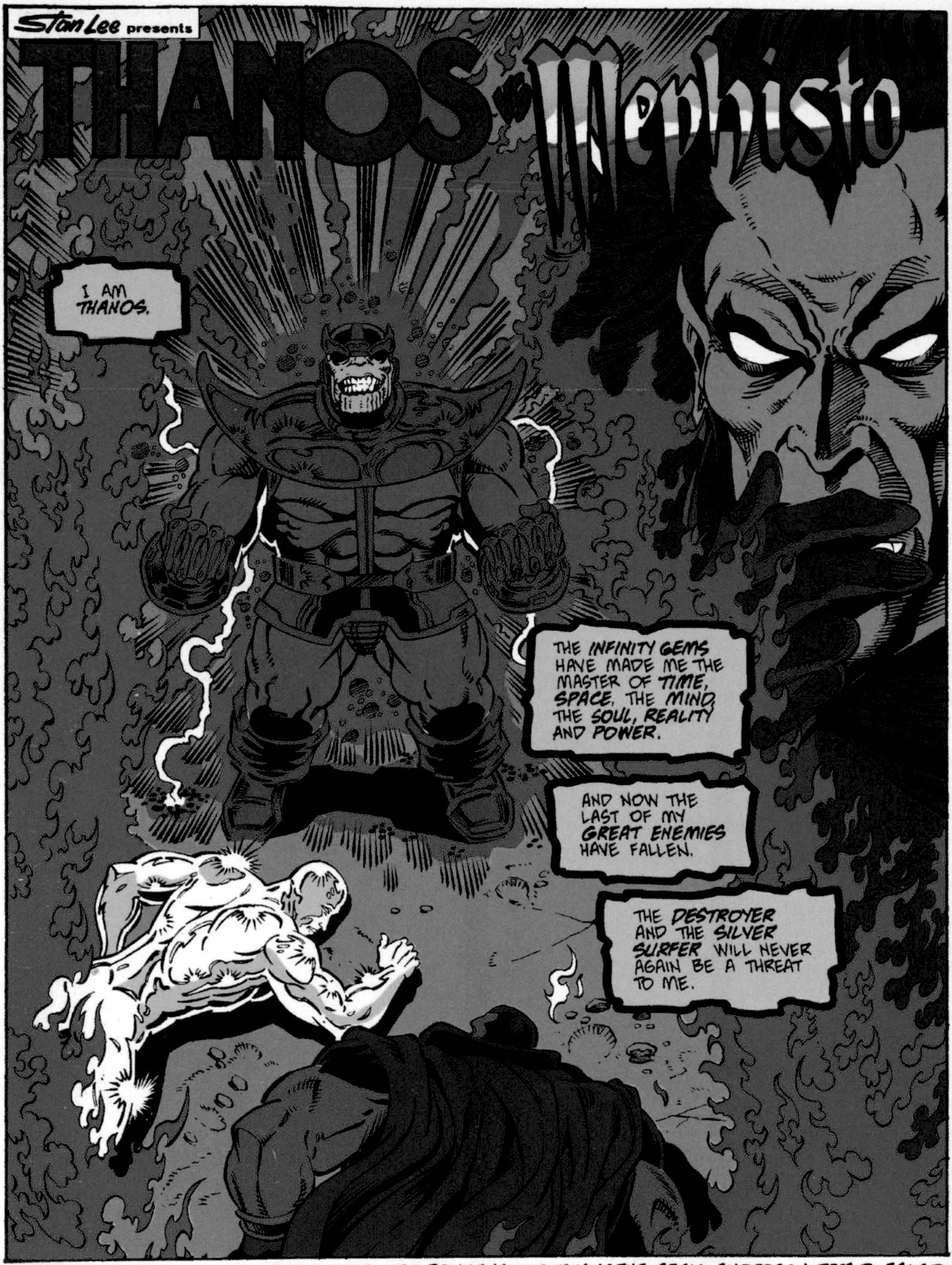
Stan Lee presents
THANOS vs Mephisto
I AM THANOS.
THE INFINITY GEMS HAVE MADE ME THE MASTER OF TIME, SPACE, THE MIND, THE SOUL, REALITY AND POWER.
AND NOW THE LAST OF MY GREAT ENEMIES HAVE FALLEN.
THE DESTROYER AND THE SILVER SURFER WILL NEVER AGAIN BE A THREAT TO ME.

JIM STARLIN · RON LIM · TOM CHRISTOPHER · KEN BRUZENAK · TOM VINCENT · CRAIG ANDERSON · TOM DeFALCO
WRITER · PENCILER · INKER · LETTERER · COLORIST · EDITOR · CHIEF

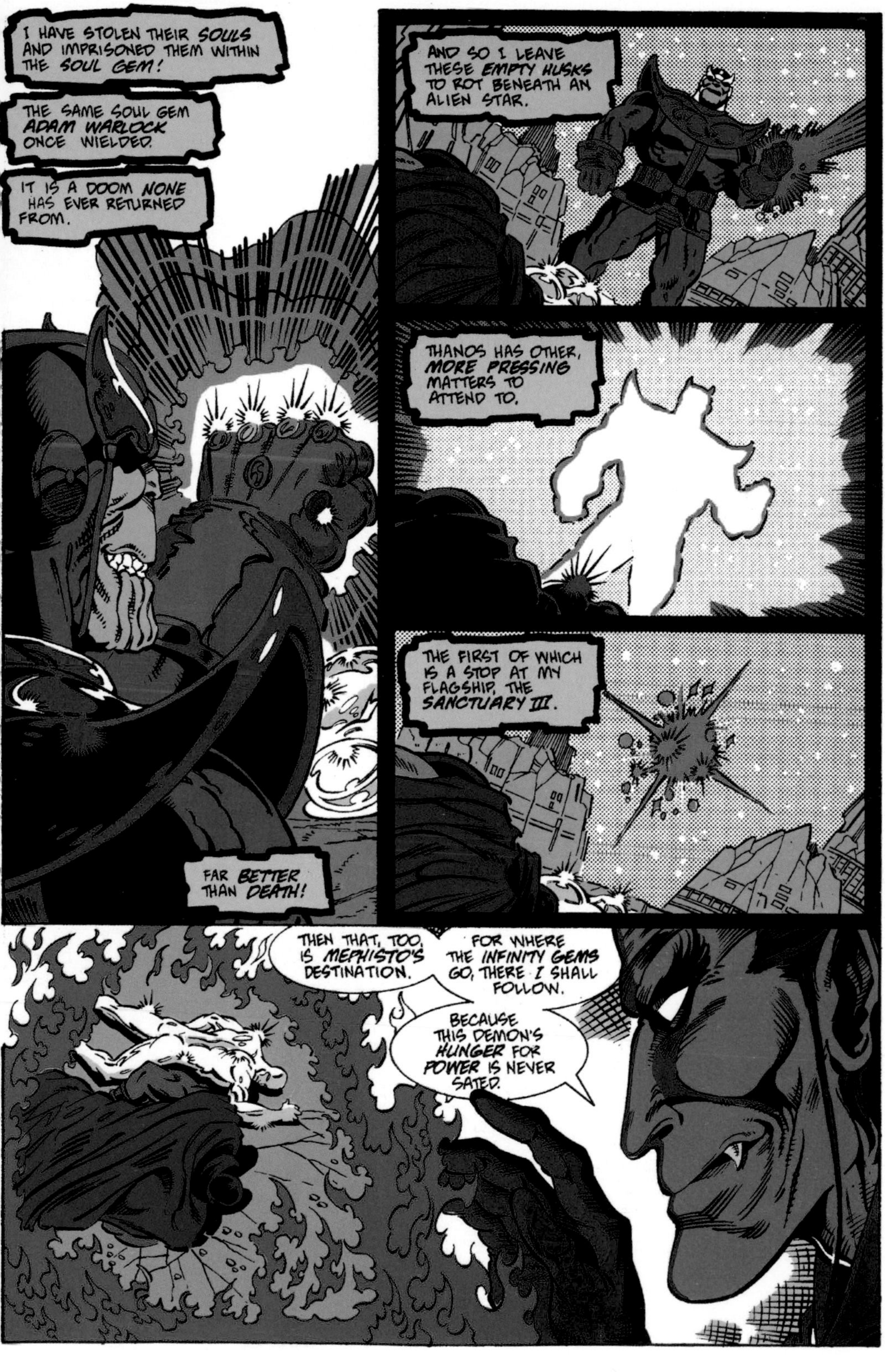
I HAVE STOLEN THEIR SOULS AND IMPRISONED THEM WITHIN THE SOUL GEM!
THE SAME SOUL GEM ADAM WARLOCK ONCE WIELDED.
IT IS A DOOM NONE HAS EVER RETURNED FROM.
FAR BETTER THAN DEATH!
AND SO I LEAVE THESE EMPTY HUSKS TO ROT BENEATH AN ALIEN STAR.
THANOS HAS OTHER, MORE PRESSING MATTERS TO ATTEND TO.
THE FIRST OF WHICH IS A STOP AT MY FLAGSHIP, THE SANCTUARY III.
THEN THAT, TOO, IS MEPHISTO'S DESTINATION.
FOR WHERE THE INFINITY GEMS GO, THERE I SHALL FOLLOW.
BECAUSE THIS DEMON'S HUNGER FOR POWER IS NEVER SATED.

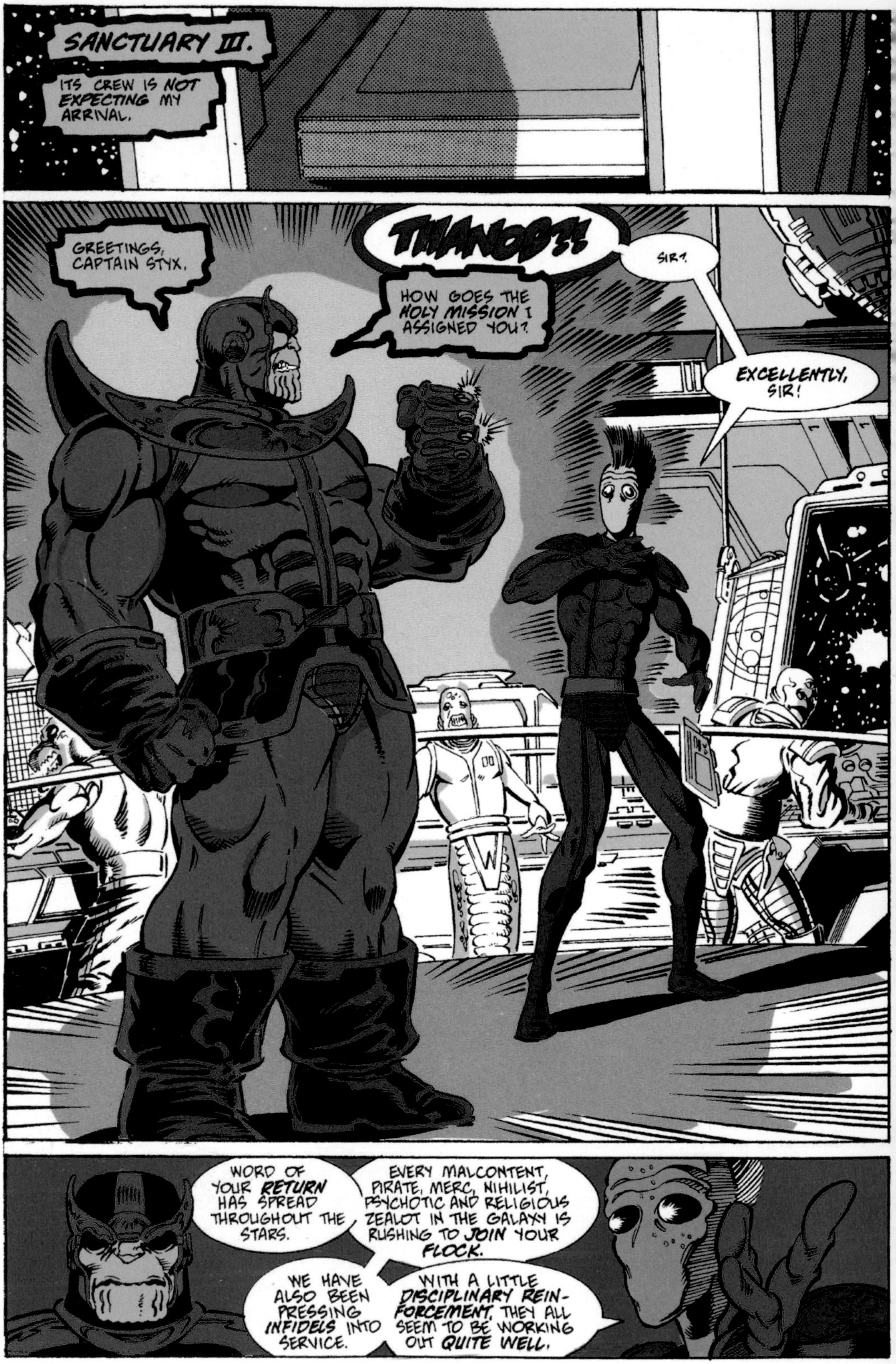

SANCTUARY III.
ITS CREW IS NOT EXPECTING MY ARRIVAL.
GREETINGS, CAPTAIN STYX.
THANOS?!
HOW GOES THE HOLY MISSION I ASSIGNED YOU?
SIR?
EXCELLENTLY, SIR!
WORD OF YOUR RETURN HAS SPREAD THROUGHOUT THE STARS.
EVERY MALCONTENT, PIRATE, MERC, NIHILIST, PSYCHOTIC AND RELIGIOUS ZEALOT IN THE GALAXY IS RUSHING TO JOIN YOUR FLOCK.
WE HAVE ALSO BEEN PRESSING INFIDELS INTO SERVICE.
WITH A LITTLE DISCIPLINARY REIN-FORCEMENT, THEY ALL SEEM TO BE WORKING OUT QUITE WELL.

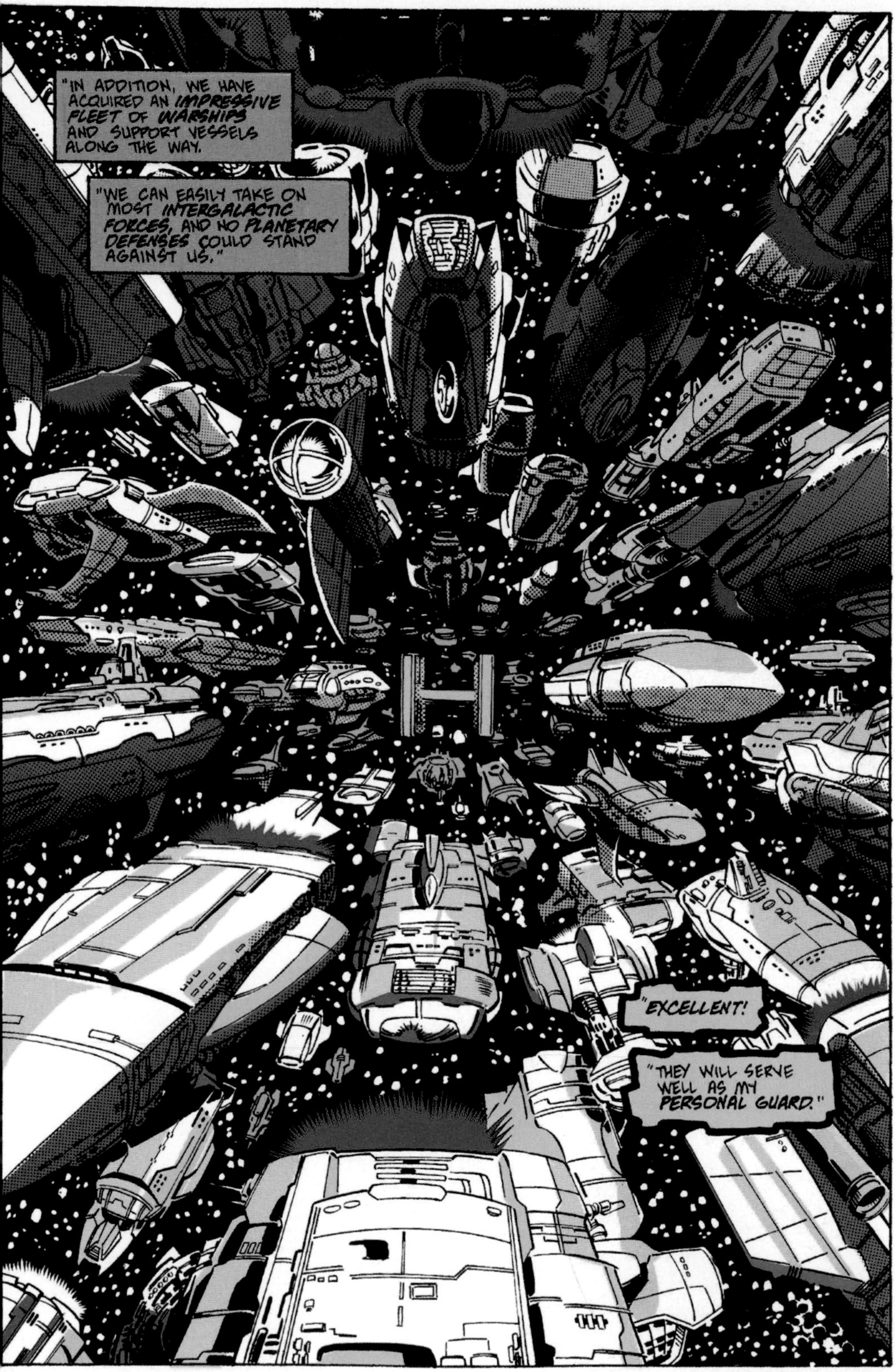
"IN ADDITION, WE HAVE ACQUIRED AN IMPRESSIVE FLEET OF WARSHIPS AND SUPPORT VESSELS ALONG THE WAY.
"WE CAN EASILY TAKE ON MOST INTERGALACTIC FORCES, AND NO PLANETARY DEFENSES COULD STAND AGAINST US."
"EXCELLENT!
"THEY WILL SERVE WELL AS MY PERSONAL GUARD."

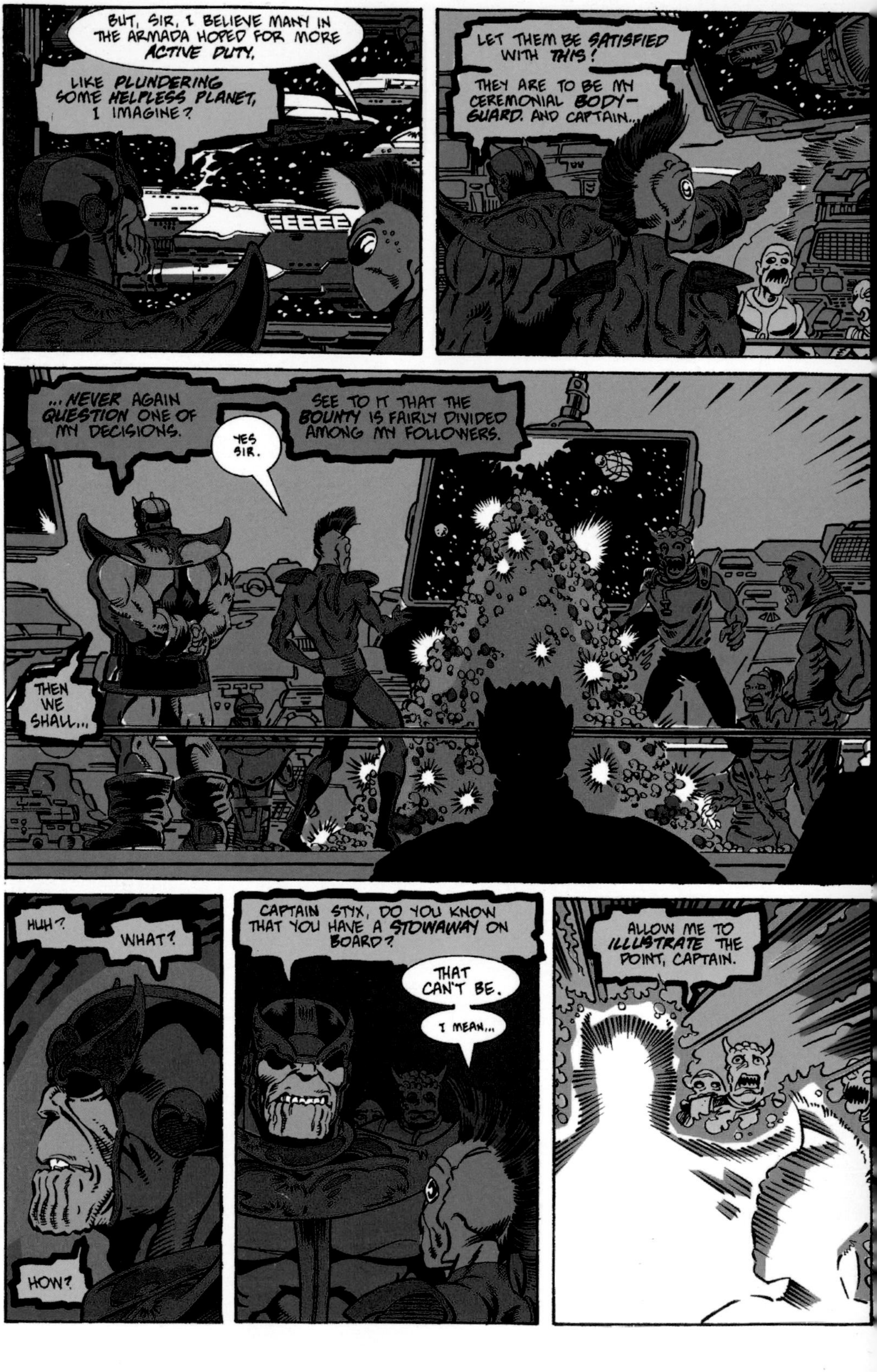
BUT, SIR, I BELIEVE MANY IN THE ARMADA HOPED FOR MORE ACTIVE DUTY.
LIKE PLUNDERING SOME HELPLESS PLANET, I IMAGINE?
LET THEM BE SATISFIED WITH THIS!
THEY ARE TO BE MY CEREMONIAL BODY-GUARD. AND CAPTAIN...
...NEVER AGAIN QUESTION ONE OF MY DECISIONS.
SEE TO IT THAT THE BOUNTY IS FAIRLY DIVIDED AMONG MY FOLLOWERS.
YES SIR.
THEN WE SHALL...
HUH?
WHAT?
HOW?
CAPTAIN STYX, DO YOU KNOW THAT YOU HAVE A STOWAWAY ON BOARD?
THAT CAN'T BE.
I MEAN...
ALLOW ME TO ILLUSTRATE THE POINT, CAPTAIN.

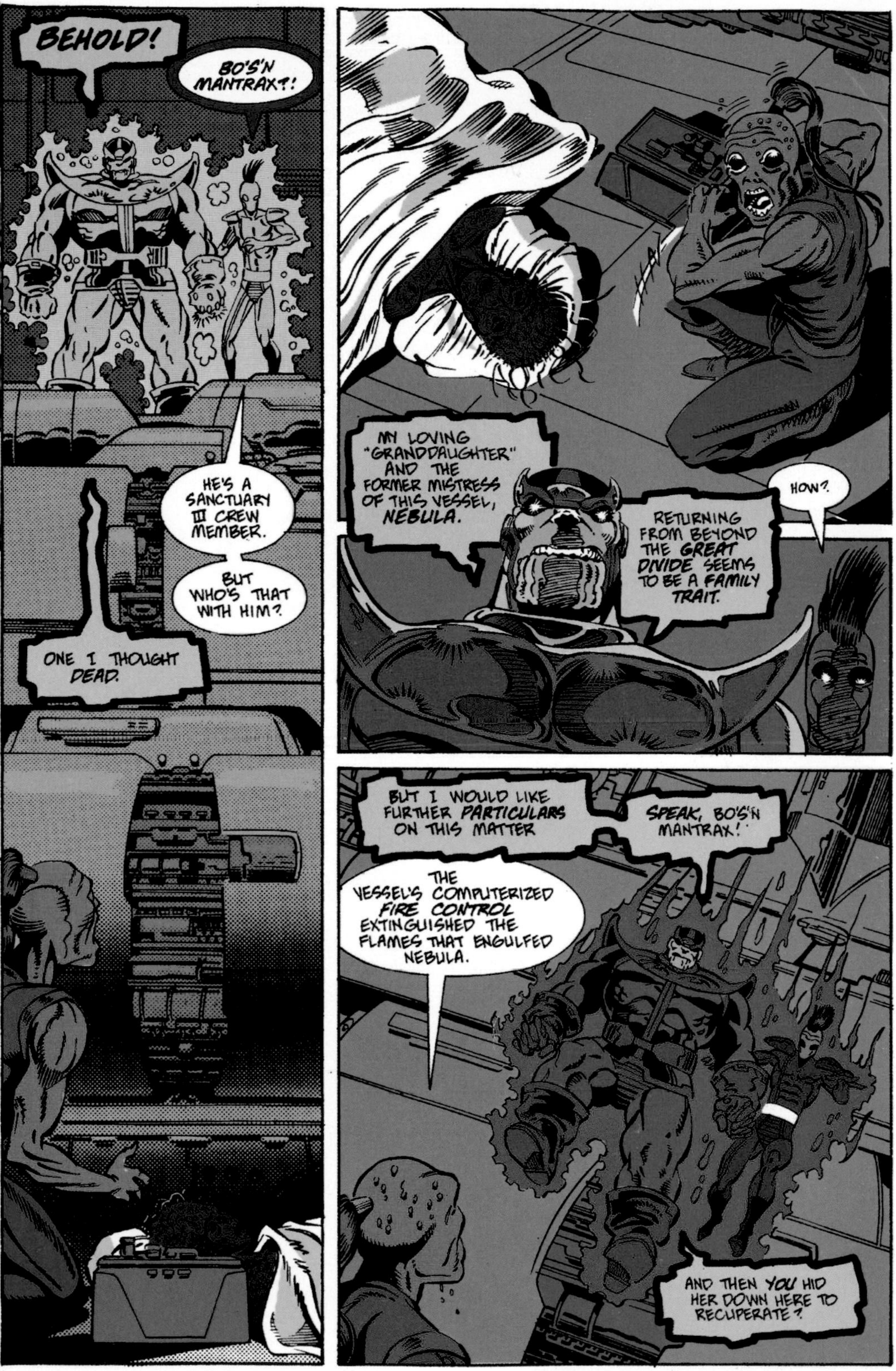
BEHOLD!
BO'S'N MANTRAX?!
HE'S A SANCTUARY III CREW MEMBER.
BUT WHO'S THAT WITH HIM?
ONE I THOUGHT DEAD.
MY LOVING "GRANDDAUGHTER" AND THE FORMER MISTRESS OF THIS VESSEL, NEBULA.
RETURNING FROM BEYOND THE GREAT DIVIDE SEEMS TO BE A FAMILY TRAIT.
HOW?
BUT I WOULD LIKE FURTHER PARTICULARS ON THIS MATTER
SPEAK, BO'S'N MANTRAX!
THE VESSEL'S COMPUTERIZED FIRE CONTROL EXTINGUISHED THE FLAMES THAT ENGULFED NEBULA.
AND THEN YOU HID HER DOWN HERE TO RECUPERATE?

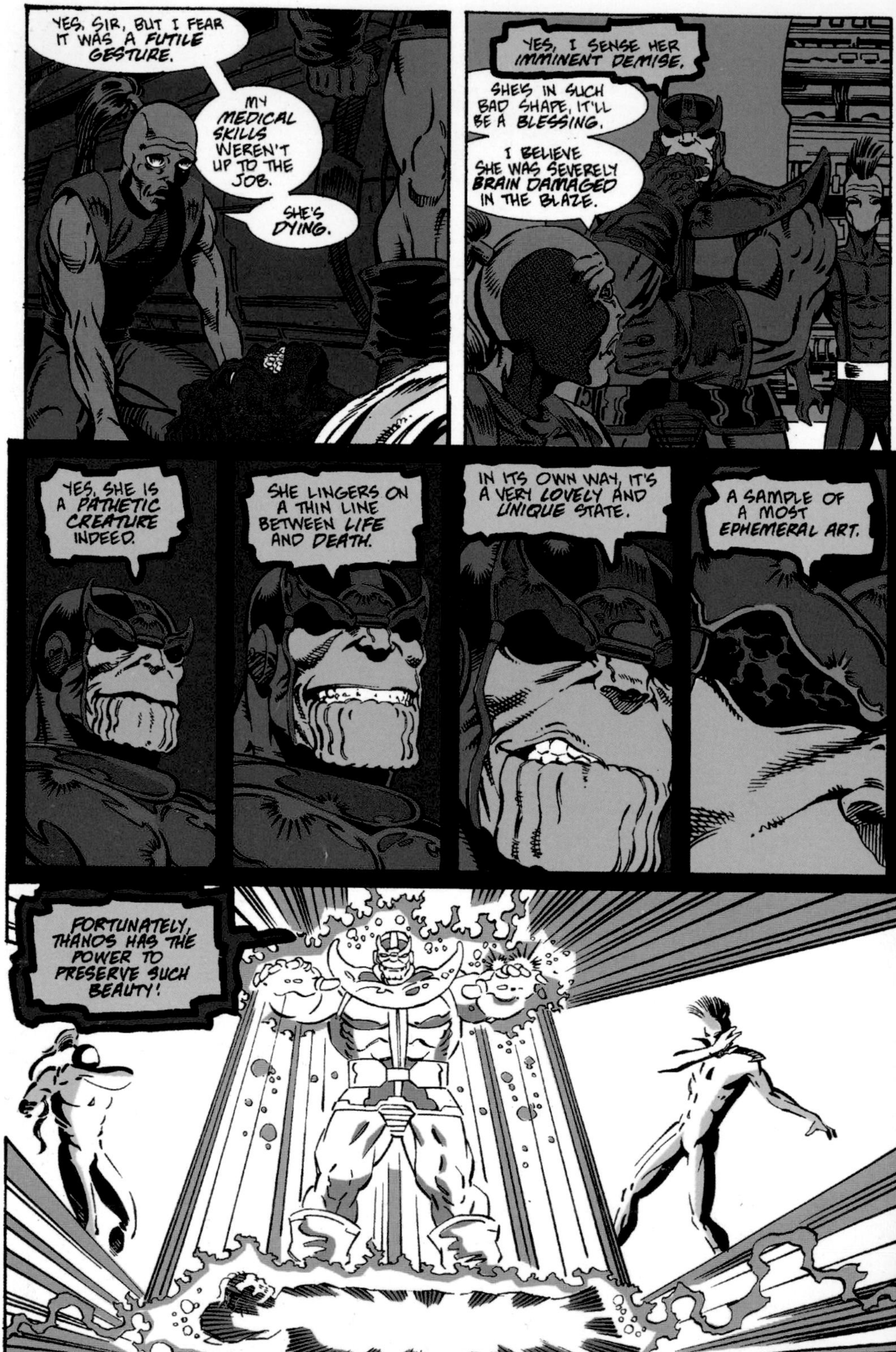
YES, SIR, BUT I FEAR IT WAS A FUTILE GESTURE.
MY MEDICAL SKILLS WEREN'T UP TO THE JOB.
SHE'S DYING.
YES, I SENSE HER IMMINENT DEMISE.
SHE'S IN SUCH BAD SHAPE, IT'LL BE A BLESSING.
I BELIEVE SHE WAS SEVERELY BRAIN DAMAGED IN THE BLAZE.
YES, SHE IS A PATHETIC CREATURE INDEED.
SHE LINGERS ON A THIN LINE BETWEEN LIFE AND DEATH.
IN ITS OWN WAY, IT'S A VERY LOVELY AND UNIQUE STATE.
A SAMPLE OF A MOST EPHEMERAL ART.
FORTUNATELY, THANOS HAS THE POWER TO PRESERVE SUCH BEAUTY!

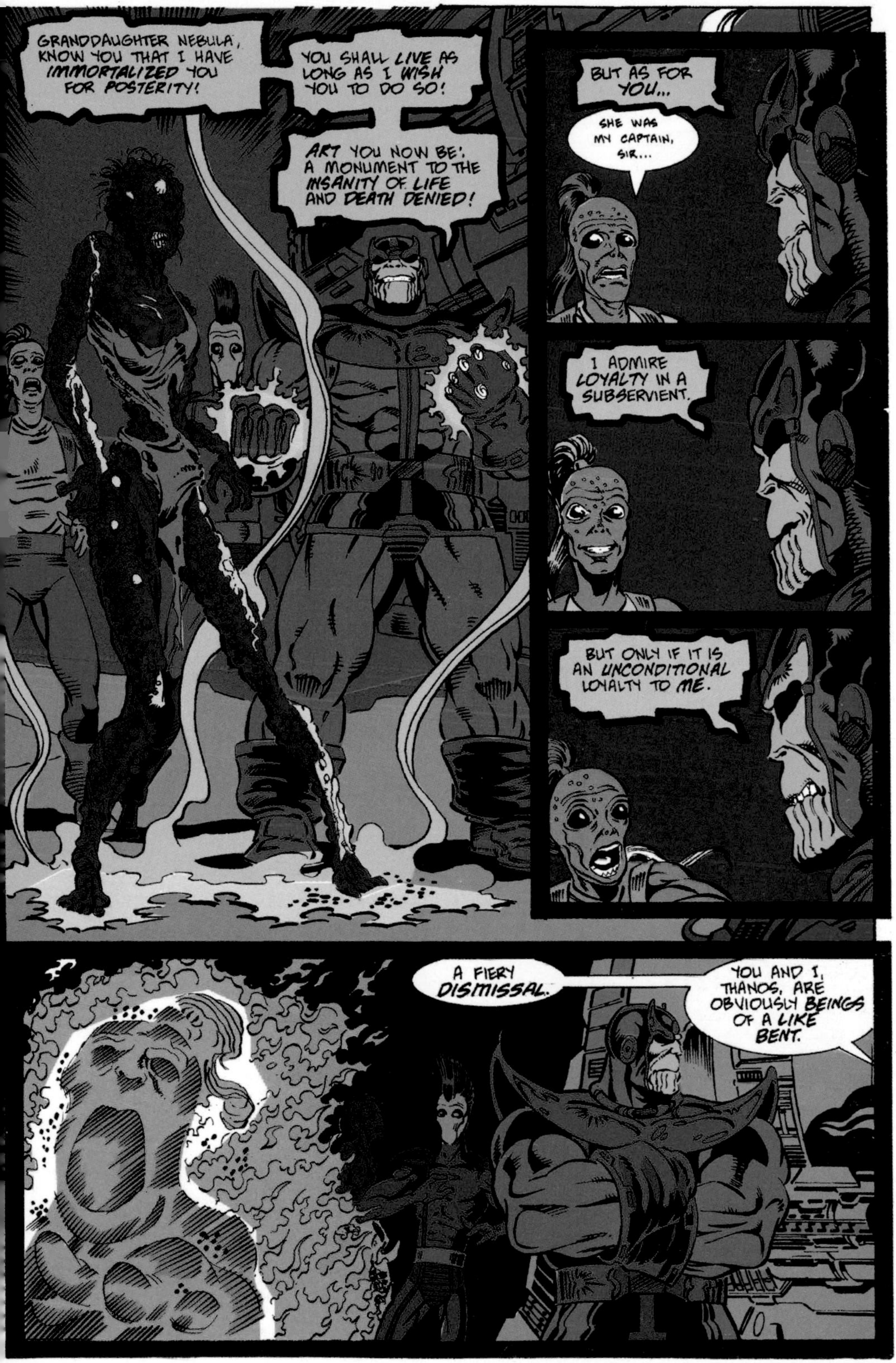
GRANDDAUGHTER NEBULA, KNOW YOU THAT I HAVE IMMORTALIZED YOU FOR POSTERITY!
YOU SHALL LIVE AS LONG AS I WISH YOU TO DO SO!
ART YOU NOW BE: A MONUMENT TO THE INSANITY OF LIFE AND DEATH DENIED!
BUT AS FOR YOU...
SHE WAS MY CAPTAIN, SIR...
I ADMIRE LOYALTY IN A SUBSERVIENT.
BUT ONLY IF IT IS AN UNCONDITIONAL LOYALTY TO ME.
A FIERY DISMISSAL.
YOU AND I, THANOS, ARE OBVIOUSLY BEINGS OF A LIKE BENT.

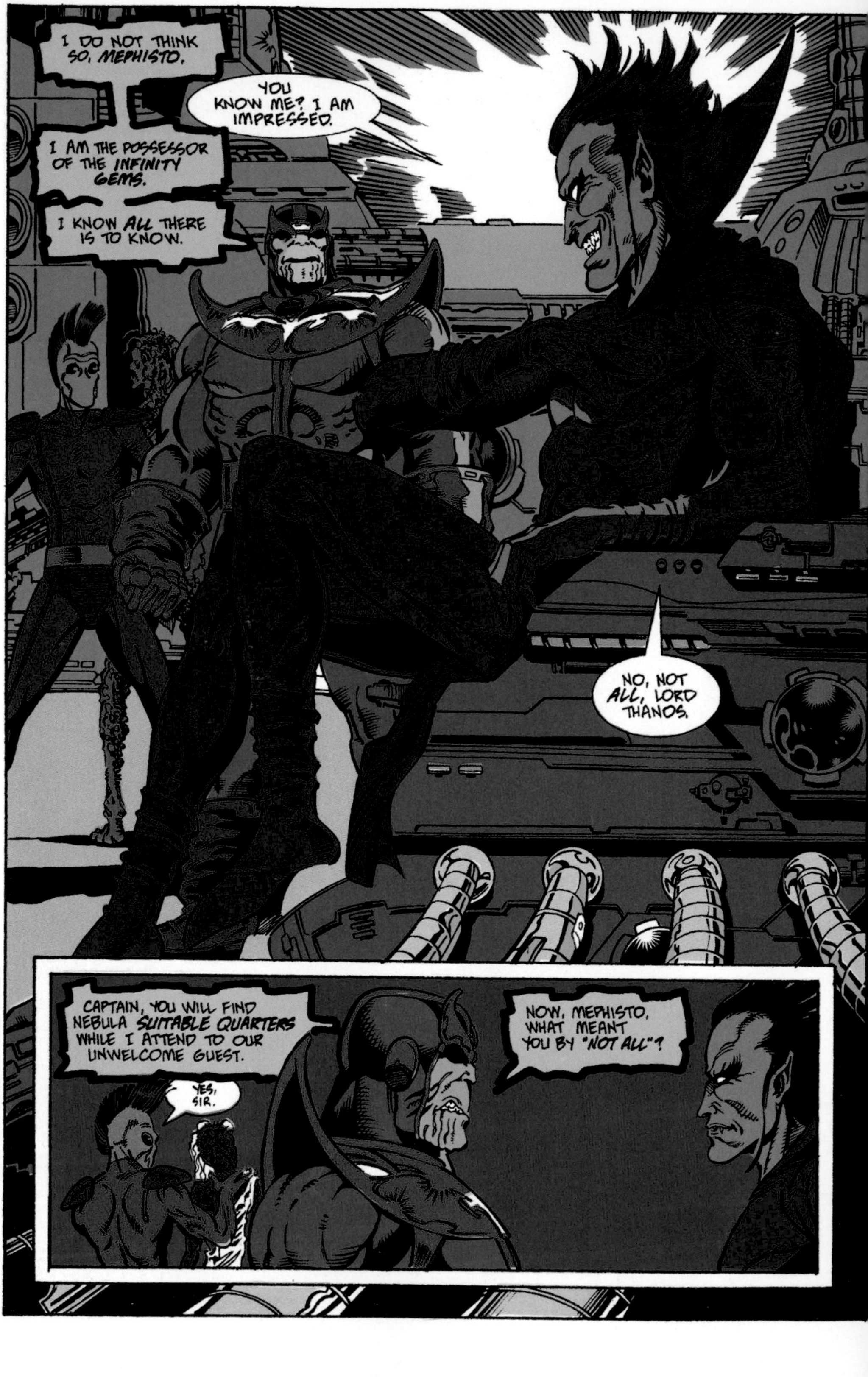

I DO NOT THINK SO, MEPHISTO.
YOU KNOW ME? I AM IMPRESSED.
I AM THE POSSESSOR OF THE INFINITY GEMS.
I KNOW ALL THERE IS TO KNOW.
NO, NOT ALL, LORD THANOS.
CAPTAIN, YOU WILL FIND NEBULA SUITABLE QUARTERS WHILE I ATTEND TO OUR UNWELCOME GUEST.
YES, SIR.
NOW, MEPHISTO, WHAT MEANT YOU BY "NOT ALL"?

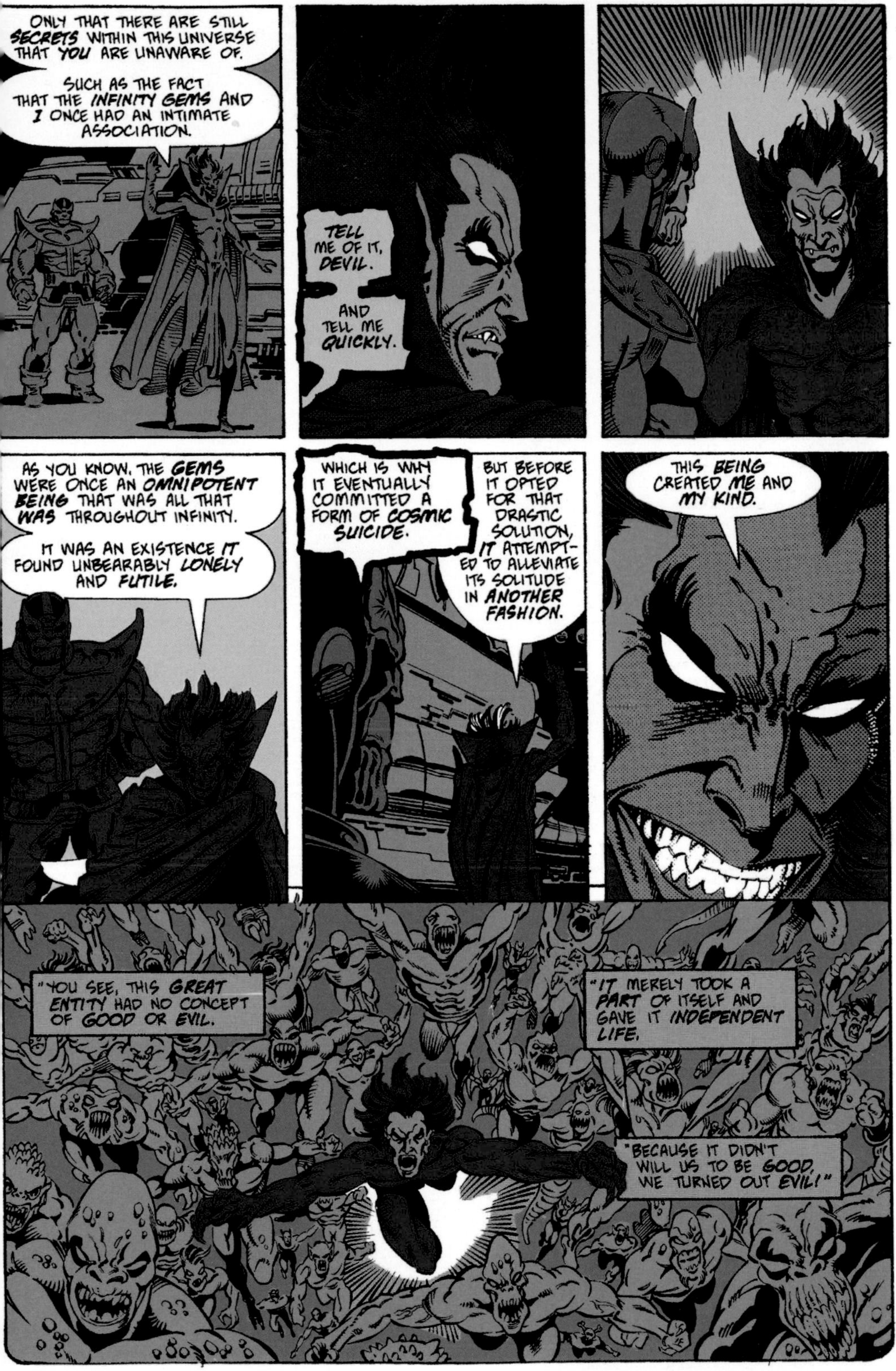
ONLY THAT THERE ARE STILL SECRETS WITHIN THIS UNIVERSE THAT YOU ARE UNAWARE OF.
SUCH AS THE FACT THAT THE INFINITY GEMS AND I ONCE HAD AN INTIMATE ASSOCIATION.
TELL ME OF IT, DEVIL.
AND TELL ME QUICKLY.
AS YOU KNOW, THE GEMS WERE ONCE AN OMNIPOTENT BEING THAT WAS ALL THAT WAS THROUGHOUT INFINITY.
IT WAS AN EXISTENCE IT FOUND UNBEARABLY LONELY AND FUTILE.
WHICH IS WHY IT EVENTUALLY COMMITTED A FORM OF COSMIC SUICIDE.
BUT BEFORE IT OPTED FOR THAT DRASTIC SOLUTION, IT ATTEMPTED TO ALLEVIATE ITS SOLITUDE IN ANOTHER FASHION.
THIS BEING CREATED ME AND MY KIND.
"YOU SEE, THIS GREAT ENTITY HAD NO CONCEPT OF GOOD OR EVIL.
"IT MERELY TOOK A PART OF ITSELF AND GAVE IT INDEPENDENT LIFE.
"BECAUSE IT DIDN'T WILL US TO BE GOOD, WE TURNED OUT EVIL!"

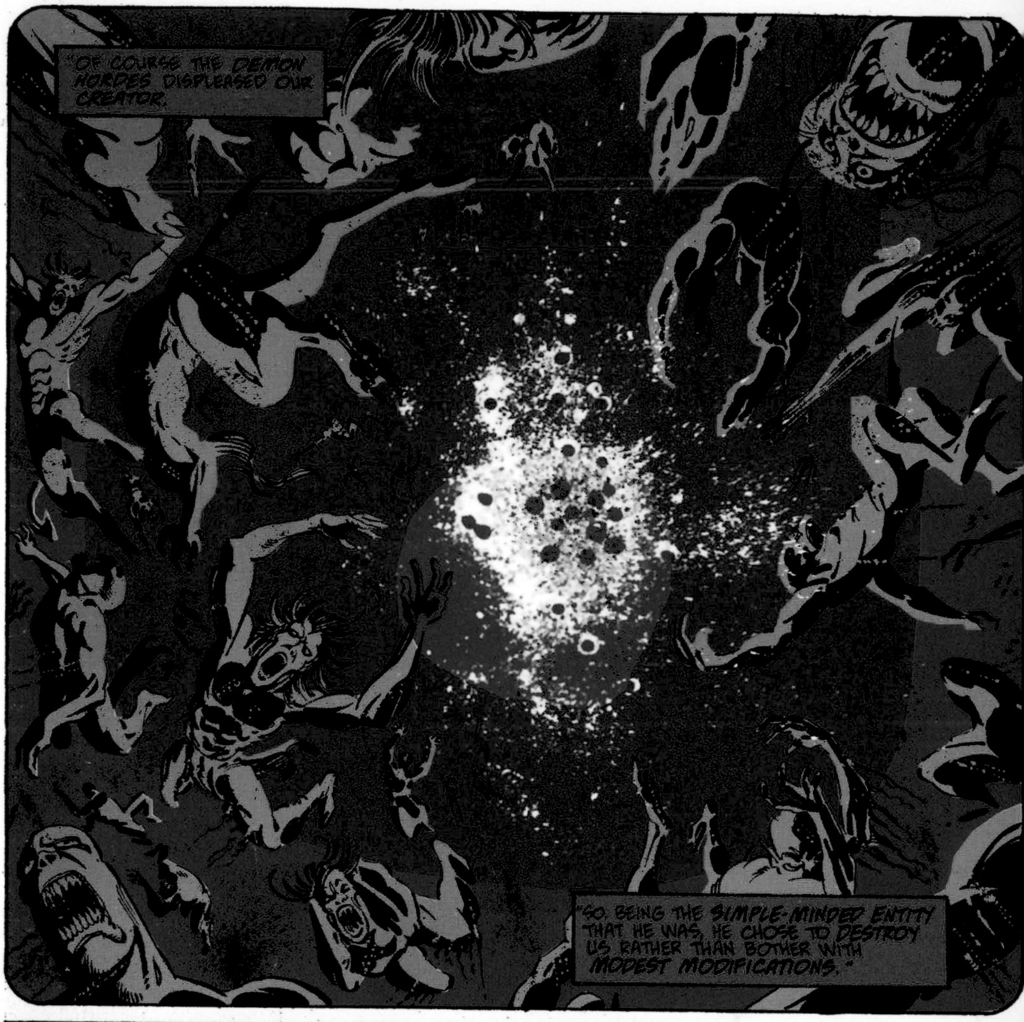
"OF COURSE THE DEMON HORDES DISPLEASED OUR CREATOR.
"SO, BEING THE SIMPLE-MINDED ENTITY THAT HE WAS, HE CHOSE TO DESTROY US RATHER THAN BOTHER WITH MODEST MODIFICATIONS."
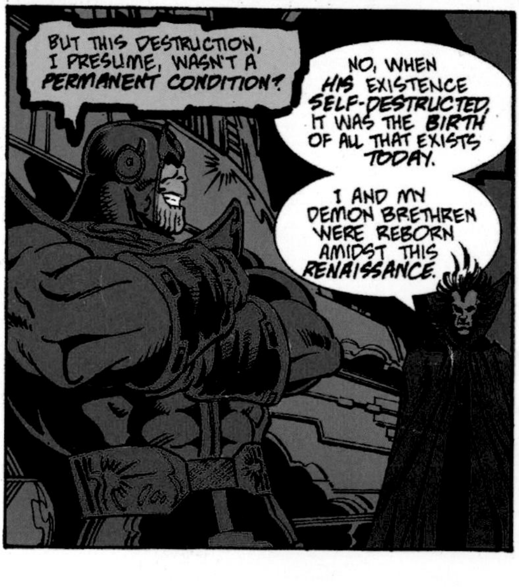
BUT THIS DESTRUCTION, I PRESUME, WASN'T A PERMANENT CONDITION?
NO, WHEN HIS EXISTENCE SELF-DESTRUCTED, IT WAS THE BIRTH OF ALL THAT EXISTS TODAY.
I AND MY DEMON BRETHREN WERE REBORN AMIDST THIS RENAISSANCE.
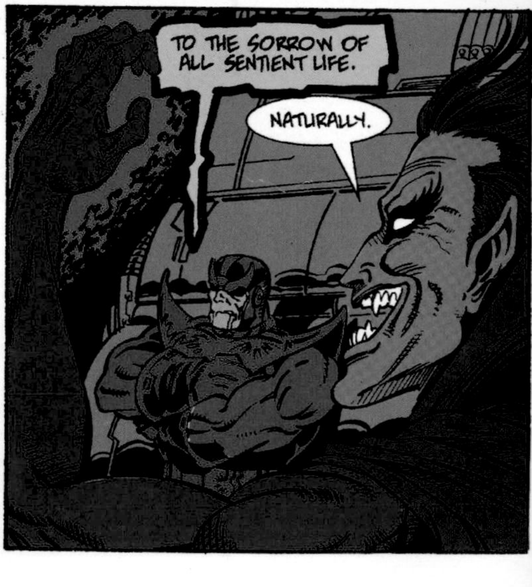
TO THE SORROW OF ALL SENTIENT LIFE.
NATURALLY.

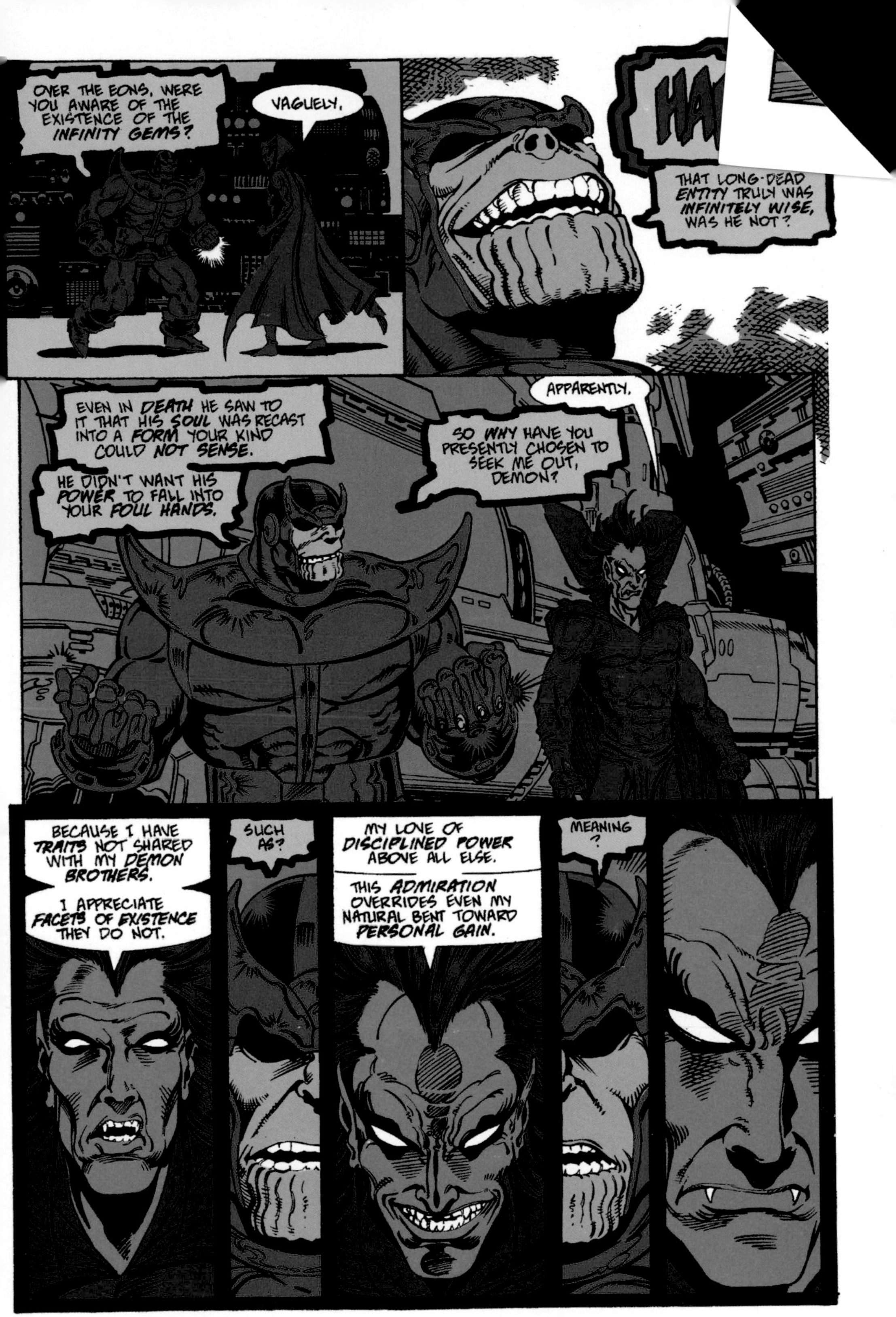

OVER THE EONS, WERE YOU AWARE OF THE EXISTENCE OF THE INFINITY GEMS?
VAGUELY.
THAT LONG-DEAD ENTITY TRULY WAS INFINITELY WISE, WAS HE NOT?
EVEN IN DEATH HE SAW TO IT THAT HIS SOUL WAS RECAST INTO A FORM YOUR KIND COULD NOT SENSE.
HE DIDN'T WANT HIS POWER TO FALL INTO YOUR FOUL HANDS.
APPARENTLY.
SO WHY HAVE YOU PRESENTLY CHOSEN TO SEEK ME OUT, DEMON?
BECAUSE I HAVE TRAITS NOT SHARED WITH MY DEMON BROTHERS.
I APPRECIATE FACETS OF EXISTENCE THEY DO NOT.
SUCH AS?
MY LOVE OF DISCIPLINED POWER ABOVE ALL ELSE.
THIS ADMIRATION OVERRIDES EVEN MY NATURAL BENT TOWARD PERSONAL GAIN.
MEANING?

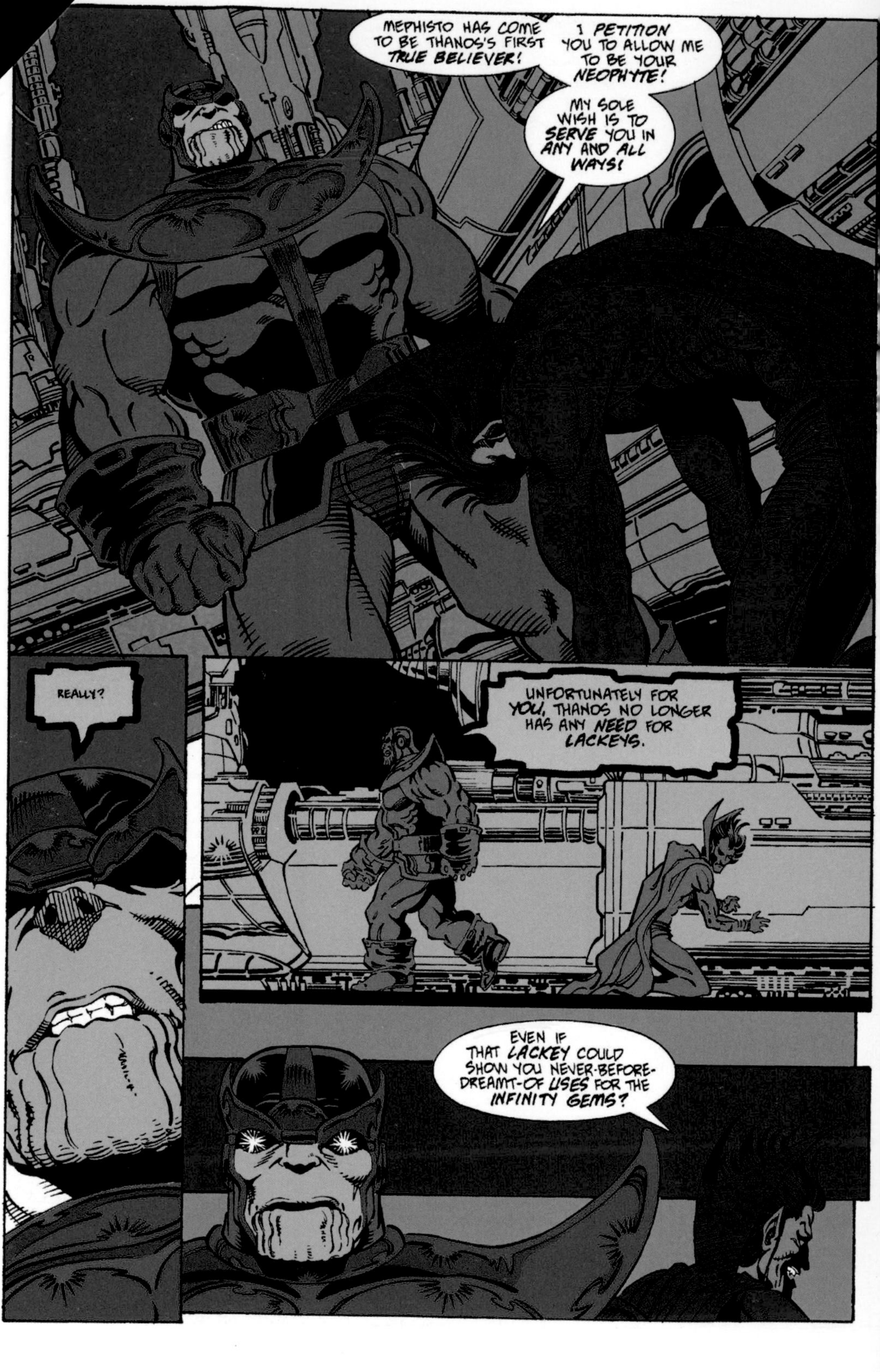
MEPHISTO HAS COME TO BE THANOS'S FIRST TRUE BELIEVER!
I PETITION YOU TO ALLOW ME TO BE YOUR NEOPHYTE!
MY SOLE WISH IS TO SERVE YOU IN ANY AND ALL WAYS!
REALLY?
UNFORTUNATELY FOR YOU, THANOS NO LONGER HAS ANY NEED FOR LACKEYS.
EVEN IF THAT LACKEY COULD SHOW YOU NEVER-BEFORE-DREAMT-OF USES FOR THE INFINITY GEMS?

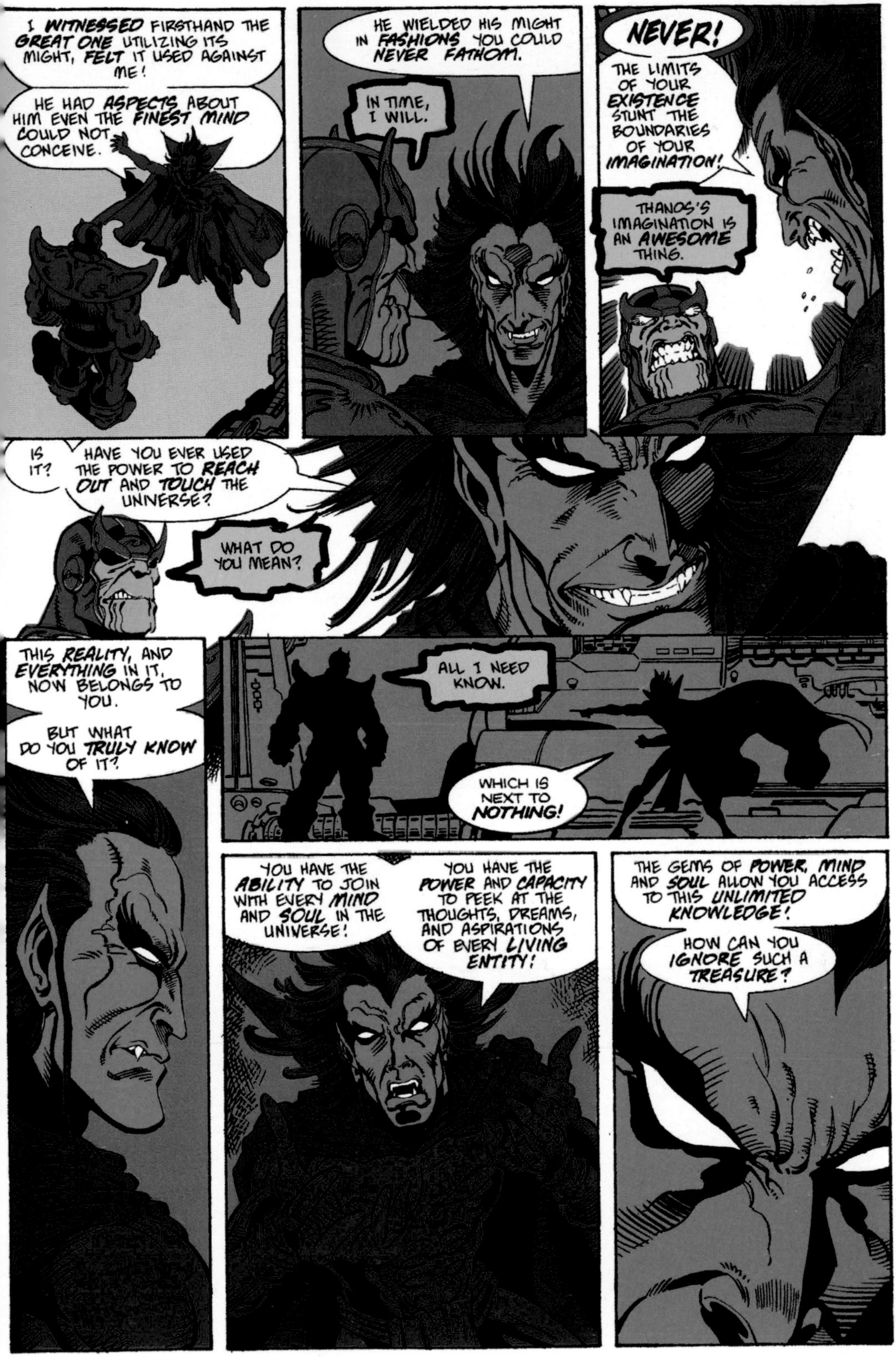
I WITNESSED FIRSTHAND THE GREAT ONE UTILIZING ITS MIGHT, FELT IT USED AGAINST ME!
HE HAD ASPECTS ABOUT HIM EVEN THE FINEST MIND COULD NOT CONCEIVE.
HE WIELDED HIS MIGHT IN FASHIONS YOU COULD NEVER FATHOM.
IN TIME, I WILL.
NEVER!
THE LIMITS OF YOUR EXISTENCE STUNT THE BOUNDARIES OF YOUR IMAGINATION!
THANOS'S IMAGINATION IS AN AWESOME THING.
IS IT?
HAVE YOU EVER USED THE POWER TO REACH OUT AND TOUCH THE UNIVERSE?
WHAT DO YOU MEAN?
THIS REALITY, AND EVERYTHING IN IT, NOW BELONGS TO YOU.
BUT WHAT DO YOU TRULY KNOW OF IT?
ALL I NEED KNOW.
WHICH IS NEXT TO NOTHING!
YOU HAVE THE ABILITY TO JOIN WITH EVERY MIND AND SOUL IN THE UNIVERSE!
YOU HAVE THE POWER AND CAPACITY TO PEEK AT THE THOUGHTS, DREAMS, AND ASPIRATIONS OF EVERY LIVING ENTITY!
THE GEMS OF POWER, MIND AND SOUL ALLOW YOU ACCESS TO THIS UNLIMITED KNOWLEDGE!
HOW CAN YOU IGNORE SUCH A TREASURE?

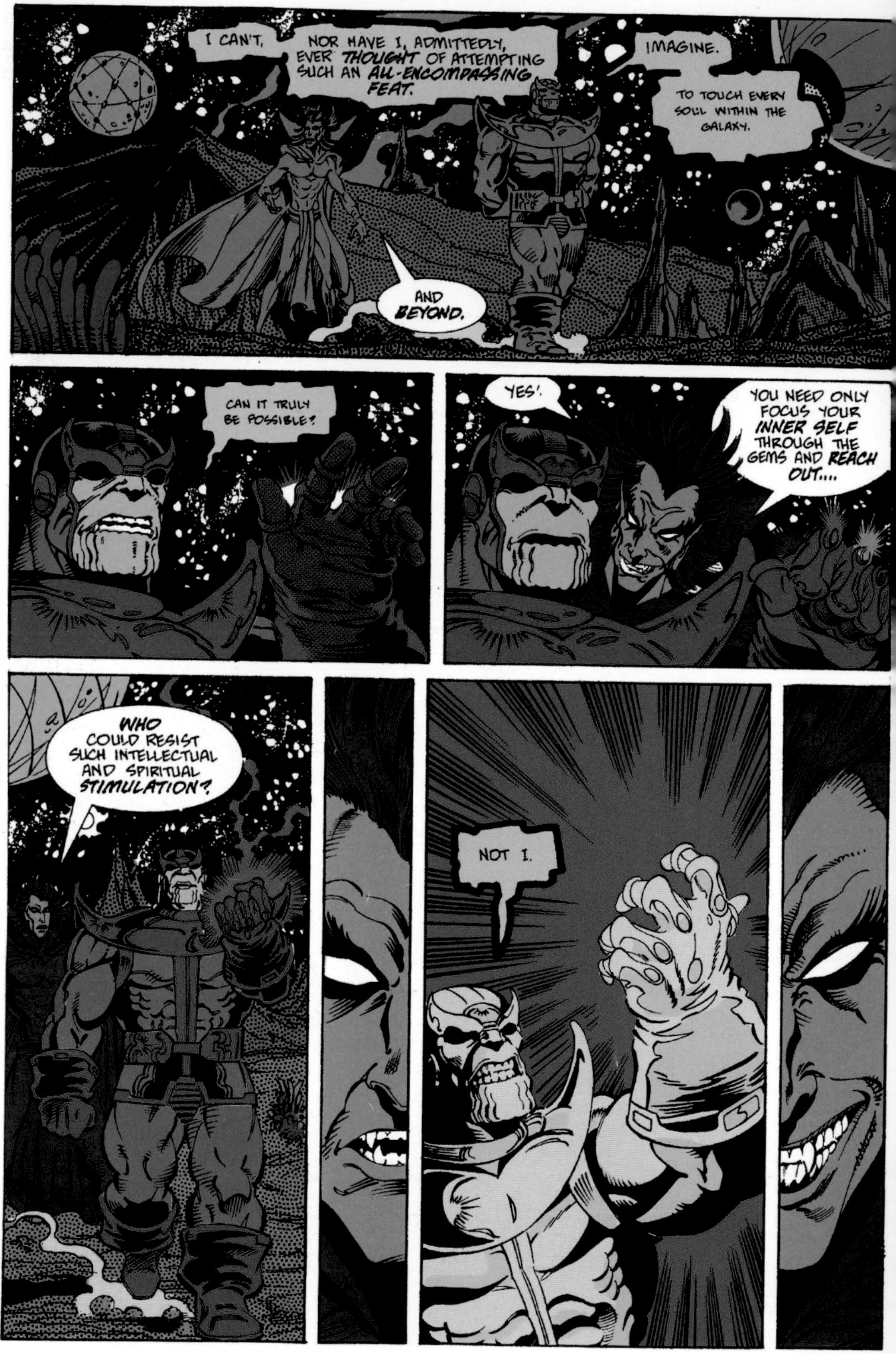
I CAN'T.
NOR HAVE I, ADMITTEDLY, EVER THOUGHT OF ATTEMPTING SUCH AN ALL-ENCOMPASSING FEAT.
IMAGINE.
TO TOUCH EVERY SOUL WITHIN THE GALAXY.
AND BEYOND.
CAN IT TRULY BE POSSIBLE?
YES!
YOU NEED ONLY FOCUS YOUR INNER SELF THROUGH THE GEMS AND REACH OUT....
WHO COULD RESIST SUCH INTELLECTUAL AND SPIRITUAL STIMULATION?
NOT I.

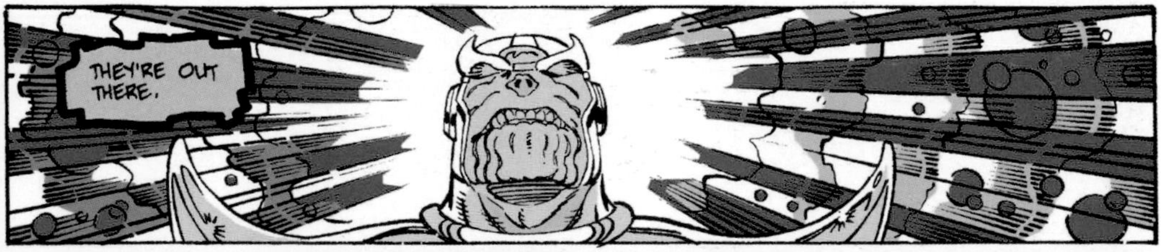
THEY'RE OUT THERE.

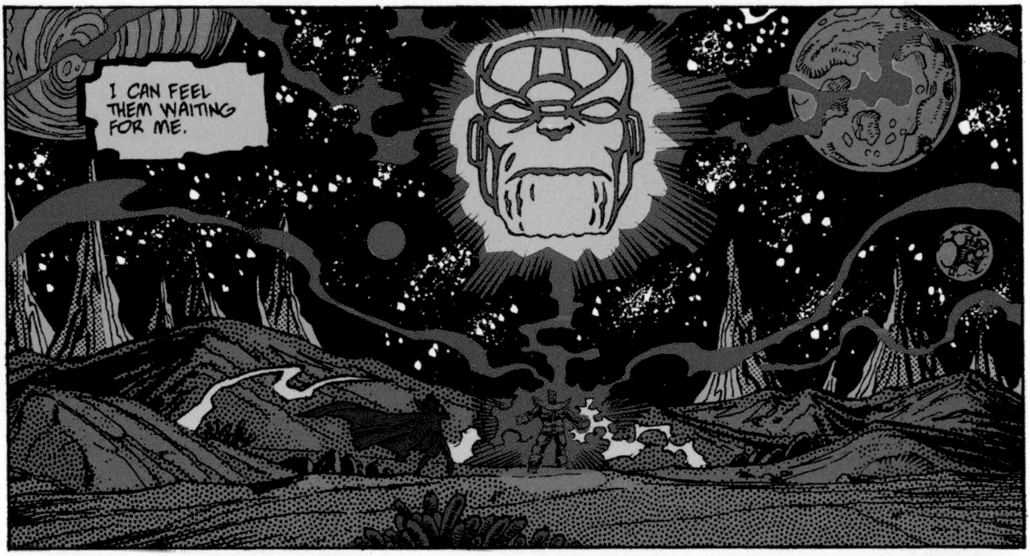
I CAN FEEL THEM WAITING FOR ME.

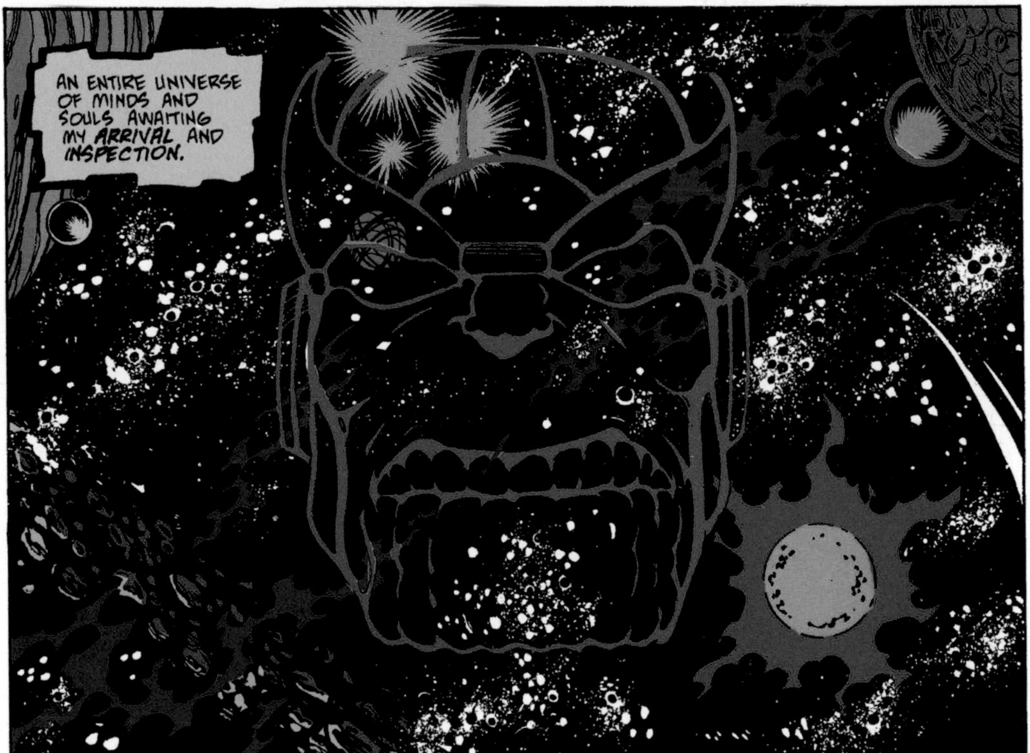
AN ENTIRE UNIVERSE OF MINDS AND SOULS AWAITING MY ARRIVAL AND INSPECTION.

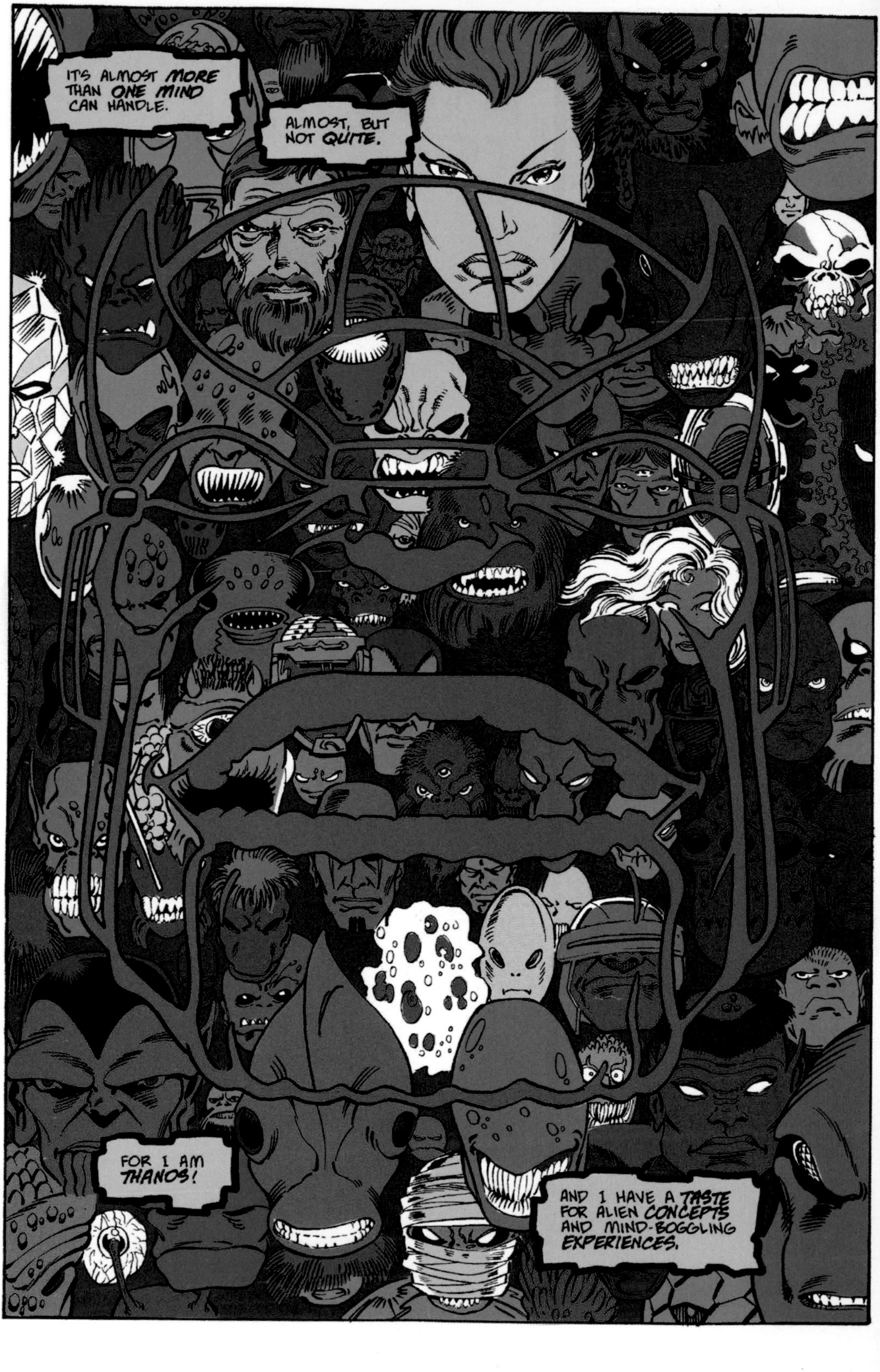
IT'S ALMOST MORE THAN ONE MIND CAN HANDLE.
ALMOST, BUT NOT QUITE.
FOR I AM THANOS!
AND I HAVE A TASTE FOR ALIEN CONCEPTS AND MIND-BOGGLING EXPERIENCES.

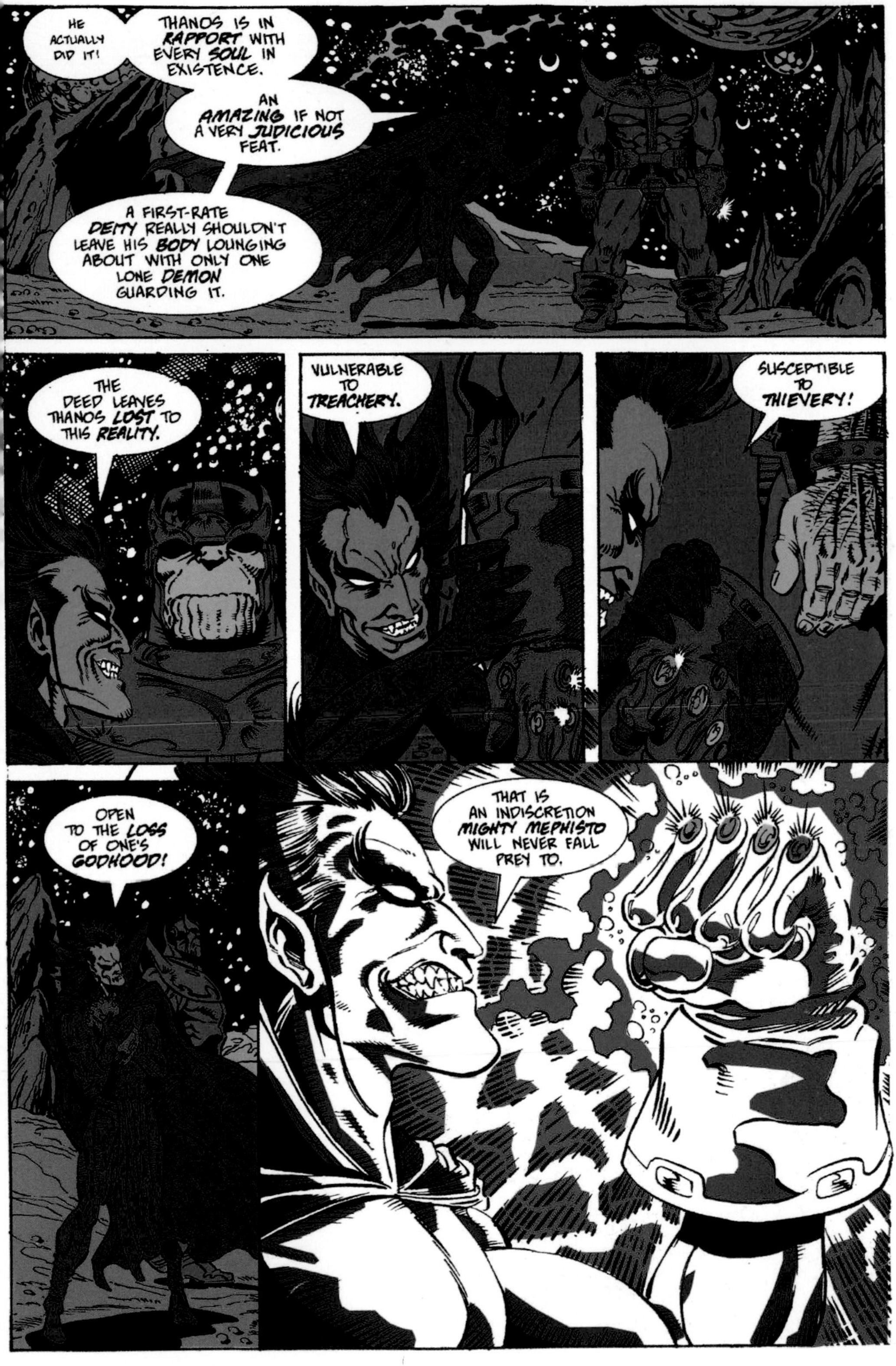
HE ACTUALLY DID IT!
THANOS IS IN RAPPORT WITH EVERY SOUL IN EXISTENCE.
AN AMAZING IF NOT A VERY JUDICIOUS FEAT.
A FIRST-RATE DEITY REALLY SHOULDN'T LEAVE HIS BODY LOUNGING ABOUT WITH ONLY ONE LONE DEMON GUARDING IT.
THE DEED LEAVES THANOS LOST TO THIS REALITY.
VULNERABLE TO TREACHERY.
SUSCEPTIBLE TO THIEVERY!
OPEN TO THE LOSS OF ONE'S GODHOOD!
THAT IS AN INDISCRETION MIGHTY MEPHISTO WILL NEVER FALL PREY TO.

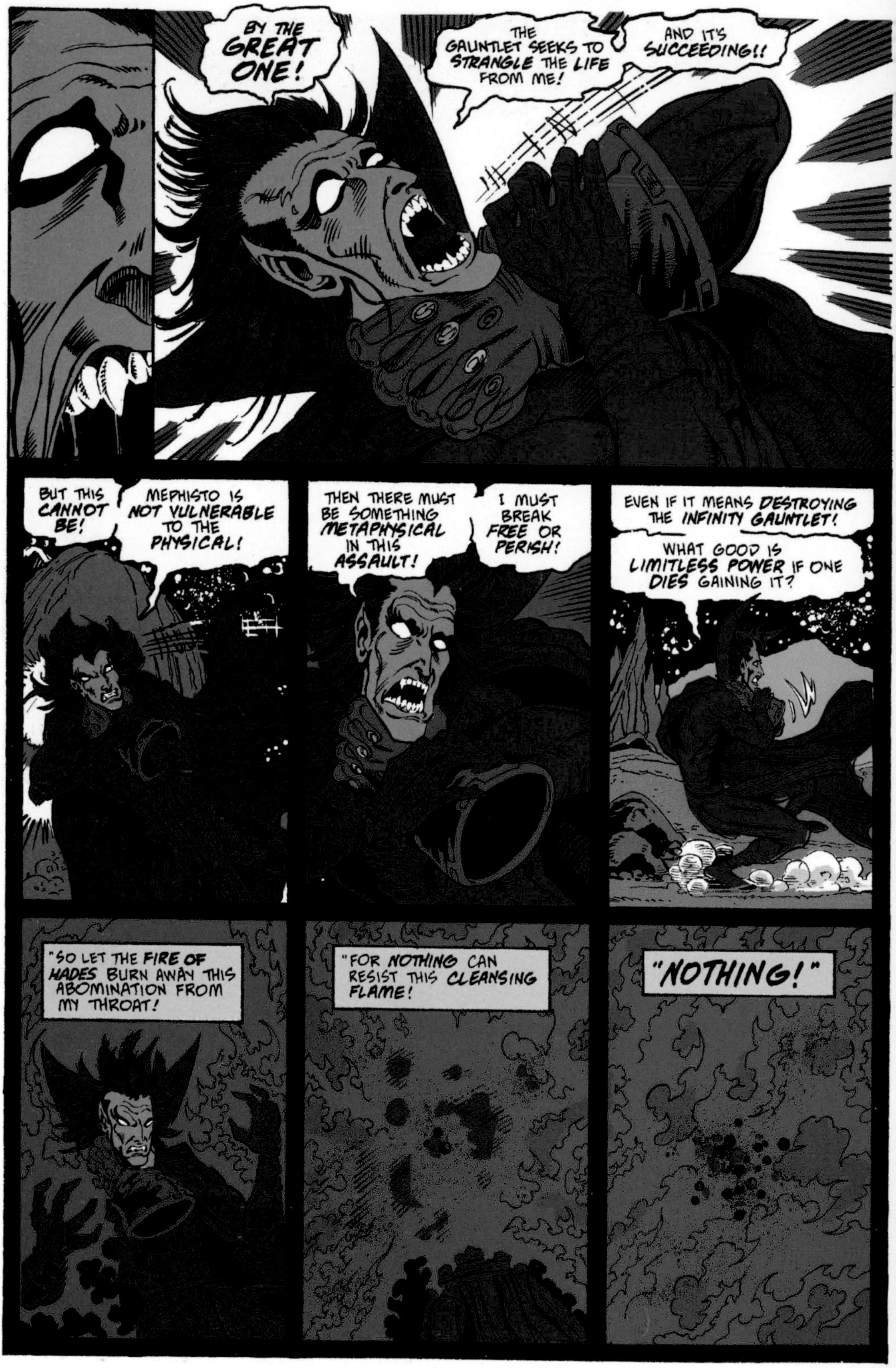
BY THE GREAT ONE!
THE GAUNTLET SEEKS TO STRANGLE THE LIFE FROM ME!
AND IT'S SUCCEEDING!!
BUT THIS CANNOT BE!
MEPHISTO IS NOT VULNERABLE TO THE PHYSICAL!
THEN THERE MUST BE SOMETHING METAPHYSICAL IN THIS ASSAULT!
I MUST BREAK FREE OR PERISH!
EVEN IF IT MEANS DESTROYING THE INFINITY GAUNTLET!
WHAT GOOD IS LIMITLESS POWER IF ONE DIES GAINING IT?
"SO LET THE FIRE OF HADES BURN AWAY THIS ABOMINATION FROM MY THROAT!
"FOR NOTHING CAN RESIST THIS CLEANSING FLAME!
"NOTHING!"

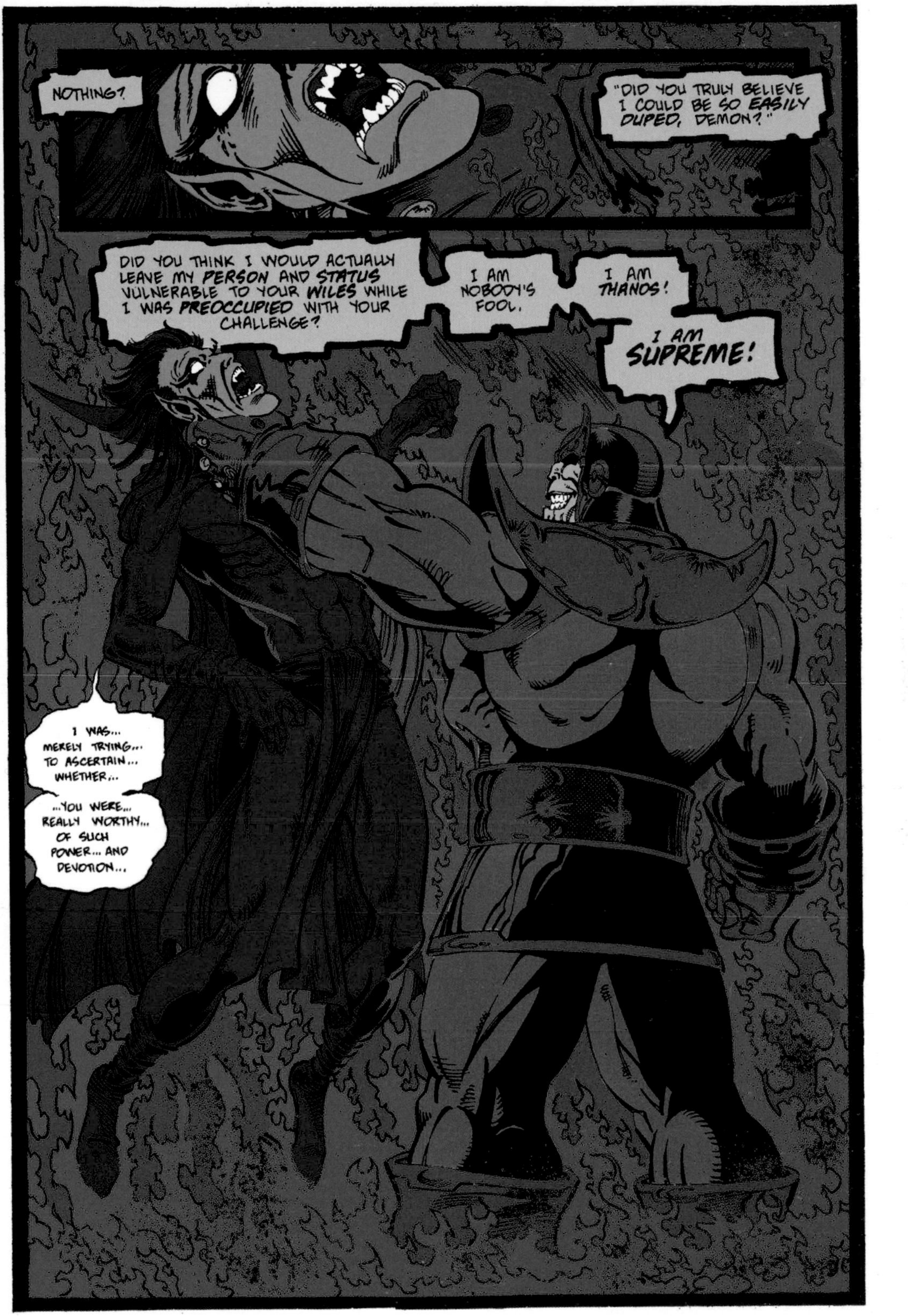
NOTHING?
"DID YOU TRULY BELIEVE I COULD BE SO EASILY DUPED, DEMON?"
DID YOU THINK I WOULD ACTUALLY LEAVE MY PERSON AND STATUS VULNERABLE TO YOUR WILES WHILE I WAS PREOCCUPIED WITH YOUR CHALLENGE?
I AM NOBODY'S FOOL.
I AM THANOS!
I AM SUPREME!
I WAS... MERELY TRYING... TO ASCERTAIN... WHETHER...
...YOU WERE... REALLY WORTHY... OF SUCH POWER... AND DEVOTION...

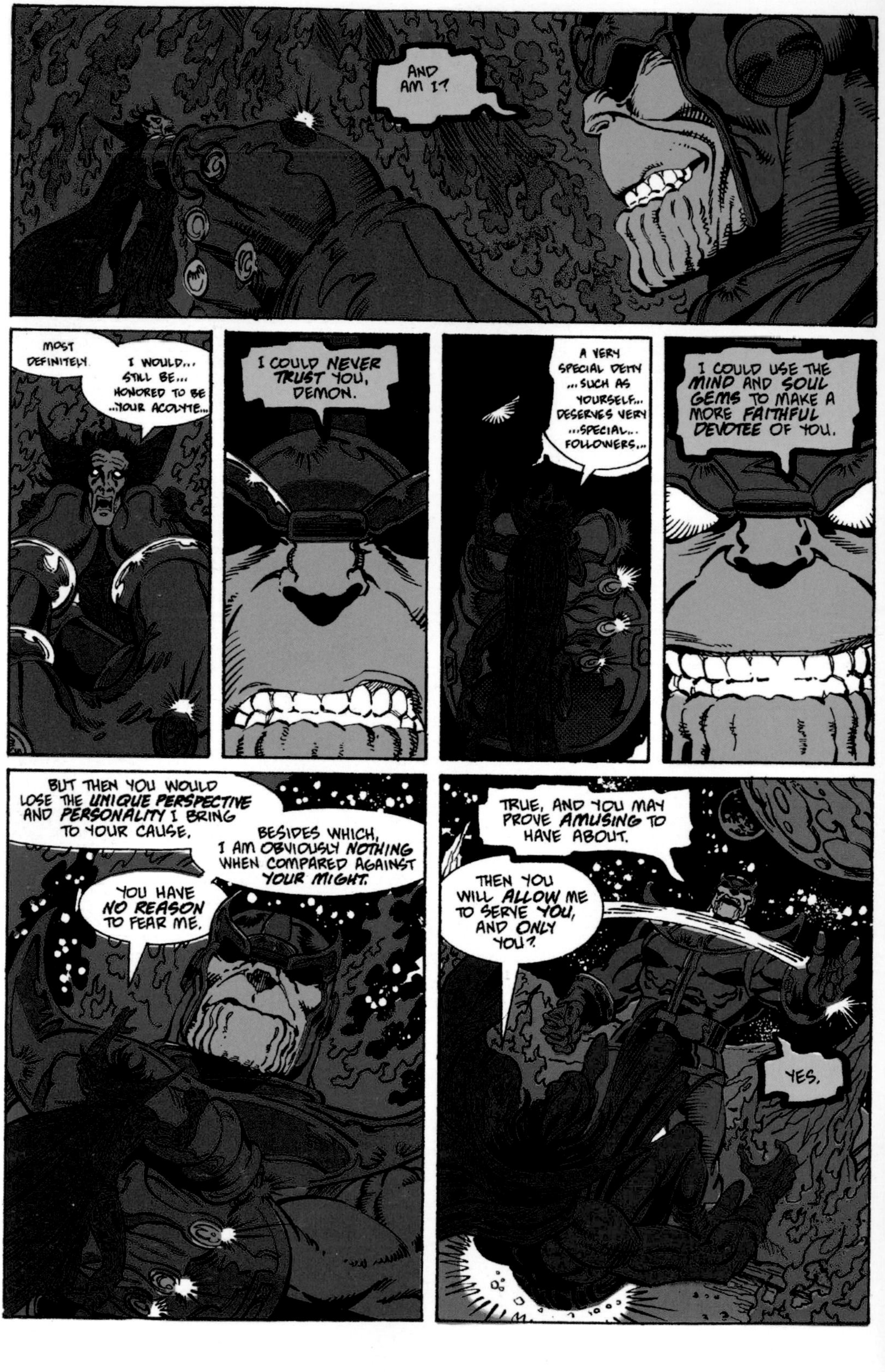
AND AM I?
MOST DEFINITELY.
I WOULD... STILL BE... HONORED TO BE ...YOUR ACOLYTE...
I COULD NEVER TRUST YOU, DEMON.
A VERY SPECIAL DEITY ...SUCH AS YOURSELF... DESERVES VERY ...SPECIAL... FOLLOWERS...
I COULD USE THE MIND AND SOUL GEMS TO MAKE A MORE FAITHFUL DEVOTEE OF YOU.
BUT THEN YOU WOULD LOSE THE UNIQUE PERSPECTIVE AND PERSONALITY I BRING TO YOUR CAUSE.
BESIDES WHICH, I AM OBVIOUSLY NOTHING WHEN COMPARED AGAINST YOUR MIGHT.
YOU HAVE NO REASON TO FEAR ME.
TRUE, AND YOU MAY PROVE AMUSING TO HAVE ABOUT.
THEN YOU WILL ALLOW ME TO SERVE YOU, AND ONLY YOU?
YES.

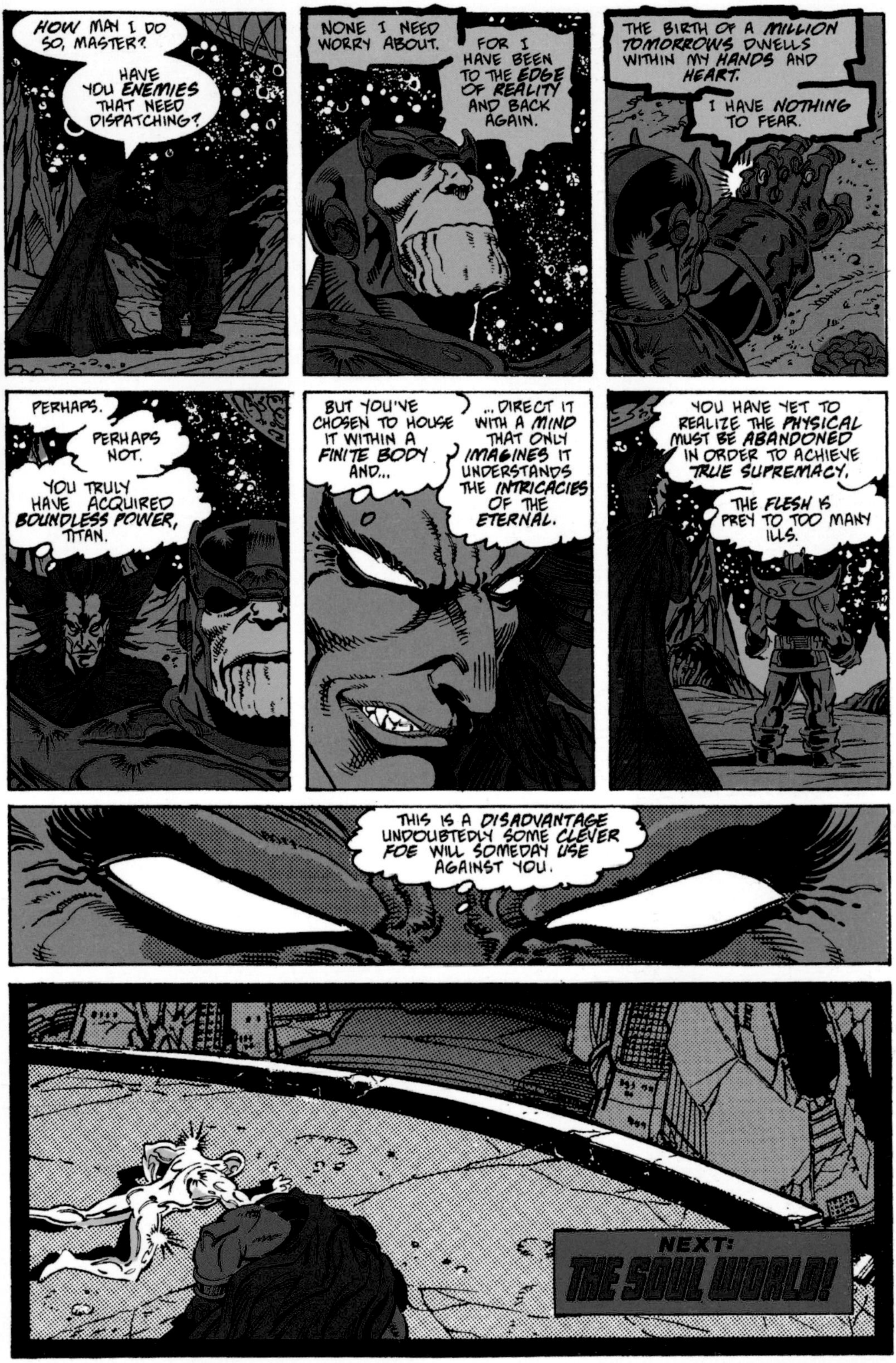

HOW MAY I DO SO, MASTER?
HAVE YOU ENEMIES THAT NEED DISPATCHING?
NONE I NEED WORRY ABOUT.
FOR I HAVE BEEN TO THE EDGE OF REALITY AND BACK AGAIN.
THE BIRTH OF A MILLION TOMORROWS DWELLS WITHIN MY HANDS AND HEART.
I HAVE NOTHING TO FEAR.
PERHAPS.
PERHAPS NOT.
YOU TRULY HAVE ACQUIRED BOUNDLESS POWER, TITAN.
BUT YOU'VE CHOSEN TO HOUSE IT WITHIN A FINITE BODY AND...
...DIRECT IT WITH A MIND THAT ONLY IMAGINES IT UNDERSTANDS THE INTRICACIES OF THE ETERNAL.
YOU HAVE YET TO REALIZE THE PHYSICAL MUST BE ABANDONED IN ORDER TO ACHIEVE TRUE SUPREMACY.
THE FLESH IS PREY TO TOO MANY ILLS.
THIS IS A DISADVANTAGE UNDOUBTEDLY SOME CLEVER FOE WILL SOMEDAY USE AGAINST YOU.
NEXT:
THE SOUL WORLD!

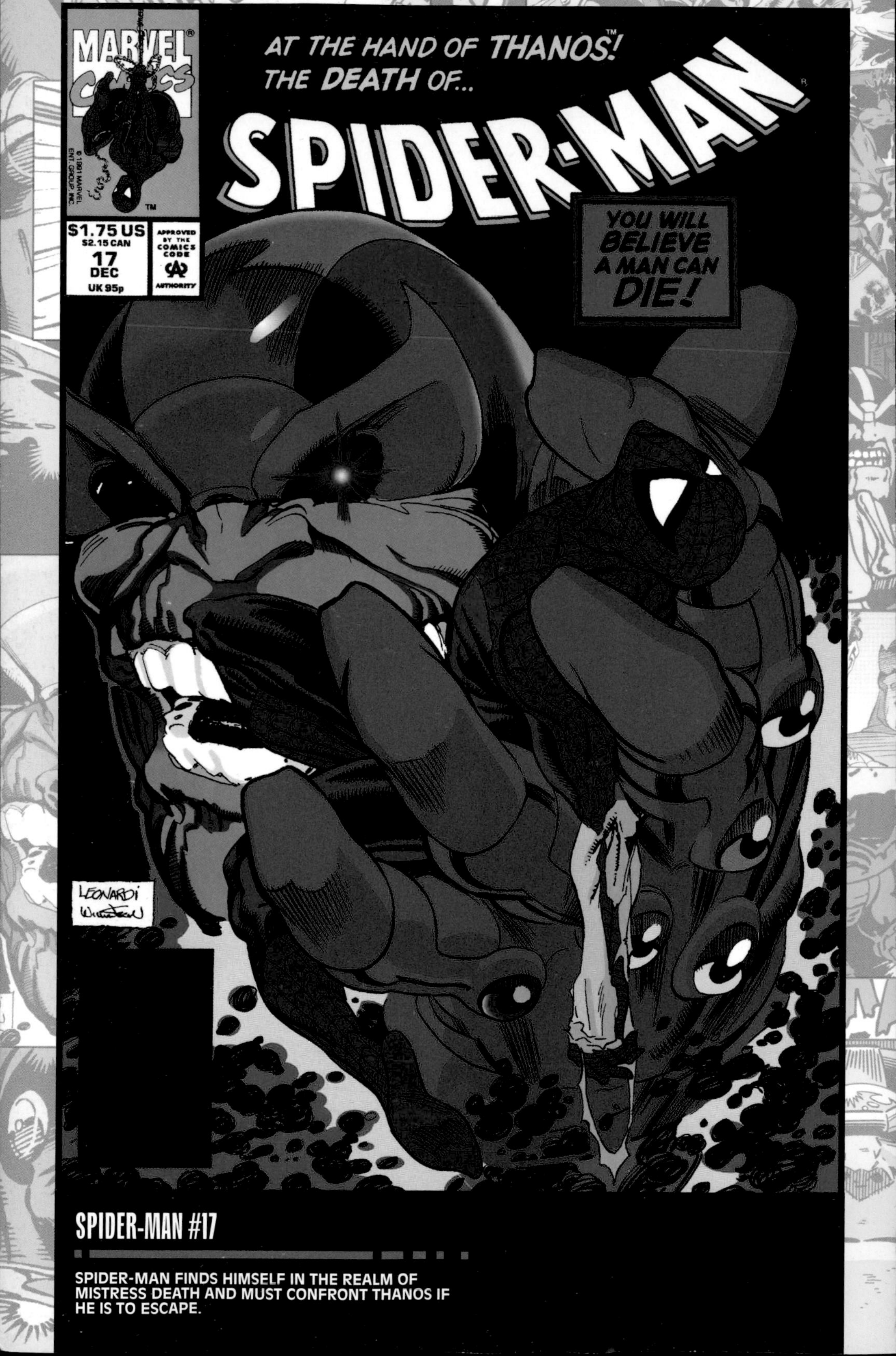
MARVEL COMICS
AT THE HAND OF THANOS!
THE DEATH OF...
SPIDER-MAN
YOU WILL BELIEVE A MAN CAN DIE!
$1.75 US
$2.15 CAN
17
DEC
UK 95p
APPROVED BY THE COMICS CODE AUTHORITY
LEONARDI

SPIDER-MAN #17

SPIDER-MAN FINDS HIMSELF IN THE REALM OF MISTRESS DEATH AND MUST CONFRONT THANOS IF HE IS TO ESCAPE.

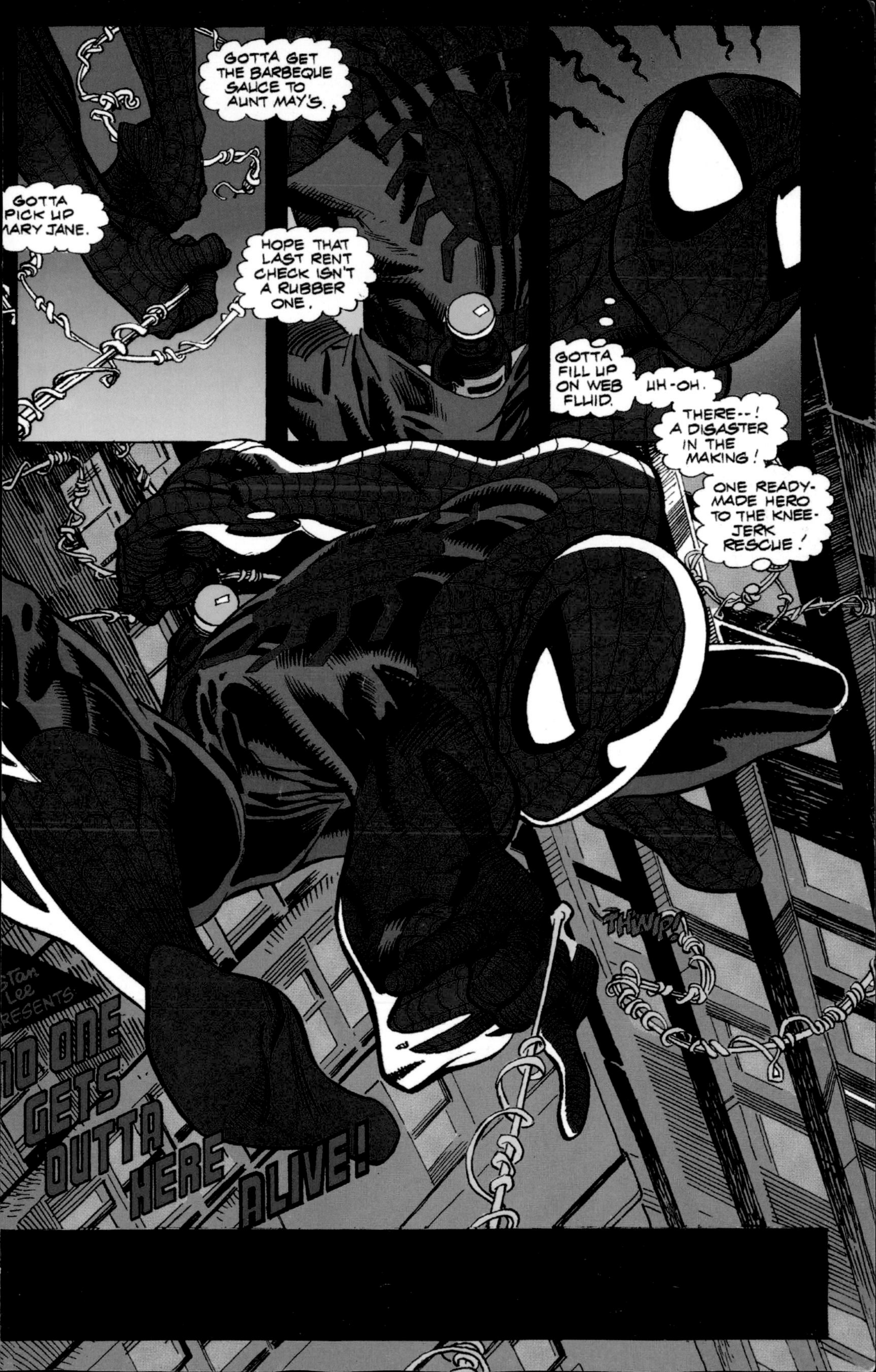
GOTTA GET THE BARBEQUE SAUCE TO AUNT MAY'S.
GOTTA PICK UP MARY JANE.
HOPE THAT LAST RENT CHECK ISN'T A RUBBER ONE.
GOTTA FILL UP ON WEB FLUID.
UH-OH.
THERE--! A DISASTER IN THE MAKING!
ONE READY-MADE HERO TO THE KNEE-JERK RESCUE!
THWIP!
STAN LEE PRESENTS
NO ONE GETS OUTTA HERE ALIVE!
[redacted]

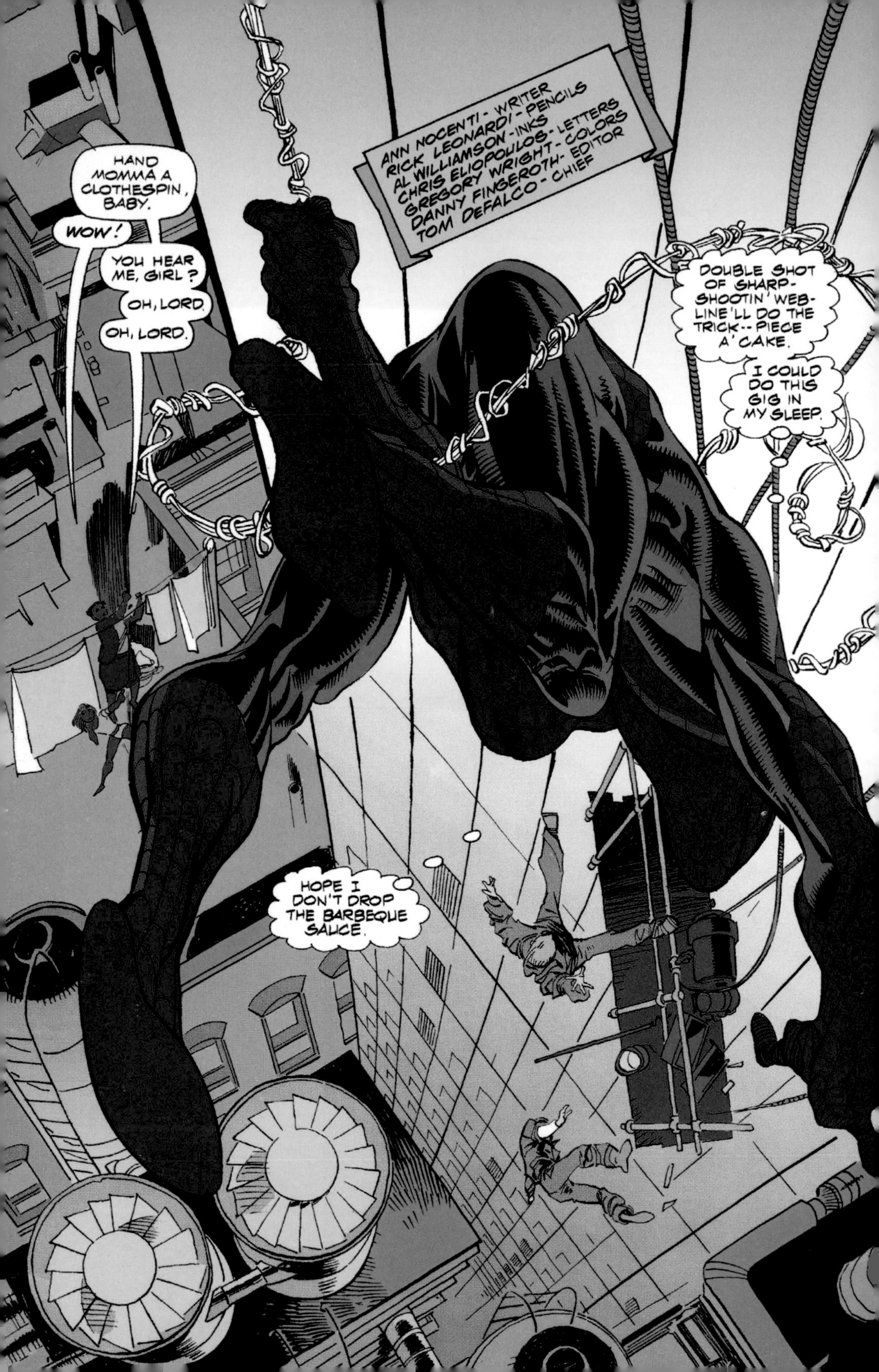
ANN NOCENTI - WRITER
RICK LEONARDI - PENCILS
AL WILLIAMSON - INKS
CHRIS ELIOPOULOS - LETTERS
GREGORY WRIGHT - COLORS
DANNY FINGEROTH - EDITOR
TOM DEFALCO - CHIEF
HAND MOMMA A CLOTHESPIN, BABY.
WOW!
YOU HEAR ME, GIRL?
OH, LORD.
OH, LORD.
DOUBLE SHOT OF SHARP-SHOOTIN' WEB-LINE'LL DO THE TRICK-- PIECE A' CAKE.
I COULD DO THIS GIG IN MY SLEEP.
HOPE I DON'T DROP THE BARBEQUE SAUCE.

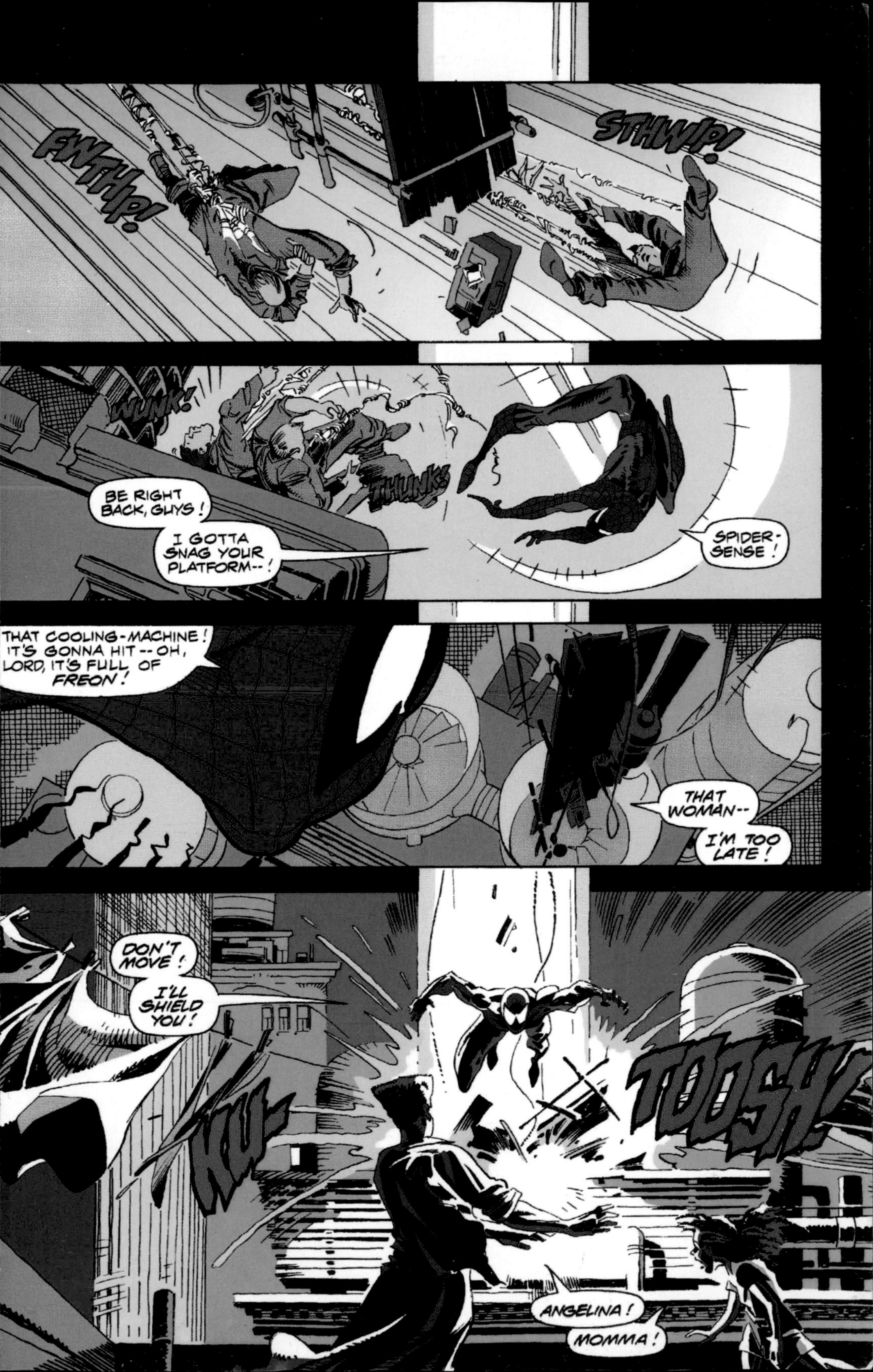
FWTHP!
STHWIP!
WUNK!
THUNK!
BE RIGHT BACK, GUYS!
I GOTTA SNAG YOUR PLATFORM--!
SPIDER-SENSE!
THAT COOLING-MACHINE! IT'S GONNA HIT -- OH, LORD, IT'S FULL OF FREON!
THAT WOMAN--
I'M TOO LATE!
DON'T MOVE!
I'LL SHIELD YOU!
KA-
TOOSH!
ANGELINA!
MOMMA!

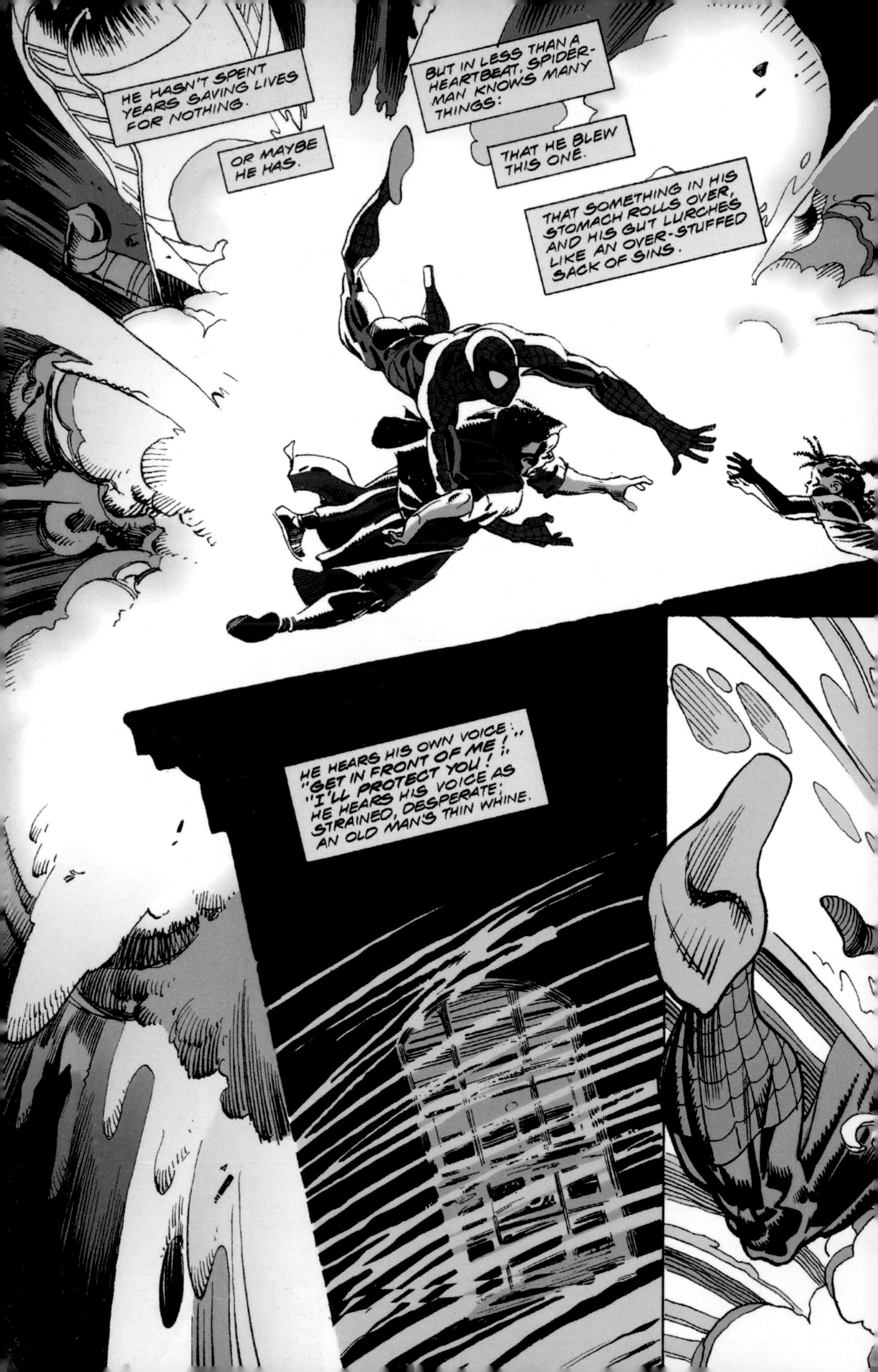
HE HASN'T SPENT YEARS SAVING LIVES FOR NOTHING.
OR MAYBE HE HAS.
BUT IN LESS THAN A HEARTBEAT, SPIDER-MAN KNOWS MANY THINGS:
THAT HE BLEW THIS ONE.
THAT SOMETHING IN HIS STOMACH ROLLS OVER, AND HIS GUT LURCHES LIKE AN OVER-STUFFED SACK OF SINS.
HE HEARS HIS OWN VOICE: "GET IN FRONT OF ME!" "I'LL PROTECT YOU!" HE HEARS HIS VOICE AS STRAINED, DESPERATE: AN OLD MAN'S THIN WHINE.

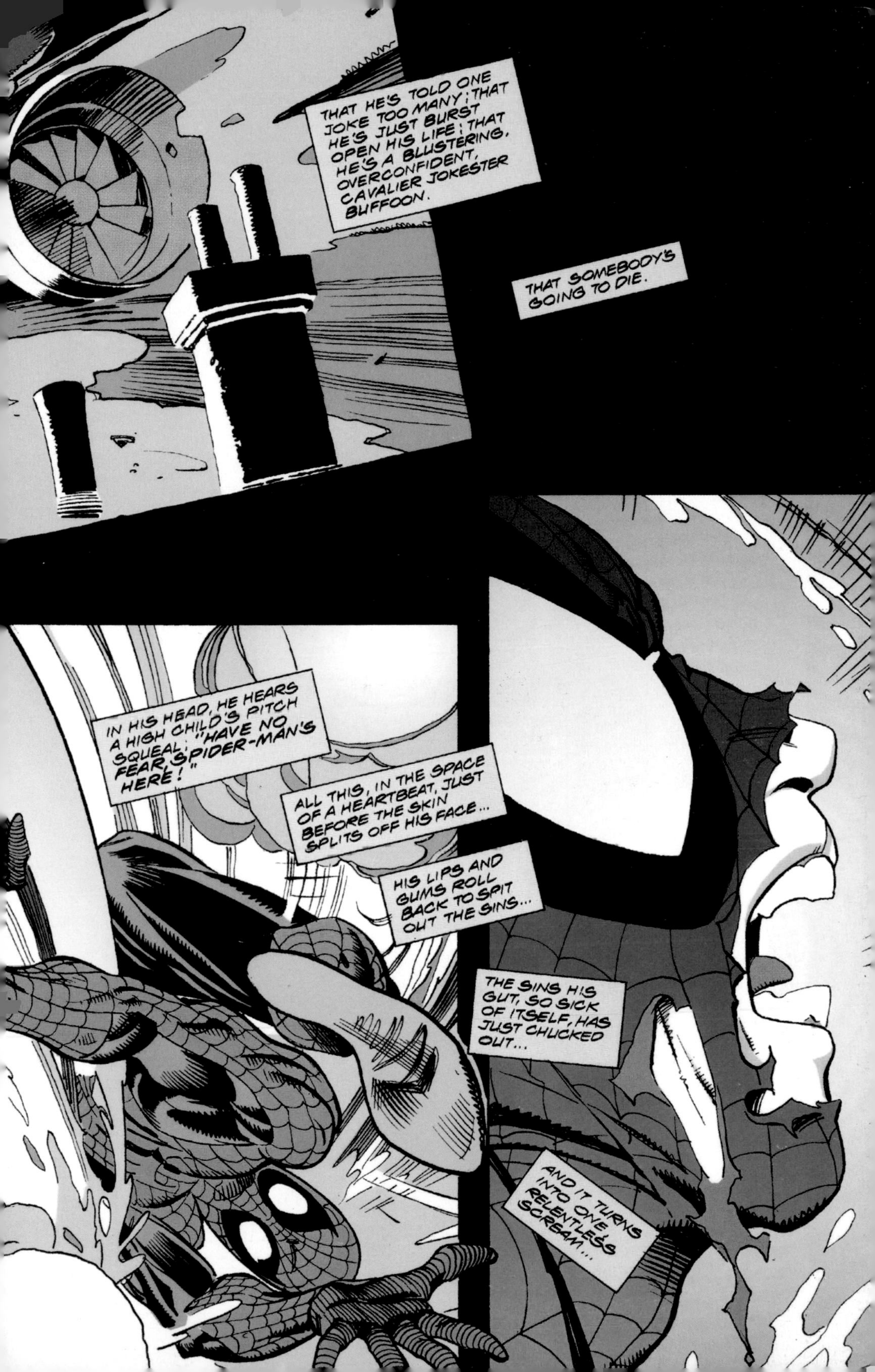
THAT HE'S TOLD ONE JOKE TOO MANY; THAT HE'S JUST BURST OPEN HIS LIFE; THAT HE'S A BLUSTERING, OVERCONFIDENT, CAVALIER JOKESTER BUFFOON.
THAT SOMEBODY'S GOING TO DIE.
IN HIS HEAD, HE HEARS A HIGH CHILD'S PITCH SQUEAL: "HAVE NO FEAR, SPIDER-MAN'S HERE!"
ALL THIS, IN THE SPACE OF A HEARTBEAT, JUST BEFORE THE SKIN SPLITS OFF HIS FACE...
HIS LIPS AND GUMS ROLL BACK TO SPIT OUT THE SINS...
THE SINS HIS GUT, SO SICK OF ITSELF, HAS JUST CHUCKED OUT...
AND IT TURNS INTO ONE RELENTLESS SCREAM...

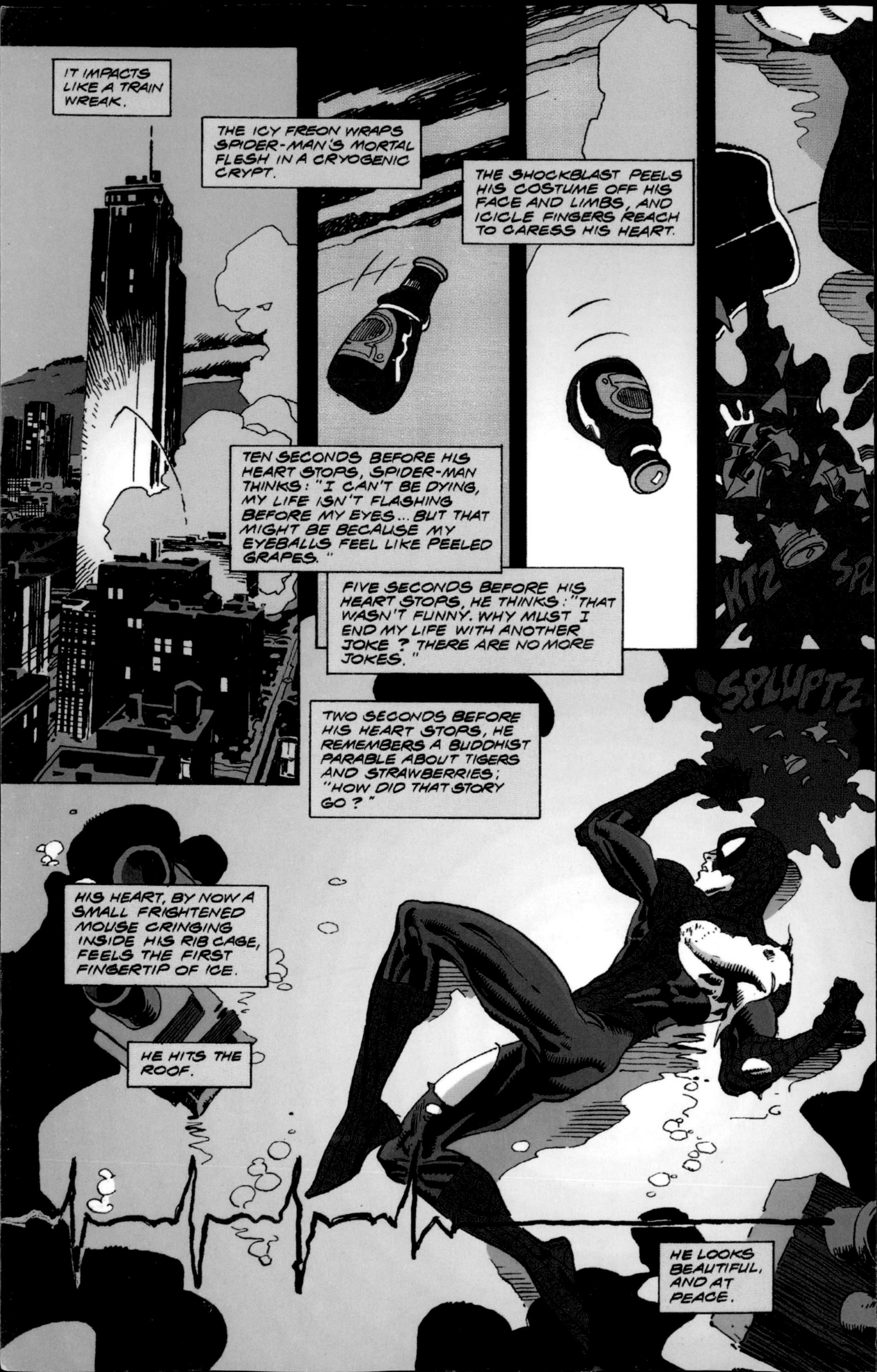
IT IMPACTS LIKE A TRAIN WREAK.
THE ICY FREON WRAPS SPIDER-MAN'S MORTAL FLESH IN A CRYOGENIC CRYPT.
THE SHOCKBLAST PEELS HIS COSTUME OFF HIS FACE AND LIMBS, AND ICICLE FINGERS REACH TO CARESS HIS HEART.
TEN SECONDS BEFORE HIS HEART STOPS, SPIDER-MAN THINKS: "I CAN'T BE DYING, MY LIFE ISN'T FLASHING BEFORE MY EYES... BUT THAT MIGHT BE BECAUSE MY EYEBALLS FEEL LIKE PEELED GRAPES."
FIVE SECONDS BEFORE HIS HEART STOPS, HE THINKS: "THAT WASN'T FUNNY. WHY MUST I END MY LIFE WITH ANOTHER JOKE? THERE ARE NO MORE JOKES."
SPLUPTZ
TWO SECONDS BEFORE HIS HEART STOPS, HE REMEMBERS A BUDDHIST PARABLE ABOUT TIGERS AND STRAWBERRIES; "HOW DID THAT STORY GO?"
HIS HEART, BY NOW A SMALL FRIGHTENED MOUSE CRINGING INSIDE HIS RIB CAGE, FEELS THE FIRST FINGERTIP OF ICE.
HE HITS THE ROOF.
HE LOOKS BEAUTIFUL, AND AT PEACE.

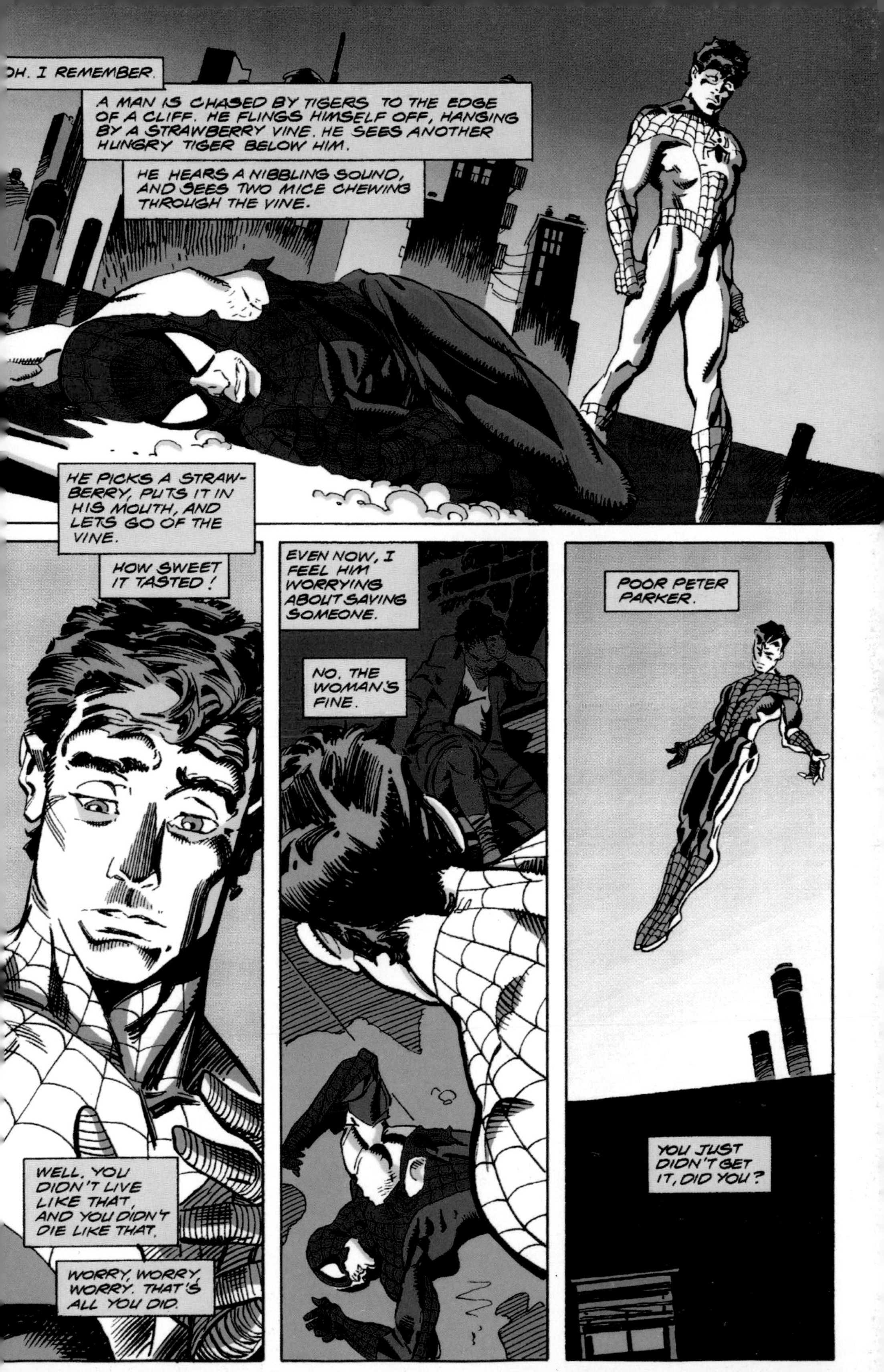
OH. I REMEMBER.
A MAN IS CHASED BY TIGERS TO THE EDGE OF A CLIFF. HE FLINGS HIMSELF OFF, HANGING BY A STRAWBERRY VINE. HE SEES ANOTHER HUNGRY TIGER BELOW HIM.
HE HEARS A NIBBLING SOUND, AND SEES TWO MICE CHEWING THROUGH THE VINE.
HE PICKS A STRAW-BERRY, PUTS IT IN HIS MOUTH, AND LETS GO OF THE VINE.
HOW SWEET IT TASTED!
WELL, YOU DIDN'T LIVE LIKE THAT, AND YOU DIDN'T DIE LIKE THAT.
WORRY, WORRY, WORRY. THAT'S ALL YOU DID.
EVEN NOW, I FEEL HIM WORRYING ABOUT SAVING SOMEONE.
NO, THE WOMAN'S FINE.
POOR PETER PARKER.
YOU JUST DIDN'T GET IT, DID YOU?

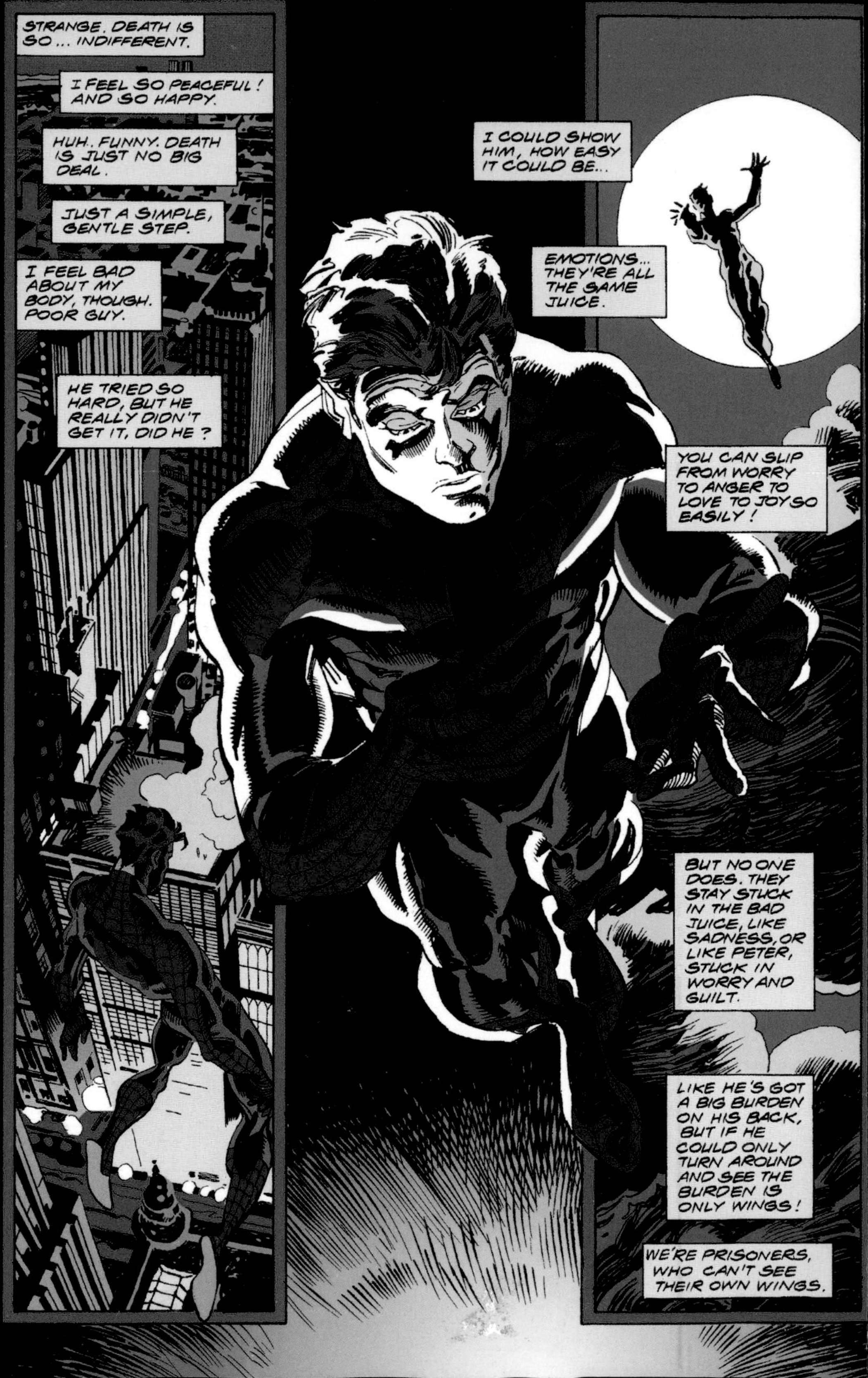
STRANGE. DEATH IS SO ... INDIFFERENT.
I FEEL SO PEACEFUL! AND SO HAPPY.
HUH.. FUNNY. DEATH IS JUST NO BIG DEAL.
JUST A SIMPLE, GENTLE STEP.
I FEEL BAD ABOUT MY BODY, THOUGH. POOR GUY.
HE TRIED SO HARD, BUT HE REALLY DIDN'T GET IT, DID HE?
I COULD SHOW HIM, HOW EASY IT COULD BE...
EMOTIONS... THEY'RE ALL THE SAME JUICE.
YOU CAN SLIP FROM WORRY TO ANGER TO LOVE TO JOY SO EASILY!
BUT NO ONE DOES. THEY STAY STUCK IN THE BAD JUICE, LIKE SADNESS, OR LIKE PETER, STUCK IN WORRY AND GUILT.
LIKE HE'S GOT A BIG BURDEN ON HIS BACK, BUT IF HE COULD ONLY TURN AROUND AND SEE THE BURDEN IS ONLY WINGS!
WE'RE PRISONERS, WHO CAN'T SEE THEIR OWN WINGS.

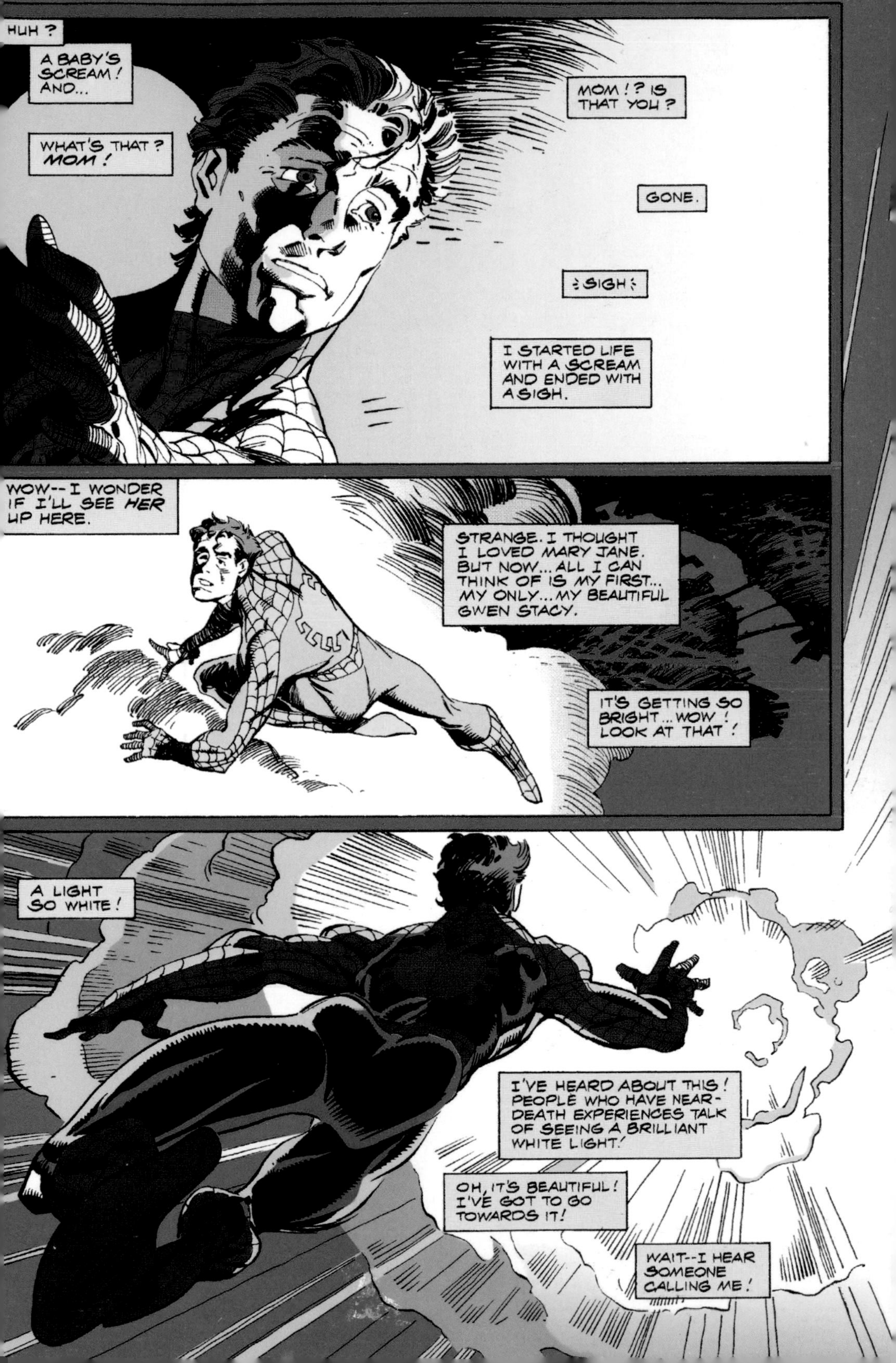
HUH ?
A BABY'S SCREAM ! AND...
WHAT'S THAT ? *MOM* !
MOM !? IS THAT YOU ?
GONE.
SIGH
I STARTED LIFE WITH A SCREAM AND ENDED WITH A SIGH.
WOW-- I WONDER IF I'LL SEE *HER* UP HERE.
STRANGE. I THOUGHT I LOVED MARY JANE. BUT NOW... ALL I CAN THINK OF IS MY FIRST... MY ONLY... MY BEAUTIFUL GWEN STACY.
IT'S GETTING SO BRIGHT... WOW ! LOOK AT THAT !
A LIGHT SO WHITE !
I'VE HEARD ABOUT THIS ! PEOPLE WHO HAVE NEAR-DEATH EXPERIENCES TALK OF SEEING A BRILLIANT WHITE LIGHT !
OH, IT'S BEAUTIFUL ! I'VE GOT TO GO TOWARDS IT !
WAIT--I HEAR SOMEONE CALLING ME !

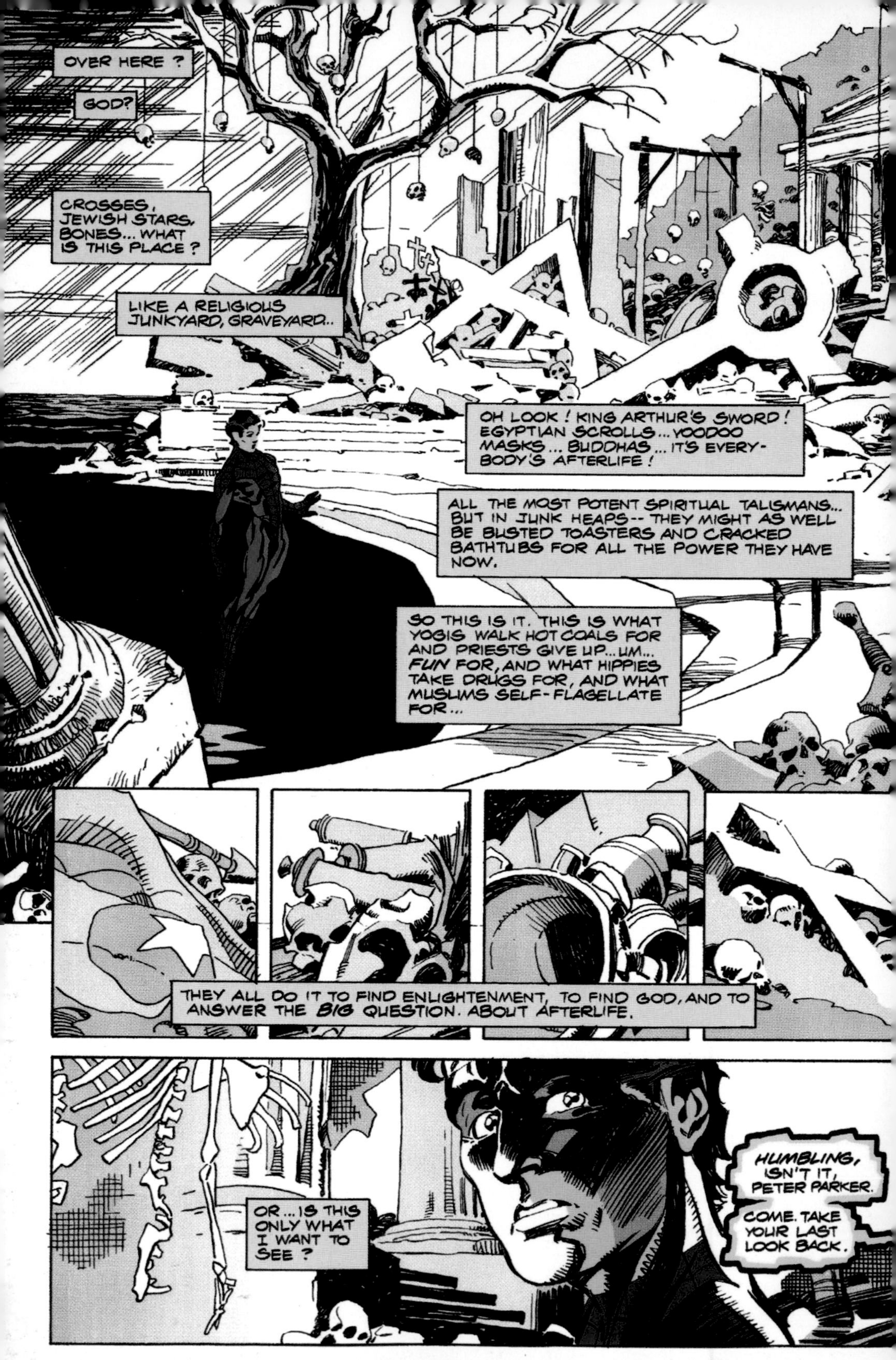
OVER HERE ?
GOD?
CROSSES, JEWISH STARS, BONES... WHAT IS THIS PLACE ?
LIKE A RELIGIOUS JUNKYARD, GRAVEYARD..
OH LOOK ! KING ARTHUR'S SWORD ! EGYPTIAN SCROLLS... VOODOO MASKS... BUDDHAS... IT'S EVERY-BODY'S AFTERLIFE !
ALL THE MOST POTENT SPIRITUAL TALISMANS... BUT IN JUNK HEAPS-- THEY MIGHT AS WELL BE BUSTED TOASTERS AND CRACKED BATHTUBS FOR ALL THE POWER THEY HAVE NOW.
SO THIS IS IT. THIS IS WHAT YOGIS WALK HOT COALS FOR AND PRIESTS GIVE UP...UM... FUN FOR, AND WHAT HIPPIES TAKE DRUGS FOR, AND WHAT MUSLIMS SELF-FLAGELLATE FOR...
THEY ALL DO IT TO FIND ENLIGHTENMENT, TO FIND GOD, AND TO ANSWER THE BIG QUESTION. ABOUT AFTERLIFE.
OR... IS THIS ONLY WHAT I WANT TO SEE ?
HUMBLING, ISN'T IT, PETER PARKER.
COME. TAKE YOUR LAST LOOK BACK.

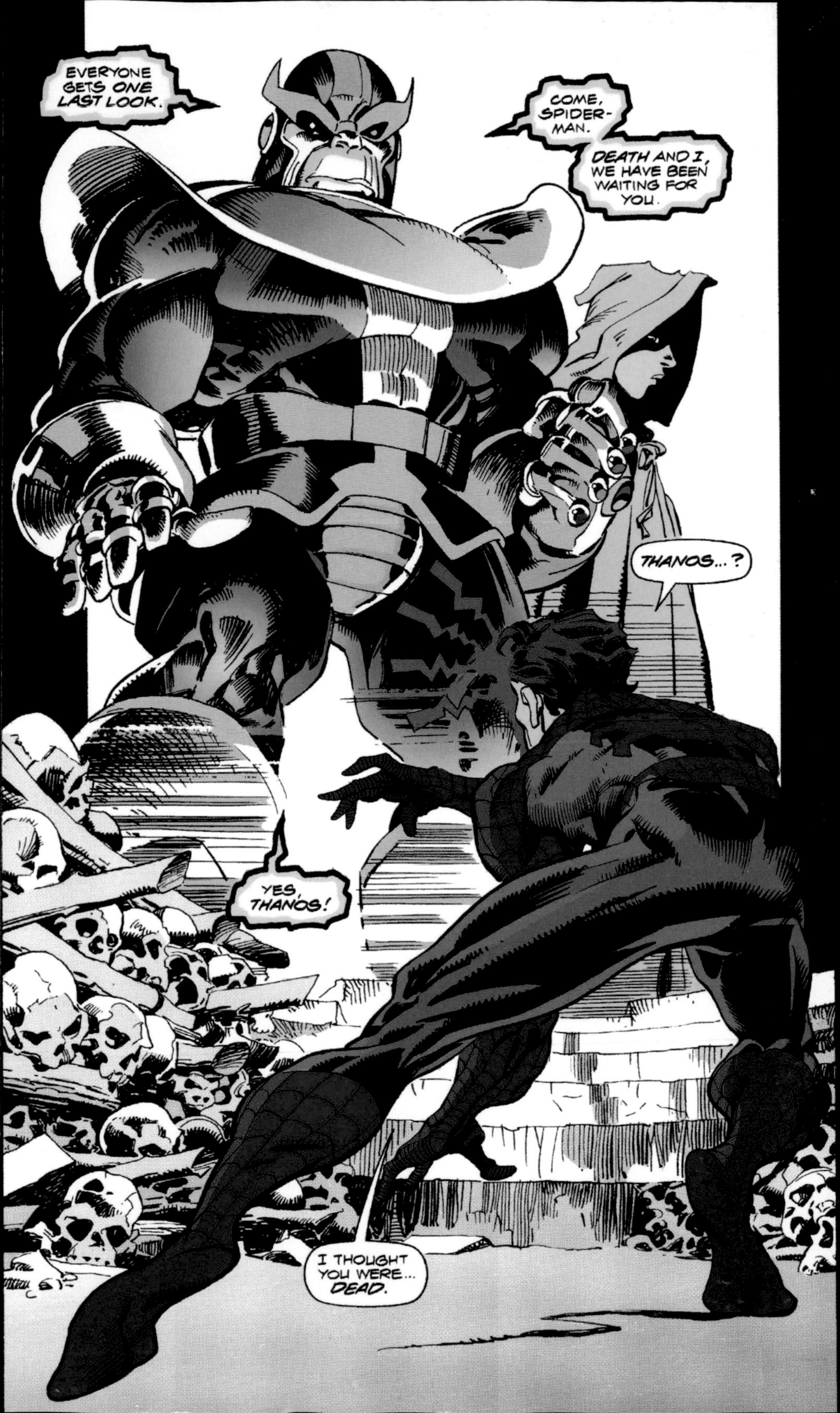
EVERYONE GETS ONE LAST LOOK.
COME, SPIDER-MAN.
DEATH AND I, WE HAVE BEEN WAITING FOR YOU.
THANOS...?
YES, THANOS!
I THOUGHT YOU WERE... DEAD.

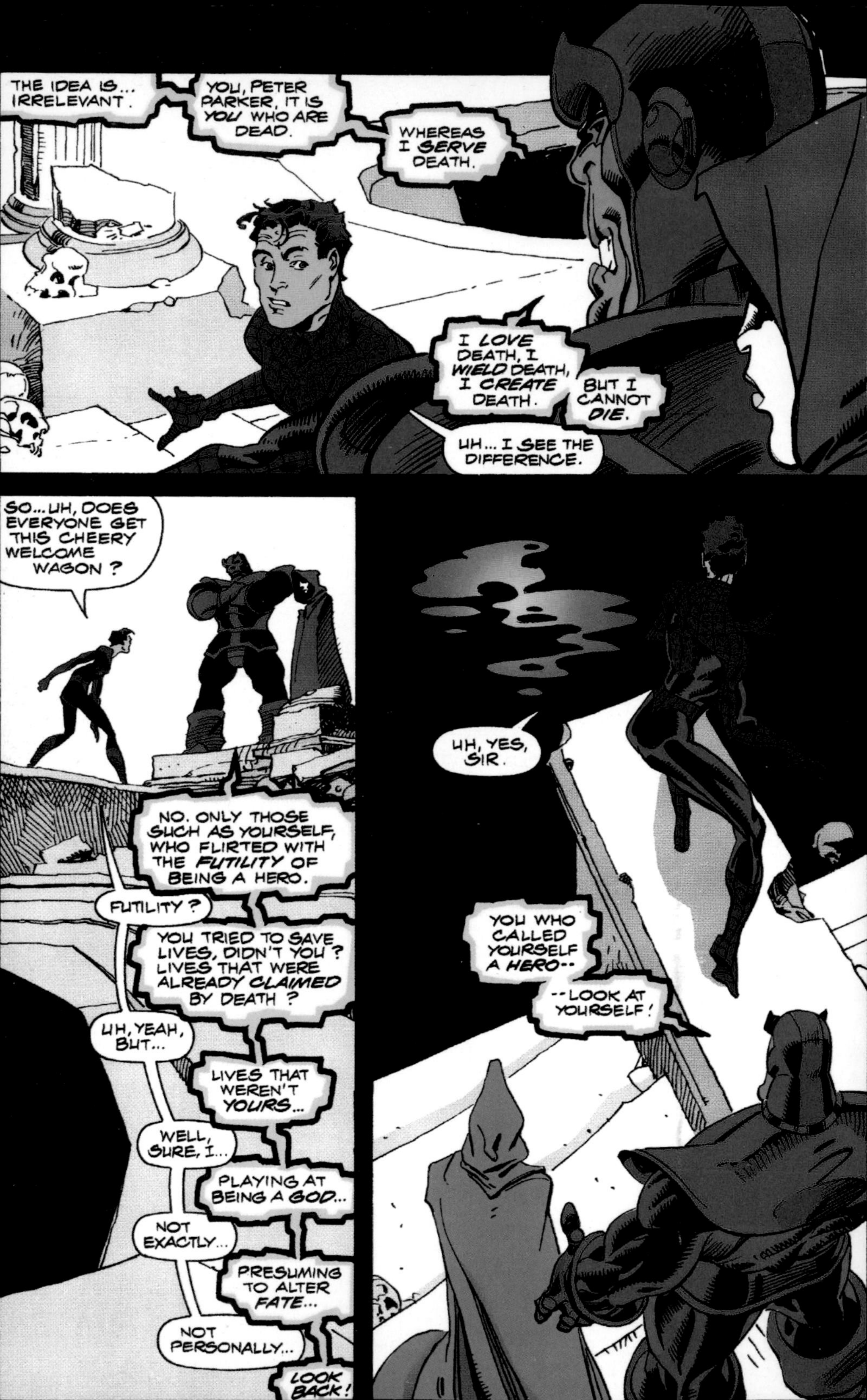
THE IDEA IS... IRRELEVANT.
YOU, PETER PARKER, IT IS YOU WHO ARE DEAD.
WHEREAS I SERVE DEATH.
I LOVE DEATH, I WIELD DEATH, I CREATE DEATH.
BUT I CANNOT DIE.
UH... I SEE THE DIFFERENCE.
SO...UH, DOES EVERYONE GET THIS CHEERY WELCOME WAGON?
NO. ONLY THOSE SUCH AS YOURSELF, WHO FLIRTED WITH THE FUTILITY OF BEING A HERO.
FUTILITY?
YOU TRIED TO SAVE LIVES, DIDN'T YOU? LIVES THAT WERE ALREADY CLAIMED BY DEATH?
UH, YEAH, BUT...
LIVES THAT WEREN'T YOURS...
WELL, SURE, I...
PLAYING AT BEING A GOD...
NOT EXACTLY...
PRESUMING TO ALTER FATE...
NOT PERSONALLY...
LOOK BACK!
UH, YES, SIR.
YOU WHO CALLED YOURSELF A HERO--
--LOOK AT YOURSELF!

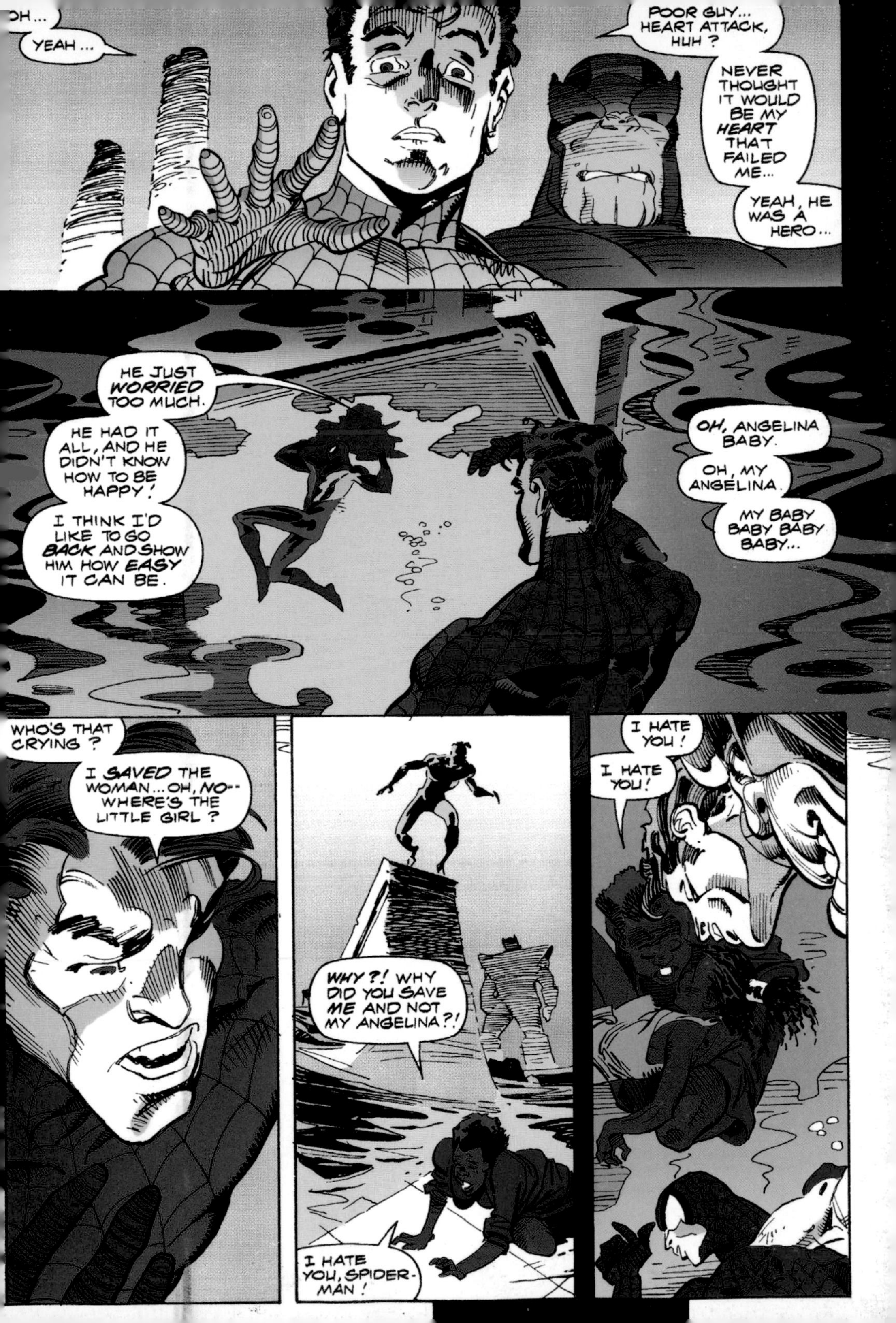
OH...
YEAH...
POOR GUY... HEART ATTACK, HUH?
NEVER THOUGHT IT WOULD BE MY HEART THAT FAILED ME...
YEAH, HE WAS A HERO...
HE JUST WORRIED TOO MUCH.
HE HAD IT ALL, AND HE DIDN'T KNOW HOW TO BE HAPPY!
I THINK I'D LIKE TO GO BACK AND SHOW HIM HOW EASY IT CAN BE.
OH, ANGELINA BABY.
OH, MY ANGELINA.
MY BABY BABY BABY BABY BABY...
WHO'S THAT CRYING?
I SAVED THE WOMAN... OH, NO-- WHERE'S THE LITTLE GIRL?
WHY?! WHY DID YOU SAVE ME AND NOT MY ANGELINA?!
I HATE YOU, SPIDER-MAN!
I HATE YOU!
I HATE YOU!

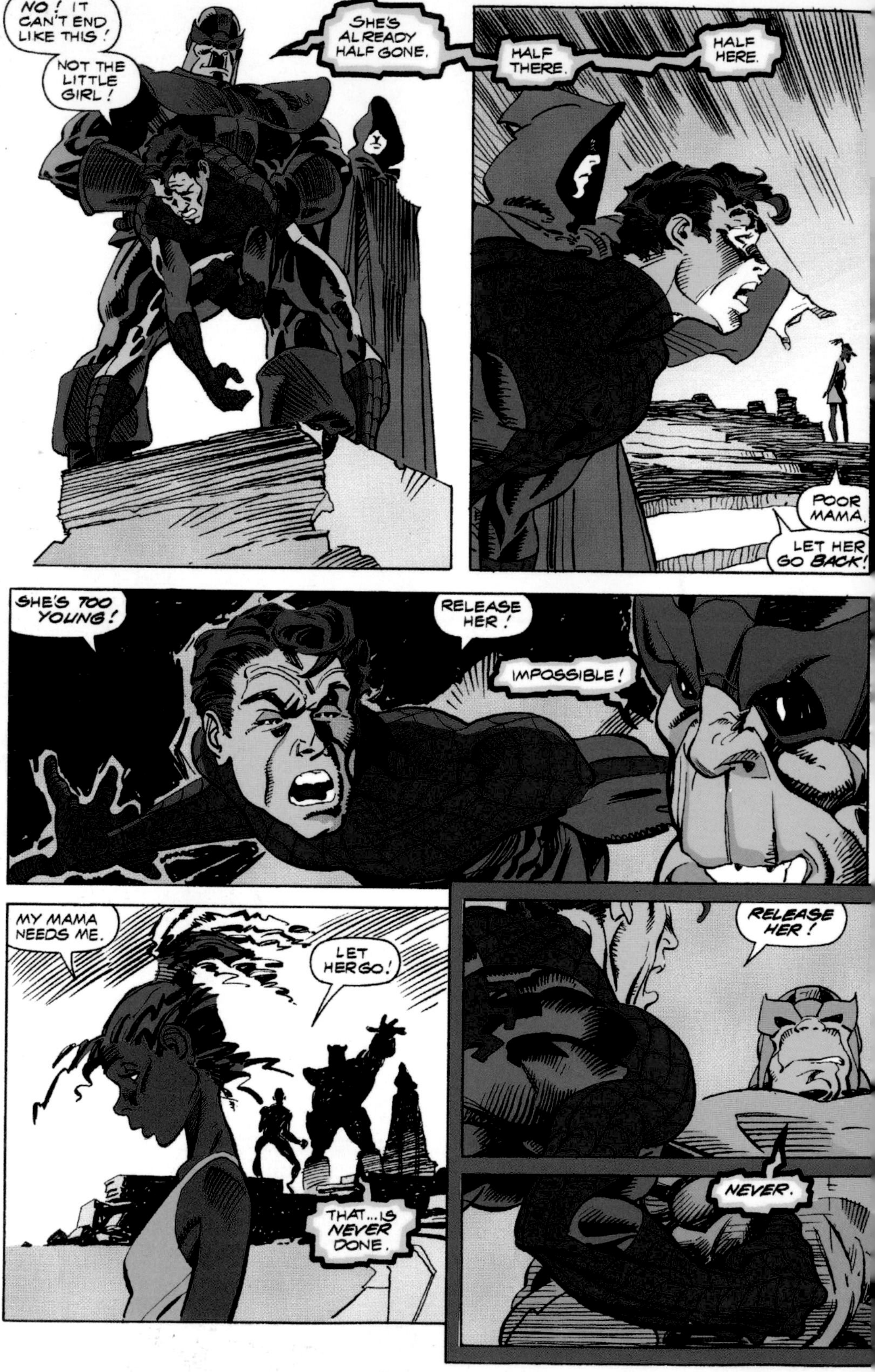

NO! IT CAN'T END LIKE THIS!
NOT THE LITTLE GIRL!
SHE'S ALREADY HALF GONE.
HALF THERE.
HALF HERE.
POOR MAMA.
LET HER GO BACK!
SHE'S TOO YOUNG!
RELEASE HER!
IMPOSSIBLE!
MY MAMA NEEDS ME.
LET HER GO!
THAT... IS NEVER DONE.
RELEASE HER!
NEVER.

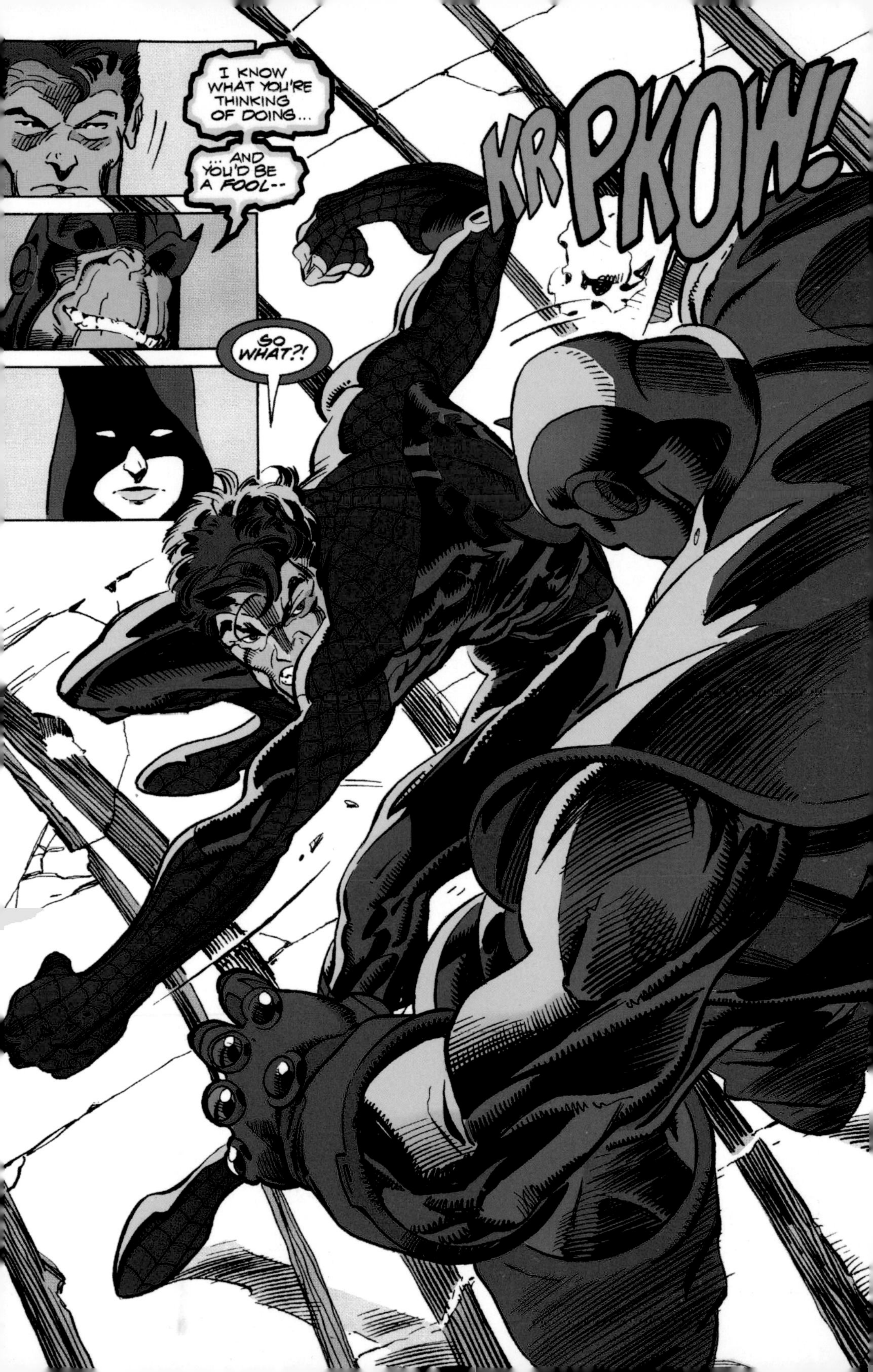
I KNOW WHAT YOU'RE THINKING OF DOING...
... AND YOU'D BE A *FOOL*--
SO WHAT?!
KRPKOW!

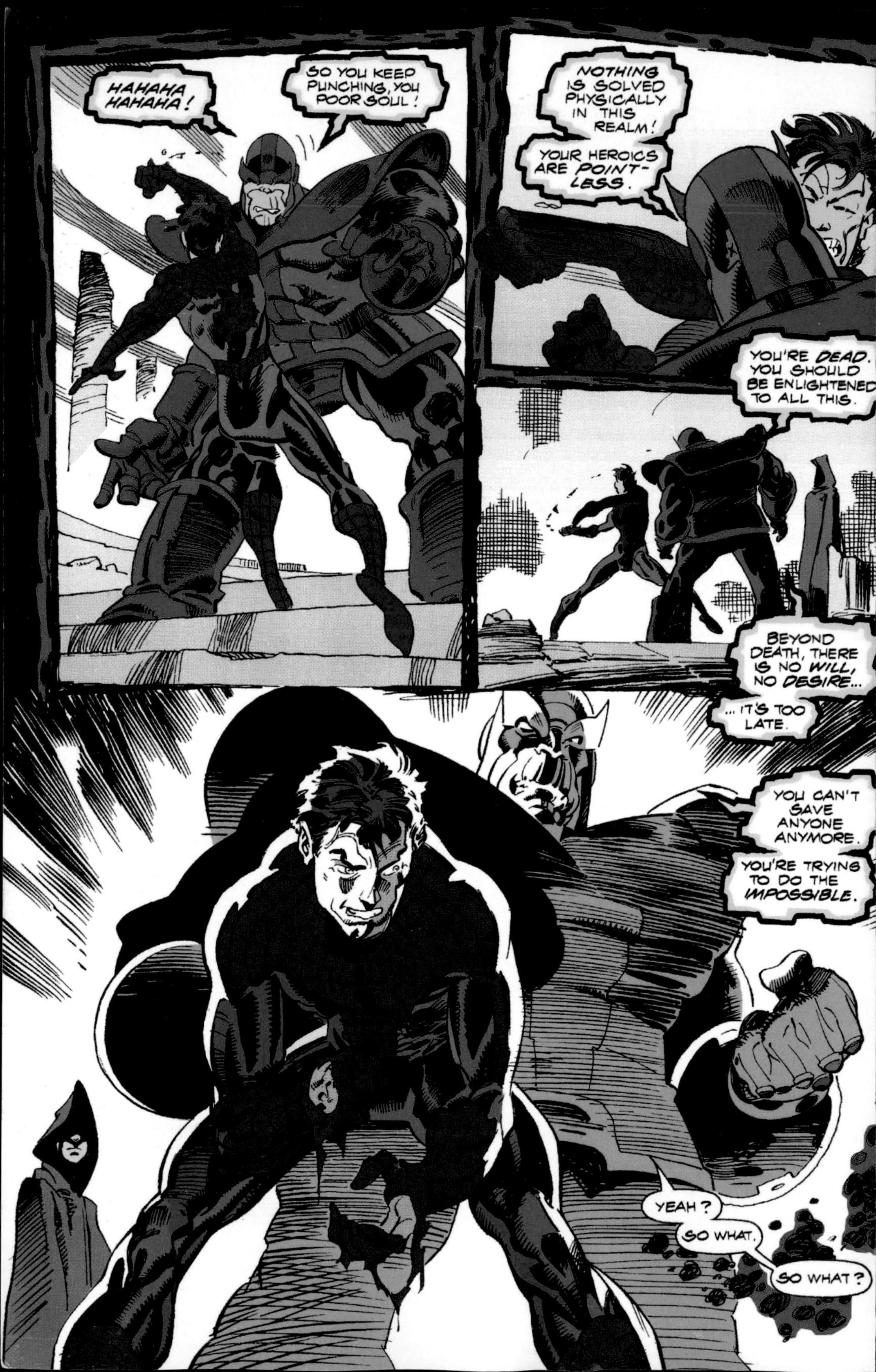
HAHAHA HAHAHA!
SO YOU KEEP PUNCHING, YOU POOR SOUL!
NOTHING IS SOLVED PHYSICALLY IN THIS REALM!
YOUR HEROICS ARE POINTLESS.
YOU'RE DEAD. YOU SHOULD BE ENLIGHTENED TO ALL THIS.
BEYOND DEATH, THERE IS NO WILL, NO DESIRE...
...IT'S TOO LATE.
YOU CAN'T SAVE ANYONE ANYMORE.
YOU'RE TRYING TO DO THE IMPOSSIBLE.
YEAH?
SO WHAT.
SO WHAT?

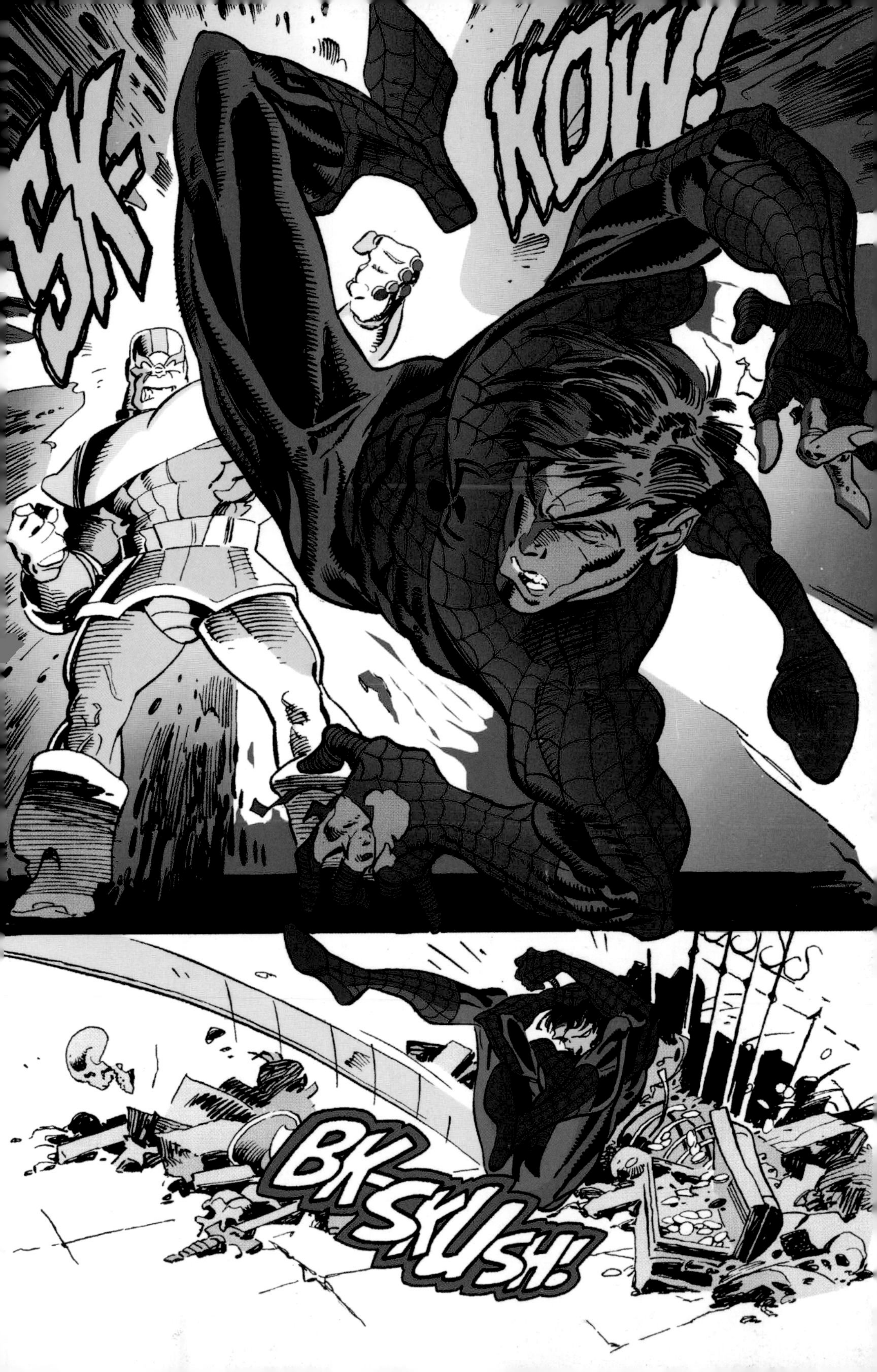
SKKOW!
BKSSHH!

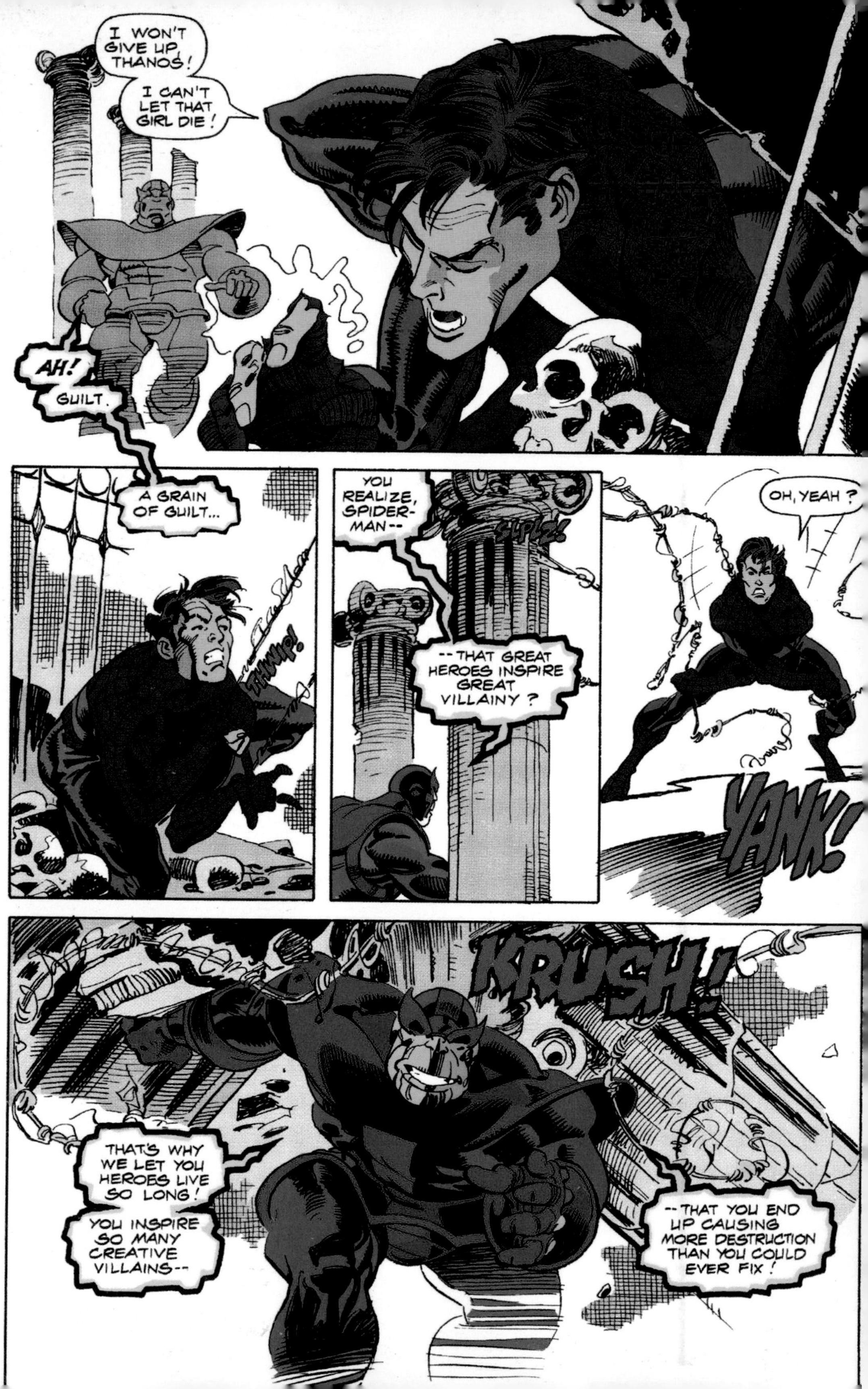
I WON'T GIVE UP THANOS!
I CAN'T LET THAT GIRL DIE!
AH!
GUILT.
A GRAIN OF GUILT...
THWIP!
YOU REALIZE, SPIDER-MAN--
--THAT GREAT HEROES INSPIRE GREAT VILLAINY?
OH, YEAH?
YANK!
KRUSH!
THAT'S WHY WE LET YOU HEROES LIVE SO LONG!
YOU INSPIRE SO MANY CREATIVE VILLAINS--
--THAT YOU END UP CAUSING MORE DESTRUCTION THAN YOU COULD EVER FIX!

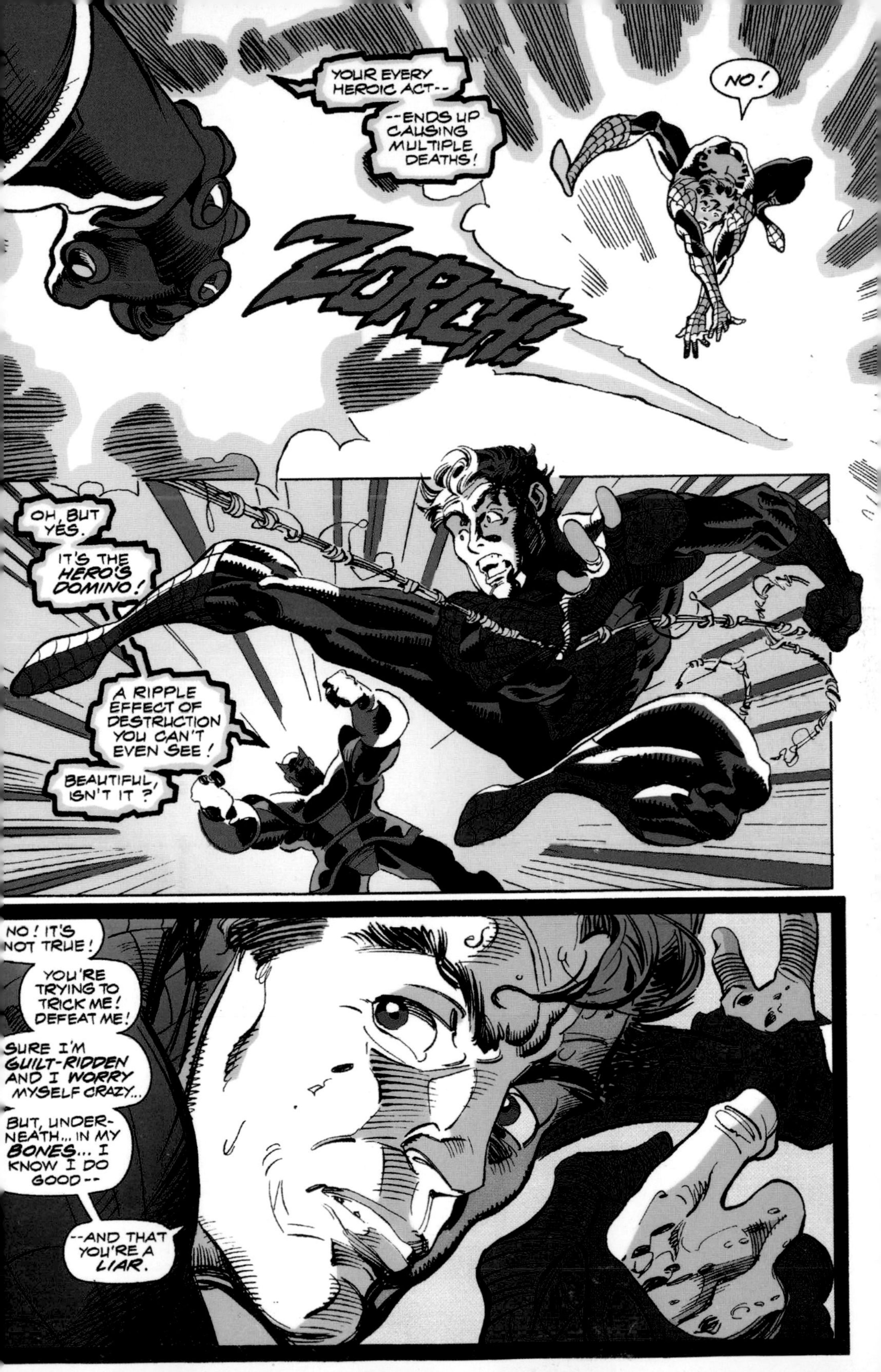

YOUR EVERY HEROIC ACT--
--ENDS UP CAUSING MULTIPLE DEATHS!
NO!
ZORCH!
OH, BUT YES.
IT'S THE HERO'S DOMINO!
A RIPPLE EFFECT OF DESTRUCTION YOU CAN'T EVEN SEE!
BEAUTIFUL, ISN'T IT?
NO! IT'S NOT TRUE!
YOU'RE TRYING TO TRICK ME! DEFEAT ME!
SURE I'M GUILT-RIDDEN AND I WORRY MYSELF CRAZY...
BUT, UNDER-NEATH... IN MY BONES... I KNOW I DO GOOD--
--AND THAT YOU'RE A LIAR.

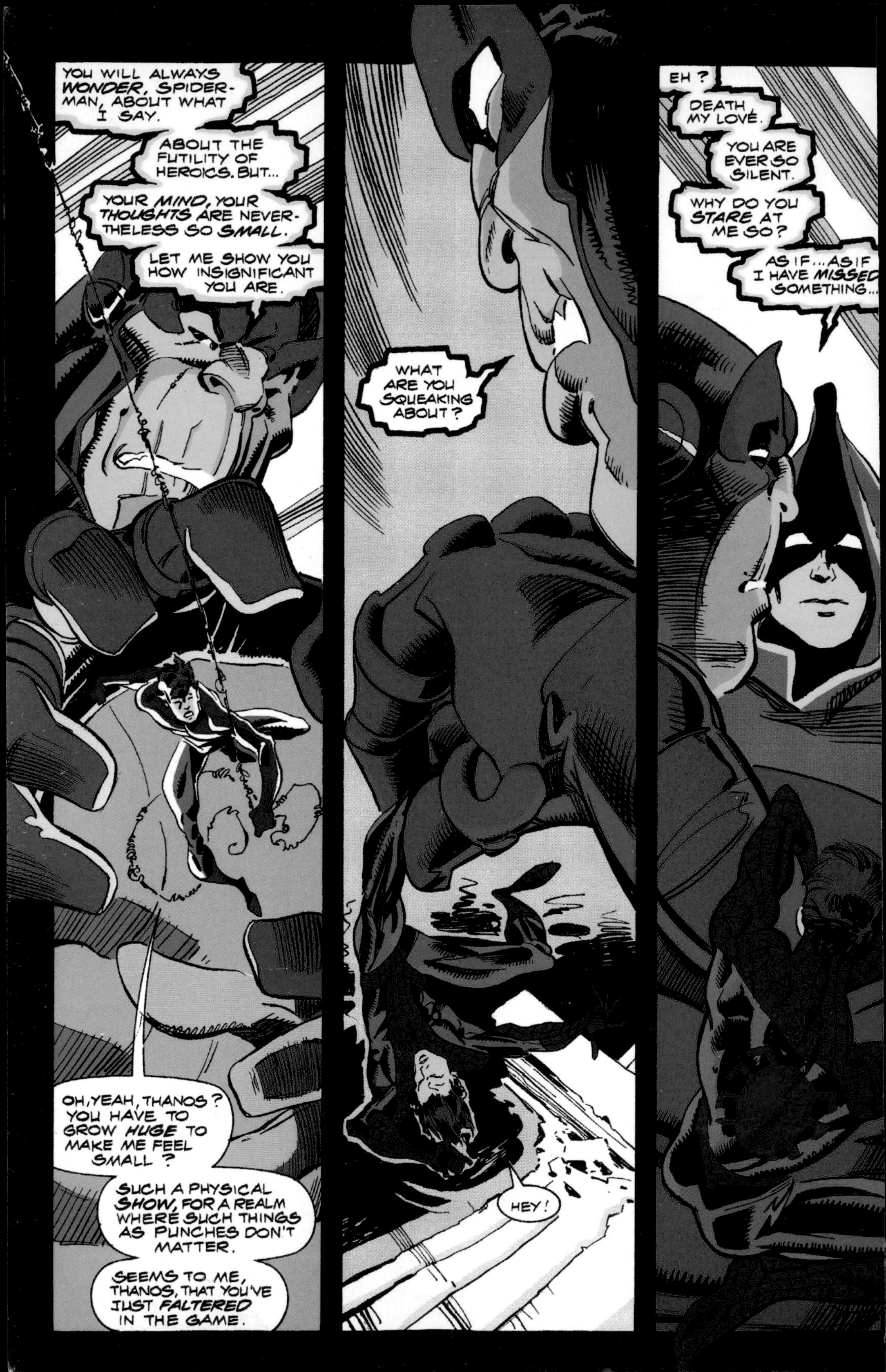
YOU WILL ALWAYS WONDER, SPIDER-MAN, ABOUT WHAT I SAY.
ABOUT THE FUTILITY OF HEROICS. BUT...
YOUR MIND, YOUR THOUGHTS ARE NEVER-THELESS SO SMALL.
LET ME SHOW YOU HOW INSIGNIFICANT YOU ARE.
OH, YEAH, THANOS? YOU HAVE TO GROW HUGE TO MAKE ME FEEL SMALL?
SUCH A PHYSICAL SHOW, FOR A REALM WHERE SUCH THINGS AS PUNCHES DON'T MATTER.
SEEMS TO ME, THANOS, THAT YOU'VE JUST FALTERED IN THE GAME.
WHAT ARE YOU SQUEAKING ABOUT?
HEY!
EH?
DEATH, MY LOVE.
YOU ARE EVER SO SILENT.
WHY DO YOU STARE AT ME SO?
AS IF... AS IF I HAVE MISSED SOMETHING...

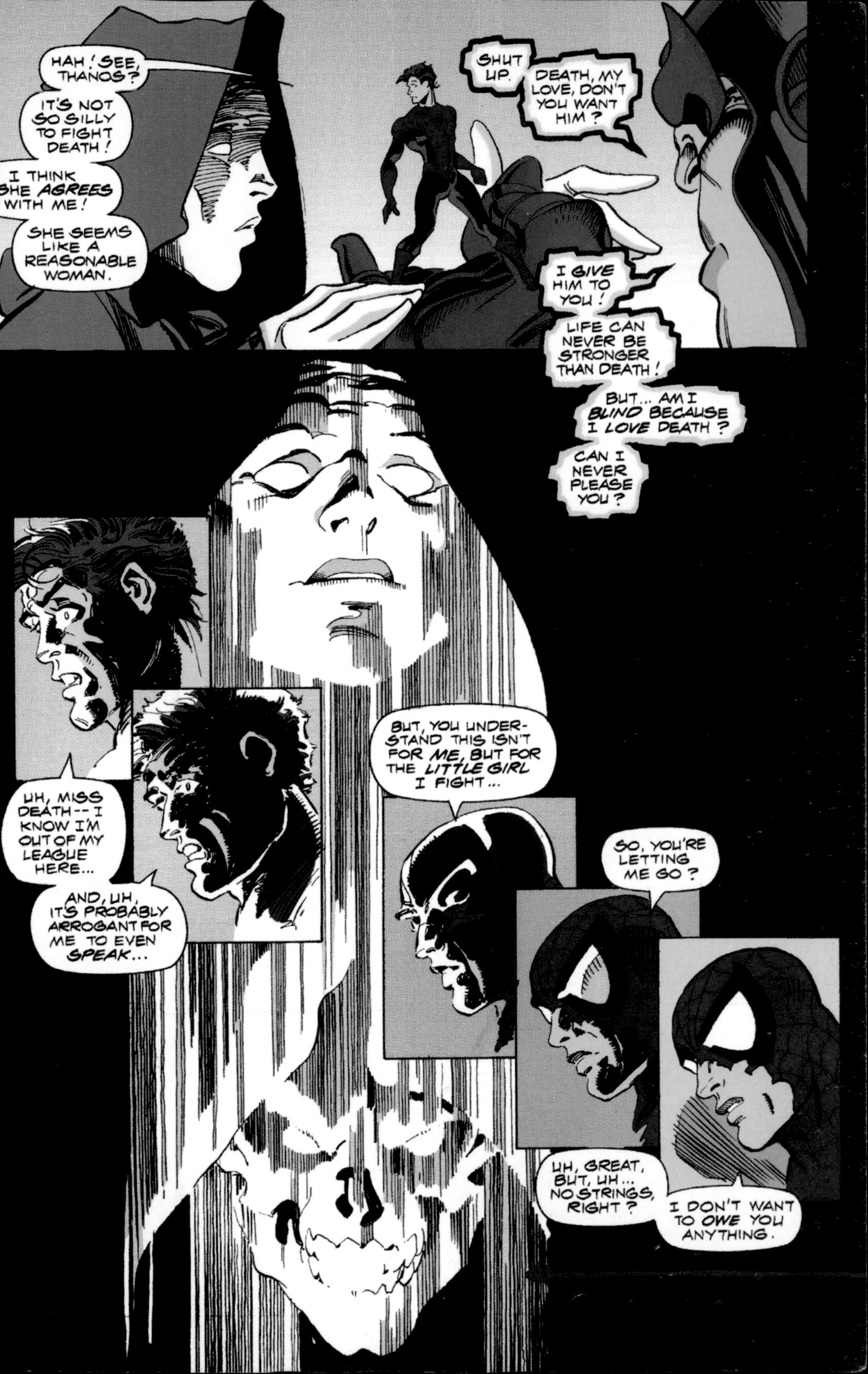
HAH! SEE, THANOS?
IT'S NOT SO SILLY TO FIGHT DEATH!
I THINK SHE AGREES WITH ME!
SHE SEEMS LIKE A REASONABLE WOMAN.
SHUT UP.
DEATH, MY LOVE, DON'T YOU WANT HIM?
I GIVE HIM TO YOU!
LIFE CAN NEVER BE STRONGER THAN DEATH!
BUT... AM I BLIND BECAUSE I LOVE DEATH?
CAN I NEVER PLEASE YOU?
UH, MISS DEATH-- I KNOW I'M OUT OF MY LEAGUE HERE...
AND, UH, IT'S PROBABLY ARROGANT FOR ME TO EVEN SPEAK...
BUT, YOU UNDERSTAND THIS ISN'T FOR ME, BUT FOR THE LITTLE GIRL I FIGHT...
SO, YOU'RE LETTING ME GO?
UH, GREAT, BUT, UH... NO STRINGS, RIGHT?
I DON'T WANT TO OWE YOU ANYTHING.

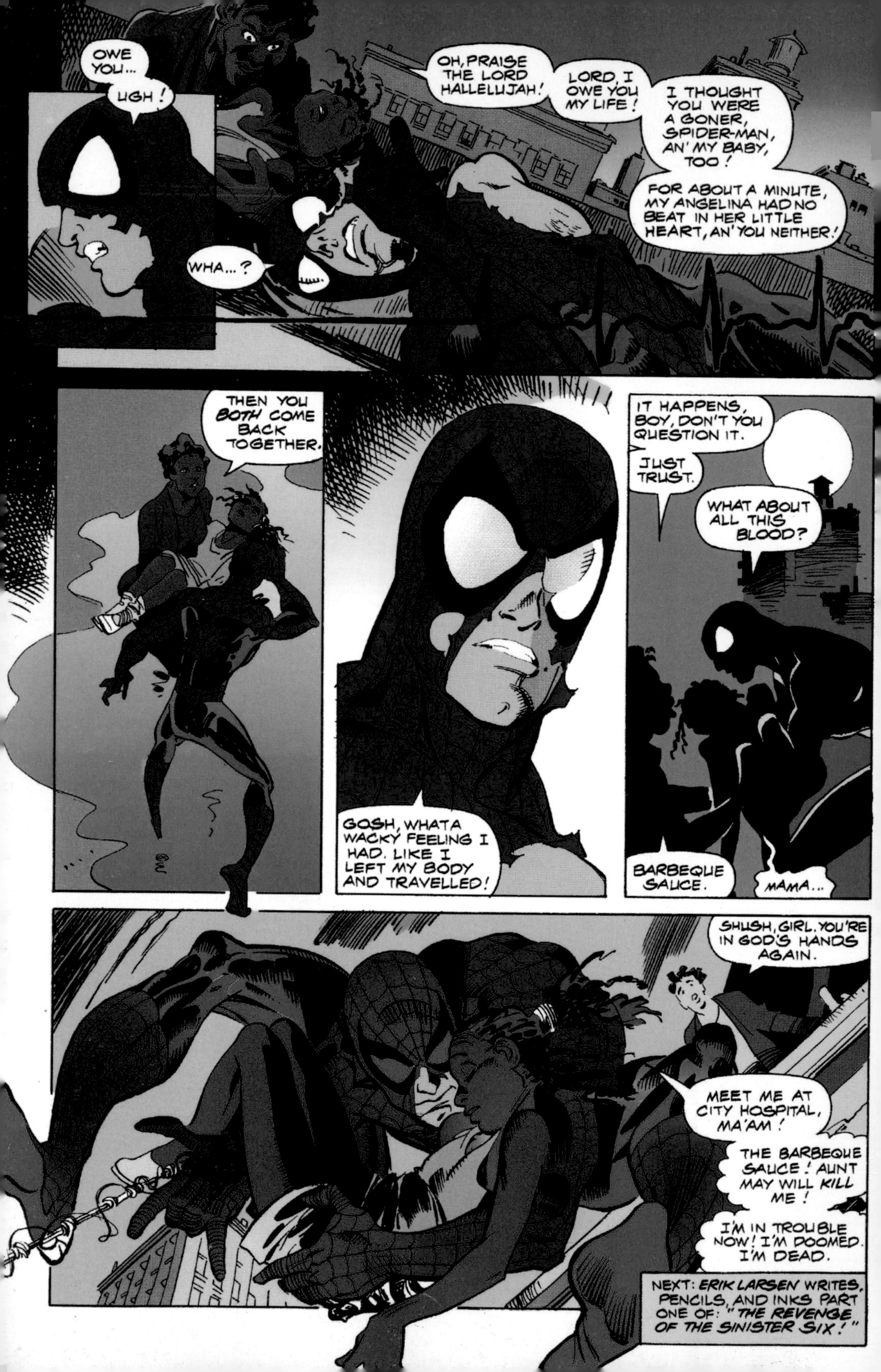
OWE YOU... UGH!
WHA...?
OH, PRAISE THE LORD HALLELUJAH!
LORD, I OWE YOU MY LIFE!
I THOUGHT YOU WERE A GONER, SPIDER-MAN, AN' MY BABY, TOO!
FOR ABOUT A MINUTE, MY ANGELINA HAD NO BEAT IN HER LITTLE HEART, AN' YOU NEITHER!
THEN YOU BOTH COME BACK TOGETHER.
GOSH, WHATA WACKY FEELING I HAD. LIKE I LEFT MY BODY AND TRAVELLED!
IT HAPPENS, BOY, DON'T YOU QUESTION IT.
JUST TRUST.
WHAT ABOUT ALL THIS BLOOD?
BARBEQUE SAUCE.
MAMA...
SHUSH, GIRL. YOU'RE IN GOD'S HANDS AGAIN.
MEET ME AT CITY HOSPITAL, MA'AM!
THE BARBEQUE SAUCE! AUNT MAY WILL KILL ME!
I'M IN TROUBLE NOW! I'M DOOMED. I'M DEAD.
NEXT: ERIK LARSEN WRITES, PENCILS, AND INKS PART ONE OF: "THE REVENGE OF THE SINISTER SIX!"

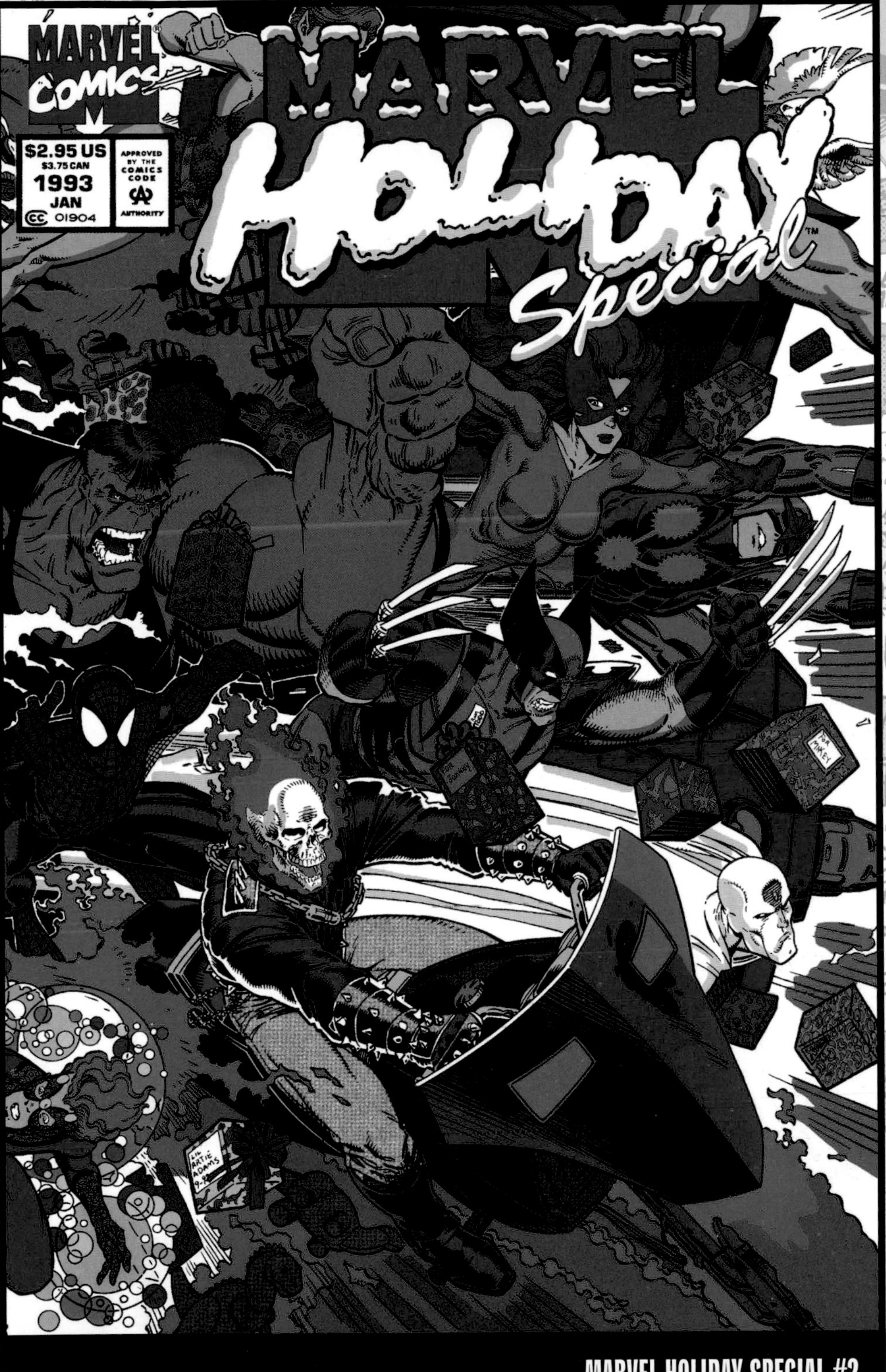
MARVEL COMICS
$2.95 US
$3.75 CAN
1993
JAN
01904
APPROVED BY THE COMICS CODE AUTHORITY
MARVEL
HOLIDAY
Special

MARVEL HOLIDAY SPECIAL #2

SEE A DIFFERENT SIDE OF THANOS AS HE CELEBRATES THE HOLIDAYS WITH HIS "DAUGHTER" GAMORA.

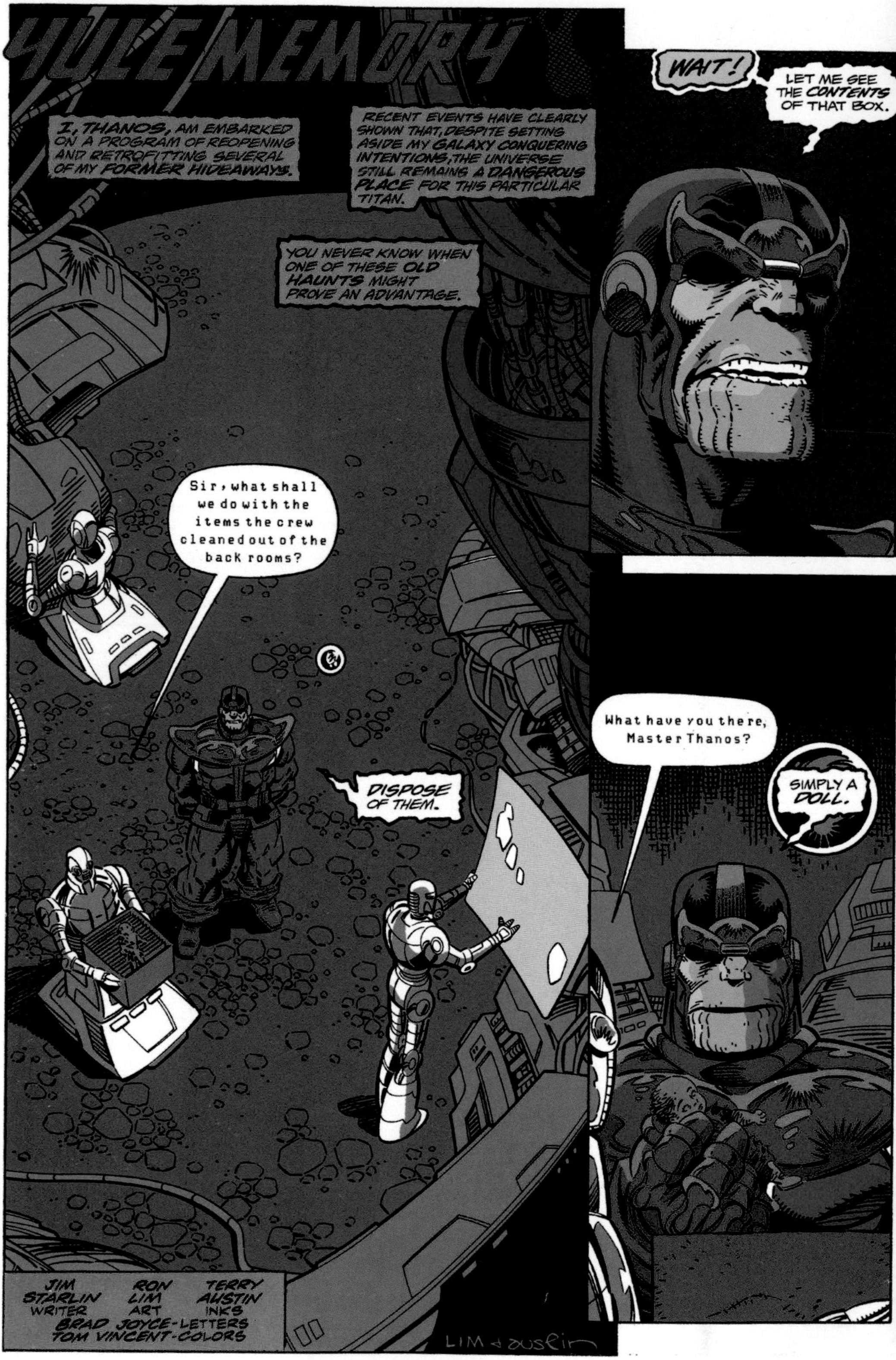
YULE MEMORY
I, THANOS, AM EMBARKED ON A PROGRAM OF REOPENING AND RETROFITTING SEVERAL OF MY FORMER HIDEAWAYS.
RECENT EVENTS HAVE CLEARLY SHOWN THAT, DESPITE SETTING ASIDE MY GALAXY CONQUERING INTENTIONS, THE UNIVERSE STILL REMAINS A DANGEROUS PLACE FOR THIS PARTICULAR TITAN.
YOU NEVER KNOW WHEN ONE OF THESE OLD HAUNTS MIGHT PROVE AN ADVANTAGE.
Sir, what shall we do with the items the crew cleaned out of the back rooms?
DISPOSE OF THEM.
JIM STARLIN WRITER
RON LIM ART
TERRY AUSTIN INKS
BRAD JOYCE-LETTERS
TOM VINCENT-COLORS
LIM & austin
WAIT!
LET ME SEE THE CONTENTS OF THAT BOX.
What have you there, Master Thanos?
SIMPLY A DOLL.

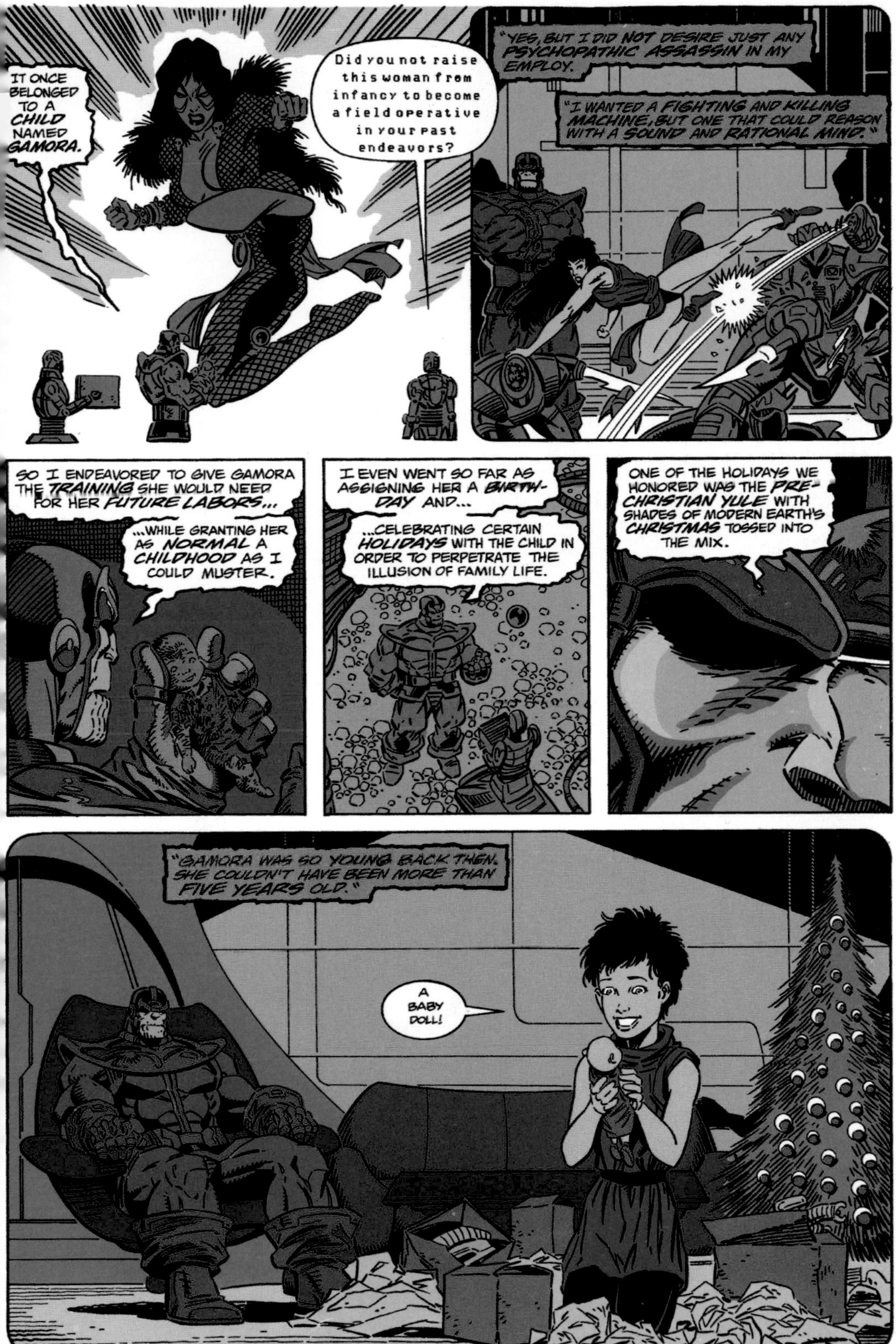

IT ONCE BELONGED TO A CHILD NAMED GAMORA.
Did you not raise this woman from infancy to become a field operative in your past endeavors?
"YES, BUT I DID NOT DESIRE JUST ANY PSYCHOPATHIC ASSASSIN IN MY EMPLOY.
"I WANTED A FIGHTING AND KILLING MACHINE, BUT ONE THAT COULD REASON WITH A SOUND AND RATIONAL MIND."
SO I ENDEAVORED TO GIVE GAMORA THE TRAINING SHE WOULD NEED FOR HER FUTURE LABORS...
...WHILE GRANTING HER AS NORMAL A CHILDHOOD AS I COULD MUSTER.
I EVEN WENT SO FAR AS ASSIGNING HER A BIRTH-DAY AND...
...CELEBRATING CERTAIN HOLIDAYS WITH THE CHILD IN ORDER TO PERPETRATE THE ILLUSION OF FAMILY LIFE.
ONE OF THE HOLIDAYS WE HONORED WAS THE PRE-CHRISTIAN YULE WITH SHADES OF MODERN EARTH'S CHRISTMAS TOSSED INTO THE MIX.
"GAMORA WAS SO YOUNG BACK THEN. SHE COULDN'T HAVE BEEN MORE THAN FIVE YEARS OLD."
A BABY DOLL!

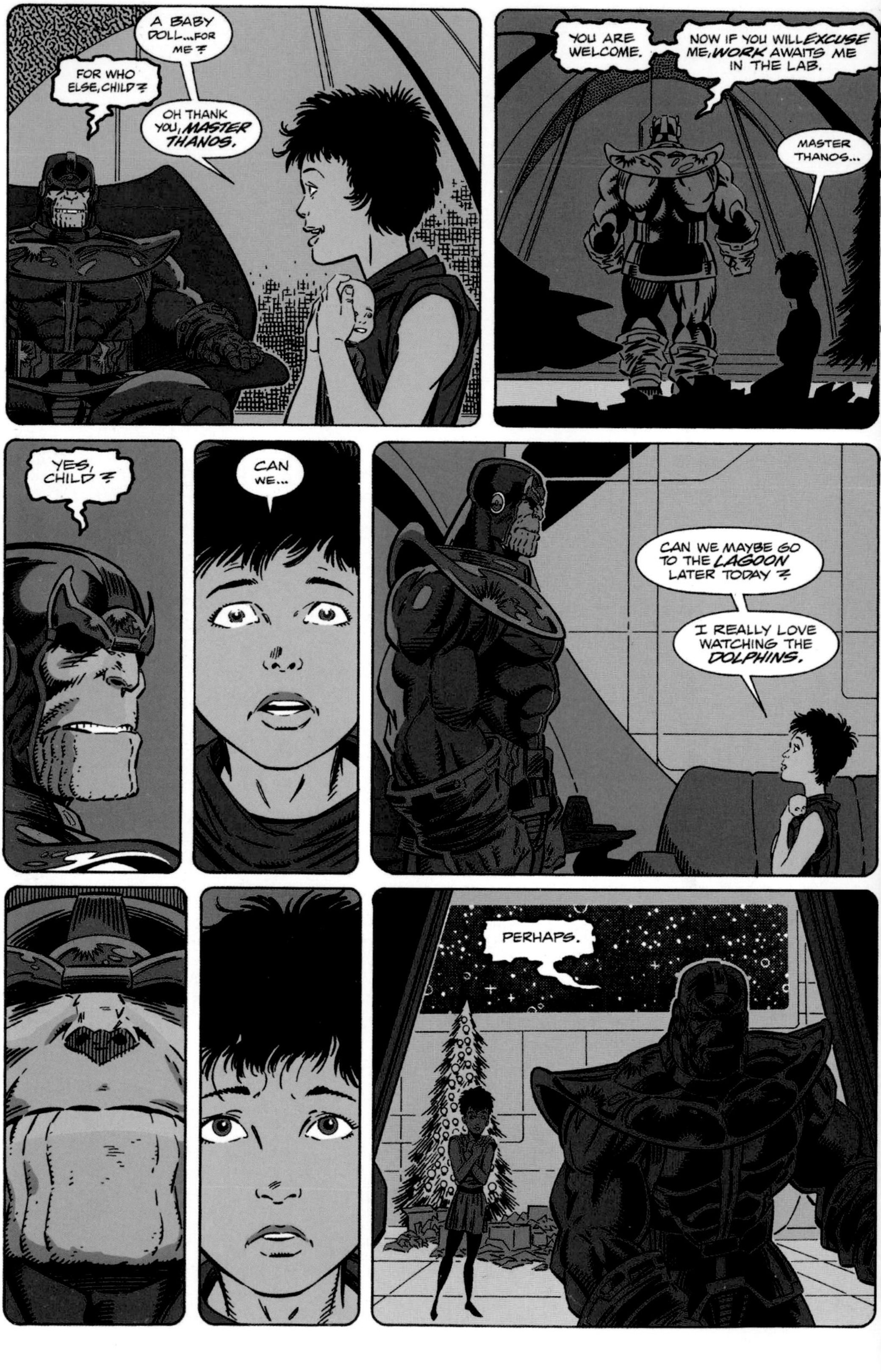
A BABY DOLL...FOR ME?
FOR WHO ELSE, CHILD?
OH THANK YOU, MASTER THANOS.
YOU ARE WELCOME.
NOW IF YOU WILL EXCUSE ME, WORK AWAITS ME IN THE LAB.
MASTER THANOS...
YES, CHILD?
CAN WE...
CAN WE MAYBE GO TO THE LAGOON LATER TODAY?
I REALLY LOVE WATCHING THE DOLPHINS.
PERHAPS.

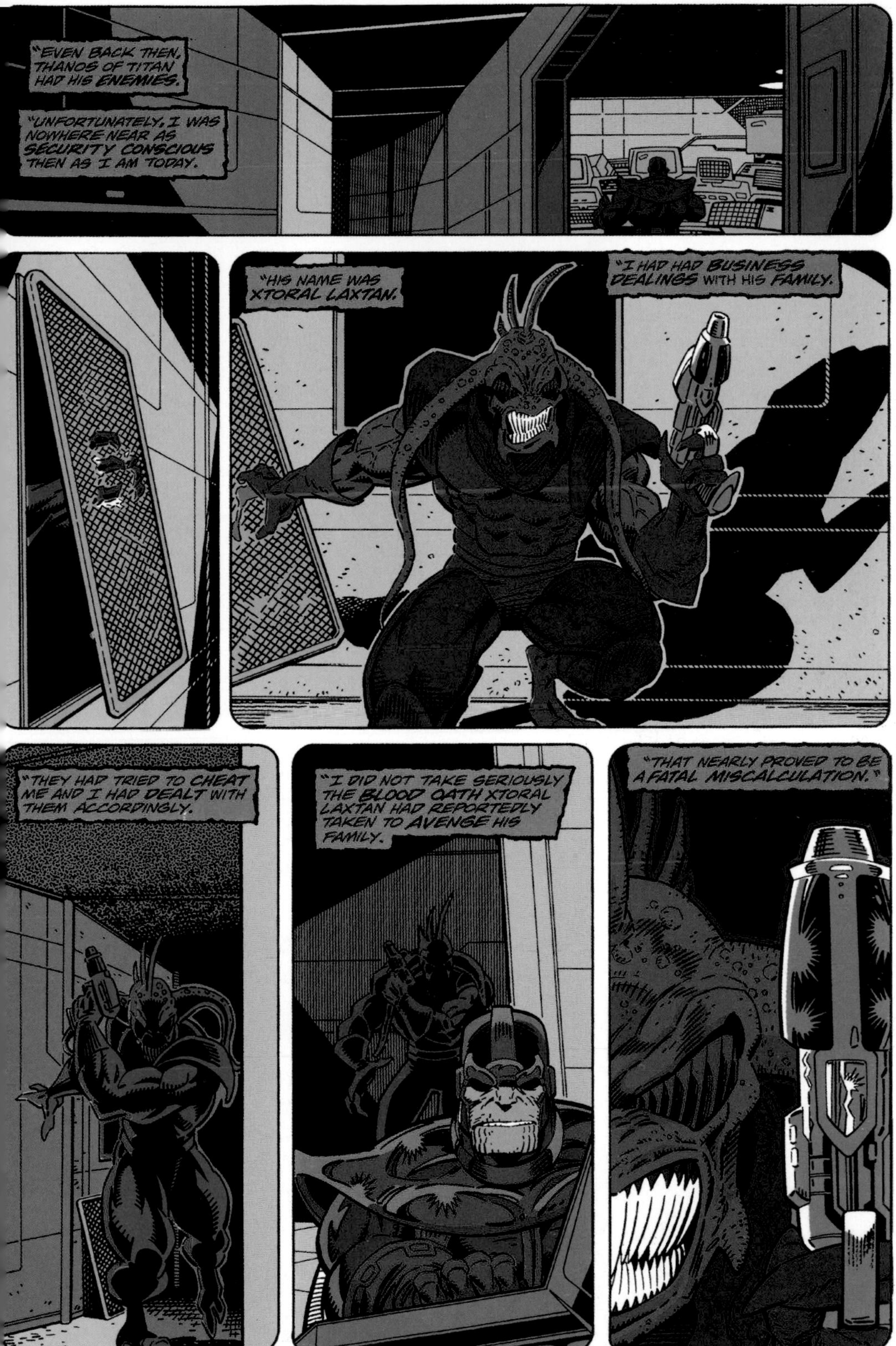
"EVEN BACK THEN, THANOS OF TITAN HAD HIS ENEMIES.
"UNFORTUNATELY, I WAS NOWHERE NEAR AS SECURITY CONSCIOUS THEN AS I AM TODAY.
"HIS NAME WAS XTORAL LAXTAN.
"I HAD HAD BUSINESS DEALINGS WITH HIS FAMILY.
"THEY HAD TRIED TO CHEAT ME AND I HAD DEALT WITH THEM ACCORDINGLY.
"I DID NOT TAKE SERIOUSLY THE BLOOD OATH XTORAL LAXTAN HAD REPORTEDLY TAKEN TO AVENGE HIS FAMILY.
"THAT NEARLY PROVED TO BE A FATAL MISCALCULATION."

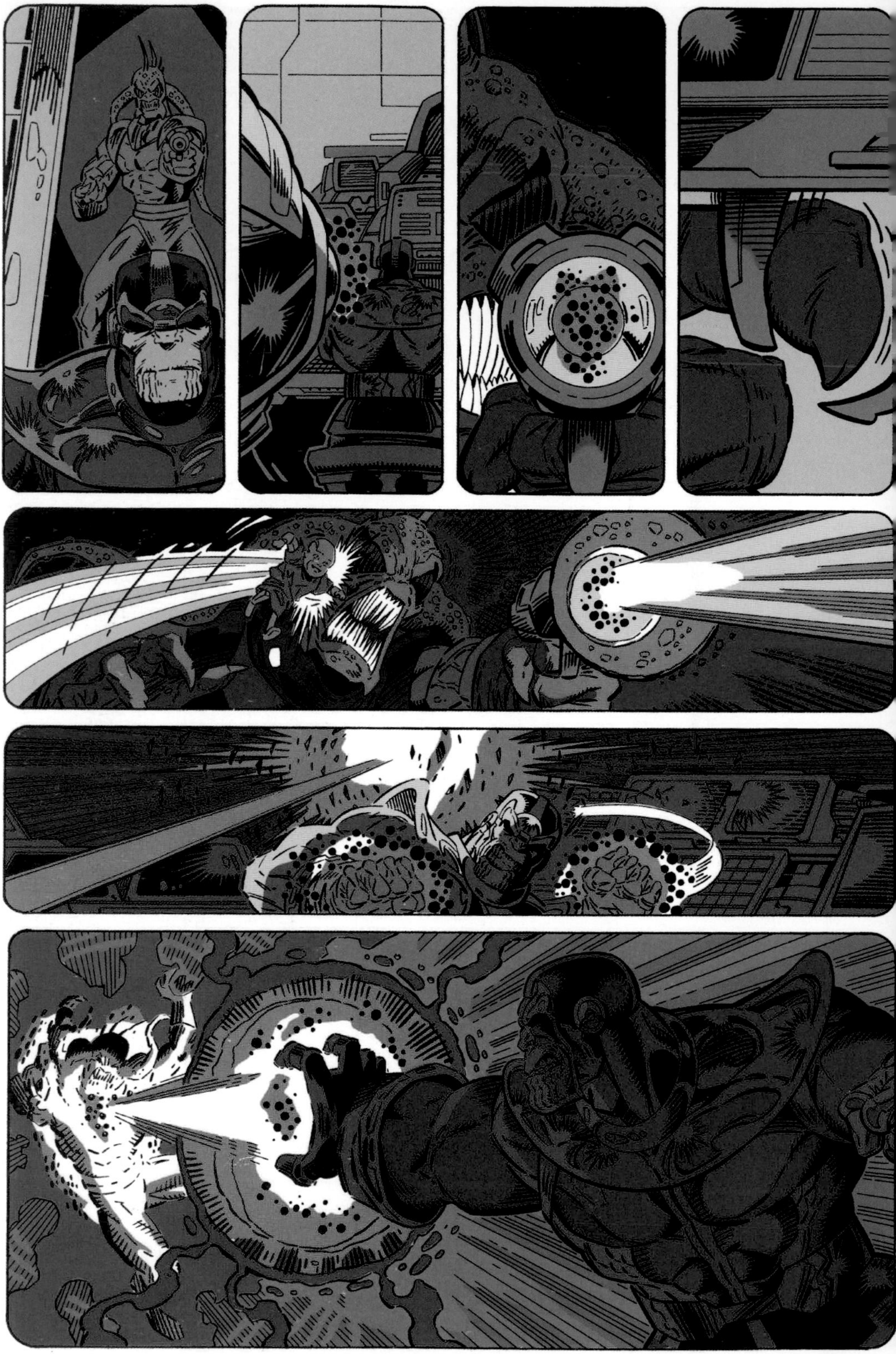

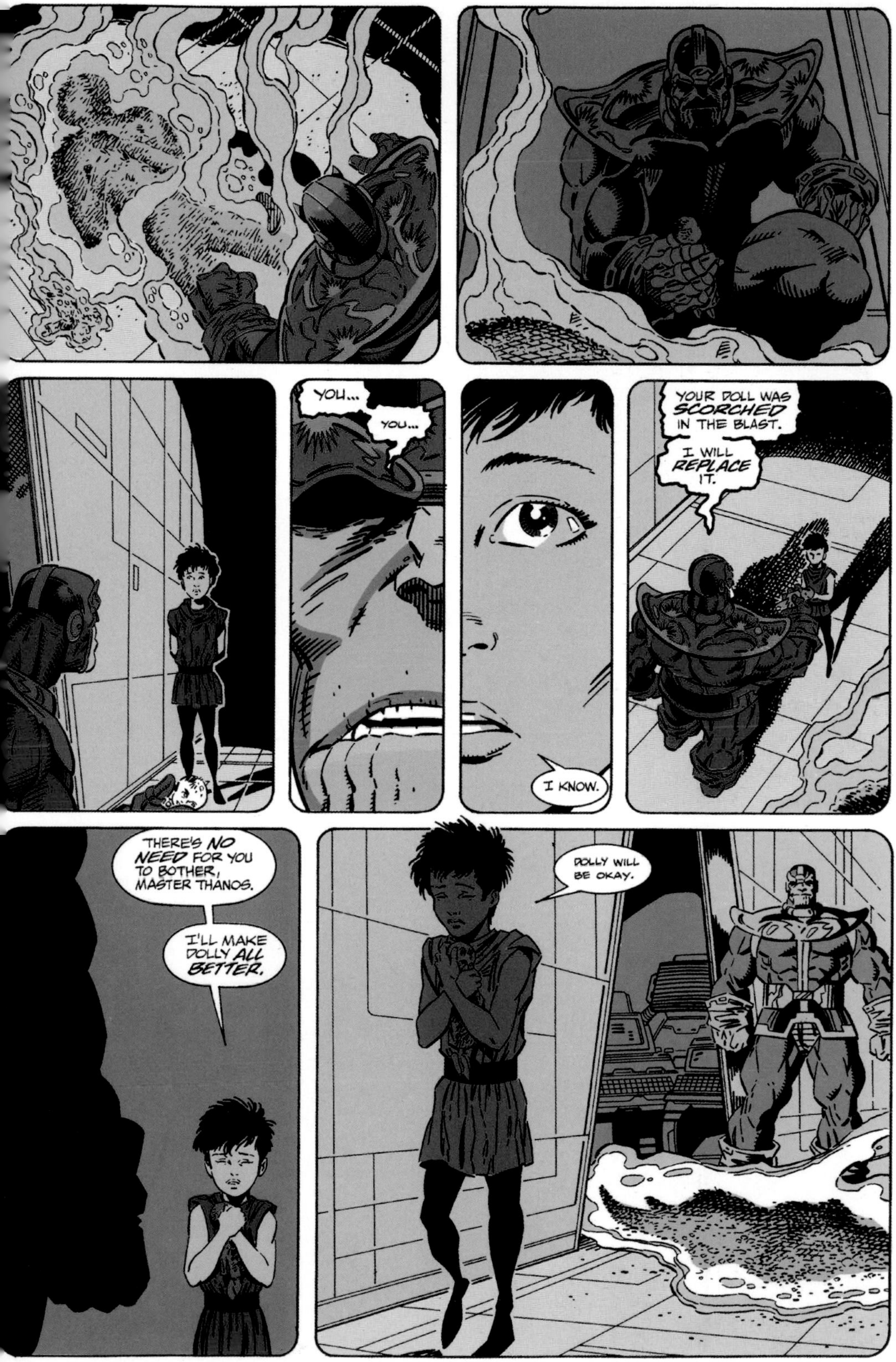
YOU...
YOU...
I KNOW.
YOUR DOLL WAS SCORCHED IN THE BLAST.
I WILL REPLACE IT.
THERE'S NO NEED FOR YOU TO BOTHER, MASTER THANOS.
I'LL MAKE DOLLY ALL BETTER.
DOLLY WILL BE OKAY.

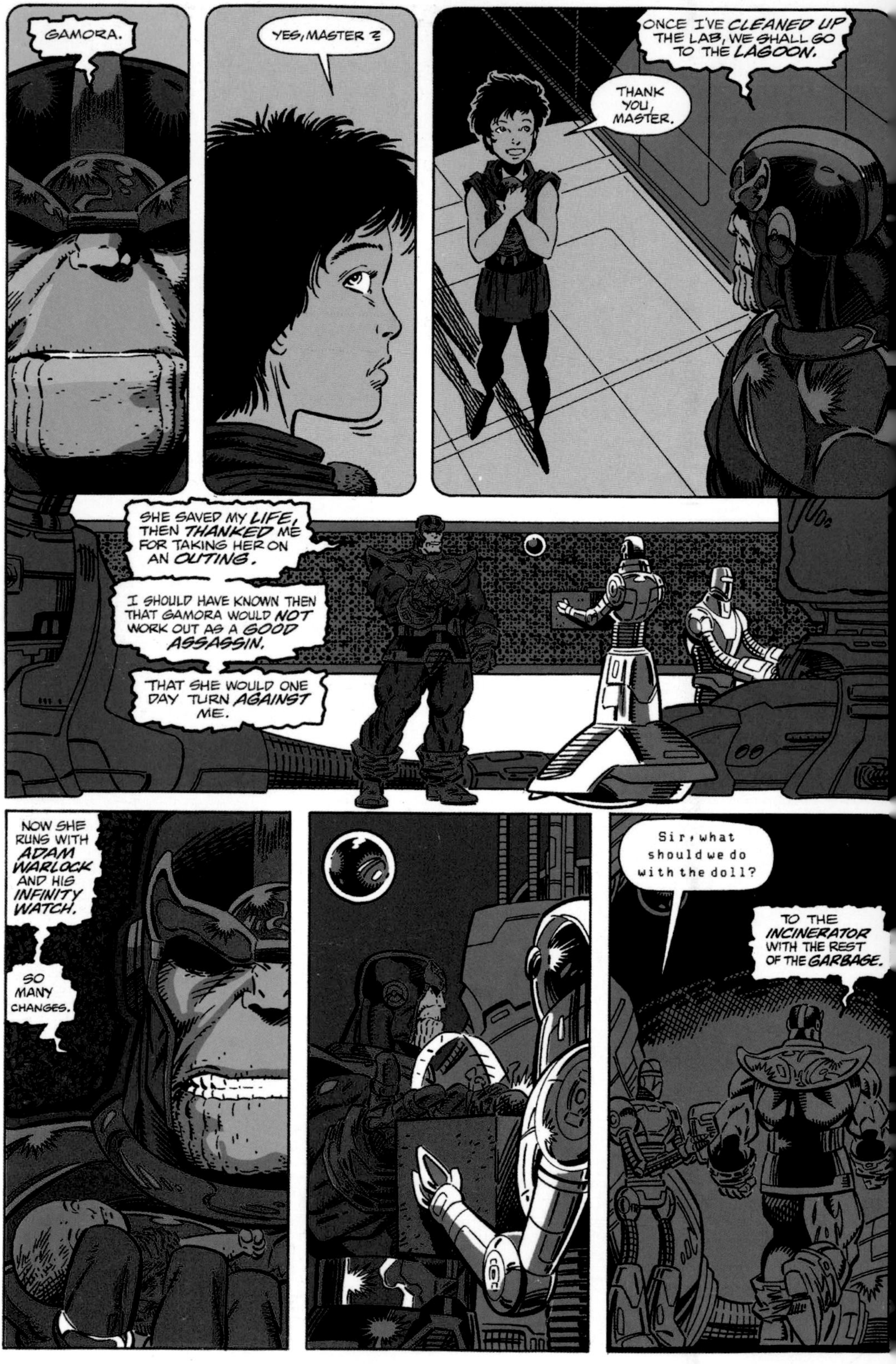
GAMORA.
YES, MASTER?
ONCE I'VE CLEANED UP THE LAB, WE SHALL GO TO THE LAGOON.
THANK YOU, MASTER.
SHE SAVED MY LIFE, THEN THANKED ME FOR TAKING HER ON AN OUTING.
I SHOULD HAVE KNOWN THEN THAT GAMORA WOULD NOT WORK OUT AS A GOOD ASSASSIN.
THAT SHE WOULD ONE DAY TURN AGAINST ME.
NOW SHE RUNS WITH ADAM WARLOCK AND HIS INFINITY WATCH.
SO MANY CHANGES.
Sir, what should we do with the doll?
TO THE INCINERATOR WITH THE REST OF THE GARBAGE.

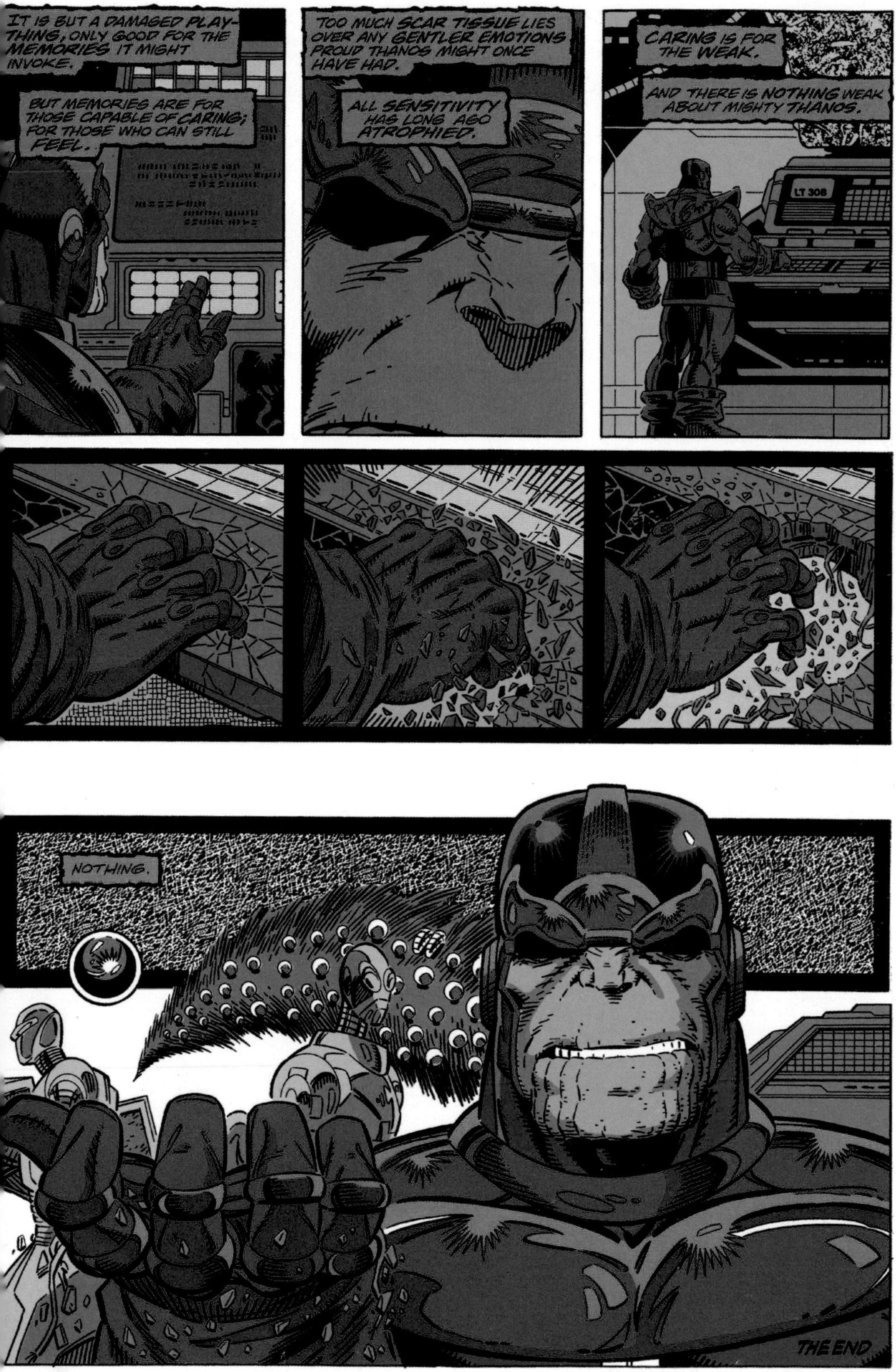
IT IS BUT A DAMAGED PLAYTHING, ONLY GOOD FOR THE MEMORIES IT MIGHT INVOKE.
BUT MEMORIES ARE FOR THOSE CAPABLE OF CARING; FOR THOSE WHO CAN STILL FEEL.
TOO MUCH SCAR TISSUE LIES OVER ANY GENTLER EMOTIONS PROUD THANOS MIGHT ONCE HAVE HAD.
ALL SENSITIVITY HAS LONG AGO ATROPHIED.
CARING IS FOR THE WEAK.
AND THERE IS NOTHING WEAK ABOUT MIGHTY THANOS.
LT 308
NOTHING.
THE END

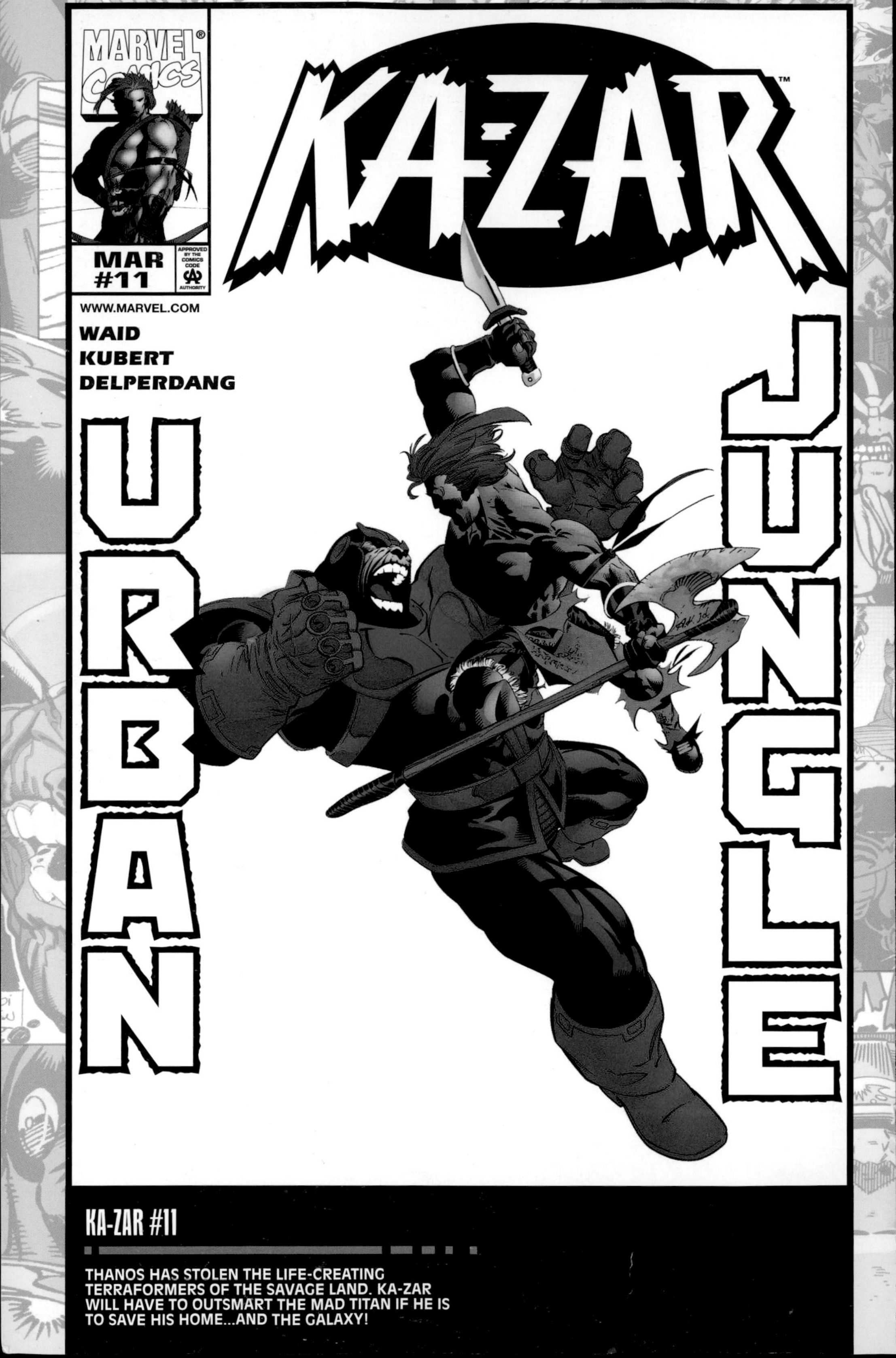
MARVEL COMICS
KA-ZAR™
MAR
#11
APPROVED BY THE COMICS CODE AUTHORITY
WWW.MARVEL.COM
WAID
KUBERT
DELPERDANG
URBAN
JUNGLE

KA-ZAR #11

THANOS HAS STOLEN THE LIFE-CREATING TERRAFORMERS OF THE SAVAGE LAND. KA-ZAR WILL HAVE TO OUTSMART THE MAD TITAN IF HE IS TO SAVE HIS HOME...AND THE GALAXY!

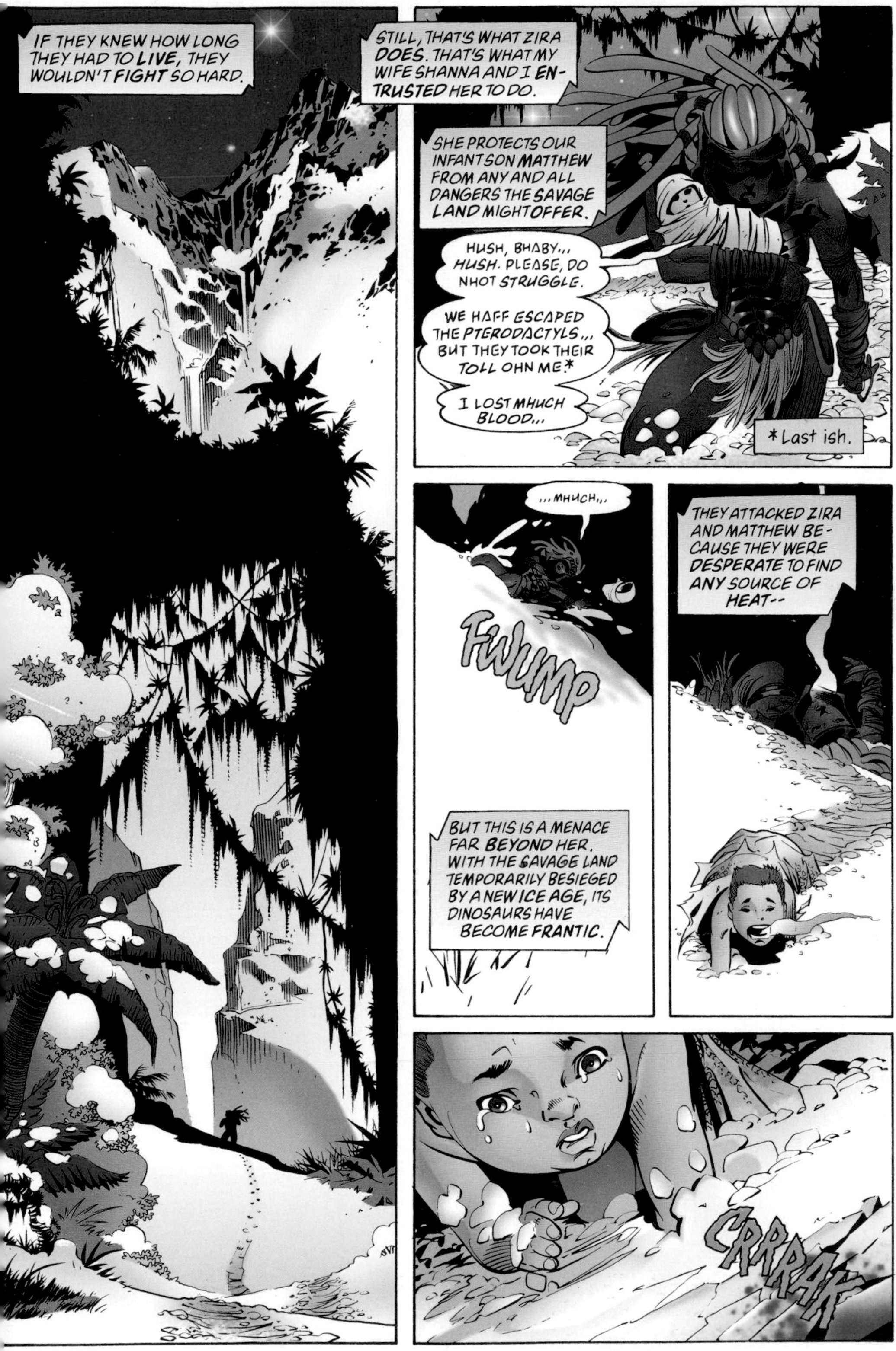
IF THEY KNEW HOW LONG THEY HAD TO LIVE, THEY WOULDN'T FIGHT SO HARD.
STILL, THAT'S WHAT ZIRA DOES. THAT'S WHAT MY WIFE SHANNA AND I ENTRUSTED HER TO DO.
SHE PROTECTS OUR INFANT SON MATTHEW FROM ANY AND ALL DANGERS THE SAVAGE LAND MIGHT OFFER.
HUSH, BHABY... HUSH. PLEASE, DO NHOT STRUGGLE.
WE HAFF ESCAPED THE PTERODACTYLS... BUT THEY TOOK THEIR TOLL OHN ME.*
I LOST MHUCH BLOOD...
*Last ish.
...MHUCH...
FWUMP
THEY ATTACKED ZIRA AND MATTHEW BECAUSE THEY WERE DESPERATE TO FIND ANY SOURCE OF HEAT--
BUT THIS IS A MENACE FAR BEYOND HER. WITH THE SAVAGE LAND TEMPORARILY BESIEGED BY A NEW ICE AGE, ITS DINOSAURS HAVE BECOME FRANTIC.
CRRRAK

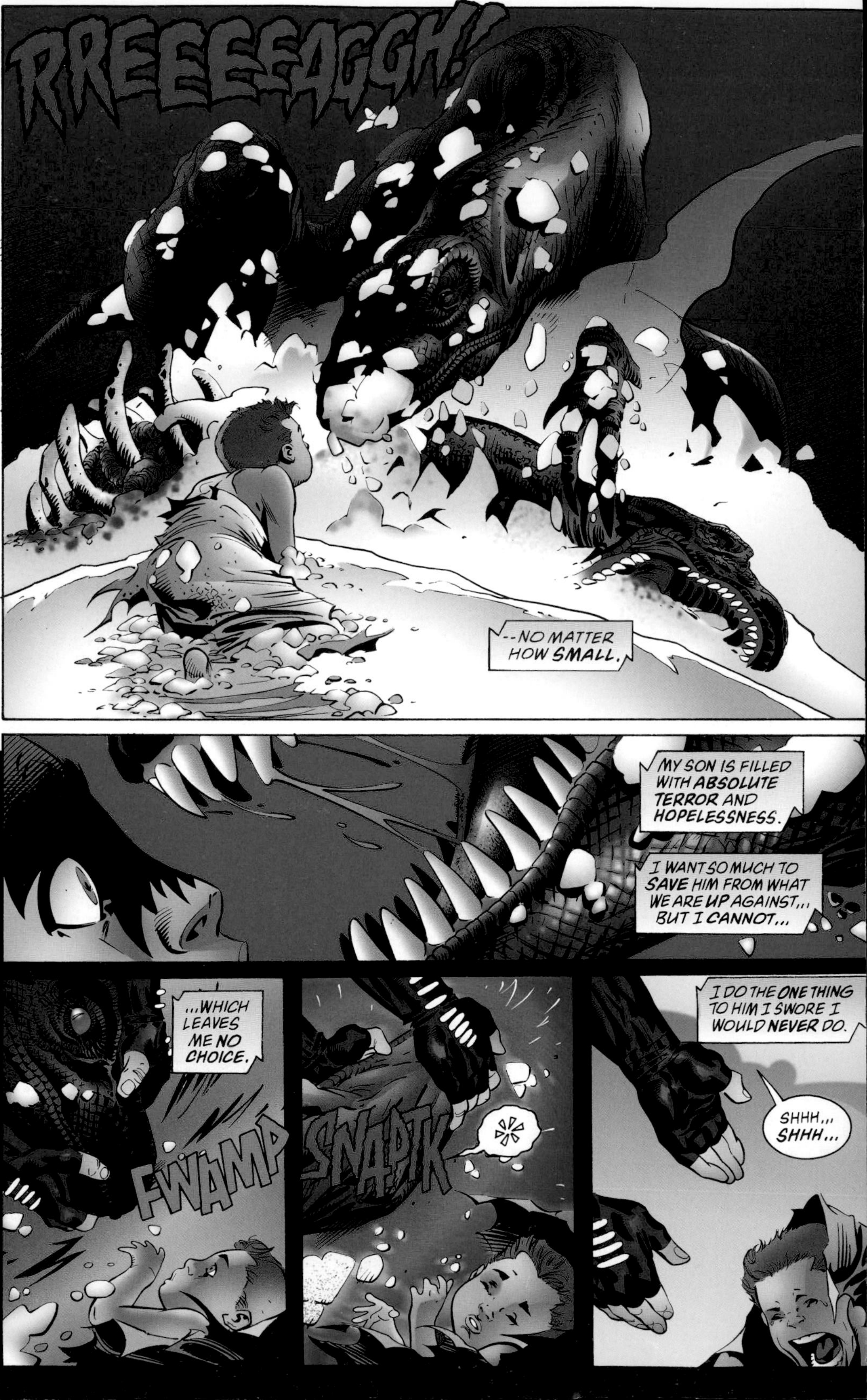
RREEEEAGGH!
--NO MATTER HOW SMALL.
MY SON IS FILLED WITH ABSOLUTE TERROR AND HOPELESSNESS.
I WANT SO MUCH TO SAVE HIM FROM WHAT WE ARE UP AGAINST... BUT I CANNOT...
...WHICH LEAVES ME NO CHOICE.
FWAMP
SNAPTK
I DO THE ONE THING TO HIM I SWORE I WOULD NEVER DO.
SHHH... SHHH...

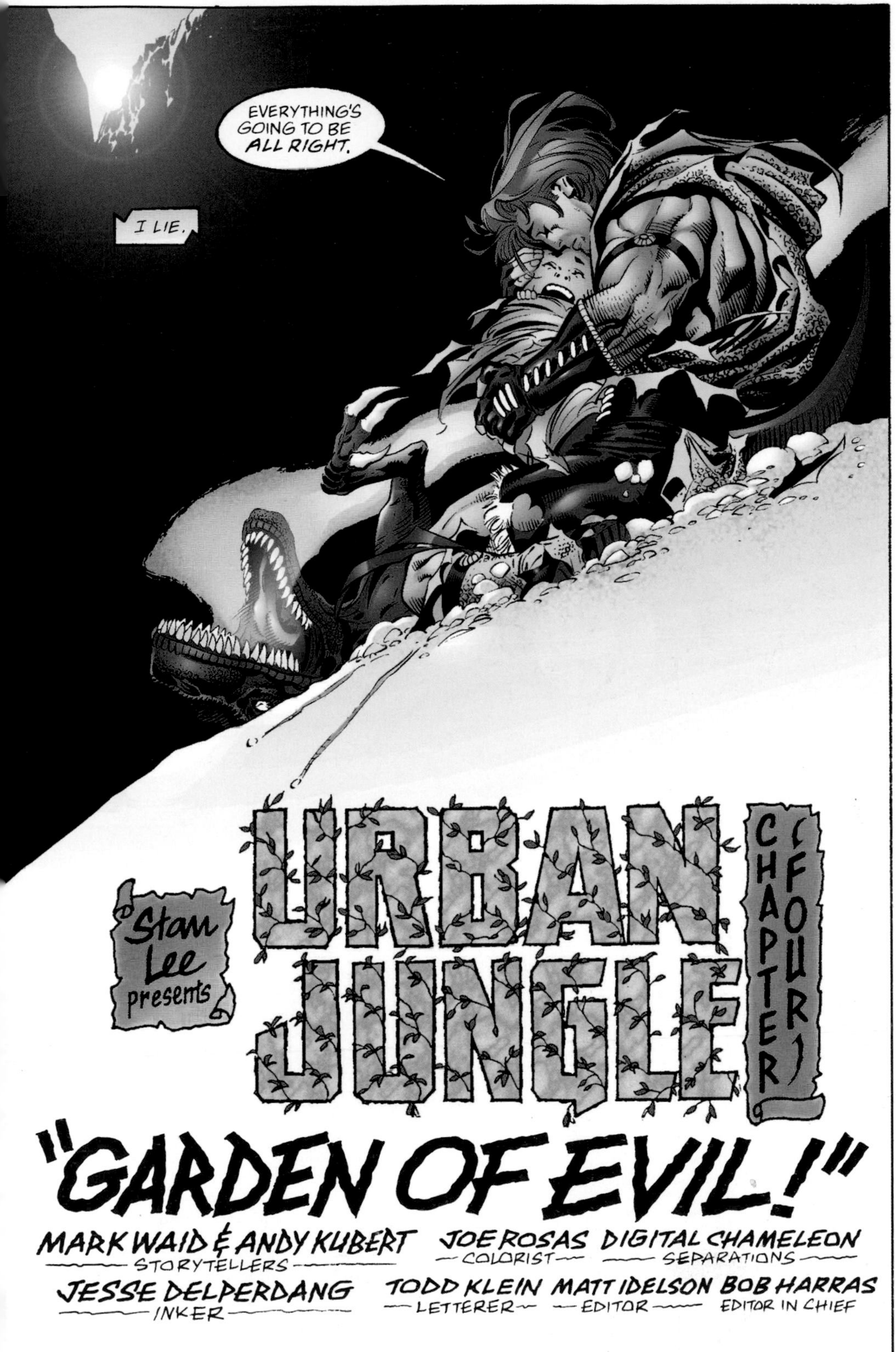
EVERYTHING'S GOING TO BE ALL RIGHT.
I LIE.
Stan Lee presents
URBAN JUNGLE
(CHAPTER FOUR)
"GARDEN OF EVIL!"
MARK WAID & ANDY KUBERT — STORYTELLERS
JOE ROSAS — COLORIST
DIGITAL CHAMELEON — SEPARATIONS
JESSE DELPERDANG — INKER
TODD KLEIN — LETTERER
MATT IDELSON — EDITOR
BOB HARRAS — EDITOR IN CHIEF

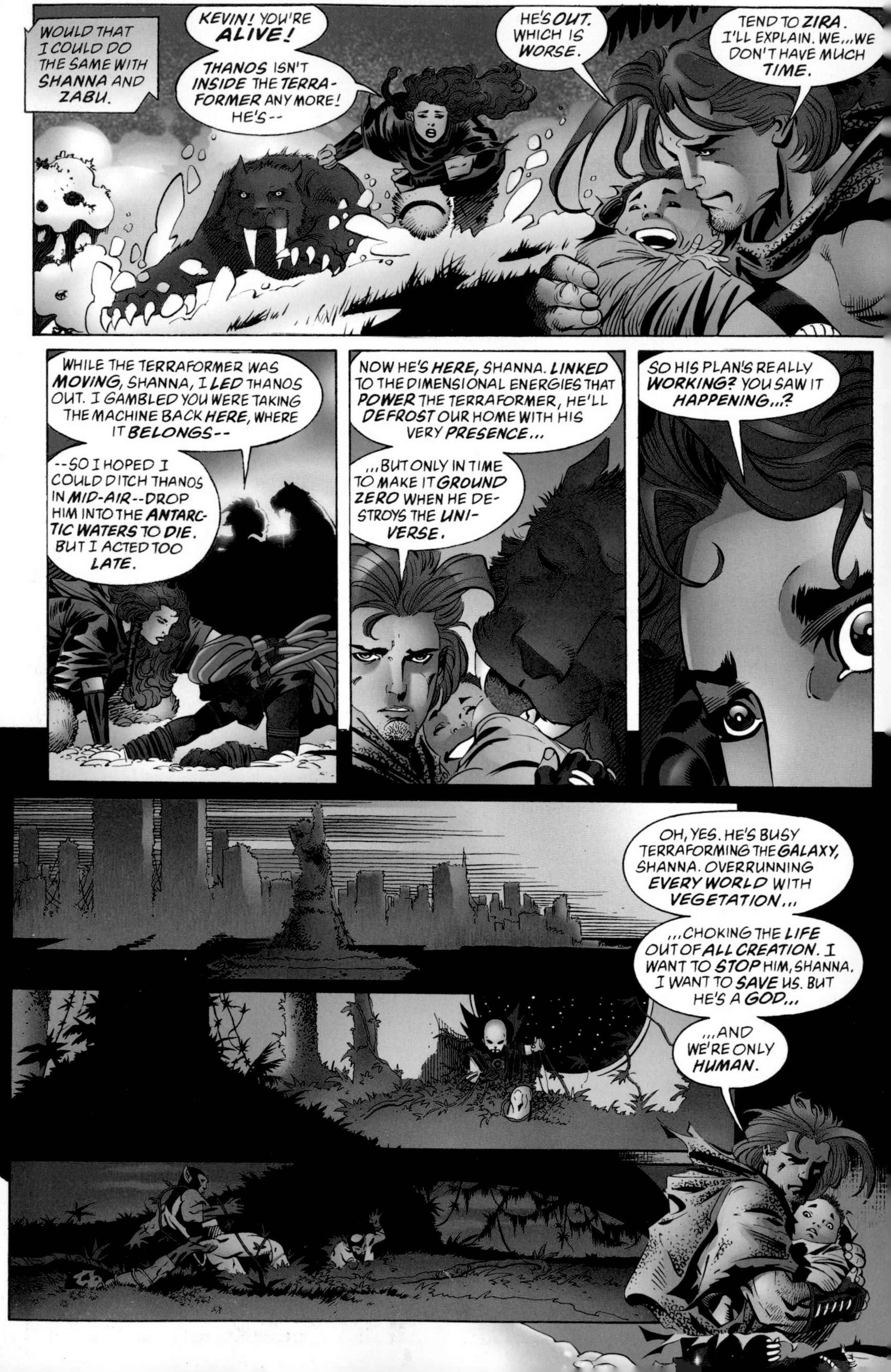
WOULD THAT I COULD DO THE SAME WITH SHANNA AND ZABU.
KEVIN! YOU'RE ALIVE!
THANOS ISN'T INSIDE THE TERRA-FORMER ANY MORE! HE'S--
HE'S OUT. WHICH IS WORSE.
TEND TO ZIRA. I'LL EXPLAIN. WE...WE DON'T HAVE MUCH TIME.
WHILE THE TERRAFORMER WAS MOVING, SHANNA, I LED THANOS OUT. I GAMBLED YOU WERE TAKING THE MACHINE BACK HERE, WHERE IT BELONGS--
--SO I HOPED I COULD DITCH THANOS IN MID-AIR--DROP HIM INTO THE ANTARCTIC WATERS TO DIE. BUT I ACTED TOO LATE.
NOW HE'S HERE, SHANNA. LINKED TO THE DIMENSIONAL ENERGIES THAT POWER THE TERRAFORMER, HE'LL DEFROST OUR HOME WITH HIS VERY PRESENCE...
...BUT ONLY IN TIME TO MAKE IT GROUND ZERO WHEN HE DESTROYS THE UNIVERSE.
SO HIS PLAN'S REALLY WORKING? YOU SAW IT HAPPENING...?
OH, YES. HE'S BUSY TERRAFORMING THE GALAXY, SHANNA. OVERRUNNING EVERY WORLD WITH VEGETATION...
...CHOKING THE LIFE OUT OF ALL CREATION. I WANT TO STOP HIM, SHANNA. I WANT TO SAVE US. BUT HE'S A GOD...
...AND WE'RE ONLY HUMAN.

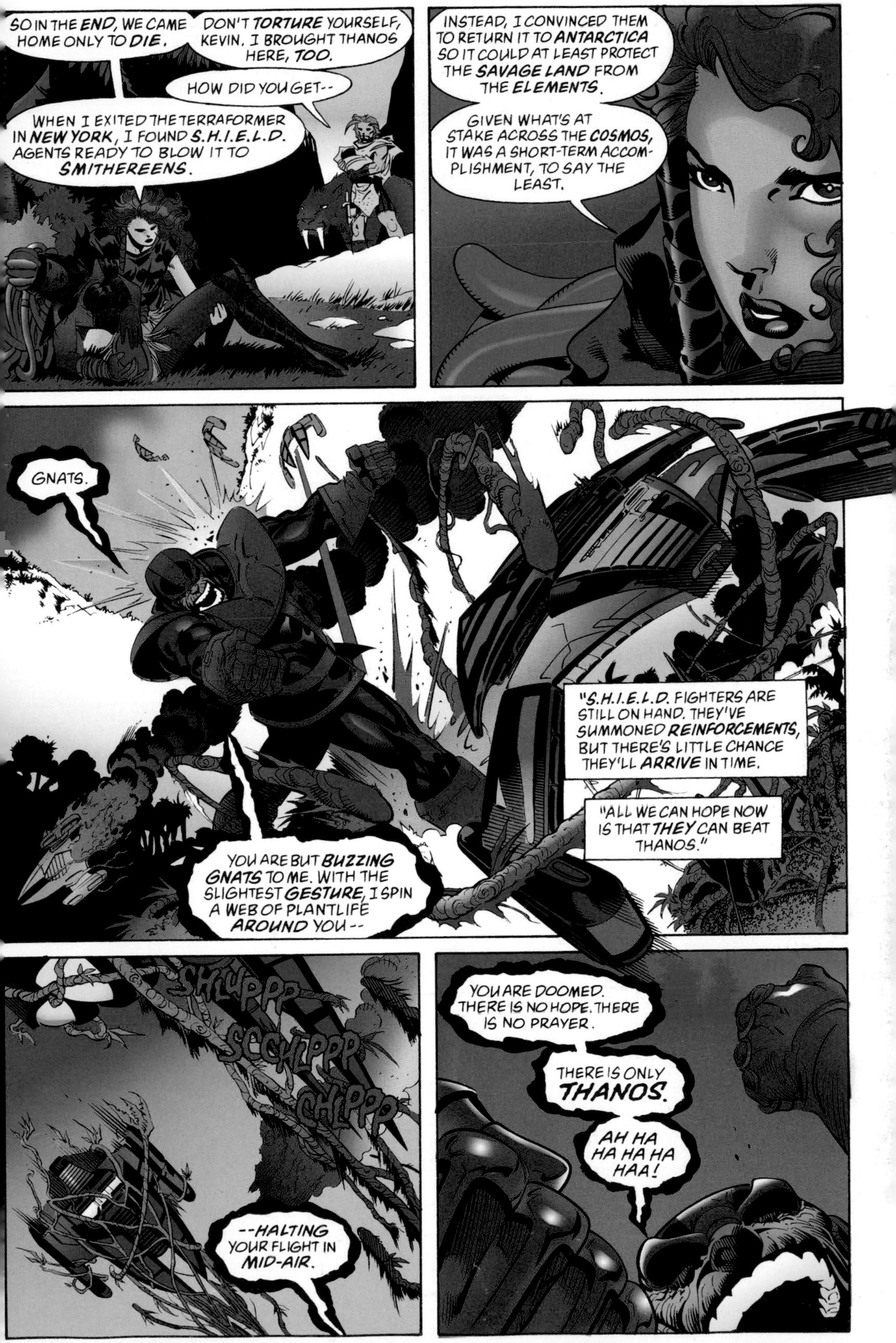
SO IN THE END, WE CAME HOME ONLY TO DIE.
DON'T TORTURE YOURSELF, KEVIN. I BROUGHT THANOS HERE, TOO.
HOW DID YOU GET--
WHEN I EXITED THE TERRAFORMER IN NEW YORK, I FOUND S.H.I.E.L.D. AGENTS READY TO BLOW IT TO SMITHEREENS.
INSTEAD, I CONVINCED THEM TO RETURN IT TO ANTARCTICA SO IT COULD AT LEAST PROTECT THE SAVAGE LAND FROM THE ELEMENTS.
GIVEN WHAT'S AT STAKE ACROSS THE COSMOS, IT WAS A SHORT-TERM ACCOMPLISHMENT, TO SAY THE LEAST.
GNATS.
"S.H.I.E.L.D. FIGHTERS ARE STILL ON HAND. THEY'VE SUMMONED REINFORCEMENTS, BUT THERE'S LITTLE CHANCE THEY'LL ARRIVE IN TIME.
"ALL WE CAN HOPE NOW IS THAT THEY CAN BEAT THANOS."
YOU ARE BUT BUZZING GNATS TO ME. WITH THE SLIGHTEST GESTURE, I SPIN A WEB OF PLANTLIFE AROUND YOU --
SHLUPPP
SCCHLPPP
CHLPPP
--HALTING YOUR FLIGHT IN MID-AIR.
YOU ARE DOOMED. THERE IS NO HOPE. THERE IS NO PRAYER.
THERE IS ONLY THANOS.
AH HA HA HA HA HAA!

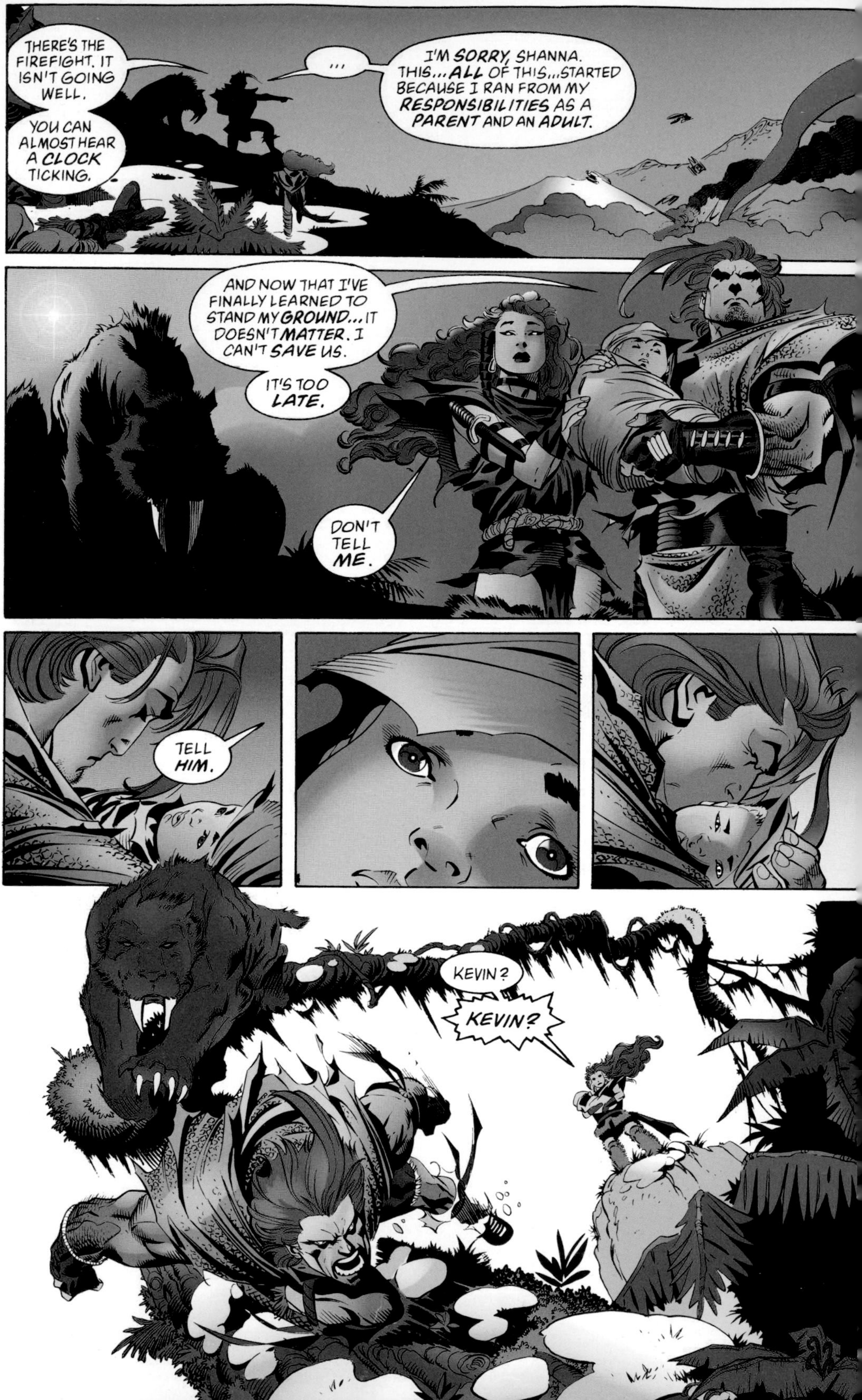
THERE'S THE FIREFIGHT. IT ISN'T GOING WELL.
YOU CAN ALMOST HEAR A CLOCK TICKING.
...
I'M SORRY, SHANNA. THIS... ALL OF THIS... STARTED BECAUSE I RAN FROM MY RESPONSIBILITIES AS A PARENT AND AN ADULT.
AND NOW THAT I'VE FINALLY LEARNED TO STAND MY GROUND... IT DOESN'T MATTER. I CAN'T SAVE US.
IT'S TOO LATE.
DON'T TELL ME.
TELL HIM.
KEVIN?
KEVIN?

NOT WITHOUT A FIGHT!

EVEN IN THE FACE OF UTTER **DEFEAT**, YOU **CONTINUE** TO WASTE MY TIME WITH **OBSTIN-ATE DEFIANCE**.

HOW PERFECTLY **EARTHLING** OF YOU.

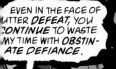

RRRAWRRR

LAY **DOWN**, MORTALS.

AH, YES. ENTER THE **NOBLE SAVAGE**.

PERHAPS I MISUNDERSTAND YOUR **LANGUAGE**.

OR PERHAPS I DID NOT **HEAR** YOU PROPERLY.

I BELIEVE YOU SAID SOMETHING ABOUT A "**FIGHT**."

NNGGGH!

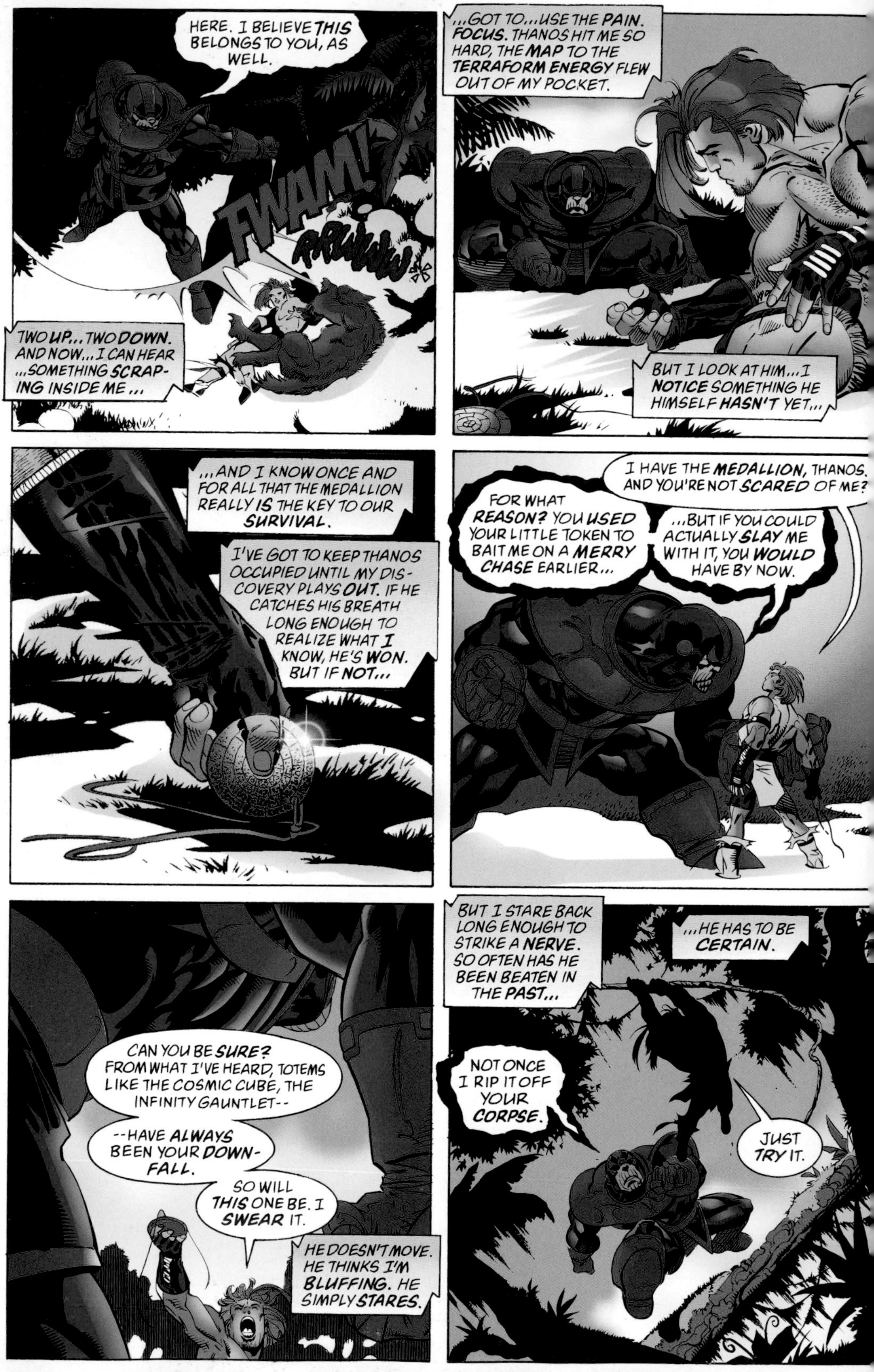
HERE. I BELIEVE THIS BELONGS TO YOU, AS WELL.
FWAM!
RRUWW
TWO UP... TWO DOWN. AND NOW... I CAN HEAR ...SOMETHING SCRAPING INSIDE ME...
...GOT TO... USE THE PAIN. FOCUS. THANOS HIT ME SO HARD, THE MAP TO THE TERRAFORM ENERGY FLEW OUT OF MY POCKET.
BUT I LOOK AT HIM... I NOTICE SOMETHING HE HIMSELF HASN'T YET...
...AND I KNOW ONCE AND FOR ALL THAT THE MEDALLION REALLY IS THE KEY TO OUR SURVIVAL.
I'VE GOT TO KEEP THANOS OCCUPIED UNTIL MY DISCOVERY PLAYS OUT. IF HE CATCHES HIS BREATH LONG ENOUGH TO REALIZE WHAT I KNOW, HE'S WON. BUT IF NOT...
I HAVE THE MEDALLION, THANOS. AND YOU'RE NOT SCARED OF ME?
FOR WHAT REASON? YOU USED YOUR LITTLE TOKEN TO BAIT ME ON A MERRY CHASE EARLIER...
...BUT IF YOU COULD ACTUALLY SLAY ME WITH IT, YOU WOULD HAVE BY NOW.
CAN YOU BE SURE? FROM WHAT I'VE HEARD, TOTEMS LIKE THE COSMIC CUBE, THE INFINITY GAUNTLET--
--HAVE ALWAYS BEEN YOUR DOWNFALL.
SO WILL THIS ONE BE. I SWEAR IT.
HE DOESN'T MOVE. HE THINKS I'M BLUFFING. HE SIMPLY STARES.
BUT I STARE BACK LONG ENOUGH TO STRIKE A NERVE. SO OFTEN HAS HE BEEN BEATEN IN THE PAST...
...HE HAS TO BE CERTAIN.
NOT ONCE I RIP IT OFF YOUR CORPSE.
JUST TRY IT.

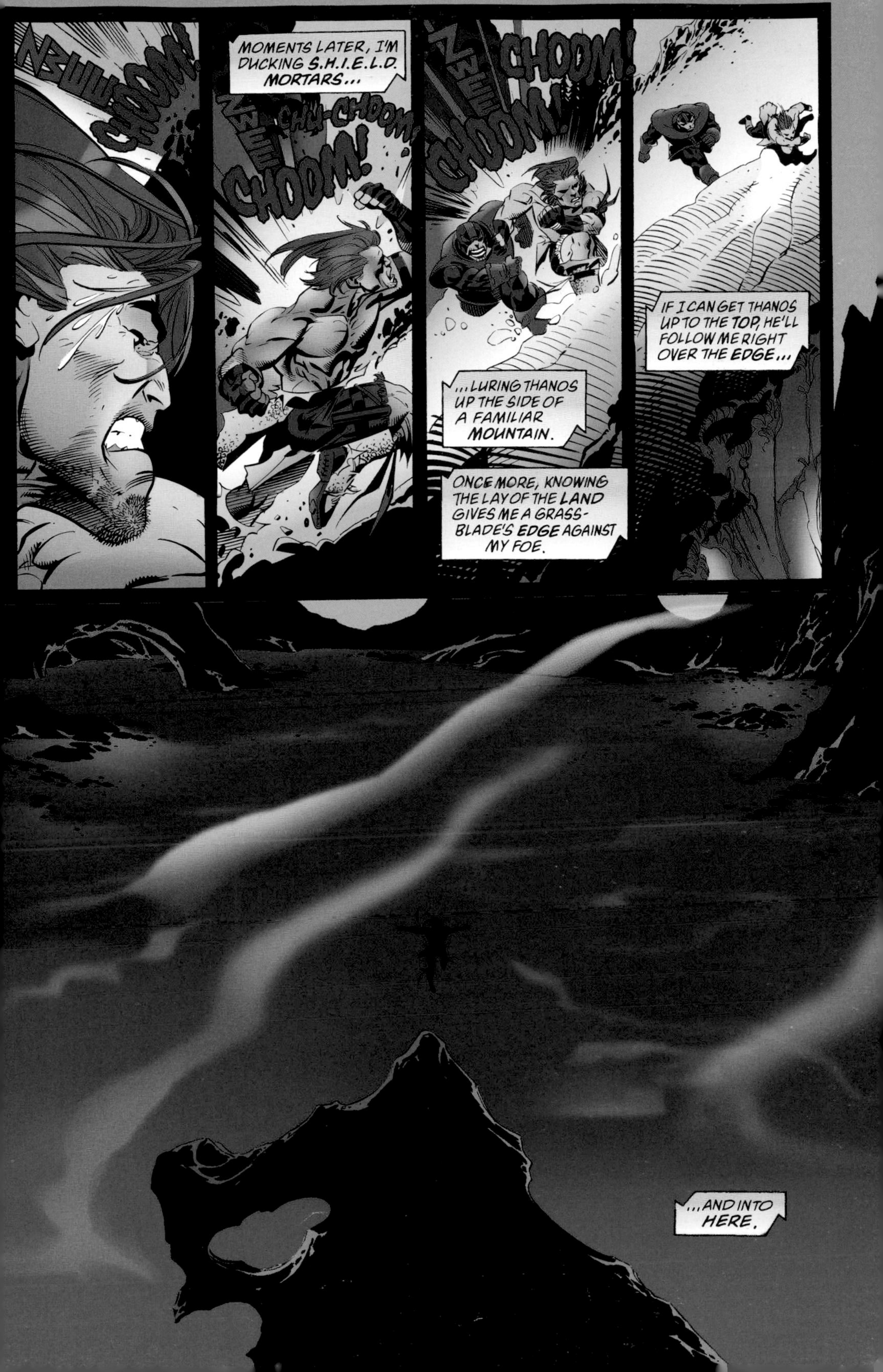
NZWEEE
CHOOM!
MOMENTS LATER, I'M DUCKING S.H.I.E.L.D. MORTARS...
ZWEE CHU-CHOOM!
CHOOM!
ZWEE
CHOOM!
CHOOM!
...LURING THANOS UP THE SIDE OF A FAMILIAR MOUNTAIN.
ONCE MORE, KNOWING THE LAY OF THE LAND GIVES ME A GRASS-BLADE'S EDGE AGAINST MY FOE.
IF I CAN GET THANOS UP TO THE TOP, HE'LL FOLLOW ME RIGHT OVER THE EDGE...
...AND INTO HERE.

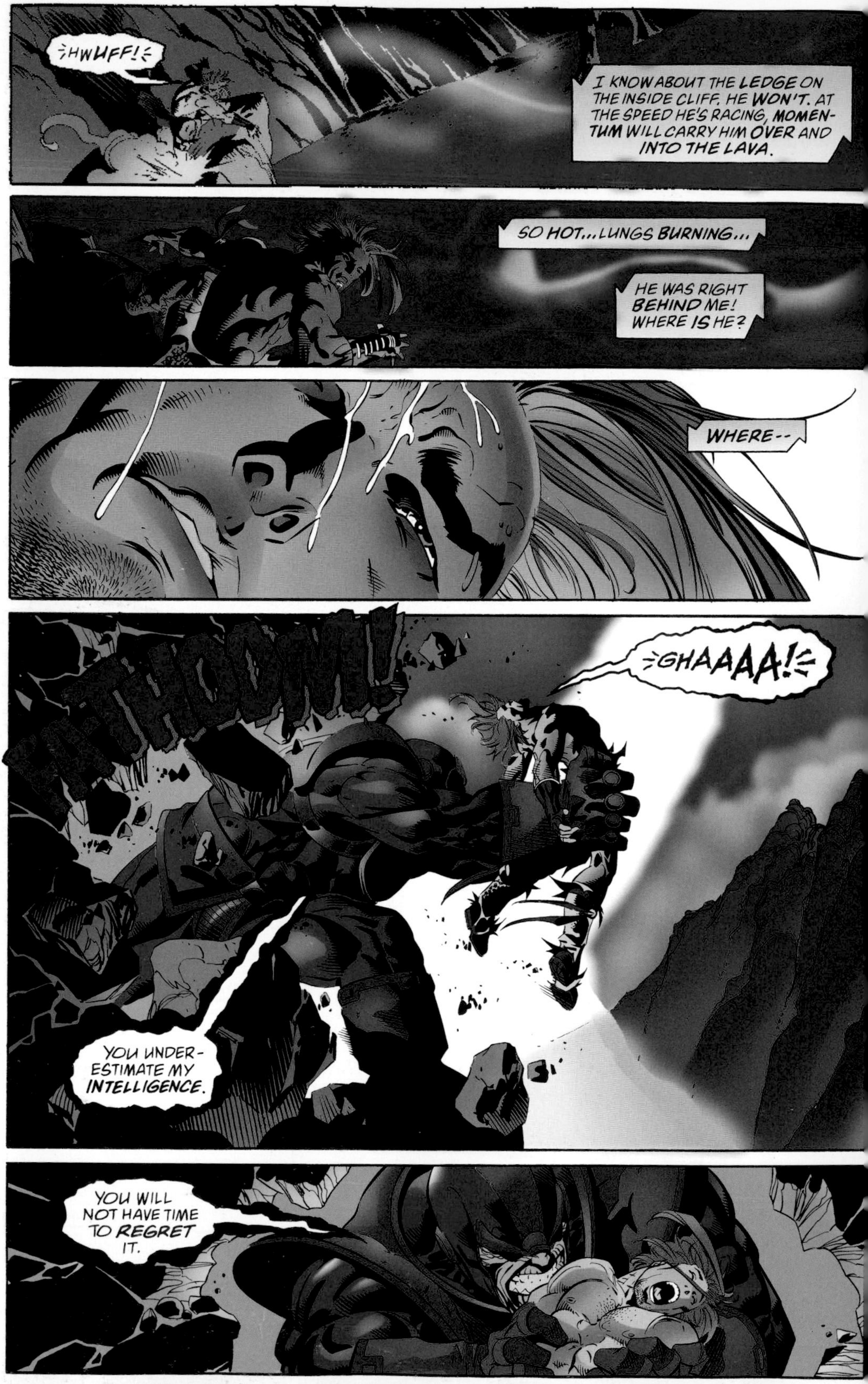
HWUFF!
I KNOW ABOUT THE LEDGE ON THE INSIDE CLIFF. HE WON'T. AT THE SPEED HE'S RACING, MOMENTUM WILL CARRY HIM OVER AND INTO THE LAVA.
SO HOT... LUNGS BURNING...
HE WAS RIGHT BEHIND ME! WHERE IS HE?
WHERE--
THOOM!
GHAAAA!
YOU UNDER-ESTIMATE MY INTELLIGENCE.
YOU WILL NOT HAVE TIME TO REGRET IT.

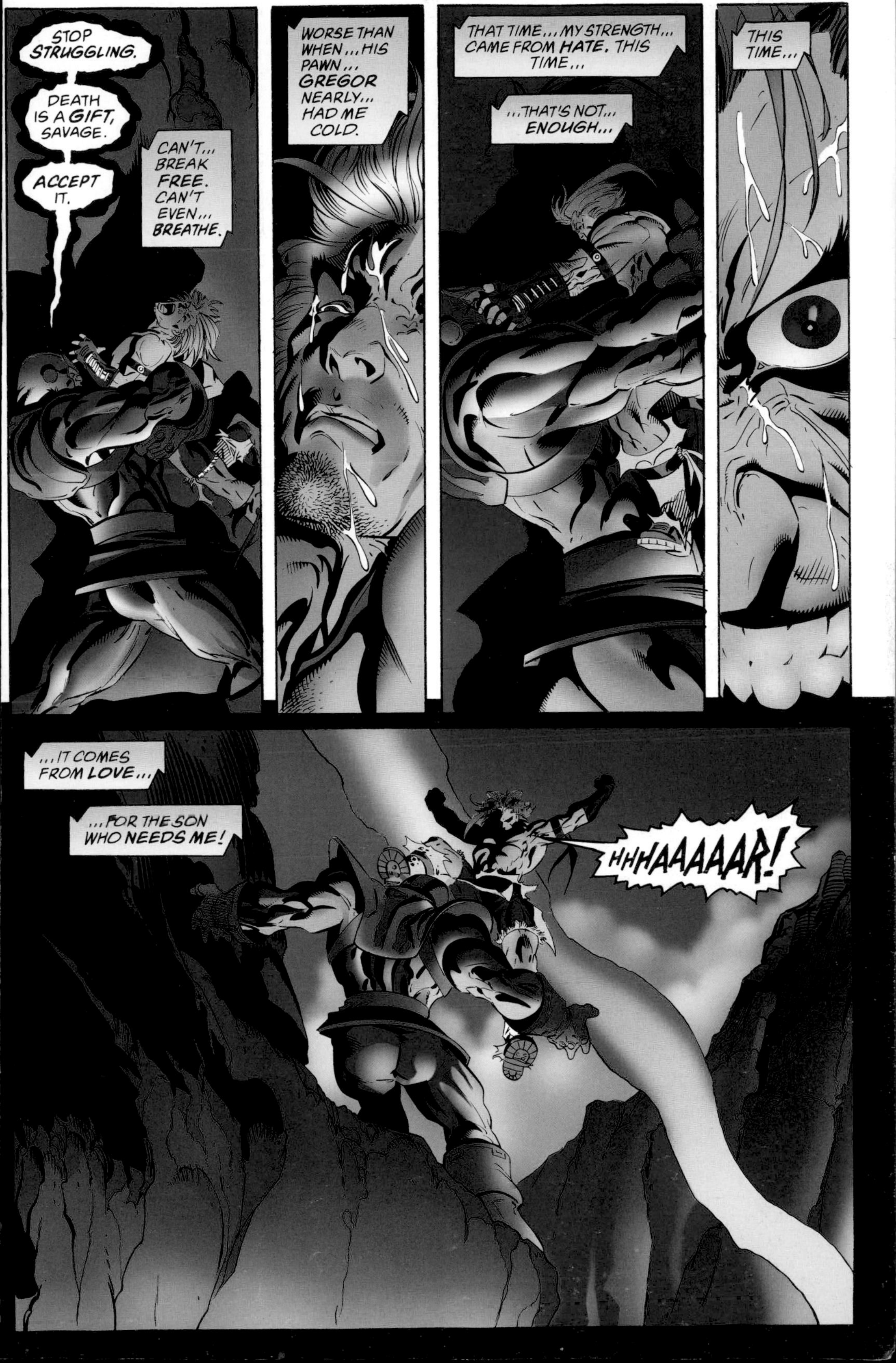
STOP STRUGGLING.
DEATH IS A GIFT, SAVAGE.
ACCEPT IT.
CAN'T... BREAK FREE. CAN'T EVEN... BREATHE.
WORSE THAN WHEN... HIS PAWN... GREGOR NEARLY... HAD ME COLD.
THAT TIME... MY STRENGTH... CAME FROM HATE. THIS TIME...
...THAT'S NOT... ENOUGH...
THIS TIME...
...IT COMES FROM LOVE...
...FOR THE SON WHO NEEDS ME!
HHHAAAAAR!

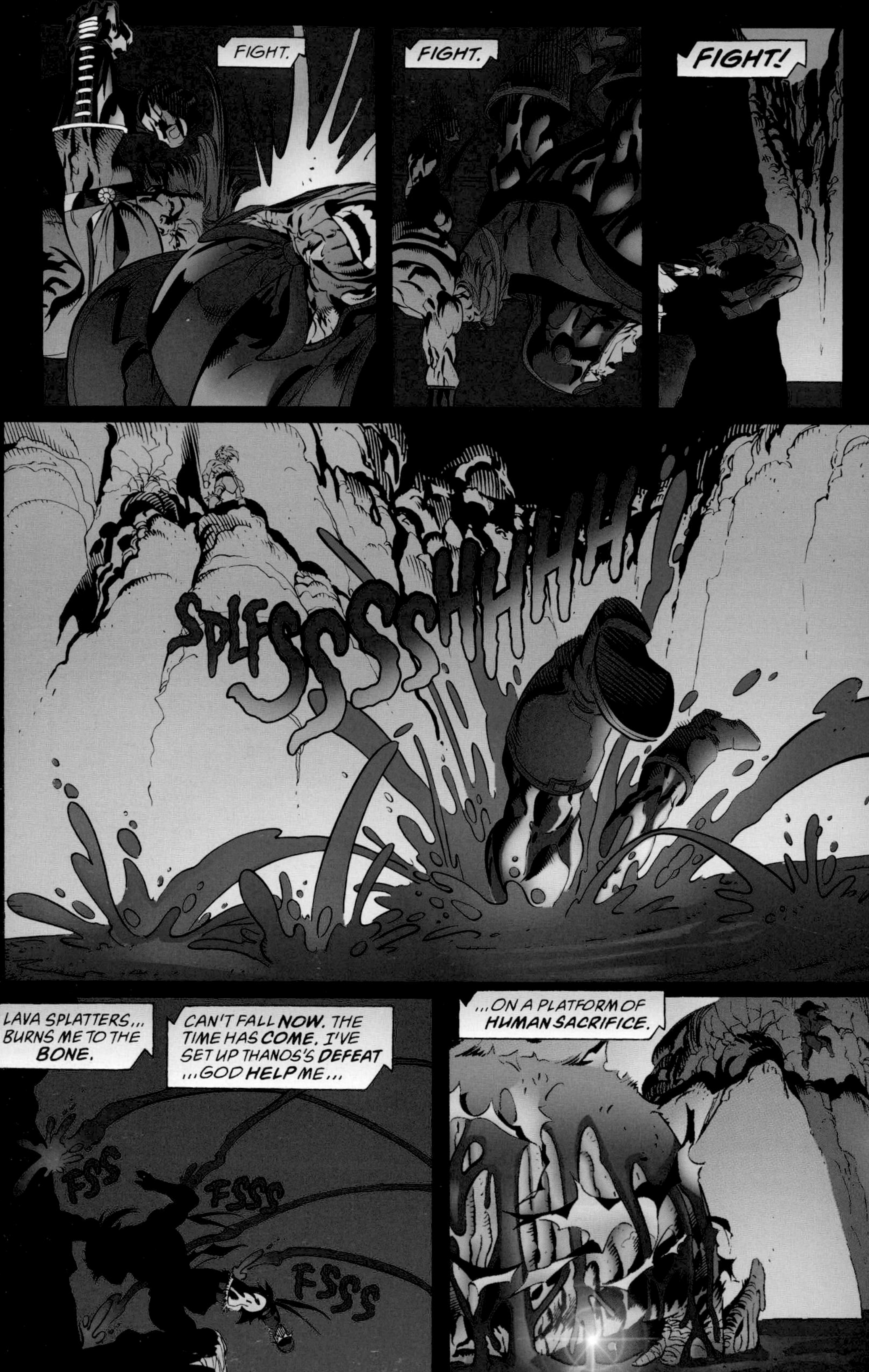
FIGHT.
FIGHT.
FIGHT!
SPLFSSSSSHHHH!
LAVA SPLATTERS... BURNS ME TO THE BONE.
CAN'T FALL NOW. THE TIME HAS COME. I'VE SET UP THANOS'S DEFEAT ...GOD HELP ME...
FSS
FSSS
FSSS
...ON A PLATFORM OF HUMAN SACRIFICE.

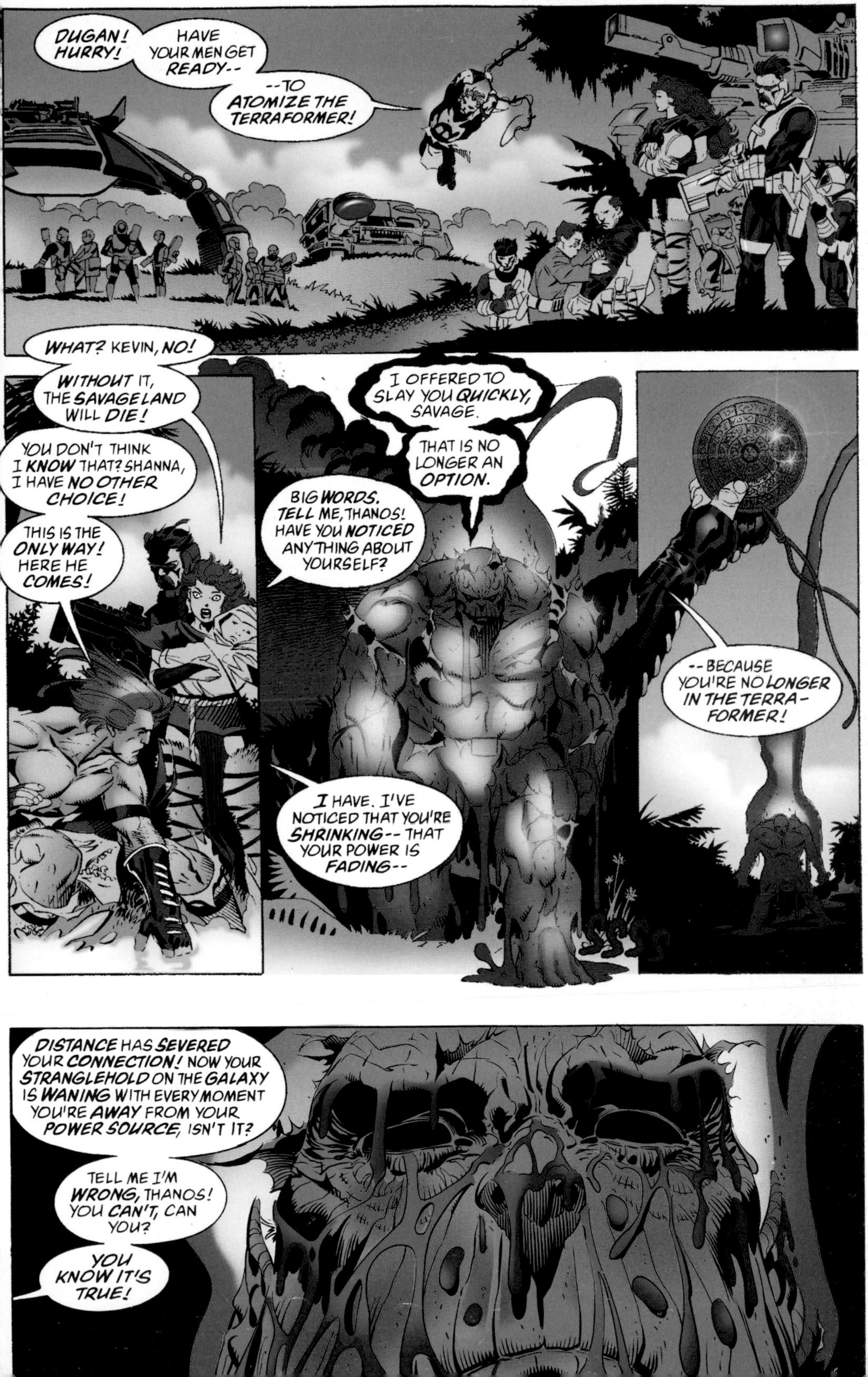
DUGAN! HURRY!
HAVE YOUR MEN GET READY--
--TO ATOMIZE THE TERRAFORMER!
WHAT? KEVIN, NO!
WITHOUT IT, THE SAVAGE LAND WILL DIE!
YOU DON'T THINK I KNOW THAT? SHANNA, I HAVE NO OTHER CHOICE!
THIS IS THE ONLY WAY! HERE HE COMES!
I OFFERED TO SLAY YOU QUICKLY, SAVAGE.
THAT IS NO LONGER AN OPTION.
BIG WORDS. TELL ME, THANOS! HAVE YOU NOTICED ANYTHING ABOUT YOURSELF?
I HAVE. I'VE NOTICED THAT YOU'RE SHRINKING-- THAT YOUR POWER IS FADING--
--BECAUSE YOU'RE NO LONGER IN THE TERRA-FORMER!
DISTANCE HAS SEVERED YOUR CONNECTION! NOW YOUR STRANGLEHOLD ON THE GALAXY IS WANING WITH EVERY MOMENT YOU'RE AWAY FROM YOUR POWER SOURCE, ISN'T IT?
TELL ME I'M WRONG, THANOS! YOU CAN'T, CAN YOU?
YOU KNOW IT'S TRUE!

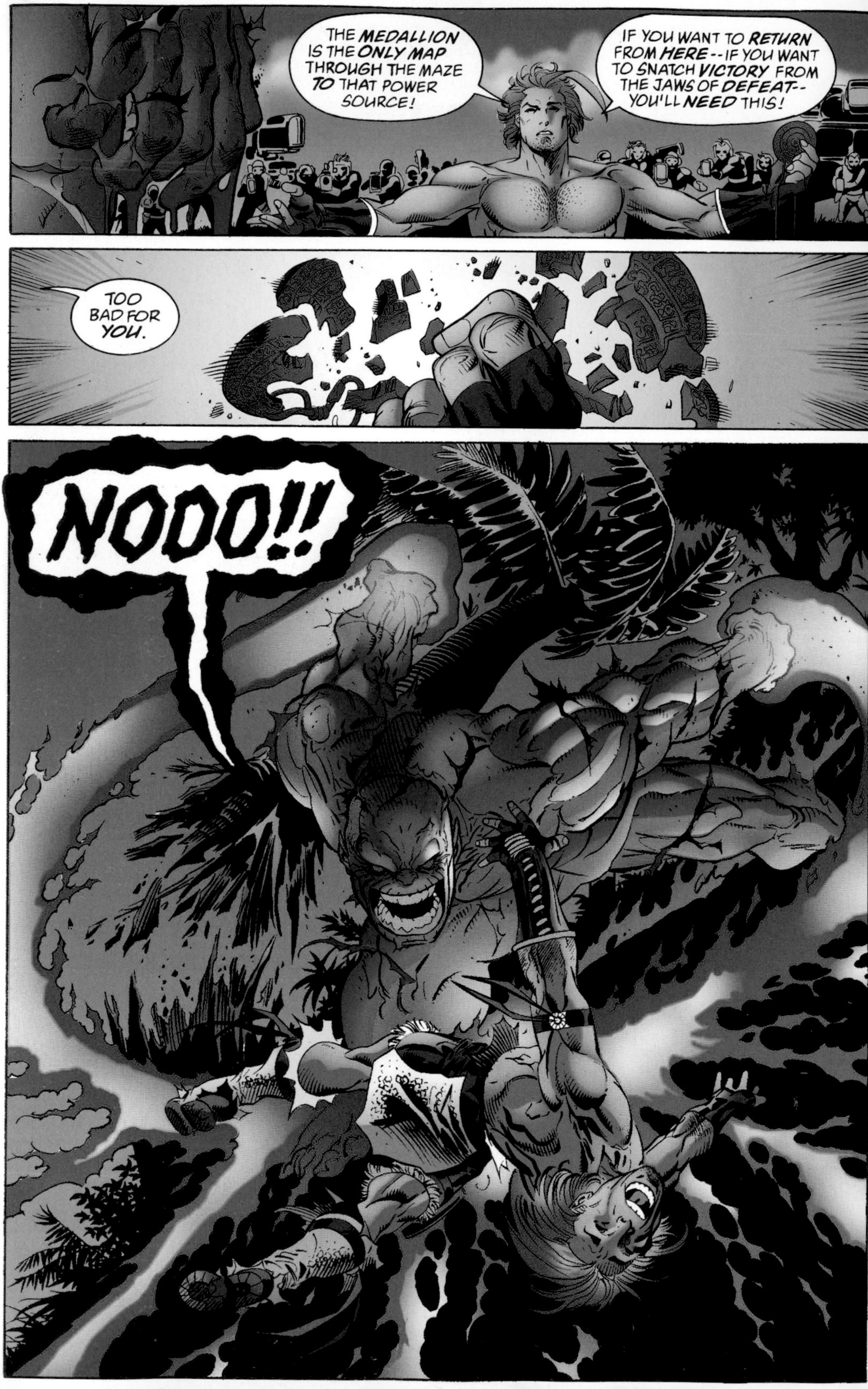
THE MEDALLION IS THE ONLY MAP THROUGH THE MAZE TO THAT POWER SOURCE!
IF YOU WANT TO RETURN FROM HERE--IF YOU WANT TO SNATCH VICTORY FROM THE JAWS OF DEFEAT--YOU'LL NEED THIS!
TOO BAD FOR YOU.
NOOO!!

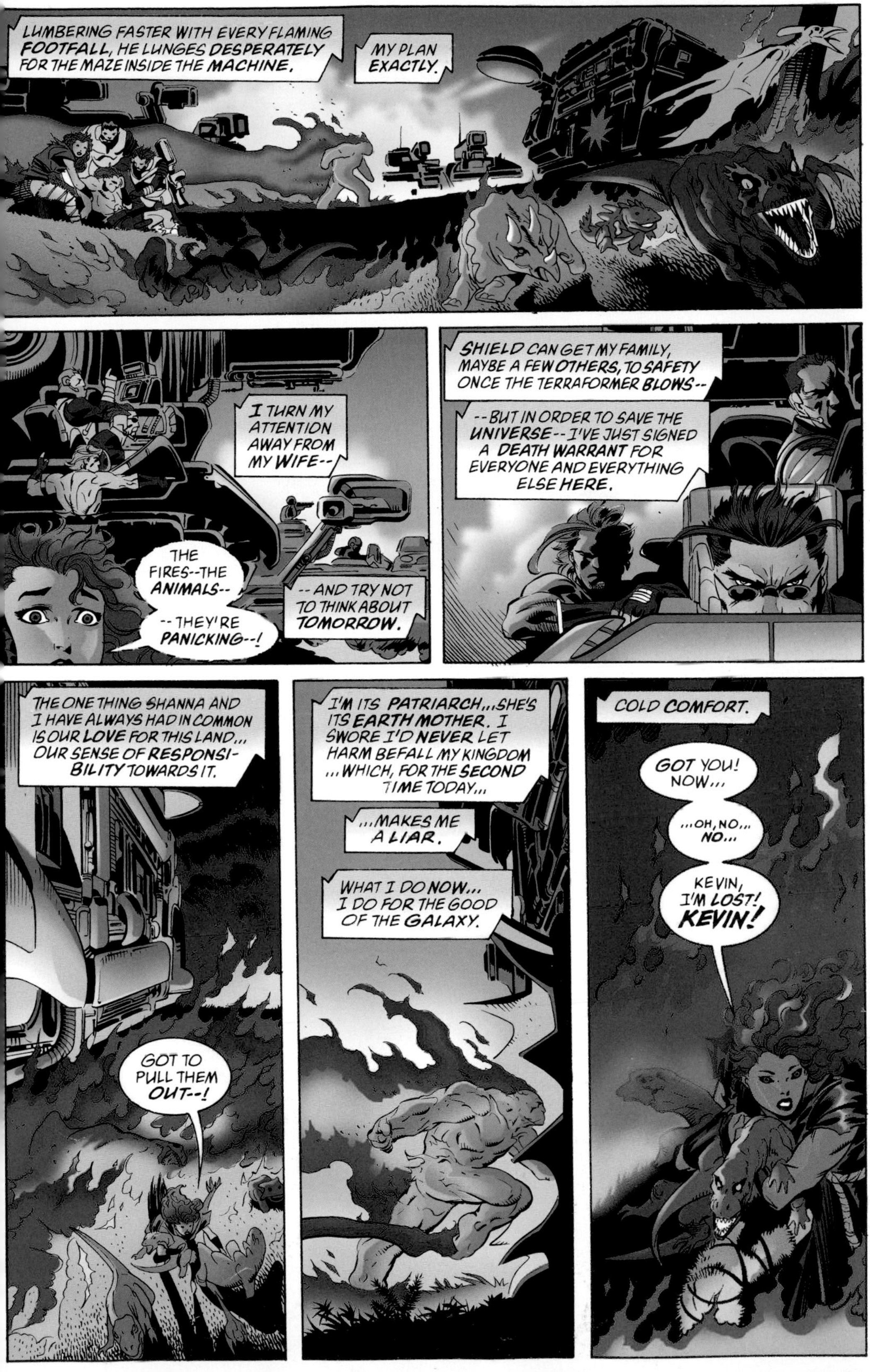
LUMBERING FASTER WITH EVERY FLAMING FOOTFALL, HE LUNGES DESPERATELY FOR THE MAZE INSIDE THE MACHINE.
MY PLAN EXACTLY.
I TURN MY ATTENTION AWAY FROM MY WIFE--
THE FIRES--THE ANIMALS--
--THEY'RE PANICKING--!
--AND TRY NOT TO THINK ABOUT TOMORROW.
SHIELD CAN GET MY FAMILY, MAYBE A FEW OTHERS, TO SAFETY ONCE THE TERRAFORMER BLOWS--
--BUT IN ORDER TO SAVE THE UNIVERSE--I'VE JUST SIGNED A DEATH WARRANT FOR EVERYONE AND EVERYTHING ELSE HERE.
THE ONE THING SHANNA AND I HAVE ALWAYS HAD IN COMMON IS OUR LOVE FOR THIS LAND... OUR SENSE OF RESPONSI-BILITY TOWARDS IT.
GOT TO PULL THEM OUT--!
I'M ITS PATRIARCH... SHE'S ITS EARTH MOTHER. I SWORE I'D NEVER LET HARM BEFALL MY KINGDOM ...WHICH, FOR THE SECOND TIME TODAY...
...MAKES ME A LIAR.
WHAT I DO NOW... I DO FOR THE GOOD OF THE GALAXY.
COLD COMFORT.
GOT YOU! NOW...
...OH, NO... NO...
KEVIN, I'M LOST! KEVIN!

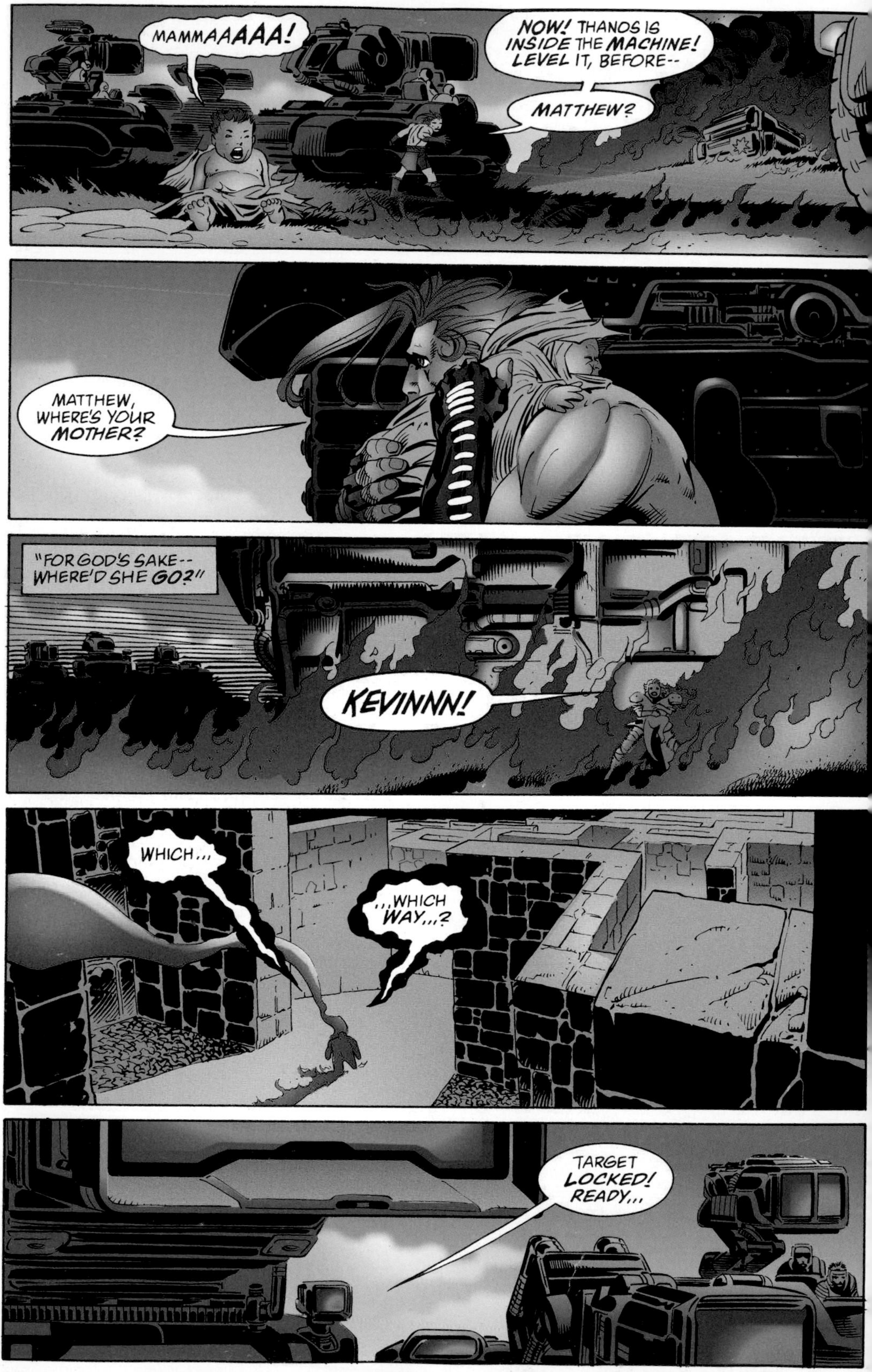
MAMMAAAAA!
NOW! THANOS IS INSIDE THE MACHINE! LEVEL IT, BEFORE--
MATTHEW?
MATTHEW, WHERE'S YOUR MOTHER?
"FOR GOD'S SAKE-- WHERE'D SHE GO?"
KEVINNN!
WHICH...
...WHICH WAY...?
TARGET LOCKED! READY...

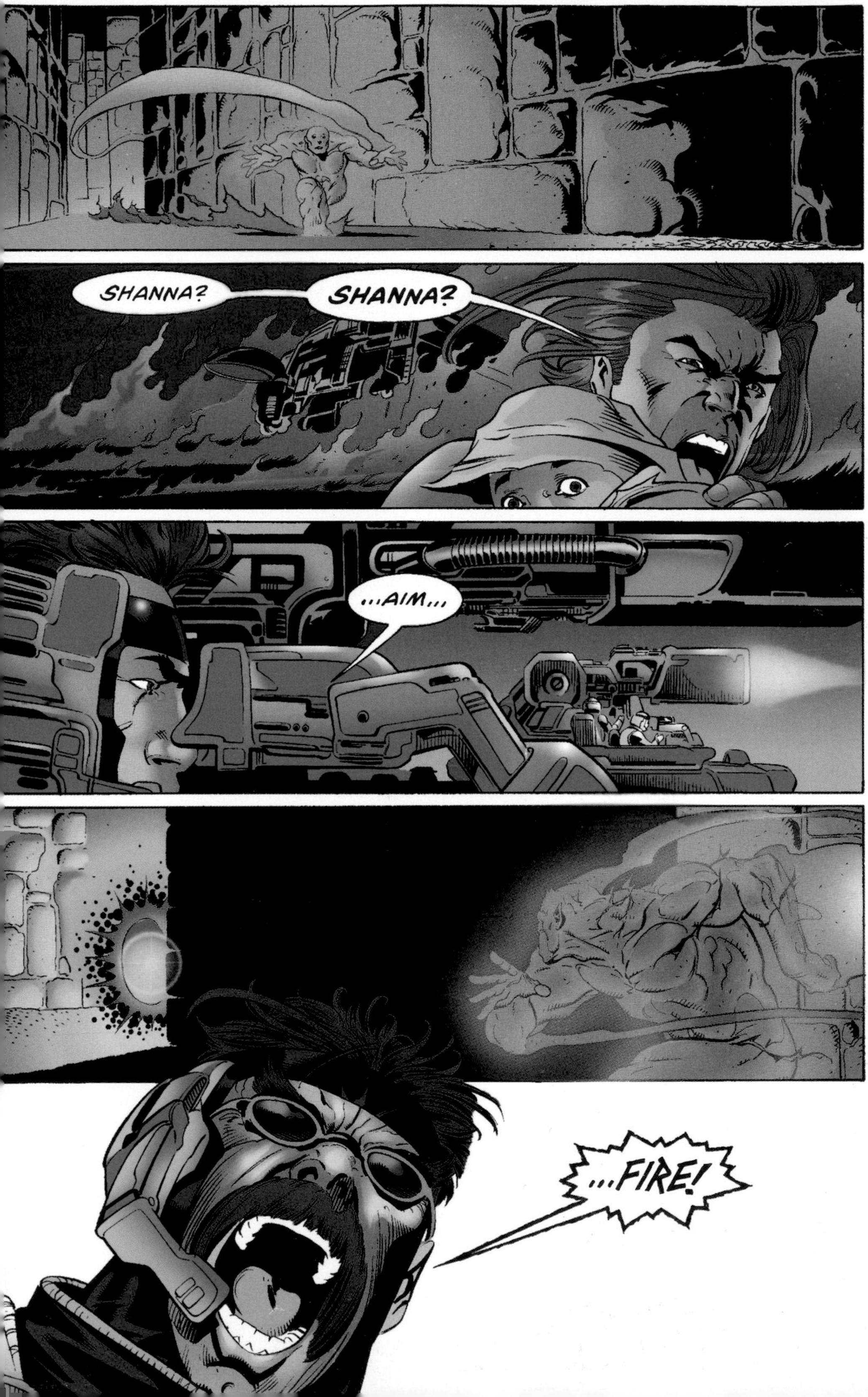
SHANNA?
SHANNA?
...AIM...
...FIRE!

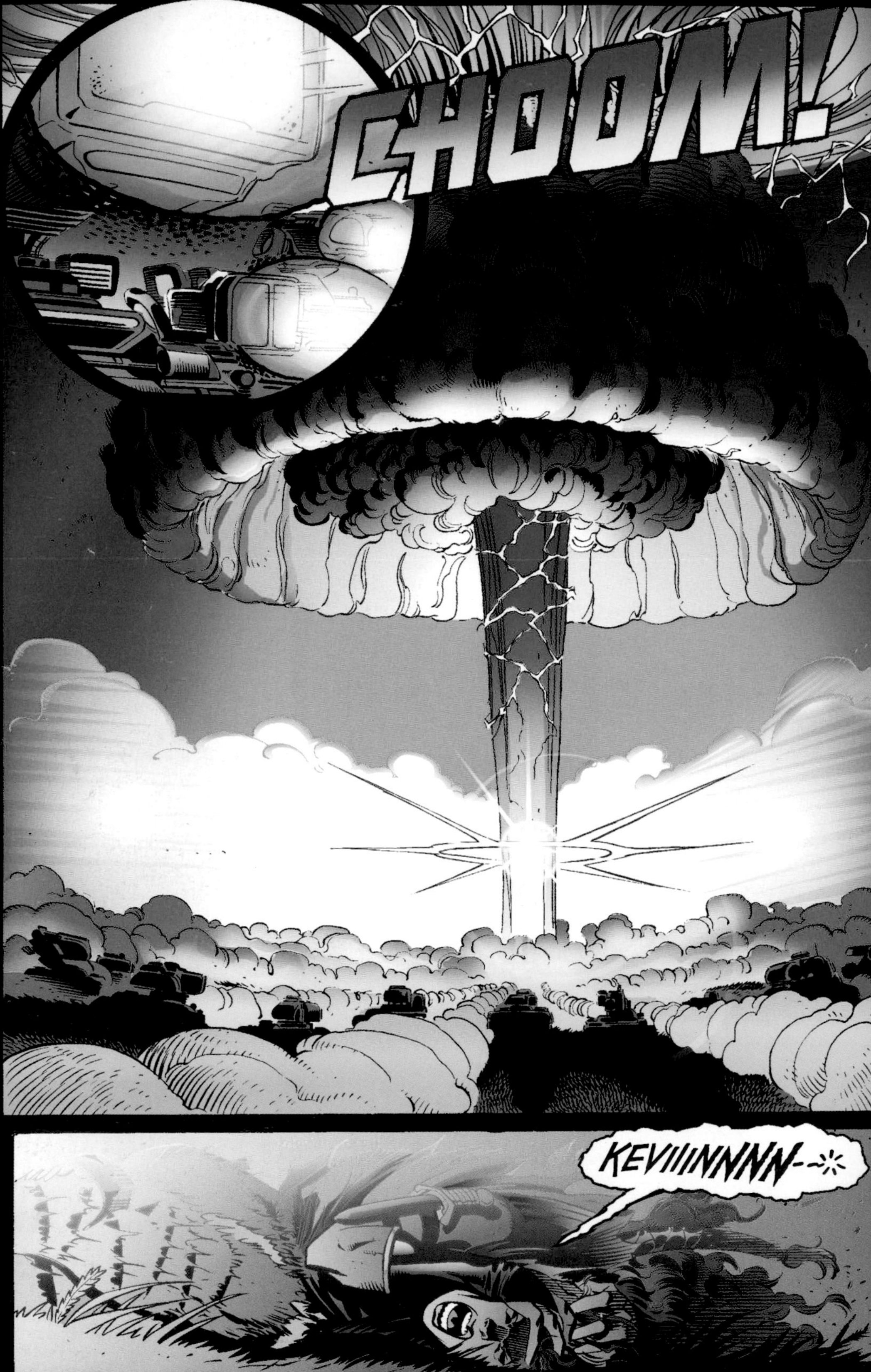
CHOOM!
KEVIIINNNN--

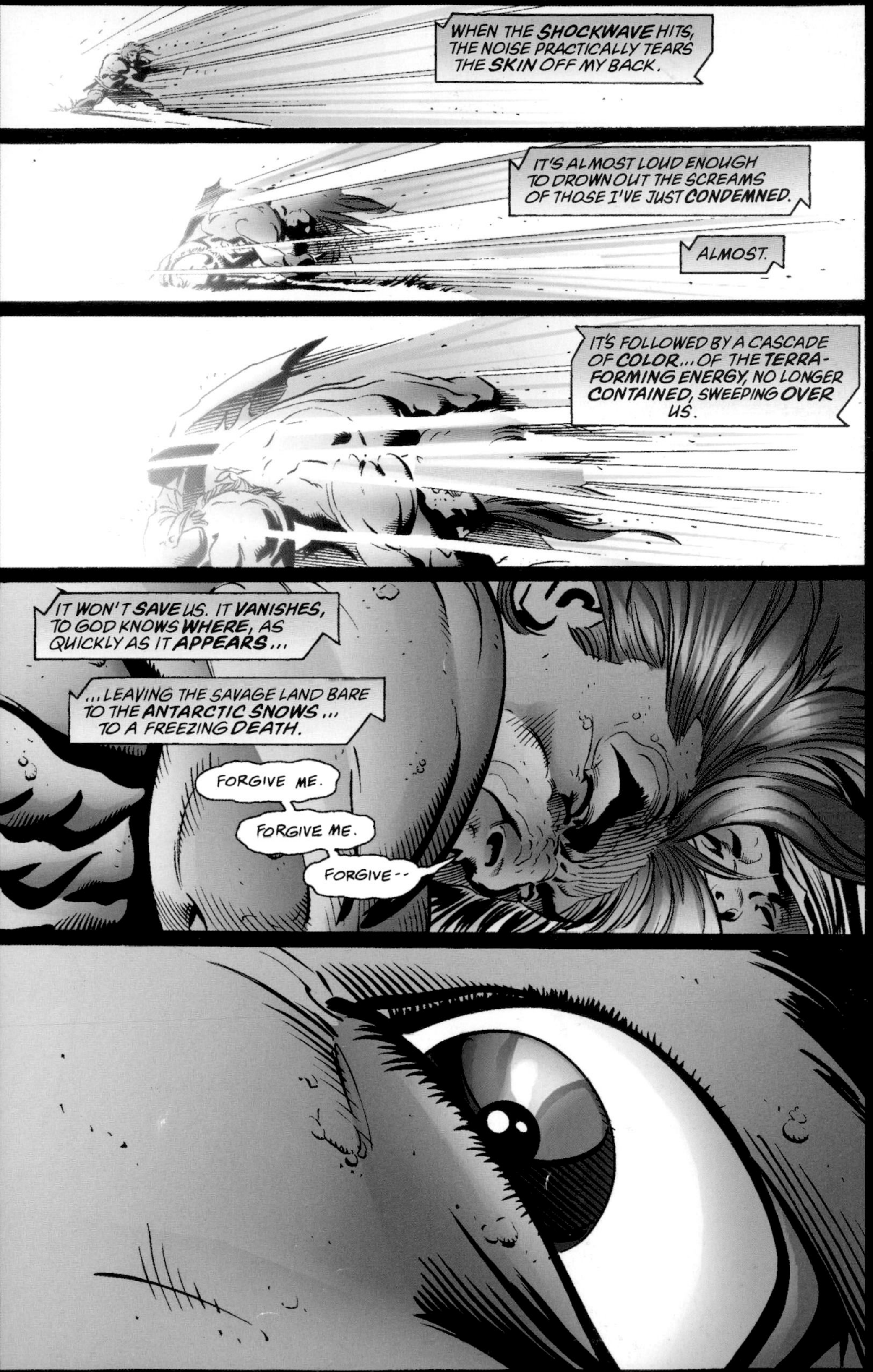
WHEN THE SHOCKWAVE HITS, THE NOISE PRACTICALLY TEARS THE SKIN OFF MY BACK.
IT'S ALMOST LOUD ENOUGH TO DROWN OUT THE SCREAMS OF THOSE I'VE JUST CONDEMNED.
ALMOST.
IT'S FOLLOWED BY A CASCADE OF COLOR... OF THE TERRA-FORMING ENERGY, NO LONGER CONTAINED, SWEEPING OVER US.
IT WON'T SAVE US. IT VANISHES, TO GOD KNOWS WHERE, AS QUICKLY AS IT APPEARS...
...LEAVING THE SAVAGE LAND BARE TO THE ANTARCTIC SNOWS... TO A FREEZING DEATH.
FORGIVE ME.
FORGIVE ME.
FORGIVE--

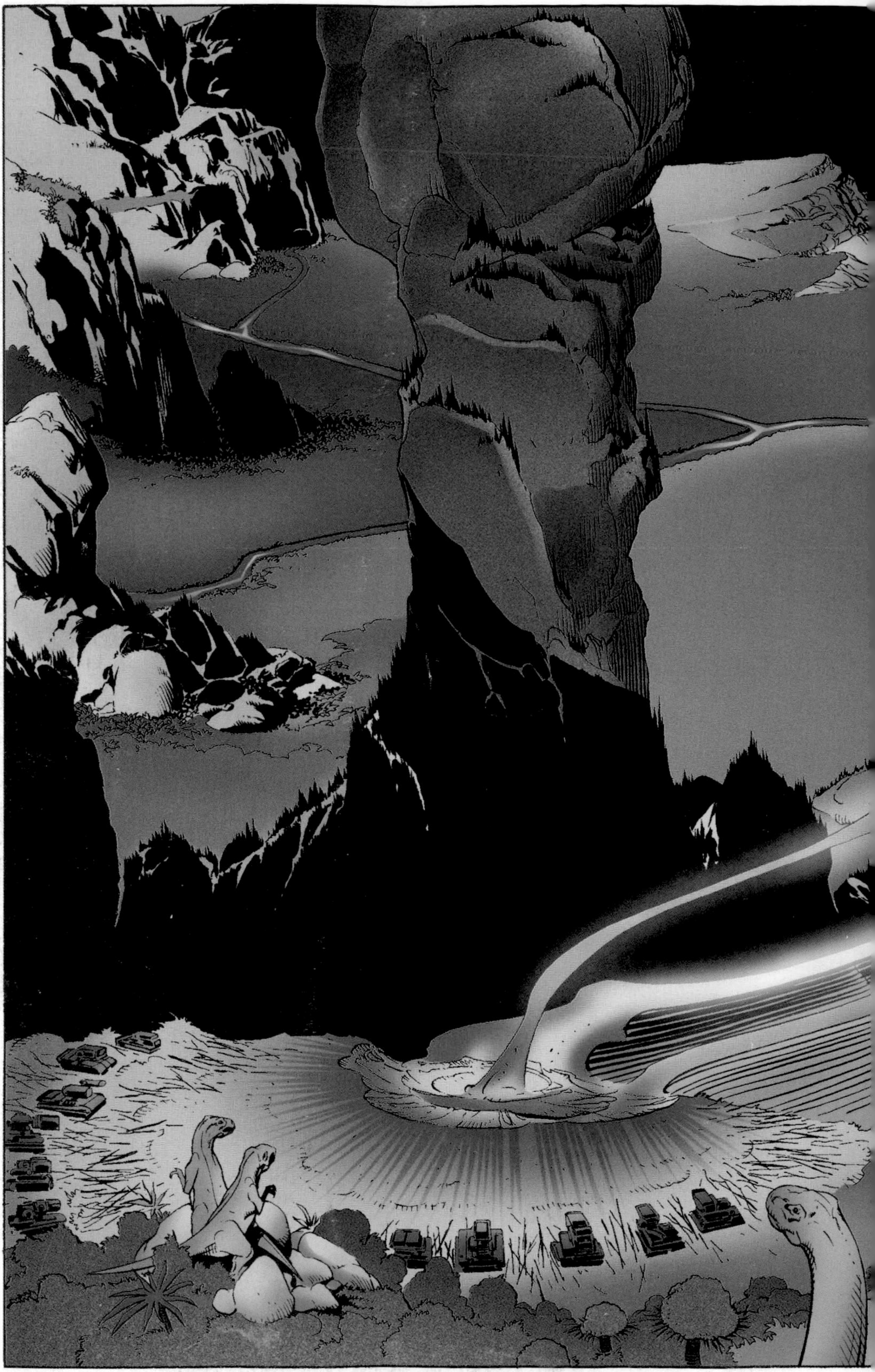

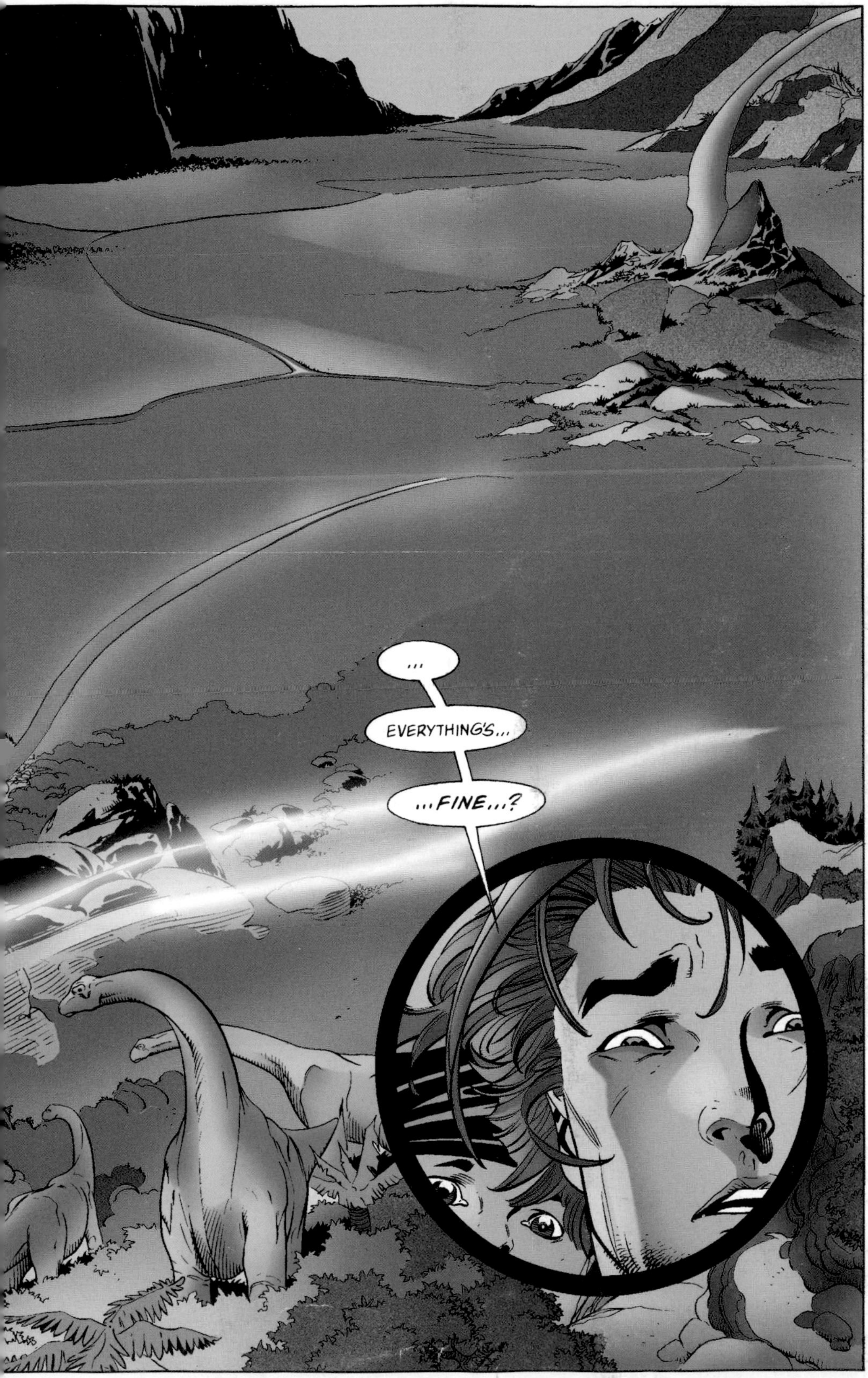
...
EVERYTHING'S...
...FINE...?

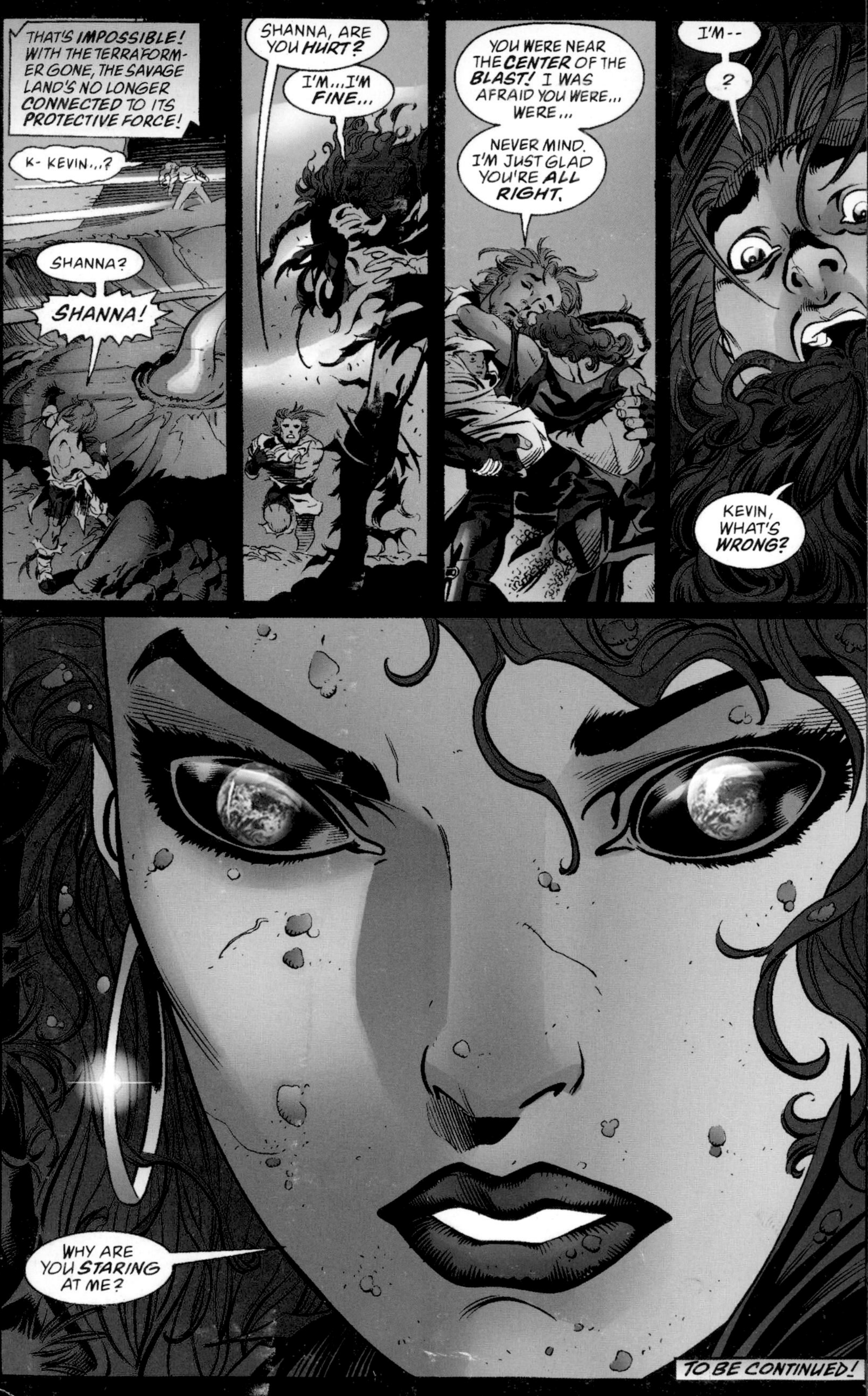
THAT'S IMPOSSIBLE! WITH THE TERRAFORMER GONE, THE SAVAGE LAND'S NO LONGER CONNECTED TO ITS PROTECTIVE FORCE!
K-KEVIN...?
SHANNA?
SHANNA!
SHANNA, ARE YOU HURT?
I'M...I'M FINE...
YOU WERE NEAR THE CENTER OF THE BLAST! I WAS AFRAID YOU WERE... WERE...
NEVER MIND. I'M JUST GLAD YOU'RE ALL RIGHT.
I'M--
?
KEVIN, WHAT'S WRONG?
WHY ARE YOU STARING AT ME?
TO BE CONTINUED!